Grand Duchy of Reme

Authors: Matt Finch, Casey Christofferson, Rhiannon Louve, Anthony Pryor, Kenneth Spencer

Editor: Jeff Harkness

Producer: Matt Finch

Project Managers: Matt Finch, Edwin Nagy

Cover Design: Charles A. Wright

Cover Art: Colin Chan

Interior Art: Julio De Carvahlo, Colin Chan, Santa Norvaisaite, Michael Syrigos

Art Direction: Casey Christofferson

Cartography: Robert Altbauer

Layout: Suzy Moseby

ADVENTURES
WORTH
WINNING

FROG GOD GAMES

ISBN: 978-1-6656-0002-6 PoD

Frog God Games is:

Bill Webb, Matthew J. Finch, Zach Glazar,

Charles A. Wright, Edwin Nagy,

Mike Badolato and John Barnhouse

Table of Contents

Introduction 7

Chapter One: Overview 10

Culture of the Loreclans 10

The Loreclan of Tabaj 10

Loreclan of the Quick Knives 11

The Kirimaji Loreclan 11

The Lore 11

The Rise of Reme 11

Sea Power 13

History 15

Pre-Hyperborean Period 15

Hyperborean Era 15

Foerdewaith Era 15

Independent World Power 16

Chapter Two: Lands of the Grand Duke 17

Overview 18

Reme, Ducal Lands 18

Government and Military 18

Religion 18

Trade and Commerce 19

Loyalties and Diplomacy 19

Locations in the Grand Ducal Territory 19

Reme, City of 19

Gilboath 19

The High Downs 19

Quintas 19

Remenos River 20

Varazath 20

White Squirrel Inn 22

Whiterush 23

Whiterush River 23

Yalendir 23

Chapter Three: The City of Reme 26

Overview of the City of Reme 27

Religion 27

Government 27

Military 27

Streets and Bridges 29

1. The Island of Heroes 29

2. Palace Complex 30

3. Stronghold of the Sea Tigress 30

4. Arcanum Collegium 31

5. Guild House 32

6. High Altar of Solanus 32

7. Lord Mayor's Manor 33

8. Temple of Mithras 33

9. Acropolis of the Four Winds 35

10. Lich's Rest 35

11. Livonia's Park 35

12. North Gate 36

13. South Gate 36

14. Underwall 36

15. Uphill 36

16. The House of Oron 36

17. House Drenwall 37

18. House Gastone-Sheshek 37

19. Fortress of the Bandi 38

20. Angry Gull 39

21. Hol-Hebar 39

22. The Blue Rooster 39

23. The Sujabi 40

24. Hauk Skarpson's Feast Hall 40

25. Lancers' Hall 41

26. Roost of the Owls 41

27. Quill House 41

28. The Pit of the Lizards 42

29. Fallenhouse 42

30. The Kujuk (Gate) 42

31. The Ice Cult 42

32. Hall of the Terriers 43

33. Field of the Sirkan Pashtars 43

34. The Quojo 43

35. Hall of the Red Thumb 44

Chapter 4: Duchy of the Northmarches 46
  Overview 47
    History and People 47
    Religion 49
    Trade and Commerce 49
    Loyalties and Diplomacy 49
    Government 49
    Military 50
    Major Threats 50
    Wilderness and Adventures 50
  Locations 51
    Albion 51
    Ashen Hills 51
    Durgam's Folly 52
    Golden Oak 52
    Gryphon Hills 53
    Crynnomar Gap 53
    Haunted Wood 53
    High Downs 53
    Ionkri Hall 53
    Ironhill 53
    Kheled'khaduin 55
    Nerimar 56
    Runya'mor 57
    Shadowhold 57
    Sternwood 57
    Tanith 58
    Wayland's Fane 58
    Wizard's Wall 58
Chapter 5: The Frontier 60
  Overview 60
  General Information 61
    Borders and Lands 61
    History and People 61
    Religion 62
    Trade and Commerce 62
    Loyalties and Diplomacy 62
    Government 62

    Military 63
    Major Threats 63
  Locations in the Frontier 63
    Acier River 63
    The Deepfells 63
    Dreikeng 63
    Endless Hills 64
    Eisenwood Forest 65
    Gauldark 65
    Harrowfar 66
    Namjan Forest 66
    Riverside 67
Chapter 6: Duchy of Waymarch 69
  Overview 69
    Borders and Lands 70
    History and People 70
    Religion 70
    Trade and Commerce 70
    Loyalties and Diplomacy 71
    Government 71
    Military 71
    Wilderness and Adventure 72
    Major Threats 72
  Locations in Waymarch 72
    Crossroads Center 72
    The Dagger & Rose 73
    Fareme 73
    Fivestones 75
    The Grimburg 76
    The Ice Tower of Kal-Tior 77
    Panetoth 77
    The Plains 83
    The Tradeway 84
Chapter 7: Duchy of Westmarch 86
  Overview 86
    History and People 86
    Religion 87
    Trade and Commerce 87

Loyalties and Diplomacy	88
Government	88
Military	88
Major Threats	88
Wilderness and Adventures	89
Locations in the Westmarches	89
Acier River	89
Baronswood	90
Caer Dire	90
The Carnival at the End of the World	91
City of Cats	96
City of the Lost	96
Dunavenwood	98
Eckland	99
Endless Hills	102
The Kingdom Beneath	102
Martyn's Nest	104
Fenria	106
Ferdozan	107
Forswen	108
The Gallows	109
Green Mountains	109
Kemresen	110
Khazfrecht	110
Knife's Edge Ridge	111
Museids	111
Quail River	113
Quail Valley	113
Seaside	114
Ruins of Sheffen Palace	114
Shining Temple	115
Silverlight	115
Tanner's Green	115
Tower of Jhedophar	116
Wessem	116
West Fortress	117
Western Akadian Forest	117
Westwood	118
The Windreft	118
Ashen Hills	119
History and People	120
Religion	120
Loyalties and Diplomacy	120
Government	120
Military	121
Major Threats	121
Wilderness and Adventures	121
Kingdoms of the Deepfells	121
History and People	121
Religion	122
Loyalties and Diplomacy	122
Government	122
Military	122
Major Threats	122
Wilderness and Adventures	123
Devil's Finger	123
Dragonbone Citadel	124
Dragonbone Peak	124
Eamonvale	124
History and People	124
Religion	125
Trade and Commerce	125
Loyalties and Diplomacy	125
Government	125
Military	125
Major Threats	125
Broadwater	126
Overview	126
Dun Eamon	126
Eamonvale Trade Road	127
River Eamon	127
The Haunted Wood	127
History and People	127
Religion	129
Trade and Commerce	129
Loyalties and Diplomacy	129
Government	129
Military	129

MAJOR THREATS	129
WILDERNESS AND ADVENTURES	129
THE HIGH DOWNS	130
HISTORY AND PEOPLE	130
RELIGION	131
TRADE AND COMMERCE	131
LOYALTIES AND DIPLOMACY	131
GOVERNMENT	131
MILITARY	131
MAJOR THREATS	132
WILDERNESS AND ADVENTURES	132
CHALKTOWN	132
ROYAL BLUFF	132
KYTHERAX'S KINGDOM	133
HISTORY AND PEOPLE	133
RELIGION	134
LOYALTIES AND DIPLOMACY	134
GOVERNMENT	134
MILITARY	134
MAJOR THREATS	135
WILDERNESS AND ADVENTURES	135
CALDERA CITADEL	135
NYCTOSEA	136
HISTORY AND PEOPLE	136
RELIGION	136
TRADE AND COMMERCE	136
LOYALTIES AND DIPLOMACY	137
GOVERNMENT	137
MILITARY	137
MAJOR THREATS	137
WILDERNESS AND ADVENTURES	137
BLACKFLAME	138
STONEAXE CAVERNS	138
HISTORY AND PEOPLE	138
RELIGION	139
TRADE AND COMMERCE	139
LOYALTIES AND DIPLOMACY	139
GOVERNMENT	139
MILITARY	140

MAJOR THREATS	140
WILDERNESS AND ADVENTURES	140
TULIDOR VALE	140
HISTORY AND PEOPLE	140
RELIGION	141
GOVERNMENT	141
MILITARY	141
MAJOR THREATS	141
WILDERNESS AND ADVENTURES	141
COUNCIL GROVE	141
APPENDIX A: PRIMARY GODS OF REME	142
APPENDIX B: ENCOUNTER TABLES	144

AUTHOR BIOGRAPHY:

Matt Finch, born November 15, 1967, is generally considered the main founder of the gaming movement known as the OSR. He won an ENNIE award in 2009 for the Swords & Wizardry game (a restatement of the rules of Original 1974-1978 Dungeons & Dragons) and is the author of the Quick Primer for Old School Gaming along with numerous other D&D resource books, including the Tome of Adventure Design. Finch is one of the founding members of Frog God Games, the successor to Necromancer Games. Matt is a graduate of Harvard College and Georgetown Law School.

GRAND DUCHY OF REME

By Matt Finch with Casey Christofferson, Rhiannon Louve, Anthony Pryor, Kenneth Spencer

INTRODUCTION

The Grand Duchy of Reme is one of the original regions of the Lost Lands campaign world, dating back to the 1970s. This book, though, is the first detailed description of the area to be published. Because of the name "grand duchy," one might assume that the country is essentially a Western European feudal culture, but in fact this is quite untrue. Reme is a unique fantasy civilization whose structure is determined by the one overriding fact of its geography: Reme is a grassland plain equivalent in size to central Asia and the American great plains, the largest Earthly examples of such an area. There are particular constraints on trade, agriculture, and communication that come into play on an essentially endless sea of grass, which is the starting point to understanding the culture of Reme.

It is a difficult trick for you to convey the feel of a fantasy culture that doesn't just default in the mind of the players to a standard Merry-England-With-Elves. Merry England can be deflected with other cultural "templates" — keywords that vary as wildly as "the Thirty Years' War," "King Kong," "Imperial China," "Ancient Egypt" — but all of these are just as likely to divert the players into a pre-existing historical fictional model without getting you anywhere farther than "Merry England" gets you. For the most part, the only way to bring the players into a truly new fantasy culture is bit by bit, tossing strange things in front of them over and over again during the course of play until their mental imagery of the world begins to reshape itself in accordance with all of these anomalous fragments of information.

Perhaps the best way to start conveying the underlying reality of Reme is to address the word "duke," which is assumed to be in the common tongue everywhere it appears in the world of the Lost Lands. The Rhemish word that translates as "duke" in the common tongue comes from an ancient root word in Kirkut which translates much more closely into "khan." All of the people in Reme, when they are referring to the dukes of the marches or to the grand duke, are actually using a word whose meaning is a hybrid of "khan" and "duke." Those who speak only the common tongue tend to perceive the "grand duchy" in feudal terms, whereas Kirkut speakers most likely assume that the "great khanate" is much more of a dictatorship than it actually is. The Kirkut speaker does not hear the implied division of power when they hear only "khan" rather than "duke." The common speaker does not perceive the extent of the grand duke's power when they hear "duke" rather than "khan." The truth resides quietly in the Rhemish language, just as the Rhemish people reside in their vast plains. They do not particularly care if they are understood, as long as they are respected and — when necessary — feared.

Another point that may be useful for reading the book is the distinction between Reme the city and Reme the country. The word for the country, culture, and people of Reme is "Rhemish," whereas the word for referring specifically to the city of Reme is "Reman."

Finally, the most significant social organizations of Reme are the Loreclans, a social grouping originating in the deep plains of Reme but that still operate in settled and urban areas. The Loreclannic culture is intermingled with the more standard-feudal Foerdewaith culture that dominated Reme politically for some time, but Loreclannic culture is slowly assimilating and adapting Foerdewaith culture to its own, completely original, uses. The Loreclannic culture is highly adaptive — it has incorporated culture and ideas from its original Hyperborean invaders and from its later Foerdewaith liege-lords without being dominated by either culture. In both cases, the invaders eventually fell or retreated, leaving behind a Loreclannic culture that took what it needed and discarded the rest.

We hope you enjoy exploring the strange lands and adventures that are to be found in the Grand Duchy — or perhaps "Grand Khanate" — of Reme.

Chapter One: Overview

The Grand Duchy of Reme is a vast realm: a network of well-settled river valleys running through enormous areas of almost-uncharted wilderness. To the west, Reme's territory extends to the Deepfells Mountains and the forbidden Green Realm of the wild elves. To the east, it reaches to the town of Fareme near the western edge of the Stoneheart Valley. Its northern border is the Wizard's Wall across the Crynnomar Gap, and to the south, the realm extends to the Whiterush River. The land borders of Reme do not tell the whole story, however, for Reme is also a seafaring nation, one of the most significant in the world. The grand duke has no colonial aspirations, but the nation has been focused on dominating trade on the Crescent Sea for centuries, and Rhemish ships venture throughout the known world from the city's great port.

In overall size, the Grand Duchy of Reme technically rivals the entire holdings of the overking of Foere and exceeds that of the actual Kingdom of Foere by quite a bit. However, most of Reme remains wild, inhabited by nomadic Loreclans rather than agrarian settlements. With the exception of river valleys, Reme is almost entirely a vast grassland prairie poorly suited to farming. The Frontier in the northwest is only nominally under the jurisdiction of the Northmarches, for the reach of the duchess at Ironfell only barely extends into this region. In the west, permanent agricultural settlements have only recently begun to form in the Windreft following the resolution of civil wars that ravaged the Westmarches for the last several decades. The civilization of Reme is powerful, but the settled population is widely scattered in pockets and along the great rivers.

Given the uneven settlement and great distances within the wild territories of Reme, the grand duchy has evolved into a number of marches providing for more local administration. Today, these are the Westmarches, the Northmarches, and Waymarch, in addition to the central lands held directly by the grand duke. The origin of power of the dukes of Reme are as Loreclannic chiefs, and their authority, developed over the course of millennia, extends to ancient Loreclannic boundaries rather than feudal grants of the land itself. The distinction between Reme's Loreclannic traditions versus Foere's feudal law is nuanced, but it is a key factor in understanding the history and the nature of the Rhemish people.

Culture of the Loreclans

Reme is dominated by its various Loreclans; a social organization akin to that of a tribe, but more complex in terms of internal organization. Loreclans usually have 500–1,000 members, but there are smaller Loreclans that have fallen upon hard times over the years, and the urban Loreclans in and around the city of Reme can number as many as 5,000. Across the vast sea of grass dominating Reme's central plains, there are vast differences between the cultures of the Loreclans — all of them respect the general tradition governing the rights of the other Loreclans, but the clans themselves are highly individual.

The Loreclans of Reme are, first of all, divided into three basic types: settled, semi-nomadic, and purely-nomadic. While the cultures of these three types are essentially the same, they live by different means, which affects how they interact with characters.

Settled Loreclans are found along the river valleys, or living in villages, towns, and even cities. Their component clans are often mixed with clans of other Loreclans in the same areas, and regions occupied by settled Loreclans are the most familiar to foreigners in terms of surface appearance. Settled Loreclans are engaged in year-round agriculture (and for the riverside Loreclans, fishing).

Semi-nomadic Loreclans are usually engaged in herding rather than pure hunting and move their herds from a summer to a winter pasture. The pastures are defined locations, and these Loreclans build permanent structures in both places. By long tradition, the purely nomadic Loreclans respect the boundaries of these pastures but are also allowed to take certain advantage of them when they are unoccupied. In their turn, the pure nomads attempt to keep wild herds away from the growing pastureland of the semi-nomadic Loreclans.

Purely-nomadic Loreclans follow the vast herds of wild cattle wherever they might go, although this is usually within territories defined by the ancient traditions of the Loreclans. There are protocols for following herds into the territory of other Loreclans, which usually avoid wars. Traditions only go so far in these cases, however, and the pure nomads of the deep plains are much more prone to warfare than the more settled Loreclans; some, indeed, have engaged in almost genocidal conflicts that have persisted for generations despite the best efforts of the dukes to break the chain of such feuds. The nomadic Loreclans of the deep plains engage in no agriculture — they are pure hunter-gatherers — which makes them extraordinarily dangerous to the enemies of Reme when they are summoned from the plains to one of Reme's infrequent wars. The skills of hunting translate directly into the skills of warfare as light cavalry, and these deep-plains' Loreclans are deadly enemies on the field of battle.

Most Loreclans are led by a "baron," a Hyperborean/Common word that in Rhemish is usually the word "tarkhan." Characters might encounter both translations. There is no permanent level of nobility between the barons/tarkhans and the dukes/khans, which leaves a vast gap for any kind of administration of Loreclan traditions, administration of justice, and mediation of potential wars.

This gap is usually filled by pashtars, a temporary title for an individual who acts in the nature of an attorney, mediator, ambassador, or temporary chieftain for more than one Loreclan at one time, usually for a single purpose. Most of the Loreclan representatives at the ducal courts are pashtars who speak for groups of Loreclans at one time. This allows a Loreclan to petition the duke without trying to move the entire Loreclan out of its traditional territory to make the petition. Anyone designated as a pashtar has an absolute right to the hospitality of tribes along the journey to a court — they are sacrosanct when acting in the capacity of pashtar.

The position of pashtar is not hereditary, although some Loreclans are known for producing a number of famous pashtars, which tends to create a cycle. These Loreclans are well-respected and often petitioned for a pashtar when nearby Loreclans feel that they need one.

To emphasize the great difference between various Loreclans, the following is a brief discussion of the culture of three of the Loreclans of Reme that characters might encounter in their adventures:

The Loreclan of Tabaj

This semi-nomadic Loreclan is highly distinct from others in that they keep a small herd of elephants along with horses and cattle. The elephants are sacred to the Tabaj and are painted with symbols and designs whose meaning is understood only within the Loreclan itself. These designs are a well-kept secret, said to add to the strength and wisdom of the Loreclan's elephantine allies. According to the Tabaj, the elephant herd is suffused with a communal spirit-mind that can communicate with the Loreclan's shaman — this is in fact how the identity of the Loreclan's shamans is determined. The spirit-mind allows the elephants to serve as scouts for the Loreclan, and it is a full member of the Loreclan's deliberations, as the spirit's voice is translated by the shaman.

The summer pasturage of the Tabaj is alongside the Remenos River, where their elephants help settled Loreclans with heavy work. Their winter pasturage is 100 miles from the summer pasturage, a large encampment with stone foundations and wooden structures that allow construction of vast, communal "tents" located in the center of what is effectively a small town of smaller family tents.

LORECLAN OF THE QUICK KNIVES

The Quick Knives are an example of a Loreclan that has stretched tradition to the breaking point and beyond, a stark contradiction to the peaceable Tabaj Loreclan. The Quick Knives are the most infamous and problematic of the Plainsfolk Loreclans in the Waymarch. Purely nomadic, the Quick Knives tend to roam the areas between the plains of the Northmarches and the River Eamon, though their members are known to hire themselves out as caravan guardians, meaning that bands of their warriors are found as far west as the city of Reme and as far east as Bard's Gate where they have been spotted in Tent City.

They are disliked and disdained by Loreclans with adjoining territories, as they have been known to raid for horses and plunder — activities that are in many cases permitted under Loreclannic tradition, but certainly not with the frequency of the Quick Knives' depredations. The Quick Knives have legendary tempers; they tend to shave the sides and back of their head, leaving only a long crop on top to grow. This is threaded with porcupine quills collected along the banks of the Eamon River to form great headdresses that further their horrific visage when they paint their bodies with rouge and greasepaint before heading into battle. The Quick Knives are careful not to raid villages and towns, for this falls immediately and squarely outside Loreclannic tradition and would be dealt with swiftly by the duke. Their favored deity is Bowbe, though it is believed that some subsets may have taken to worshipping fiends of the underworld. It is very likely that the Loreclan of the Quick Knives will be eradicated in the near future once nearby Loreclans finally join against them with the support of the duke — unless they retreat beyond the borders of Reme, as many renegade clans do.

THE KIRIMAJI LORECLAN

The Kirimaji are a Loreclan owing allegiance directly to the grand duke and are known for producing a number of famous pashtars. They are a fully-settled people who live on the banks of the Remenos River in permanent structures, and they are respected as a scholarly and serious clan. Visiting the Kirimaji territory can be intensely frustrating for outsiders, since anyone from a shopkeeper to a Loreclannic knight is fully capable of starting a discussion of philosophy or morality in the middle of a conversation about something else. Various examples might include:

- So, what is your opinion on the final destination of a soul after death?
- Do you think fish are capable of rational thought, if they are magical? If so, how would one justify eating something that is capable of thinking with only a bit of help? Here, try the trout — it's delicious when cooked this way.
- Why do you think some people prefer the color blue over other colors?
- Do you think people have free will, or is everything just a matter of destiny?

THE LORE

The "Lore" that gave rise to the name "Loreclan" was originally little more than a list of "debts" and a set of directions for moving around in the Loreclan's territory. To the untrained eye, the plains of Reme appear to be completely featureless, but there are a number of natural and purposely-built landmarks that can be followed from one place to another, and that delineate the ancient borders within the plains. These landmarks can include streams, of course, but also include small depressions in the ground, the occasional tree (usually painted with symbols), a boulder, and in many cases patterns of rocks deliberately set into the ground. These are the highways of the Loreclans, and as long as one has a guide from within one of the clans, that guide can take strangers quickly through the Loreclan's territory to the border. Members of foreign Loreclans can often spot the landmarks but can't interpret how to follow them (unless it is on one of the few well-known and neutral highways through the plains). As long as they are of a friendly Loreclan, the usual procedure for visitors is to reach the border of a Loreclan's territory and then light a small signal fire to indicate that visitors are present and would like a guide. Then they must wait, which can easily take a couple of days.

The original version of a book of "debts" was a record of any potential feuds the Loreclan might have, along with a list of friendly Loreclans that rendered assistance in the past and should be especially favored. Over time, the lore of a clan has also come to include tales, stories, and ballads of the clan's heroes — these are predominantly an oral tradition, for an odd reason. The Loreclans know that their stories and tradition would disappear with the clan itself if they were ever to be wiped out (or "eradicated" under the orders of a duke for significant violations of Loreclannic tradition). By keeping their oral traditions at risk to this possibility, the Loreclans leave a part of their existence in question. They like to know that if they are lost to the world, so will their stories be lost to the world. It is an attitude completely foreign to most cultures in the world of the Lost Lands, but it is deeply tied in to the strange culture of the Loreclans.

THE RISE OF REME

The original, primordial people of Reme were nomads, trading with the Hundaei tribes of the northern region beyond Reme itself, an area now called the Haunted Steppes. The Rhemish Loreclans of the deep plains speak a dialect of Kirkut and share many cultural features with the Haunted Steppes' tribes, whom they consider distant relatives. They are not, however, an offshoot of the Hundaei — whatever contact there may have been in the distant past was merely one long-ago factor in the development of cultures and traditions on the great plateaus of Reme. Before the coming of the Hyperboreans, the plains of Reme contained a number of semi-nomadic peoples in the river valleys who subsisted on fishing and agriculture and a larger number of purely-nomadic Loreclans in the deeper plains who lived primarily by following vast herds of wild cattle.

The city of Reme — then called "Remenos" — originated as a trading post for horse Loreclans, where the two great islands of the estuary offered an obvious neutral ground for Loreclannic emissaries to meet and trade. The three Loreclans involved in this trade eventually settled on the banks of the river and changed their focus from hunting to agriculture, fishing, and maintaining their control of the river crossing. The narrow points of the river were bridged, and the towns of these Loreclannic settlements merged slowly together into a single, wide-flung city — not always peaceably, for the Loreclans maintained their separate identities. Today, the Remish appear to be the epitome of civilization: highly-urbanized, with their academy of magic, their banking, and their empire of sea-borne trade. All of this, however, is grafted onto a far more fundamental reality of ancient Rhemish culture — the horse-riding nomad. The Rhemish do not think of land as a thing to own, merely as a region to control when control is necessary. The idea of "planting a flag" is quite foreign to Rhemish thinking. The question — to the Rhemish mind — is whether you can exert power to the places where you need it. If so, it doesn't matter whose flag flies over the place.

This explains a number of events in Rhemish history that simply can't be understood otherwise: the willingness to abandon expanses of land in the face of an invasion until the time is ready to strike; complete lack of interest in expanding the country's rule to the south, beyond the plateaus and plains; the "islands" of civilization that exist in Reme instead of a neatly-defined "forward expansion" of civilization for historians to follow year by year. Finally, too, the relationship between the settled, urban Rhemish and the horse barbarians of the plains. These represent two different subcultures of the same people, which is utterly misunderstood by most observers — it is obscured by the periodic, vicious wars on the frontiers — but the status quo between the Loreclans and the towns of Reme is a state of peace. When war breaks out, it is not a war between strangers — which makes it no less ferocious, for the Rhemish are deadly in war. As one observer puts it, "In the breast of Reme, there beats a barbaric heart."

In −87 I.R., the Hyperboreans arrived at Remenos and established a fort on the larger of the two islands in the estuary of the Remenos River: the Island of Heroes. This garrison established a single set of laws to govern the Loreclans under the single authority of the garrison commander, whose role was quickly expanded to the rank of imperator as the Remish Loreclans expanded into control of Reme. It is from this point in time that Remenos can be seen as a true city rather than a close affiliation of three Loreclannic systems clustered into a single area. The Hyperboreans followed a simple process for assimilating the Loreclans: They declared the garrison commander to be the "grand duke," the existing three Loreclannic leaders to be "dukes," and established that successors to the Loreclannic dukes would be chosen by vote from eligible members of the ducal families, with the electors being the Loreclan's "knights." Loreclannic knights are a Rhemish concept similar to the feudal concept of a knight, simply meaning a member of the Loreclan that has proven their courage and received a specific name based on whatever was done to prove that worth. It might appear that the Hyperboreans effected a major change by establishing a hereditary system from one that was originally based solely on merit — Loreclannic chieftains were chosen by acclamation rather than parentage before the Hyperboreans arrived. However, the practice of adopting children from one clan to another was so common that it did not occur to any of the Loreclans that membership in a specific "family" would ever create a problem for any great warrior on the rise to prominence. Indeed, adoption remains a common practice in Reme, confounding foreigners bred in more hidebound feudal systems.

Nevertheless, this switch from acclamation to heredity was the origin of the system that was to take hold in Reme: the creation of Reme's three families of high nobility and the title of grand duke — which would eventually give rise to a fourth high noble family as well once the title of grand duke remained with the imperator. Eventually these families would come to hold their power in the form of the three march dukedoms and the grand ducal lands.

The other key figure in the Hyperborean capture of Reme was a wizard by the name of Iesharos, attached to the garrison, who by all accounts was a highly unstable individual. Released from his service to the garrison in consequence of some crime not recorded by history, Iesharos set himself up as the "supreme arcane" of the settlement and took on a number of apprentices from the resident Loreclans. This core of fledgling wizards was to alter the history of Reme for all time.

The power of the open plain lies with the horse, and the mostly-agricultural Loreclans of Reme never mastered the art of mounted combat to anything like the degree achieved by the Loreclans of the inland plains. Magic, however — even in a very basic form — turned the newly-united city of Remenos into a regional military powerhouse. With the help of the Hyperboreans garrisoned in Remenos, Rhemish rivercraft sailed northward into the fertile river valley and then beyond into the plains themselves. The Rhemish forces built fortified "herding-towns" in the plains and broke the power of the nomadic Loreclans with small, mounted units of wizards protected by large cavalry troops. While the mounted Loreclans of the plains could easily have destroyed ordinary Rhemish cavalry in virtually any numbers, the presence of wizardry on the battlefield changed the equation entirely. The completely-nomadic Loreclans were swept out of the river valleys and the settled Loreclans were assimilated into Reme's Loreclannic-feudal empire, leaving the city of Reme in complete control of the vast river systems of the plateau. The deeper plains were left untouched for two reasons. First, there was the simple fact that Remenos glutted itself with conquest in its early years and lacked the manpower to expand further. Second, the Loreclans of the deeper plains, faced with the threat of battlefield magic, began to employ witchcraft and shamanic magic to a far greater degree than before. Even a few minor defeats against the nomads were enough to cause Remenos to pull back and consolidate its gains.

Small settlements were generally assigned by the garrison commander (later the imperator) to the administrative responsibility of one of the dukes, which, to the Hyperborean garrison commander, meant that the matter was handled. From the Rhemish perspective, though, the matter still needed considerable negotiation before the Rhemish Loreclannic duke could exert any formal control over a settlement held by another Loreclan. The greatest risk was simply that the semi-nomadic village might pick up and move — not something that the Hyperboreans even considered. In general, the capture of semi-nomadic villages gave rise to a situation in which the Rhemish Loreclannic dukes offered to raise the local Loreclannic chiefs into barons — another term quickly adapted for use from the Hyperboreans — and took the entire lands of the conquered Loreclan under their protection. Thus, what appeared to the Hyperboreans to be a feudal expansion across the plateaus of Reme was actually the creation of three Loreclannic nations each composed of a huge number of Loreclans, each Loreclan with its "baron," and each baron with a complement of Loreclannic knights. Foreigners are to be forgiven for thinking that Reme is a feudal country, for the Loreclans deliberately fit their organization into the terminology of Hyperborea, a terminology that does not precisely convey the way Reme's Loreclannic-feudal system actually operates.

The Rhemish Loreclannic-Feudal System

Loreclannic Knights

Knighthood in Reme is an honor and status that stems from the Loreclans rather than from the nobility, which is the reason for avoiding the basic term "knight" to refer to the backbone of Reme's governmental and military system. The term should not by any means conjure up a barbarian warrior; Loreclannic knights from the settled regions are little different from their counterparts in any feudal realm. It is true that Loreclannic knights from the deep plains are likely to be "barbarians," but these knights have the same social standing as a glittering chevalier from the city of Reme. Moreover, both of these individuals — the glittering chevalier and the barbarian raider — fully acknowledge the equivalence of their social status in Reme. The social distinction that might exist in Foere based on money and landholdings does not carry over into the society of the Rhemish Loreclannic knights.

In Reme, knights are raised to this status by whatever procedures a Loreclan has used over the course of its centuries of history. In most cases, there is some kind of agreement between the baron (essentially a Loreclannic chief) and the Loreclan's knights, with either the baron approving the decision of the knights or vice versa. Variations exist among the Loreclans; a very few allow their barons to appoint knights without some kind of approval, while some Loreclans appoint knights by vote of the entire Loreclan without reference to the baron or the existing knights.

Rhemish Barons

Rhemish barons are not the "owners" of land; they are the leaders of a particular Loreclan, and their territory is the ancestral Loreclannic land (subject to the occasional adjustment by the duke based on population and other considerations) in which all members of the Loreclan have certain rights. Barons generally take quite a lot of the surplus — this varies from Loreclan to Loreclan — but it is usually far less than the amount taken by a traditional feudal baron. Barons who becomes too greedy could easily lose the loyalty of their Loreclannic knights, and it is the Loreclannic knights who form the real power of a baron. There are several instances in Rhemish history where a baron hired mercenaries to counterbalance the power of Loreclannic knights, only to have one of these Loreclannic knights declare himself baron and be supported by other barons, or even by the duke. The true power in Reme lies with the Loreclannic knights, not with the title of "baron" or even of "duke," simply because the people of Reme do not place much value upon the "law" when it comes into conflict with "justice" or "Loreclan values."

Rhemish Dukes

The dukes of Reme are essentially the protectors of various Loreclans and are pledged to defend ancient Loreclannic customs, administer disputes, reallocate Loreclannic land in the case of plagues or other great changes to the needs of the Loreclans, and coordinate defense. In all cases, the allegiance of the Loreclans is still to the grand duke, but the dukes of the marches have a status in the Loreclannic-feudal system that gives them tremendous power.

The "herding-towns" of the rapidly-growing Hyperborean-Rhemish empire were not, for the most part, slotted into the feudal system the Hyperboreans thought they were creating. These towns were governed directly by appointees of the garrison commander (later the imperator) and were considered the property of the imperator in his capacity of grand duke. In many cases, they are now self-governed by charter.

Sea Power

Simply by virtue of its harbor and the city's location at the end of an immense river system, the city of Reme was basically destined to become a trading power in the region of the Crescent Sea. However, Reme's advantages also included the fact that, in the very early history of Remenos, there was a quantity of unclaimed land between the three trading posts of the Loreclans of Reme. Most of this land was assigned to the ownership of the Hyperborean Empire, but a significant portion was also assigned to the three Loreclans as a group rather than individually. The intention, on the part of Hyperborea, was to give the Loreclans a common interest to prevent feuding. However, it had an effect on later development because the Loreclannic dukes chose to assign small committees of their Loreclannic knights to administer these properties, with each group composed of knights from each Loreclan. Each committee, over a very long period, became in effect a company as the members of the committee purchased the interests of the Loreclans. The trading companies that developed from this slow purchase of jointly-held property were the precursors of Reme's great merchant houses. The merchant houses still maintain considerable real estate in Reme, but for generation upon generation they invested their land-ownership profits into ships. Not having any specific Loreclannic affiliation, they tended to shy away from land in the plateaus, which was dominated by the Loreclannic-feudal system that excluded non-Loreclannic investors. The only opportunity for investing beyond the borders of Reme itself was overseas trading. Here, the mixed Loreclannic identities of the mercantile houses proved a great benefit, for they had contacts with all three of the major Loreclans and could recruit experienced sailors from all the Loreclans. The clan-owned and individually-owned vessels of other towns on the Crescent Sea tended to fall behind the more "corporate" financial, negotiating, and recruiting resources of the mercantile houses — which in turn allowed Reme to field a much-larger merchant fleet than the city's competitors. The city's early advantage in trade allowed Reme to gain more of a lead in dominating sea trade on the Crescent, which led to the city's status as a dominating trade presence on the world stage.

These developments lead us to present-day Reme: a vast expanse of plains, with villages and towns in the river valleys but wilderness stretching to the far horizons. A city with world-spanning trade centered upon its Island of Heroes where the ashes of legendary barbarian kings reside. A grand duke with strong ties to the barbarians of the plains. The slow collapse of the Empire of Foere, and the rise of Bard's Gate to the east. The Rhemish see these events with the cold eyes of foreigners, the dispassion of those who live in regions that devour invaders. Their land is eternal; their culture can be forced back to the plains but abides there in immortality; they are — as a people — the ultimate hunters. The fall of Foere is like the fall of an antelope upon the plains; the rise of Bard's Gate is little more than the stepping-up of jackals before the body. The city of Reme waits and watches — for Reme is the dwelling-place of the wolves.

Timeline

I.R.	Event
–87	Reme is founded under the name of Remenos by Polemarch Oerson during the Hyperborean conquest of Akados.
–60	Loreclans of Reme begin extending power into the river-valleys, creating a semi-feudal Loreclannic hierarchy in the name of the Hyperborean Empire
–26	The rank of "garrison commander" of Reme is raised to "imperator" to reflect the territory absorbed by the Remish Loreclans.
40	The majority of Reme's river valleys are brought under the control of the three Remish Loreclans and the imperator (in the capacity of the "grand duke"). A far-slower period of expansion begins into the cattle-lands of the deeper plains.
48	A half-strength Hyperborean legion is isolated and destroyed in the deep plains when its horses stampede and their supply lines are wiped out. The starved, dehydrated forces are slaughtered in the Massacre of Starvation. The imperator abandons ordinary Hyperborean tactics on the high plains and shifts to the light-cavalry tactics employed by the three urban Loreclans, using auxiliaries drawn from friendly Loreclans rather than imported Hyperborean infantry.
717	Remenos extends territory north, clear-cutting forests for shipment to Reme.
753	Construction of Durgam's Folly by Hyperborean Captain Durgam Volmsmer begins.
1013	Frontier War begins and ends as a Hyperborean legion marches into the Frontier, determined to put the unruly centaurs in their place, and is decimated.
1548	Hobgoblin invasion of Northern Reme from the Deepfells. The invasion moves forward despite heavy losses from dehydration caused by ambushed supply chains and light cavalry raids under the leadership of Loreclannic knights. The nomadic Loreclans of the region fall back slowly, taking few losses while raiding deep into the territory taken by the hobgoblin horde.
1557	Loreclans of the Northmarches fall back entirely into the territory of the other march dukes; hobgoblins occupy the entirety of the Northmarches, albeit with constant losses from raiding bands from the displaced Loreclans.
1564	Adventurers infiltrate Dragonbone Peak and discover warlord-to-be hobgoblin demigod Kakobovia.
1573	Adventurers infiltrate Dragonbone Peak while forces are depleted from war in Arcady and strike at Kakobovia. Half are killed, while the rest flee magically to the High Downs; Kakobovia gathers the remaining forces of Dragonbone and launches an all-out attack on High Downs; adventurers' ploy works, and Kakobovia leads his army into a trap at Battle of Ironhill. Grand Duke Borell I of Reme defeats hobgoblins of Dragonbone and personally banishes the incarnation of Kakobovia from the Material Plane. Rhemish Loreclans rapidly reclaim the Northmarches.
2499	Hyperboreans abandon their western empire. The imperator of Reme resigns the title but remains in Reme in his capacity of grand duke. He declares Reme independent and changes the name of the capital from Remenos (the Hyperborean name) to Reme.
2840	Foerdewaith settlers push through Crynnomar Gap.
2841	Macobert brings the Grand Duchy of Reme under the sway of the Foerdewaith by negotiated settlement with Grand Duke Altharus Oersi III and the Oersi, the ruling family of Reme.
2843	Twin royal heirs Kennet and Cale born to Overking Paulus.
2854	Grand Duke Yajot Oersi Windflame falls sick; a succession war threatens the Oersi rulership of Reme, with Loreclans of the ducal lands beginning to form sides behind a number of possible successors.
2857	Negotiations begin between the Oersi of Reme and the overking of Foere regarding the possibility of Cale's adoption into the Rhemish Oersi as the successor to the ailing grand duke.
2858	Cale abdicates his claim to the throne and is given port of Reme.
2859	Grand Duke Yajot Oersi Windflame dies of sickness; Cale Oersi Macobert assumes the title and leadership of Reme based upon his adoption into the Oersi, with little opposition.
2861	Cale leads Great Colonization of Great Steppes.
2931	Caleen colonies reach shore of Lake Hali; humanoid attacks begin.
2947	Shadow walkers lead humanoid hordes from Lost Mountains; Caleen colonies destroyed; Wizard's Wall raised at Crynnomar Gap.
3213	Foerdewaith Wars of Succession begin.
3233	Grand Duchy of Reme gains independence from Foere; the "Short War" with Castorhage results in a decisive victory for Reme.
3517	The current year.

HISTORY

PRE-HYPERBOREAN PERIOD

Pre-Hyperborean Rhemish history is recorded only in the oral traditions of the Loreclans, although most of the main stories have been put to writing, expanded upon, and even turned into scripts for plays in the famed Remish theaters. The inhabitants of the Rhemish plains were nomadic Loreclans, some agricultural, some purely nomadic.

HYPERBOREAN ERA

The lands of Reme have been governed to one extent or another from the city of Reme since it was founded under the name of Remenos by Polemarch Oerson in the earliest years of the Hyperborean conquest of Akados. Boasting an excellent natural harbor and central location on trade routes, Remenos quickly became the premier port on the Crescent Sea, and the lands under its sway expanded to the west and east. For many years, any expansion north was held in check by the wild elves of the Green Realm, whose domain then extended to forests north of the High Downs. Then in the early Eighth Century I.R., war-bands from humanoid tribes in the Great Steppes began to pour through the Crynnomar Gap to make war on the elves. Fearing that the humanoids, if not stopped, would threaten their homelands farther to the west in the Green Realm, in 712 I.R. the elves moved up to the Crynnomar Gap to make it their line of defense, emptying their lands farther south. Noting the withdrawal of the elves, the imperator of Remenos took the opportunity to move into the forests north of the High Downs. When the elves finally beat back the humanoids and returned from the Gap in 725 I.R., they found Hyperborean legions entrenched and loggers clearcutting their former forest homes. Already disorganized and depleted after their war with the humanoids, the wild elves lacked the will for further battle and withdrew west deeper into the Green Realm, leaving Remenos in possession of the northern lands all the way to the Crynnomar Gap.

In 1548 I.R., hobgoblin raiding parties from the Deepfells Mountains fell upon the northern fringes of Reme. Survivors reported that a new hobgoblin kingdom led by a seemingly unbeatable warlord had arisen among the clans of Dragonbone Peak. The armies of the Northmarches staggered under the onslaught, and by 1557 I.R. fell to the hobgoblin hordes. The Hobgoblin Kingdom of the Deepfells claimed everything north of the High Downs, so Reme set a defensive line between the High Downs and the Green Mountains. Several years later, a group of adventurers infiltrated Dragonbone Peak and discovered that the warlord of the hobgoblins was in fact the demigod Kakobovia.

In 1571 I.R., an army of Deepfells hobgoblins and allied orcs invaded Arcady in the Feirgotha Plateau in the midst of the Stoneheart Mountains, only to be destroyed in a magical attack the following year. Kakobovia survived, however, and gathered the remaining forces of Dragonbone to launch an all-out attack on the High Downs. At the Battle of Ironhill, the forces of Reme lured the hobgoblin army into a trap and destroyed it. Grand Duke Borell I of Reme himself led the army and is said to have personally banished Kakobovia from the Material Plane.

The Rhemish nomads flooded back into their homelands after Ironhill, harrying and destroying any remaining outposts of the hobgoblin horde, and quickly re-established their rule over the homelands from which they had retreated.

In 2496 I.R., the Hyperborean capital of Curgantium was destroyed in a wildfire that spread and burned the Plains of Suilley and Matagost Forest. Three years later, the imperial capital moved to Tircople in Libynos, and the Hyperboreans abandoned their western empire. In the absence of an imperator, the grand duke declared himself sovereign and Reme independent, and changed the name of the capital from Remenos (the Hyperborean name) to Reme.

When the Hyperboreans began their retreat from the west in 2499 I.R., Imperator Barthorios Deciandos was ordered to return to the empire with the imperial garrison, which was mostly composed of diplomats and two Rhemish cavalry legions. Deciandos, who had spent the majority of his life in Reme, was disinclined to leave. He consulted with the Loreclannic dukes and with the high priests and priestesses of Dame Torren, Mithras, and Solanus in a series of counsels known today as the Council of Deciandos. Imperator Deciandos argued that Hyperborean withdrawal from the region would cause tremendous upheaval, and that if it was necessary for the Hyperboreans to withdraw, then something needed to be done to fill the ensuing power vacuum. At the end of the Council of Deciandos, the decision was made that the imperator would resign his post and be acclaimed grand duke in his own right by the Loreclans, accepting a sovereign position over Reme. In the end, only a very few of the Hyperboreans in Reme actually departed for the east, as the majority of the Hyperborean power structure simply changed its name — from the service of the imperator to the service of the grand duke.

FOERDEWAITH ERA

This period of independence barely lasted 200 years. In the early part of the 28th Century I.R., envoys of King Macobert of Foere came to Reme with a proposition: Swear fealty or prepare for war. The canny Grand Duke Altharus III, recognizing the benefits that would come from allying with Macobert as well as the importance to Foere of a secure harbor on the Crescent Sea, sent diplomats to negotiate a favorable treaty. And he obtained a deal that granted Reme substantial independence in exchange for an oath of fealty, Foere's access to the port, and a small annual payment to the crown.

Overking Paulus of Foere died in 2858 I.R., leaving behind twin sons, Kennet and Cale, though no one knew which was the elder. Different factions of the empire supported each of the brothers, and the possibility of a civil war loomed.

Reme faced a similar situation, where Grand Duke Yajot Oersi Windflame suffered from a wasting sickness that would clearly prove fatal at some time in the near future. As in Foere, but due to a lack of obvious heirs rather than too many, a succession war threatened the Oersi rulership of Reme, with Loreclans of the ducal lands forming sides behind a number of possible successors.

The twin heirs of Foere, showing a wisdom beyond their years, chose a course of action that solved both problems. Foere had too many heirs, and Reme too few, although the clarity of the problem must not have been nearly as clear at the time Reme and Foere actually had to deal with it. It is most likely that the solution to the problem evolved slowly in the minds of the various nobles involved, but eventually someone must have noticed the opportunity inherent in the long Rhemish tradition of adopting outsiders into their Loreclannic structure. In preparation for the eventual death of Grand Duke Yajot Oersi Windflame, Cale Macobert entered the Oersi Loreclan as Cale Oersi Macobert, adopted by the dying grand duke as a son and heir. This gave the Loreclans of Reme time to accept Cale as their future leader, and for the Oersi to overcome (either by negotiation or by combat) the claims of other potential Oersi successors.

In Foere, Kennet was eventually crowned as the sole overking of the Hyperborean monarchy. Cale, meanwhile, abdicated his claim to the throne, and succeeded to the title of grand duke of Reme. The arrangement united the two realms more closely for many years to come and aligned the new Oersi dynasty in Reme with the royal lineage of Foere. Cale's adoption remained a point of friction for decades among many of the Rhemish Loreclans, but to deny its validity would clearly fly in the face of centuries of Rhemish Loreclannic tradition. So-called "conservatives" who pointed to the fact that Cale had no Rhemish blood received little help from equally conservative Loreclannic leaders who sought to adhere closely to Rhemish traditions. Ultimately, the voices of opposition wavered and grew silent.

With the full support and resources of Courghais at his disposal, Cale began the Great Colonization, a mass migration of settlers through the Crynnomar Gap into the fertile and largely unoccupied grasslands of the Great Steppes. Little was known in Reme of the battles that the elves had fought at the Gap more than two millennia before, and such rumors as were remembered were generally dismissed — the Rhemish are quite aware that their campfire tales of valor and war contain a bit of poetic license. Unfortunately, in this case the fireside tales were fairly accurate. During the Great Colonization, the Foerdewaith military provided all the protection that the colonists needed against the few bands of Shattered Folk and disorganized humanoid tribes that were occasionally seen upon the plains beyond Reme.

Within 70 years, a string of settlements sprang up along the base of the surrounding mountains and in an unbroken chain across the steppes to the western coast more than a thousand miles away. Then the colonists reached the shores of Lake Hali in the far northwest where they found better organized and aggressive tribes of humanoids that suddenly descended in hordes onto the Great Steppes. The widely scattered settlements were ill-prepared, and many were sacked and burned before the Foerdewaith were even aware of the threat. With additional military assistance from Courghais, the colonists fortified their steadings and slowly pushed back the humanoid marauders until a tense stalemate settled in.

The stalemate did not last long. Less than two decades later, the floodgates opened once again as a horde poured forth from the Lost Mountains in numbers not seen since the great elven defense of the Crynnomar Gap, and this time new horrors never seen by the men of Foere accompanied the horde, creatures of shadow only whispered of in the old tales of the Northlands and the Ancient Ones. The horde descended in a tide that rolled south, burning and destroying settlements as it went. Finally, at the Crynnomar Gap, the legion of Cale and the remaining colonial irregulars met the humanoids and shadow walkers. But against this new threat, the steel pikes and heavy cavalry of Foere proved little worth, and the legion fell where it stood with tens of thousands dead. Among the missing was Grand Duke Cale himself.

Refugees from the settlements poured into Reme, and the army of the Foerdewaith prepared to march north to try to stop the oncoming horde. In this time of Reme's greatest need, the powerful archmages Margon and Alycthron appeared out of legend, having vanished from the knowledge of men more than 10 centuries before. At the Crynnomar Gap, where the gathering legions of Foere stared across a field at seemingly endless numbers of humanoids, the wizards called upon ancient and forgotten magics. The ground before the legions broke and tilted steeply backward, creating a slope where only a flat plain had stood before. The hordes beyond the break watched as the tilted ground rose in a massive escarpment of earth and stone before them and rose hundreds of feet and stretched all the way from the flanks of the Stoneheart Mountains, across the Crynnomar Gap, to the flanks of the Deepfells more than 500 miles distant. With such an unscalable height — thereafter known as the Wizard's Wall — blocking their path into the human lands, the humanoid hordes were turned back.

Despite their victory, the legions were saddened by the loss of the colonies and anyone trapped below on the plains beyond the Wizard's Wall. Still, the soldiers of Foere turned their backs upon the House of Cale and began the long march home. Garrisons were left along the length of the broken escarpment to ensure no attempts were made to scale the wall and sneak into the human lands beyond, but never again, swore the folk of Foere, would they cross the Crynnomar Gap and enter what became known as the Haunted Steppes beyond.

Between 2960 I.R. and 3207 I.R., the Foerdewaith embarked on four great crusades to Libynos in efforts to control the ancient city of Tircople and the holy Sacred Table. Many of the forces sent on these crusades left from the port of Reme, and both Grand Duke Tobiah and his son and heir Crown Duke Jesper were lost at sea in the sinking of the Third Great Crusade's fleet. Ultimately unsuccessful, the aggregate effect of these crusades was to drain the resources of Foere of manpower and gold. By 3213 I.R., Ramthion Island declared its independence from Foere, marking the beginning of the Foerdewaith Wars of Succession.

Independent World Power

In 3233 I.R., the grand duke of Reme, with the concurrence of the Lords' Council of Reme, declared its independence from Foere. By this time, the overking was unable to do much other than complain and attempt, without avail, to pressure other monarchs not to recognize the grand duchy's independence. Caught between the two, the young king Luceus of Castorhage managed to offend both nations and soon found himself in the decisive Short War with Reme. In seven months, Reme soundly defeated Castorhage's navy and forestalled Castorhage's attempts to regain control of Tandril Island and the Forest Coast, its former possessions. In the next year, the Free States declared their independence in the Forest Coast, and the Grand Duchy of Reme became the first to recognize this new state.

Civil Unrest in the Westmarches

Over the last 500 years, various families have fought for dominance in the Westmarches, which has led to civil unrest and, in a few circumstances, outright rebellion against the grand duke. Recently, the last of the disobedient families was brought to heel, leaving the grand duke in firm control of the Westmarches. As a result, areas under the domain of the duke in Eckland that were formerly largely inaccessible, such as the Windreft, became fertile ground for new settlers.

Ethnicity and Culture

Roughly a third of the humans in the grand duchy have some degree of Foerdewaith ancestry, although these are clustered mostly in cities, towns, and other substantial settlements. Adoption of bits and pieces of Foerdewaith culture is more widespread in Reme than actual Foerdewaith ancestry, for the cultural impact of Reme's alliance of convenience with Foere extended into the Loreclans of the plains as well as the cities. The common tongue is used as a trade language to overcome Loreclannic dialects of Kirkut, jewelry is heavily influenced by Foerdewaith craftsmanship, and — perhaps oddly, perhaps not — plays and music from Foere are performed enthusiastically by amateur troupes even deep in the plains, by purely nomadic Loreclans.

The Loreclans and the Shattered Folk

Every 50 years, tribal families from the Shattered Folk beyond the Crynnomar Gap are permitted to petition for a right to settle in the Rhemish plains, and a lottery is held to determine who may immigrate. These families are incorporated into their Loreclans, for most tribes of the Shattered Plains have at least some representatives in the Rhemish Plateaus that have been granted their own Loreclannic lands by one or the other of the Rhemish dukes.

Loreclans owing allegiance directly to the grand duke hold the southern and central portions of Reme. Note that the relative population of Foerdewaith ancestry is high because this region contains the city of Reme but the composition of Loreclannic ancestry is little different from the other parts of Reme.

The eastern boundary of the grand duke's territory is the Northway Road, the Northernmost reach is the city of Vazarath, the westernmost border is the Road of Horses, and the southern border is the Whiterush River.

Overview

Reme, Ducal Lands

Alignment: Neutral Good

Capital: City of Reme

Ruler: His Far-Reaching Presence Iltobarus, Grand Duke (Kirkut: Great Khan) of Reme, Wave-Rider of the Crescent Sea and Wind-Rider of the Marches

Government: Monarchy with a Loreclannic-feudal organization

Population: 4,341,000 (including only grand ducal lands) (Rhemish Loreclannic, in Reme itself completely urbanized 2,186,200, Foerdewaith 1,738,500, halfling 162,400, mountain dwarf 71,100, hill dwarf 66,500, gnome 59,500, half elf 31,400, high elf 17,300, half-orc 7,300, other 800)

Monstrous: Hobgoblins and orcs (Deepfells), goblins, orcs, trolls, rocs and green dragons (Green Mountains and Quail Valley), dire hyenas and gnolls (Westwood and the Endless Hills), creatures of shadow (Haunted Wood), orcs (Ashen Hills), kobolds (High Downs), sabosan, greenskin orcs and ettins (Whiterush River region)

Languages: Common, Rhemish, Kirkut, Elven

Religion: Solanus, Dame Torren, Mithras (city); Archeillus, Sefagreth, Vanitthu, Belon the Wise, Muir, Thyr; Kamien, Freya, Telophus, Ceres (countryside)

Resources: Wine, baleen oil, grain, lumber, salt, trade

Currency: Rhemish

Technology Level: Renaissance (city of Reme), Medieval (cities), High Middle Ages (rural areas)

Demonym/Adjectival Demonym: Reman (for the city specifically), Rheman/Rhemish for the people of the entire country

Government and Military

Government

The Grand Duchy of Reme is a hereditary, feudal monarchy ruled by a grand duke or grand duchess if one translates into the common tongue, but in Rhemish a title that means "grand khan" in the Kirkut linguistic roots. For purposes of understanding Reme's structure of government, as opposed to its culture, the term "duke" is probably the better fit. The grand duke's powers are more limited than those of a Hundaei-culture khan to the north of Reme, but they are limited by Loreclannic conventions and ancient ancestral promises, not by the abstract laws that purport to restrain feudal rulers in other cultures such as Foere. Nevertheless, restrained as they are by these conventions and ancestral promises, the grand dukes of Reme interfere very little in the affairs of the dukes of the Waymarch, Westmarch, and Northmarches.

Local authority in the Marches is devolved to the respective dukes of the Northmarches, the Westmarches, and the Waymarch as the protectors of Loreclans that have sworn fealty to them as groups. Although the position of duke by tradition passes down to the predecessor's first heir, the grand dukes can remove and appoint dukes, a right they have exercised on only a few, very rare occasions. Below the dukes (or, in the case of the ducal lands, the grand duke), civilized regions are usually divided into baronies (a title for chiefs of Loreclans conquered by the three original Loreclans of the city of Reme), with small communities also held by "Loreclannic knights" — a close analogy to the status of knighthood elsewhere in the Lost Lands.

The grand dukes have long ruled with the guidance of a high council made up of the dukes of the Marches and a group of chosen advisors. The advisors generally include one or more of the ruling members of the prominent merchant houses such as Drenwall, Oron, and Gastone-Sheshek.

Military

Given the size of the territory of Reme, it is unsurprising that the duchy maintains a sizable military contingent at all times. The grand duke draws forces from the grand ducal lands and from the forces of the dukes, who are obliged to provide a certain number of warriors to their monarch each year. The navy of Reme also owes allegiance directly to the grand duke, and warships continually venture around the Crescent Sea and beyond the Mouth of Akados to protect shipping lanes and deter pirates. Command of the ships of the Reman navy is vested in the lord high admiral of Reme, a direct appointee of the grand duke.

Each of the dukes of Reme also maintains an army drawn from their own landholdings and from their feudal vassals. The Northmarches and Waymarch both have sizable standing militias, in the former case largely to protect against incursions from the Haunted Wood and the Deepfells, and in the latter case principally to protect trade. The Westmarches are slowly rebuilding their military now that decades of civil war have finally come to an end.

Reme's military tends to focus on heavy infantry with large contingents of the light cavalry of Loreclannic warriors. Light infantry has little use in Reme's open interior. Large-scale battles are few and far between, with most combat taking place between light cavalry units of varying sizes. The heavy infantry is almost always used in battles against settlements or fortifications that have failed to screen civilian retreats from the Rhemish light cavalry; such battles are virtually always a mopping-up operation. The Rhemish tactic against invasions such as the great hobgoblin incursions or large-scale banditry is more to cut off supply lines, weaken opposing forces, and in many cases simply to wait until invaders become lost on the open plain rather than to engage enemies that are at full strength. In foreign wars, the most significant contribution is, again, to contribute large forces of mounted archers clad in light armor of high quality.

Rhemish military forces are called "legions" in the Hyperborean tradition, but even during Reme's Hyperborean Era the composition of legions operating on the Rhemish plains was vastly different than that of the traditional Hyperborean legion, as the imperator adapted strategy to the wide-open plain. Rhemish legions, as noted above, usually consist of relatively small heavy infantry contingents that operate as an auxiliary to the legion's core, a much-larger number of light cavalry units augmented with one or two troops of heavy knights that operate in tandem with the heavy infantry. Ordinarily, the advance of a Rhemish legion is more like a naval operation, with a cloud of cavalry troops operating over a wide area around the heavy infantry, which lags far behind the legion's leading edge, only coming up to finish off opponents who have been weakened by cavalry operations designed to cut supply lines and remove advance units.

Religion

Although temples to many gods may be found within the walls of the city of Reme, Solanus, Dame Torren, and Mithras are the matron/patron deities of the city, and their worship is predominant among the residents. The worship of Mithras is almost exclusively limited to the cities and settlements, having been an import of the Hyperborean legions that did not catch on among the nomadic Loreclans.

In addition to the three most prominent deities, other gods (mainly of the Hyperborean or native Loreclannic pantheons) are worshiped throughout the grand duchy. Merchants and travelers pray to Sefagreth or Belon the Wise, many soldiers and city guards venerate Vanitthu, and Kamien, Freya, Telophus and Ceres have devotees throughout the countryside. Given the dedication to Solanus throughout Reme, this is one of the few regions on Akados that has proven resistant to the growth of the faith of Mitra.

The Loreclans usually worship Halatra the Horse, and many Loreclannic knights also worship Bowbe, god of battle-ragers. The worship of Bowbe is more common in the eastern regions of the plains but is found scattered throughout the Loreclans across the country.

Trade and Commerce

The city of Reme sits at the western end of the Tradeway, a critical trade road that in the east passes through Bard's Gate, thence to Freegate, a port city on the Gulf of Akados, and beyond. The Tradeway has existed since the days of the Hyperborean Empire and provides a direct travel route that does not require a detour through the heart of the Foerdewaith empire.

The city of Reme also boasts one of the best harbors on the Crescent Sea, with merchant traffic arriving from and departing to all of the known ports of Akados and beyond.

As a result, nearly anything can be bought or sold in the markets of Reme. Most of the trade throughout the grand duchy is controlled by several powerful merchant houses, each of which has a representative on the Council of Merchant Houses and Guilds that, with a lord mayor, governs the city of Reme.

Loyalties and Diplomacy

Reme has no colonies beyond its traditional, ancient borders. In part, this is due to a distaste for foreign conquest arising from the painful memory of the terrors that nearly overran the grand duchy from the Haunted Steppes after the disastrous attempt to colonize those lands during the reign of Grand Duke Cale. But even without that impetus, with the excellent harbor at the city of Reme, vast lands providing ample food and other resources, and a central location in Akados unmatched by any other power, it really has no need to look elsewhere for conquest or colonization. Reme's entire political structure is based upon the ancestral lands of its Loreclans, and there are no ancestral lands that Reme has not already reached and protected. If Reme were ever to lose control of lands claimed by one or more of its Loreclans, however, the reprisal would be savage and involve hordes of mounted cavalry in numbers far beyond what most feudal leaders could possibly mobilize.

As a result of this general attitude of peacefulness beyond the borders, the grand duchy seeks to be on good terms with other realms of the Lost Lands, so long as they do not threaten the sovereignty of Reme's lands or the security of its trade. Stability is the primary goal sought by the grand dukes. As a result, it is on friendly terms with Foere, the Kingdom of the North Heath, the Kingdom of the Vast, the Principality of Olduvar, the Kingdom of Suilley, Bard's Gate, the Borderland Provinces, and the Kingdom of Oceanus. It has particularly good relations with the Tycho Free States and has been instrumental in ensuring their ongoing independence. Reme trades with various cities in the Northlands throughout Libynos. Reme even has good — albeit wary — relations with Castorhage.

To protect its interests, the grand dukes have agents and spies in nearly every country and major city on Akados, and even in many locales in Libynos. The slow but steady deterioration of Foere is of great concern to Reme, particularly the growing chaos in the Borderland Provinces and Sundered Kingdoms. This concern is a large part of the reason that the grand dukes encouraged the alliance between the Duchy of Waymarch and Bard's Gate, as this secures the Tradeway and the eastern border of the grand duchy.

In terms of actual political threats to the country, Reme has few concerns at this time in its history. The civil unrest historically seen in the Westmarches has recently been resolved in Reme's favor. There are, of course, tribes of humanoids in the realm, particularly in the Green Mountains and in the far north amid the Haunted Wood and the Deepfells. But none of those poses any real threat to the security of the Rhemish heartland. The Haunted Steppes beyond the Crynnomar Gap also poses a theoretical danger, but the Wizard's Wall continues to be an impassable barrier to those of ill intent who might wish to cross.

Locations in the Grand Ducal Territory

Reme, City of

See Chapter 3: The City of Reme

Gilboath

Alignment: Neutral Good
Ruler: Mayor Aerin Sarporond
Government: Mayor and Town Council
Population: 2,220 (Foerdewaith 1,104, human mixed ethnicity 868, halfling 225, half-elf 23)
Languages: Common
Religion: Muir
Resources: Grain, wine
Technology Level: Medieval

Gilboath is a small town about 150 miles north of the city of Reme. Its main business, were it not for one fact, would be agriculture. Rich fields and vineyards can be found in the surrounding region. Farmers and vintners come into town to sell their wares and to buy goods from elsewhere.

The town's great claim to fame, however, is its most famous son, Gerrant of Gilboath, a Justicar of Muir and one of the last two members of that holy order. Gerrant was lost in the Battle of Tsar between the Army of Light and the Disciples of Orcus in 3209 I.R. Sometime after that, a shrine to Muir was established in Gilboath. The townsfolk spared no expense in building the temple, which is constructed of beautiful white marble and houses six falcons, Muir's sacred animal. It is said that the falconer can read portents from the goddess in the flights of his raptors. Pilgrims from near and far come to the shrine to worship Muir and to seek the intercession of her holy paladin Gerrant.

The High Downs

The High Downs are technically an independent kingdom and are described in full in the chapter "Beyond the Borders."

Quintas

Alignment: Lawful Neutral
Ruler: Earl Darvel Arcunas
Government: Feudal
Population: 21,378 (Foerdewaith 15,173, half-elf 244, human mixed ethnicity 4,331, halfling 160, gnome 629, hill dwarf 841)
Languages: Common
Religion: Freya, Telophus, Archeillus
Resources: Trade (cattle), grain
Technology Level: Medieval

Quintas sits at the crossing of three important trade roads, with one leading north to Ironhill and the Northmarches, one east to Broadwater, the gateway to Eamonvale, and the last south to Yalendir and the rest of the grand duchy. The Earl Arcunas has profited greatly from this location and the amount of tradegoods that pass through the city's gates. As a result, the earl is a very wealthy man. Fortunately for the folk of Quintas and the rest of the county, the earl is also a thoughtful shepherd of his wealth and ensures that his demesne is well run with as little corruption as possible.

The Mustering Field is a large, open area outside the city walls. Although it would make for good farmland, it is always kept unsown. According to local legend, the field was used for the mustering of the armies of Reme in 1573 I.R. on their way to the Battle of Ironhill with the forces of Dragonbone Peak, and again of the Foerdewaith legions heading north to the Crynnomar Gap during the war against the humanoid and shadow hordes from the Haunted Plains in 2947 I.R. It is said that so long as the field remains available for the use of the Rhemish army, the grand duchy will never fall.

The Pit of Yar-Mith

West of Quintas, one finds a mysterious, giant hole shattered through the stony ground to the very bedrock. A castle was once here, a towering affair of gleaming white stone with tall, turreted towers waving brightly-colored pennants in the soft breeze. This castle is now a tumbled mass of broken masonry and shattered lives.

The castle of Yar-Mith was to be the wonder of its age, a fortification as functional as it would be beautiful. This perfect blend of palace and castle was constructed 200 years ago by Grand Duke Traiv as a country estate (and potential refuge in times of strife). Although the grand duchy was at peace and had been for some time, Traiv was a cautious, almost paranoid person. He saw plots and schemes in every corner of his court, save for in the hearts of his wife and children. His rule, especially in the city of Reme, was unquestionably marked by cruelties: He had suspects arrested and tortured until they revealed their crimes, real or imagined. Sometimes people would simply disappear, with the duke's justices coming and taking them away without explanation. The great noble and merchant houses of the grand duchy were forced to walk a fine line, displaying public support for the grand duke, but not too much, for even that could trigger his suspicions. Certainly, the grand duke expected some kind of revolt at any moment, and thus he ordered a castle that would serve as a pleasant home for his family, a place of safety while he brought wrath down upon the traitors he spied in every shadow.

The construction of such a magnificent castle strained the coffers of the grand duchy, and Traiv levied new taxes to pay for it. When these caused complaints, the resistance only reinforced his belief that a great conspiracy was under way. Traiv fled to the half-completed castle when a part of the Northmarches rose up in revolt — even though the uprising was a small and unrelated rebellion of peasants and commoners that was quickly put down by the local lords. He shut himself up in it with his family and servants to await an army of imagined traitors who never came.

The duke of the Northmarches himself came to inform the grand duke that the rebellion had been put down, but he took the duke's advance guard to be an approaching host and ordered the gates barred. Days passed as the duke's entourage camped outside the castle and sent messenger after messenger, gaining no response. Days turned into weeks, and then months. The duke of the Northmarches departed, and the nobility of Reme became greatly concerned about the realm's stability.

Grand Duke Traiv kept himself and his family shut up inside the castle of Yar-Mith for 10 months. During this time, he did not allow any to leave, nor did he allow any to enter. Supplies ran short, and one by one the servants deserted him. Even his most loyal guards saw the signs of madness growing, and many fled. A handful remained at their posts out of duty and loyalty — or in some cases because they had committed such crimes at his command that if the grand duke fell, so too would their own heads.

Matters came to a head one night when the grand duke accused his own wife of poisoning him (he claimed his rat pie tasted odd). In a rage, he ordered his guards to take her away to the dungeon, but the guards refused to obey. They took no action against their liege, though, and Traiv stormed off into the dark, unfinished parts of the castle. Fearing some mad and rash act, as well as being worn down by the "siege" and its privations, the Loreclannic knights of the ducal guard bundled up the grand duchess and her children, then fled the castle.

Traiv was too busy with his mad work to notice the flight of his family. Secretly, he had engaged a number of wizards to put an enchantment on the castle's bedrock before its construction even began. As a last resort, if he and his family were to be captured by traitors and likely face some inglorious death, the entire castle would collapse into a pit that formed beneath it. This powerful enchantment needed the blood of a monarch, or a grand duke as the case would be, to evoke itself into power. Rooting around in the lowest dungeons of the half-finished castle, Traiv found the seal to activate the enchantment. Cackling madly, he flung himself on it and impaled his body on a spindle jutting from the seal's center.

With a roar, the castle collapsed into the ground, leaving nothing behind save a cloud of dust and a gaping maw in the earth. Few people visit these ruins, for many tales tell of the mad duke who haunts the environs. Those who do can see the gleam of old weathered stone studding the walls of the pit. Some talk of the great hoard that the grand duke collected and stored in his refuge; others say that disturbing the dead to quest for buried treasure is foolish. Yet others wonder if the grand duke had other enchantments placed upon the castle, and if they are still to be found there, and what horrors might spill out if they are disturbed. The history of the pit is also one of the early instances of a certain weakness in the line of the Decian grand dukes, a weakness destined to lead to their eventual decline, infertility, and inability to produce heirs of suitable mental stability.

Remenos River

The city of Reme sits astride the Remenos River, which makes its slow, peaceful way through the fields of Reme from the Stoneheart Mountains located 1,000 miles to the northeast. The Remenos is navigable virtually all the way to the Stonehearts and is regularly used to transport goods upriver and downriver.

Use the **River (General) Encounter Table** for random encounters on the Remenos River.

Varazath

Alignment: Lawful Neutral
Ruler: Commander Alforce Berallo and Baron Midiera Nais
Government: Feudal
Population: 16,248 (human mixed ethnicity 12,185, Foerdewaith 2,956, halfling 811, half-elf 296)
Languages: Common
Religion: Freya, Telophus, Sefagreth
Resources: Trade, cattle
Technology Level: Medieval

Varazath represents the northern extent of the lands of the grand duke. The city stands alongside the relatively minor trade route between central Reme and the Frontier at the northern extent of the Road of Horses. The city is located on a small rise and is divided into two parts: the ducal city, which is held directly by the grand duke, and the baronial city, which comprises the feudal village that has now joined with the city as the city grew. The city walls now encompass both subsections, with the baronial city occupying the outer bailey and the smaller ducal city occupying the inner bailey, which also contains the ducal castle. The castle is a fortress rather than a residence, essentially a military installation intended to keep intruders from the mountains and the High Downs from entering the territory of the grand duke. Since the fortress is as isolated as one can get in the grand duchy, it is neither a desired posting nor particularly efficient. Slovenly, in fact, would be the word chosen by most of the duke's commanders to describe the condition of the fortress and its garrison. The city reflects the relative poverty of its trade route but is by no means in the poor condition of the garrison that ostensibly protects it.

N
VARAZATH
GRAND DUCHY OF REME

White Squirrel Inn

Cursed by a wandering warlock to "never be anywhere," the White Squirrel has become a popular stop for wealthy travelers, adventurers, and those seeking the strange or bizarre. The inn is not tied to any one location: It shifts and moves about seemingly at random, disappearing in one place and reappearing in another. While this has limited business somewhat, most people visiting inns are trying to get from one place to another, so it has drawn in many who desire to experience this oddity or who just want to gamble on taking a shortcut across the Grand Duchy of Reme.

Twenty years ago, a wandering warlock visited the inn seeking a hot meal and a warm bed. He found neither, for the inn was full and the proprietor did not like the looks of the shaggy and ill-kempt vagabond. The warlock pleaded for at least a bowl of stew and warm straw in the stable, but the innkeeper refused. The disturbance brought out some of the nobles staying at the inn, who ordered their retainers to beat and drive the warlock away. In revenge for this treatment, the warlock cursed the inn, proclaiming that those inside would never see their homes again.

The visiting nobles who had filled the inn and treated the warlock so shabbily never did, indeed, return to their homes — at least not in any meaningful way. They found themselves consumed with wanderlust, and in their travels were all eventually killed by strange accidents, kidnapped by foes, or otherwise destroyed. The innkeeper and his staff were already home, but the curse manifested itself by shifting the inn to a new location, hundreds of miles away. Since that time, the inn has wandered across the grand duchy, still subject to the warlock's strange curse. Sometimes it remains in one place for a few days, other times for a number of months; but sooner or later, the inn disappears to appear elsewhere.

Which is, of course, bad for business. The owner, Hirik Mathers, tried to escape only to be teleported back into the inn the next time it shifted locations. His servers, cooks, stable boys, and maids experienced the same when they fled. Moving from one location to another made getting supplies difficult, and after a few travelers were accidently transported to the far end of the grand duchy, business essentially stopped.

In desperation, Mathers sold the inn, curse and all, to Sira Karst. A dabbler in the arcane arts herself, Karst was unfazed by the inn's curse and tendency to wander. For several months she experimented with the inn, tracking its relocations, charting when and where and most importantly why, it relocated, and even firing two maids to see if that freed them from the curse. Much like Mathers, once the maids were no longer formally associated with the inn, the curse no longer seemed to affect them.

Satisfied that she had a handle on the whole "teleporting inn" situation, Karst reopened the White Squirrel and began a campaign to promote it across the grand duchy. She hired troubadours to write songs extolling the mystery of the inn and made sure to mention the likely locations to find it (also copper ale night, the third night after any relocation). She also paid several adventurers to travel the grand duchy and purchase the land where the inn tended to relocate, putting up signage nearby and marking out the "landing point."

Because of these efforts, the inn grew in fame and popularity. Karst increased the rates for everything from the ale (save on copper ale night), the rooms, and even the stabling. Only the wealthy, or at least well off, could afford to stay in the White Squirrel, but even the middling classes could manage a meal in the common room. Mysterious, cursed, and famed in song, the White Squirrel became the place to go for the rich and powerful of the grand duchy — even the grand duke and duchess have spent the night there (to the grand duchess's disappointment, the inn remained in place).

Karst has spent her profits wisely, paying her staff high wages to compensate for the curse, upgrading the rooms and kitchens, and adding to the inn. New structures belonging to the inn are teleported right alongside those that existed when the curse was levied, as Karst learned by adding a second privy out back. While most of the difficulty of supplying the inn has been taken care of thanks to Karst's tracking of the regular landing points of the inn, she has also added several outbuildings for times when the inn reappears far from civilization.

The White Squirrel is a sprawling complex enclosed by a stout stone wall (the inn has reappeared in the Deepfells a few times). The main building is a three-story, timber-and-stone structure. The main floor houses the common room and kitchen. Sixteen private rooms (with locks on doors and windows) fill the upper two floors, though one large double room on the second floor serves as Karst's home and office. Flanking the main building and forming a three-sided courtyard in front are a stable and a two-story structure housing another dozen rooms. Behind the main building is a bathhouse, brewery, cold house, dormitory for the staff, a fromagerie, granary, laundry, stone-lined privies, and a well. The well, as far as anyone can tell, seems to grow its own water supply when the inn relocates.

Relocating the White Squirrel Inn

1d12	Location
1	Five miles north of Albion
2	On the edge of Tanners Green
3	A previously unknown side alley in Reme
4	Across the road from the Dagger & Rose
5	10 miles due west of Quintas
6	Deep in the Deepfells
7	A mile south of the Wizard's Wall
8	On the Tradeway *exactly* halfway between Reme and Panetoth
9	Atop a hill in the High Downs
10	At the confluence of River Wren and Quail River
11	An island 25 miles south of Martyn's Nest; Karst keeps two small boats and a folding dock in storage for when this happens
12	Far away; you decide where the inn relocates.

If the party visits the inn or seeks it out, roll 1d100. This is the number of days the inn spends at its current location. Roll on the table above to determine where the inn ends up; any result of its present location means that the inn vanishes from sight and then reappears a few minutes later at the same place.

White Squirrel Menu

Food and Drink

Squirrel Tail Ale	4 cp
Now You See It Lager	4 cp
Now You Don't Stout	6 cp
Local ales, lagers, and stouts (varies by location)	8 cp
River Wren Wines	3 sp
Local vintages (varies by location)	4 sp
Imported beverages (from outside the grand duchy)	4–10 sp

Meals

Sausage and onions, with bread and sauce	5 cp
Mutton, ham, or other meat with stewed vegetables	2 sp
Dessert of the Place (varies by location)	6 cp
Break-Fast and Go (porridge, sausage, ham, eggs)	4 cp
Private meals by request	1–50 gp

Rooms and Stabling

Common room	1 sp/ night
(includes straw mattress and blanket, pillow rental 1 cp)	
Private room	4 gp/night
Stabling	1–4 gp depending on steed

WHITERUSH

Alignment: Neutral Good
Ruler: Lord Breldin Greaves
Government: Feudal
Population: 4,220 (Foerdewaith 2,104, human mixed ethnicity [mostly Loreclannic] 1,868, halfling 225, half-elf 23)
Languages: Common
Religion: Kamien, Freya, Telophus
Resources: Trade, timber, fishing
Technology Level: Medieval

Whiterush is a trade town located where the Poitres Road crosses the Whiterush River just above the Whiterush Falls. Lord Breldin Greaves holds title to the city and most of the nearby river valley. Lord Breldin spent his youth enjoying wine, women, and sausages, and today is a doddering old man with a prominent paunch and a permanently addled expression on his wrinkled face. The Quinns, a local family, control much of the trade going through Whiterush. The land here is generally peaceful, although rumor says that a tribe of orcs lives nearby in the forests to the north of town.

WHITERUSH RIVER

The Whiterush River flows through a lightly forested river valley running from the Old Tors to Rimeth Sound. It is navigable for most of its length and is economically important to southern Reme.

Use the **River (General) Encounter Table** for random encounters on the Whiterush.

YALENDIR

Alignment: Neutral Good
Ruler: Lady Belestra Vorns
Government: Governor appointed by the grand duke
Population: 36,422 (Foerdewaith 18,671, half-elf 111, Loreclannic 16,696, halfling 944)
Languages: Common
Religion: Freya, Telophus, Kamien
Resources: Trade, grains, glass
Technology Level: Medieval

OVERVIEW

Yalendir is a key trade city located at the fork of the Remenos River and the River Eamon and sits astride the Trade Road from Panetoth in the south to Quintas and Broadwater in the north. As a result, a large portion of the goods heading to and from the Northmarches and the Stoneheart Mountains must pass through its gates.

Lady Belestra Vorns was granted the lucrative governance of Yalendir seven years ago after retiring from a highly successful career as a captain in the Rhemish navy. Having had enough of the sea for several lifetimes, she asked for a demesne far from the ocean and was thus vested in lands outside Yalendir and appointed the city's governor. She is a thoughtful ruler with little experience in administration who relies heavily on her advisors. Perhaps too heavily, as several take advantage of their position, and a bit of corruption now plagues the city. Increasingly, bribery is required to get anything accomplished. There is little doubt that the Lady Vorns would put a stop to this behavior if she knew of it. So far, it is relatively confined and, given the wealth that passes through the city, has not risen to the level where she might take notice.

Yalendir is recognized throughout Reme for the wonderful stained glass manufactured here. While the sand must be brought in via the river, certain plants found on the river's shore here are processed into dyes that produce magnificent colors in the glass. The secrets of the glassworks are closely held by the glassworkers' guild here and are never shared with anyone other than another master or one's apprentice.

DESCRIPTION

Nestled on the banks of the green valley of the River Eamon, the city itself is surrounded by a high ditch and levy system to protect against spring flooding. The levy itself is topped with compact, 20-foot-high stone walls quarried in the Stoneheart Mountains to the north and ferried downriver. A large keep sits in the northern half of the city where it keeps watch over the northern frontier and serves to remind locals of the dangers posed by beasts of the Stoneheart as well as the ancient threat of the things that dwell beyond the Wizard's Wall.

The city structures are of Foerdewaith design, though they are thatch roofed due to the great quantities of sturdy blue stem prairie grass that abounds in the region. Most of the residences are two to three stories tall and contain an open common room, a storage room on the ground floor with a hearth, and two to four rooms located on the upper floors. Wealthier citizens also have a root cellar where they hide in the event of tornados that flare up on the prairie during spring and summer. Meals are cooked at the hearth or outside during the summer to avoid the boiling temperatures that can occur. Families are often made up of four to six members of varying ages, with the elderly often living with their children in houses that have been passed down for several generations.

GOVERNMENT

Lady Belestra Vorns fairly recently took custody of Yalendir Keep and the administration of the city.

Sir Froederic Gethe, Lady Belestra's chamberlain, is the power behind the pennant in Yalendir. The advisor to the former governor, Sir Gethe assumed he would be next in line for the lordship of Yalendir and chafes at playing second fiddle to a sea captain who is unfamiliar with the intricacies of local government and the monetary value to be gained from controlling this bottleneck of overland and river trade. Sir Gethe appointed Sheriff Oelwein as the city's main tax-collector, an arrangement that allows him to siphon money away from the city. Oelwein is a corrupt lesser noble who purchased the rank of lieutenant in the Waymarch cavalry but found that hard riding across the open prairie produced saddle sores that were unsatisfactory to his comfort. Thus, fines for small infractions pile up, with money flowing from Oelwein's hand to Sir Gethe's with only a trickle hitting the tax box assigned to appease Iltobarus in Reme. Such is the current administration of the city.

CITIZENRY

The denizens of the city are most commonly Foerdewaith with smaller contingencies of visiting Plainsfolk. Very small enclaves of halflings and half-elves live within the city, and they typically find themselves working as entertainers, tinsmiths, tinkers, tradesmen, and peddlers who deal their wares to the wagon caravans of the duchy's tradeways.

MILITARY

The government of Yalendir keeps 200 guardsmen in the city watch, 600 footmen and archers to patrol the prairie around the city (and to guard Yalendir Keep), and an additional 500 cavalry of Waymarch who rotate patrols along the Trade Road, with 200 held in reserve in the city at all times. For many of the troops, these postings serve as training exercises for their eventual deployment in the Stoneheart Valley in the service of Bard's Gate.

Troops are barracked in the towers that surround Yalendir when not out on patrol.

Threats and Adventures

Organized Crime

The greatest threat to the city is the encroaching noose of organized crime hiding under the nose of Sir Gethe and Sheriff Oelwein's own corruption. Missing criminals are seldom noticed, as their bodies float on down the Eamon River and end up becoming food to river monsters long before they manage the hundreds of miles to the port of Reme.

The Red Thumb, the Gastone-Shesheks, and a newly-opened charterhouse of the Wheelwrights Guild all hide safehouses in Yalendir. The Red Thumb leadership in Yalendir chased the Gastone-Shesheks to one of their last remaining strongholds.

With the arrival of Duloth's goons, who are managed from Bard's Gate, a subtle triangle of danger now exists between the various thieves and criminals hidden just beneath the surface of the city. It is probable that the Gastone-Shesheks may pledge their allegiance to the Wheelwrights in exchange for protection from the Red Thumb. The Wheelwrights would benefit from the intelligence that the Gastone-Shesheks have to offer, but they are not strong enough yet regionally to run the table.

Adventure Hook: The Lead Mine

The stained-glass industry in Yalendir is dependent on a constant supply of lead and sand. Perfect sand from the sea is plentifully brought up from Reme. Recently, however, the lead supply took a tumble as a few of the lead mines 50 miles west of the city were overrun.

The threat is actually the result of a band of mercenary kobolds who invaded the mines at the behest of a secret benefactor. Assertive adventurers bold enough to investigate the lack of communication between the lead mines and business interests in the city may be richly rewarded by Lady Vorns for uncovering the truth. The secret benefactor is Quezooct, a highly-intelligent Xorn-Mother from the Elemental Plane of Earth, who has chosen to raise her latest brood upon a diet of lead. The broken shells from Quezooct's two clutches of eggs are still present in the lower level of the mine, and in the very lowest level the youg, small, and less-dangerous xornlings are jealously guarded by the Xorn-Mother.

Notable Locations

Docks of Yalendir

The docks thrive with activity. Barge captains sail down from Dun Eamon, while others push up from the shores of Reme as they haul barges of sand for the burgeoning trade in stained glass manufactured in Yalendir for use in the grand temple and glittering towers of Reme.

The docks have a rough reputation due to the presence of rival crime organizations of Red Thumb and Gastone-Sheshek thieves. The docks are highlighted by numerous taverns, gambling halls, and bawdy houses that are fit in between warehouses and tenement dwellings of local dockworkers.

The Rathole

Fealie Olein, a halfling who runs a few tables of dice and card games managed by the house, operates this low-stakes gambling hall. A street dwarf named Cordut and a retired human mercenary named Borgo guard the Rathole. Fealie is affiliated with the Gavestone crime organization and has a hideout under the back bar for high-ranking members of the gang who are on the run.

The Rathole serves the following goods:

See **Encounter 1** in the *Convenient Reference Guide to Reme* for NPC stats, if you need them, for Felie Olein, Borgo, and Cordut.

LeCroiy Linens

This warehouse factory is known for making linen sheets, shirts, pants, and other items from locally sourced flax. The shop factory is little more than a sweatshop that serves as one of the last remaining fronts of the Gavestone organization. The work produced here is considered superior to that of many other linen makers and is produced in a massive scale by the industrious fingers of halflings who work here for low pay. Nobles who can afford them throughout the central and southwestern Duchy of Reme use LeCroiy sheets. The warehouse is heavily guarded by Gavestone agents, and a large subterranean hideout is located below the warehouse where operations have moved since the Red Thumb's purge of Gavestone activities in Reme.

LeCroiy is a respected member of the community and has a well-guarded manor home not far from Yalendir Keep. His underworld ties are known to only a very few, including Chamberlain Gethe who is well paid for his interventions on behalf of the Gavestone organization. Gethe knows that even with the Gavestones in decline, any implication by a high-ranking member of their mob would result in his immediate execution at the hands of Lady Vorns.

See **Encounter 2** in the *Convenient Reference Guide to Reme* for NPC stats, if you need them, for LeCroiy and the Gavestone Rogues.

Sand and Flame

The Sand and Flame is an upscale purveyor of handcrafted stained glass. Leelio Fathle, a half-elf artisan, crafts the glass in panes and plates, and is considered the most gifted craftsman of the trade operating in a city known for its gorgeous stained-glass pieces. She is commissioned by many of the temples in Reme and Panetoth, as well as nobles of the marches to create windows and lampshades. Due to this, she is frequently out of the shop and leaves it attended by her apprentices. Recently, there has been a reduction in lead output and she has lost contact with one of her suppliers altogether.

Leelio pays handsomely for rare foreign dyes and minerals that can be mixed to create new and lustrous shades for her stained-glass works.

The Red Plumb

This restaurant favors selling pasta made from locally grown wheat with rich tomato sauce and hearty meatballs of beef from the herds that march through the city. A recent arrival to the city, the restaurant has quickly become an upscale favorite of the wealthier denizens who enjoy imported bottles of red wine brought up from the metropolis of Reme while listening to the music of a string quartet.

The classiness of the establishment belies the fact that it is the local front operation for the Red Thumb guild. Ambrosguie Savion is the chapter leader of Yalendir. He is broad-faced and charming and has already made the acquaintance of Lady Vorns, who is thrilled to have a touch of culture here in the high plains and frequently has Ambrosguie cater to her and her courtiers in Yalendir Keep. Unbeknownst to her, her riches and the wealth of the city are being sized up for a variety of planned heists.

Ambrosguie's entire staff is at least some form of thief with a specialty in all manner of skullduggery and robbery from second-story men, to stiff-arm criminals, to professional locksmiths and footpads.

See **Encounter 3** in the *Convenient Reference Guide to Reme* for NPC stats, if you need them, for Ambrosguie and the Red Thumb rogues.

Wheelwrights Guild Hall

This hall is barracks and home to around 50 members of the Wheelwrights who are within the city at any given time. They have begun muscling in on operations involving wagons moving into and out of the city and are working on taking control of any loading and unloading of barges in town, much to the chagrin of the Red Thumb operatives who did not expect Duloth's reach to stretch so far into their own claimed territory.

Romblad Marsalle is the head of the local Wheelwrights chapter. He was tasked with bringing three oak boxes filled with dirt from Bard's Gate and finding a place to hide them within Yalendir once he arrived. He did what was instructed of him by Duloth Armitage and had the boxes placed in the cellar of the defunct River Plains Winery warehouse in the Docks District. He has had no dealings with them since nor does he plan to as nine members of the caravan from Bard's Gate went missing during the months-long trek to Yalendir.

See **Encounter 4** in the *Convenient Reference Guide to Reme* for NPC stats, if you need them, for Romblad Marsalle and the Wheelwrights.

Yalendir Keep

The keep is situated at the northern point of the city where it commands a view of the river and the trade roads. It is home to Lady Belestra Vorns and her personal guard detail as well as military barracks and headquarters of the local law enforcement managed by Sheriff Oelwein. Oelwein appoints the guard captains, who may be bribable for petty crimes and infractions if the price is right.

The barracks house 200 heavy cavalry, 300 heavy footmen, and 200 archers armed with longbows made from hedge apple and backed with sinew.

The keep is further defended by a catapult and four ballistae.

Yalendir Pitch

The Yalendir Pitch is part of the jousting circuit and holds jousts once per month from spring through fall to provide entertainment and revelry for the locals. The events are attended by Lady Vorns, who is unaccustomed to the display of cavalry excellence but seems to enjoy them very much and feels that they are an opportunity for her to be seen by the public. She pays for several casks of wine and ale to be handed out to the crowd and has children pass out baskets of fresh bread from the castle ovens.

Two styles of jousts are held here: the Foerdewaith tradition of heavily armored knights and a lightly-armored version in which competition focuses on riding skill and more of a "touch" combat. The "touch" combat can be quite dangerous, but it reflects the style of combat found on the plains where fighting in heavy armor on slow but powerful horses simply isn't a viable military tactic against lighter and more mobile cavalry.

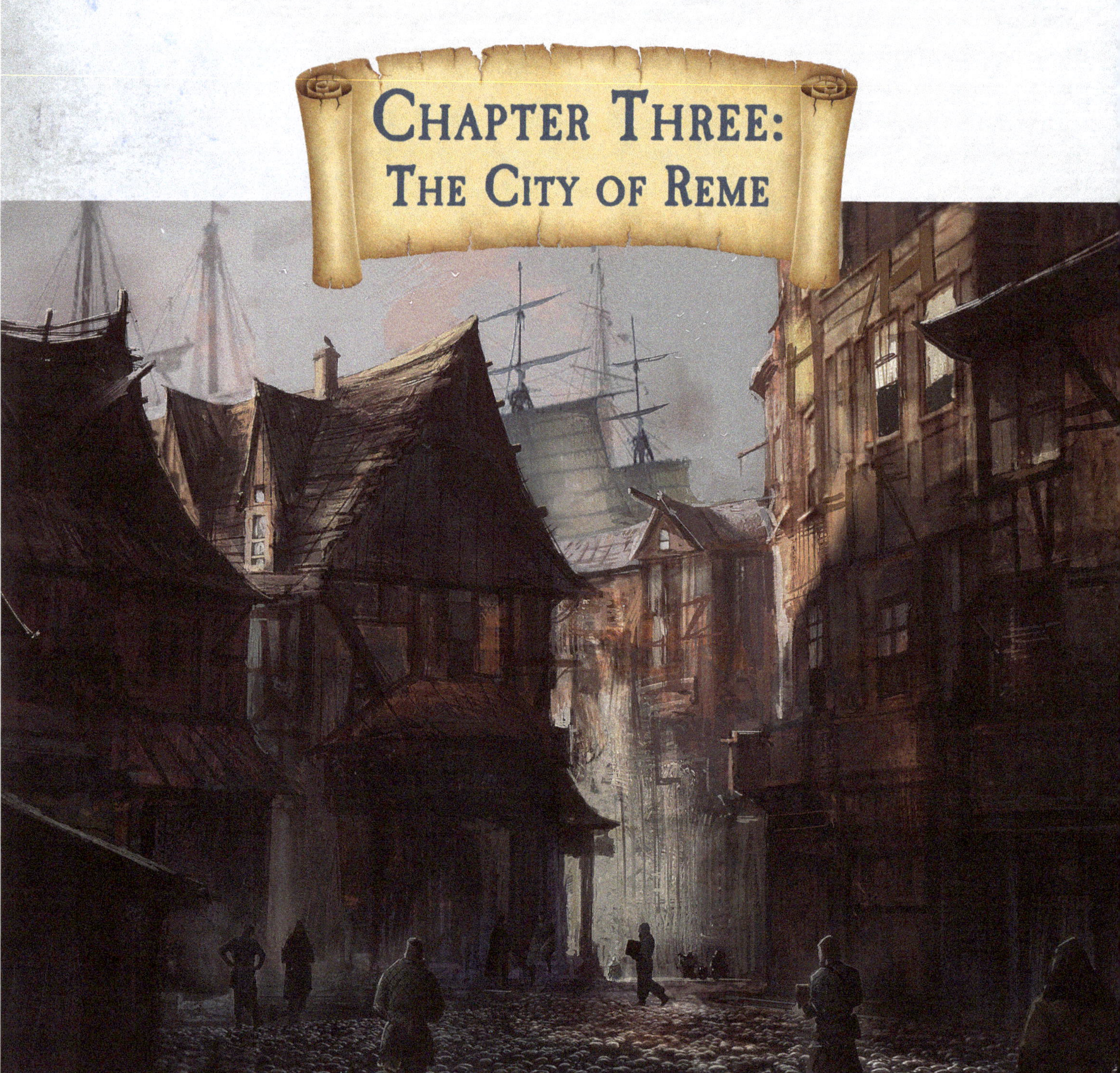

CHAPTER THREE: THE CITY OF REME

Reme is located on the estuary of the Remenos River, in a broad swath of hills below the grassy plateaus of Reme's interior.

Alignment: Neutral Good
Ruler: Lord Mayor Aldus Artaxis
Government: Mayor and Council of Merchant Houses and Guilds (appointed by and subject to the grand duke)
Population: 311,295 (Foerdewaith 154,495, human mixed ethnicity [mostly of Loreclannic origin including the original natives of the city] 93,800, halfling 18,500, half-elf 12,900, mountain dwarf 10,700, hill dwarf 9,400, gnome 6,200, high elf 5,100, other humanoid 200)
Languages: Common, Elven, Dwarven, Gnomish
Religion: Solanus, Dame Torren, Mithras
Technology Level: Renaissance

The city of Reme is one of the two most important port cities on the Crescent Sea (the other being Castorhage) and is the capital of the Grand Duchy of Reme. At its docks, merchant ships arrive from and sail to all the known ports of Akados and Libynos. It sits on the western terminus of the great Tradeway, the merchant road that runs east to Bard's Gate and then to Freegate on the Gulf of Akados. As a result, Reme is one of the great trading cities of the world where virtually anything can be bought or sold.

The city of Reme is also one of the oldest on Akados and dates back to the era before the founding of the Hyperborean empires. Originally called Remenos, it was united from Loreclannic trading posts and fortified by the Polemarch Oerson and his legions when they reached the Crescent Sea in the early years of their conquests.

The elegant walls of the city of Reme and the spires and towers rising from within can be seen for miles out to sea. Several large market squares are within the city, about which can be found merchants, traders, artisans, craftsmen, mapmakers, and scholars with few peers anywhere in the world. The city also boasts the Arcanum Collegium, one of the most prominent wizards' colleges on Akados, and several museums and art galleries. The Reman Theatre is recognized far and wide for its cadre of famous playwrights and arresting performances.

Overview of the City of Reme

Religion

The city of Reme is one of the most cosmopolitan cities of Akados, and accordingly, temples to nearly every god known may be found somewhere within its walls. However, Solanus, Dame Torren, and Mithras are the matron/patron deities of the city, and their worship is predominant among the residents. The city boasts the high altar of Solanus at the venerable Hospital of St. Jethra the Martyred, which maintains 1,220 beds and accepts the sick and infirm who seek healing from all over Akados. Prominent temples to Sefagreth, Vanitthu, Belon the Wise, Muir, and Thyr can also be found in the city, and are well-attended.

Government

The grand duke appoints the lord mayor of the city of Reme, who is charged with administering the city and enforcing its laws, and serves at the sovereign's will. Laws are approved by a council of merchant houses and guilds, the members of which are also appointed by the grand duke. That said, each of the major merchant houses and guilds of Reme has traditionally had a seat on the council, and the grand dukes pay close attention to their proposals concerning foreign trade. Even in the city, the Rhemish tradition of consensus (relative to other cities of the world) and a flat hierarchy of government (again, as a relative matter) reflects the city's Loreclannic roots, even after millennia of urban existence.

Officials below the lord mayor are typically appointed by the lord mayor, though positions of substantial authority are often subject to approval by the council. The grand duke has the right to remove or appoint any of these officials at any time, though this has been seldom exercised over the years.

Certain crimes and matters are, under the laws of Reme, subject to punishment or enforcement by the applicable merchant house or guild, but usually only if others outside the house or guild are not involved. Other matters come before magistrates appointed by the lord mayor and approved by the council.

As a general matter, the city of Reme has been well-run for centuries thanks to the appointment of qualified administrators to the role of lord mayor. Despite this, more than one active thieves' guild exists in the city, as well as other groups that operate in the shadows.

Military

Soldiers in the city of Reme fall under the authority of the grand duke and are led by the lord high commander of Reme.

The city guard is not part of the military, and is led by the guard captain of Reme, another role appointed by the lord mayor with the approval of the council.

THE CITY OF REME
Great Rise of Solanus
6
34
Street of the Sun
15
Western Reme Road
19
17
Lantern Bridge
8
Hill of Mithras
Avenue of Eternal Warning
33
10
24
18
13
N W E S
0 1/8 1/4
Mile
Street
Cattle Bridge
of Stampedes
Temple Street
16
1
Island of Heroes
2
9
Four Winds Bridge
Remenos River
21
5
The Tradeway
Street of the Martyr Lanterns
The Tradeway
12
7
27
25
4
22
11
26
28
14
35
29
32
23
30
Western Reme Road
20
31
Smoke and Urine Street
3
Street of Decadent Stenches

The City Map

Streets and Bridges

Avenue of Eternal Warning

To foreigners, the Avenue of Eternal Warning is a terrifying sight, for the long, broad street leading south from the Western Reme Road to the South Gate is paved with dense patterns of human skulls placed into the street's cobblestones. The skulls come from hundreds of Rhemish victories, but the paving of skulls was begun after the hobgoblin wars of the 1500s. Loreclans in the Northmarches collected skulls as trophies after the hobgoblin forces broke and the Loreclans retook the Northmarches, and the city of Reme undertook to purchase the skulls as a way of rebuilding some sort of commerce with the Northmarches. As a warning to those who would invade Reme, the grand duke ordered the skulls to be preserved and patterned into the long street, which was renamed to emphasize the lesson it was supposed to impart. Skulls from a number of wars later were incorporated into the street's grisly pattern, including wagonfuls from the Short War with Castorhage. Foreign diplomats always seem to be brought to view the avenue shortly after they arrive in the city.

Cattle Bridge

Cattle Bridge predates the expansion of the city walls. It was originally a crossing for smaller cattle drives along the Street of Stampedes. Since the city's expansion of the walls, it has become the city's northernmost urban bridge, joining the city's east and west banks.

Four Winds Bridge

Four Winds Bridge is one of the city's two oldest bridges, although it has been destroyed and rebuilt several times. It has connected the Island of Heroes to the east bank ever since the Hyperboreans built it to connect the Loreclannic trading posts.

Lantern Bridge

Like Four Winds Bridge, Lantern Bridge is as old as the city itself, and has been rebuilt several times — the only original part of the bridge is the ancient Hyperborean piers upon which it is constructed. Enormous lanterns hang from the base of the bridge to warn ships of the bridge's presence, for ships with high masts cannot pass beneath it. The bridge thus also demarcates the river trade to its north and the sea-trade to the south. Any ships found to the north of the bridge will be low-masted, shallow-draft keelboats engaged in traveling up and down the Remenos.

Smoke and Urine Street

As one might expect from the name, Smoke and Urine Street runs through the city's poorer districts. It is a busy harborside street, but the warehouses in this area are highly fortified, and many of the goods offloaded here are moved immediately to warehouses farther north. The docks and street are firmly in the territory of the Red Thumb thieves' guild, but this is not readily apparent to the average visitor — at least, not until after nightfall.

Street of Decadent Stenches

The Street of Decadent Stenches is the city's oldest harborside street and is named for the odd mix of smells generated by foreign cargoes. It does indeed waft with breezes of changing scents, most pleasant but some quite foul.

Street of the Martyr Lanterns

The Street of the Martyr Lanterns is in some ways the counterpart to the Avenue of Eternal Warning, for it celebrates Rhemish heroes rather than demonstrating what happens to the grand duchy's foes. Large lanterns standing in massive iron brackets along the city wall light the street. The lanterns symbolize the sacrifice of those who died in service to the grand duchy. Most of them are simply symbolic, but a few of the lanterns are lit for specific heroes, and these attract visitors who place small clay oil lamps beside the wall underneath the lantern. There is no religious or magical significance to the lanterns — very much unlike the ashes on the Island of Heroes — but visiting the actual Island of Heroes requires waiting in bridge traffic, which is inconvenient. Many city-dwellers just choose to celebrate festivals, birthdays, and other occasions by lighting a lamp here.

Street of Stampedes

The Street of Stampedes is named for its role before the extension of the city walls. Before the expansion, this was the pathway herds took outside the city walls. For obvious reasons, giant cattle drives have never been allowed into the city's narrow, crowded streets.

Street of the Sun

The Street of the Sun rises at a steep angle upward to the Great Rise of Solanus, through some of the city's most expensive real estate other than the Island of Heroes itself. The large dwellings are not, for the most part, located on the street itself. The frontage of the street is filled with expensive shops and inns, with small, well-guarded gateways leading to side streets where the manors and mansions are to be found.

Temple Street

Temple Street is the home of most of the smaller temples of Reme. The largest of these are the Temple of Kamien (located at the edge of the street closest to the river), the Temple of Belon the Wise, The Hearth of Ceres, and the Temple of Sefagreth. Walking the length of Temple Street is sometimes an exercise in patience, for the street is filled with preachers who harangue the crowd while standing on stone blocks placed for this purpose.

The Tradeway

The Tradeway reaches its terminus on the Island of Heroes. It is a major thoroughfare as wide as a market square for almost all of its length before it narrows shortly before the Four Winds Bridge. This point is, unfortunately, the city's largest bottleneck of traffic, and it can take a long time to reach the bridge.

Western Reme Road

The Western Reme Road enters the city at its northwestern gate, then splits into the Street of Stampedes and the Avenue of Eternal Warning, then reappears outside the Kujuk Gate.

1. The Island of Heroes

The ducal palace and the Castle of Reme sit upon this tall hill that overlooks the harbor. Named in honor of the Hyperboreans who built a hill fort here in eons past, the Island of Heroes is one of the first parts of the city that ships entering the harbor see. The old hill fort is long gone, as are any traces of the city's Hyperborean past. In their place stand the towering walls and towers of the castle and the ducal palace that it protects. Down the terraced slopes of the hill are the estates of the most powerful nobles of the grand duchy, mostly families related in the far past to the grand duke but so distant from the succession that they became independent noble houses long, long ago.

The Ducal Way runs from the base of the island's hill up in a spiral to terminate at the gates of the castle. The Ducal Way is a broad, tree-lined street whose gentle curves allow for a moderate slope, just barely enough to cause a fit person to be winded by the time they reach the top. Estates line the street to hang off the sides of the hill and tumble down it in rich profusion. A number of shrines are located along the way as well, but no significant temples are found other than the Acropolis of the Four Winds, which is sacred to Dame Torren. The island has always been a point of defense, tradition, and government.

The island also serves another purpose, at least in a sense. It has been the repository of the ashes of Rhemish heroes for centuries, for their bodies are traditionally burned in funeral ceremonies. It is a long-standing practice for a Loreclan to honor their most glorious heroes by sending the ashes to Reme for scattering on the Island of Heroes. It is said that the spirits of these heroes (whose ranks include great healers and users of magic) still guard the city and its traditions, and that they will rise as an ashen horde mounted on ghostly horses if the city is ever threatened.

It may strike outsiders as strange that the highest of the Reman nobility live in an area with such a mystical and ghostly aspect — and there is definitely a strange and unearthly feel to the Island of Heroes — but it makes perfect sense to Rhemish eyes and is indeed one of the things that makes living on the Island of Heroes a matter of great prestige. With absolutely no feeling of contradiction, the nobility of Reme live in ostentatious estates while carefully tending the thousands of small stones that mark the sites where the ashes of heroes were scattered. Prestige in Reme is highly dependent upon ostentatious wealth, but the highest prestige in the city is to have access to the role of a guardian of tradition. Those who have the opportunity to reach this pinnacle of prestige take it very seriously — although granted, they certainly flaunt and enjoy the elevated status.

2. Palace Complex

This cluster of high-towered fortifications includes the ducal palace and the Castle of Reme, with a cluster of semi-fortified outbuildings to house the apparatus of the ducal court and the judicial functions of the ducal court.

The Castle of Reme

The Castle of Reme stands at the pinnacle of the Island of Heroes and overlooks the city in all directions. This is the original garrison fort of the Hyperboreans, which has been tremendously expanded, century upon century, to become a powerful redoubt defended by massive walls and powerful magic. Given that no enemy has approached the castle in centuries, its main active function is to serve as a secure prison and to house the treasury.

Judiciary Complex

The palace complex also contains the duke's judiciary, which is separate from the city's judiciary and the general law-enforcement apparatus of the duke's broader realms. The judiciary also houses the duke's "lesser justices," a group that serves in many ways as a semi-secret police in the duke's service.

One potential context for adventuring in Reme is to serve the duke as members of this organization, which offers a combination of mission-sources and relative freedom of action for the adventurers. See "Duke's Lesser Justice" in the *Convenient Reference Guide to Reme* .

Adventure Hooks
Involving Lesser Justices

* While otherwise engaged in an adventure or while traveling through the grand duchy, one of the characters hears a voice cry out, "Surrender or stand in the name of the grand duke!" This is soon followed by the sound of a short, sharp fight and several running feet (or pounding hooves as necessary). Arriving on the scene of the fight, the party finds a dying lesser justice who utters just enough information to spark an adventure before expiring.

* The duke's lesser justices do not have the authority to commandeer or command people, but this doesn't stop some from trying. As the law is an esoteric matter for most, people tend to go along with the bluff. A lesser justice stops the characters and orders them to accompany him or her on a mission.

* A squad of lesser justices is on the party's tail, and they won't stop until someone is dead or their suspects are in the dungeons of the Castle of Reme. Given the way that adventurers act when loose in a city, this adventure hook is almost always available.

3. Stronghold of the Sea Tigress

This island houses the grand duke's navy and protects the city's harbor. It is the sacred precinct of the Sea Tigress Clan, an artificially-created "Loreclan." When Reme's expansion into overseas trade grew large enough to demand a navy, the imperator feared that Loreclannic relations might cause disorder among the crews of the navy. Most likely it would not have — the Hyperboreans failed to understand the Rhemish Loreclans at a fundamental level. Nevertheless, the imperator created a new Loreclan specifically for the crews of the Rhemish warships. The imperator called upon the priesthood of Dame Torren, Goddess of the Four Winds, to sanctify and establish this new Loreclan of Reme dedicated to protecting the Rhemish people on the sea. The sailors went through a shamanic ceremony to erase their prior identity, giving them a new name and a spiritual connection to the Sea Tigress, one of Dame Torren's divine lieutenants. The Sea Tigress is sometimes described as "the wind that drives the wave."

The Sea Tigress Clan is technically ruled by a duchess appointed from within the clan and approved by the priesthood of Dame Torren. In reality, the selection of the leader is a religious ceremony in which the goddess chooses the new duchess from a set of appointed candidates. The other candidates do not survive the test, and their bodies are burned as part of the crowning of the new duchess. The ceremony allows the spirit of the Sea Tigress to fuse into the soul of the new duchess, who becomes one with the extremely-powerful spirit animal. Until the duchess dies, the Sea Tigress looks out through her eyes, shares her thoughts, and assists her with the task of hunting down all those who would oppose the power of Reme on the high seas.

The duchess of the Sea Tigress Clan sits in a throne room open to the wind and overlooking the sea high in the stronghold. There, she sees visions through the eyes of members of the Sea Tigress Clan, has a limited ability to commune with Reme's captains and the spirits of their ships, and rides the wind over the sea, scouting for enemies. The duchesses of the Sea Tigress Clan seldom leave this post; most clan business is handled by her small court. Weatherworn and sharing their souls with a powerful spirit animal, the duchesses of the Sea Tigress Clan are noble figures who receive absolutely fanatical loyalty from the other members of the clan.

The Sea Tigress Clan continues to accept members from outside, although they are normally accepted in groups of a captain, crew, and followers rather than the individual acceptances that the imperator originally envisioned.

The fanatic loyalists of the Sea Tigress Clan are the foundation of the city's navy and customs. Once sailors retire from the warships, they are moved to the capacity of revenue agents who collect taxes from the city's sea trade and inspect ships to ensure that all proper taxes have been paid.

Fortifications completely cover the rocky island, and its waterline is ringed with docks for the city's warships. Smaller vessels constantly depart from and return to the stronghold as they inspect cargos and levy taxes on arriving ships. The stronghold of the Sea Tigress Clan is a dramatic sight and often visitors' first view of Reme. It is painted in a tiger-striped pattern of many colors (predominantly gray, yellow, black, and blue), with the huge, snarling visage of the Sea Tigress rising at its center. The skulls of pirates and the masts of their ships are burned once per year in the Sea Tigress' mouth at the festival of the Sea Tigress. It is believed that this burning in some way strengthens the clan's duchess in her open-air throne room where she watches over the sea. Rumors say that during the era of the great sea battles with Castorhage, living captives were burned in the Tigress' mouth to increase the duchess's ability to communicate with and to assist the warships of Reme.

4. Arcanum Collegium

The Arcanum Collegium is the direct descendant of the academy founded by the wizard Iesharos, the Hyperborean mage who attended the first Hyperborean garrison in Remenos. Iesharos committed some sort of crime that scandalized the Hyperboreans, causing them to strip him of his place in the garrison and of his Hyperborean citizenship itself. Whatever this crime might have been, it clearly caused no moral difficulties for the Loreclans of Reme, who immediately embraced the wizard as one of their own. Iesharos' teachings provided the urban Loreclans with the weapon they needed to conquer the vast plains, and they drank deeply from his store of knowledge.

The criminal beginnings of the collegium are a source of humor here, and Iesharos' crime has become a synonym for learning. When students join the collegium, they are told that they are now conspirators in "the crime of Iesharos."

The collegium offers more than just study in the mystical arts. From its founding, the overseeing Board of High Masters felt that a well-rounded education, not just technical training, was needed for its students. Toward this end, all apprentices are required to take lessons in alchemy, art, astronomy, engineering, geography, history, law, literature, logic, mathematics, medicine, natural philosophy, oratory, philosophy, planar studies, rhetoric, and theology. These courses that only tangentially apply to the working of the arcane arts allow non-magically gifted students to attend the collegium and to graduate with diplomas asserting their knowledge in any of the above subjects.

See the **Convenient Reference Guide to Reme** for information about playing a graduate of the Arcanum Collegium.

The Grounds

Tumbling down the face of the Collegium Hill in three stepped terraces, the grounds of the Arcanum Collegium are one of the great wonders of the grand duchy. Each tier is composed of solid blocks of stone welded together by engineering and magic. The bottommost tier is made from red granite with veins of gold and quartz that sparkle in the dawn. Above this is a sprawling terrace of bluestone dolerite studded with flecks of minerals that form patterns that change with each viewing. The highest tier is made from a single large block of magically-strengthened snowflake obsidian.

The main halls of the collegium are on the topmost tier, and most students take their classes on the Red Tier. The buildings here are magnificent; most are composed of a white stone that contrasts with the red granite of the tier itself. In addition to the teaching halls, this tier has three formal gardens that are enchanted to have spring-like weather year-round. The North Garden is a fragrant stand of northern firs surrounding a cool pond. Duke's Garden is a shaded glen cut into the red granite that features birch and maple as well as a waterfall. The Southern Garden has swaying palms and a pond of saltwater complete with living coral.

The Blue Tier is as far as most students and visitors are allowed to go. The Librarum Arcanum, one of the greatest libraries in the world, dominates the tier. Here, one can find texts and scrolls covering any topic and dating back to the days of the Hyperboreans. Use of the library is limited to students and faculty, but some less well-off students have made enough to cover their tuition by serving as research agents for people not connected to the collegium. While strictly against the rules, as long as none of the books goes missing or as long as the student doesn't delve into the forbidden texts' vault, a blind eye is turned to the practice. The remainder of the Blue Tier is made up of study rooms and laboratories.

The faculty of the collegium are the only ones permitted access to the Black Tier. The obsidian block raises up to a thickness of 39 feet at its center, and the private workshops, laboratories, and libraries the faculty uses are cut into the stone itself. This isolates and protects them, not so much from outsiders, as from each other. Muffled explosions, strange odors, and once a flight of winged snakes escape the confines of the Black Tier.

Student Orders

The students of the collegium long ago organized themselves into orders roughly modeled after the concept of knightly or religious orders. Dozens of orders are at the collegium, ranging from small interest-based orders such as astronomy, conjuring, geography, or linguistics, through those for students from particular areas, to the big five known as the high orders of the collegium. Not every student belongs to one of the high orders, but most do, and a great deal of student life is centered on them.

To join a high order, a student must be in good standing with the collegium and able to pay their dues (50–100 gp per year). Beyond these base requirements, each high order has its own set of criteria for judging if a student is worthy of joining. There are also a fair number of steps required to join, such as secret oaths and outlandish rituals. Each of the high orders maintains a house somewhere in town.

The most prestigious high order is the Order of the Lance, which only admits members of the aristocracy. Vying with them for dominance is the Order of the Owl, an order dedicated to arcane pursuits and the sharing of mystical knowledge. The other three are smaller, and are no threat to the Lance and Owl, at least in most years. In order of prominence, they are the Order of the Quill (open to common-born students), the Order of the Lizard (famed for their riotous banquets and for being the most social of the high orders), and the Order of the Rook (famed for their pranks and plots).

The high orders struggle to attract the largest number and most promising students, while adhering to their specific requirements. They also engage in a not-always-friendly rivalry with each other. Most of the time, this rivalry hinges around whose members achieve the most academic acclaim, but sometimes the rivalry gets out of hand, especially between the Lance and Owl. There have been brawls, riots, and the occasional death. The Bandi — members of the city's various artisan guilds — are not happy when the high orders get up to some sort of shenanigans, especially when the Rooks perpetuate one of their legendary pranks.

Faculty

The faculty of the Arcanum Collegium is diverse, though the majority are magic-workers of some kind. There are three ranks of faculty: visiting speakers, masters, and magisters. Visiting speakers tend to be those of common birth who specialize in a trade, craft, or discipline not found among the higher-ranking faculty members. A well-rounded wizard should be able to carve a wand or forge a ring, should be knowledgeable of geography and history, and should have a firm grasp on the world in general and magical theory in particular. Most masters are gifted in the arcane arts and have special knowledge of some academic discipline such as law or religion. There are eight magisters, overseen by a high magister. Each of these eight is a master of one of the common schools of magic and oversees all teaching, research, and application of that school at the collegium.

Town and Gown

The city of Reme is proud of its Arcanum Collegium, but the neighborhoods closest to the collegium are not at all fond of the disruption caused by having so many young scholars (many of whom are apprentice magic-users). When the Rooks or other high orders cause trouble, it is the collegium as a whole that gets blamed. Likewise, when a student gets drunk and breaks up a tavern, when the high orders riot, or when strange foreign ideas begin percolating through the population (or worse, the students start pushing for some kind of political or cultural change), the townsfolk blame the collegium as a whole. This ill-will runs deepest with the city's guilds; fights between apprentices and students are common, and occasionally rise to the scale of small riots.

5. Guild House

Officially known as the House of the Honorable and Skilled Masters of the City of Reme, this building is the meeting place and central office where the grandmasters of the city's guilds meet. The Guild House is an ornate and opulent building, as befits a place owned in partnership by all the guilds of the city. In addition to serving as the meeting place for the grandmasters, the Guild House contains the main armory for the Bandi, two ballrooms, an interior courtyard garden, and functions as a bank for members of any of the city's guilds. The latter is causing some problem as the House of Oron has opened their own bank and some guild members (including grandmasters) have secretly moved some or all of their assets there. This is especially troubling as the Guild House bank provides loans to guild members and uses its profits to maintain a fund to help the families of guild members when they fall on hard times. While the individual guilds do likewise, the combined wealth of all the guilds allows for a larger pool of resources to draw upon.

While the guild house bank has never been open to the public, it has long permitted certain outsiders to deposit their wealth here for safekeeping. These have all been nobles, grandmasters of aligned guilds in other cities, and occasionally very wealthy adventures who are blood relations to one of the grandmasters. The Guild House bank has, in a few cases, lent money to such individuals, but never as a regular practice. These clients have largely moved to the more commercially-oriented bank of Oron, which offers better rates and is widely considered to be better defended.

The management of the Guild House and its bank reside in an elected representative chosen from the guild grandmasters of the city. Currently, the Grandmaster of Smiths, Silanus Otiak, heads the Guild House. His annual reports on the bank's activities have been increasingly sour, something that causes the grandmasters constant worry and may have been the cause of the sudden death of Grandmaster of Potters Vulso last fall. Without a sure influx of capital, the Guild House bank may be forced to consider closing its operations.

Grandmaster of Smiths Silanus Otiak

Grandmaster of Smiths Silanus Otiak is an older man in his late 50s, but a lifetime of hammering iron in a hot forge has left him a solid layer of muscle under the spreading fat that guild masters tend to pick up. Shaven-headed, Silanus presents a towering figure of aging virility

dressed in simple but fine clothing. He wears the heavy chain of his office with pride, fights regularly for both his guild and the rights or advantages of all the other guilds (even the Terriers if truth be known), and is very popular. He is also roundly feared, for with his large frame, bald head, and bushy black beard, Silanus presents an intimidating image that quickly becomes terrifying when his cold blue eyes spark with rage.

He is also an unabashed embezzler. The Guild House bank is not empty; that would be noticed. Rather, it is greatly diminished — and not by the mismanagement of Silanus' predecessor, competition with the Oron bank, bad harvests, or any one of a dozen excuses that Silanus presents to the assembled grandmasters. For the past five years, Silanus has been quietly moving money from the Guild House bank to an estate outside of Bard's Gate. The grandmaster's plans are nearly complete, and when he is sure he has squeezed the last copper piece out of the bank he manages in trust, he will quietly slip away on a privately-owned ship and never return.

6. High Altar of Solanus

The heart of the old imperial Hyperborean worship of Solanus, the high altar in Reme is the one to which all the urban temples look. The high altar is located at the tallest crest of the Great Rise of Solanus, which was originally far beyond the city's walls, and allowed entire Loreclans or clans to camp upon the rise when they made pilgrimages here. The city has since grown to encompass the rise and incorporate the high ground as part of the city wall. Nevertheless, the high altar at the crest of the hill remains one of the city's most visible landmarks.

The high altar is a truly massive edifice that benefitted from being one of the dominant faiths of Akados for centuries. Seven spires, each representing one of the seven rays of wisdom, rise from a central sanctuary. A series of low walls surround the sanctuary and enclose the offices of the Solari Templars and Order of St. Jethra, as well as the Hospital of St. Jethra the Martyred.

Unlike many of the Hyperborean deities, the worship of Solanus caught on quickly across the plains of Reme, and the worship of the sun goddess is widespread throughout the realm. Although Solanus has waned in popularity across Akados, Reme is a single exception to this trend.

Hospital of St. Jethra the Martyred

The Hospital of St. Jethra the Martyred hosts 1,220 beds and is a center not just for hospital care, but also the study of the healing arts throughout Akados. Yellow Robes from the hospital teach classes on healing and medicine at the Arcanum Collegium, and maintain a small but comprehensive library in a building within the hospital grounds. The Order of St. Jethra the Martyred is very small but well-regarded in the city. The bead-worked pectorals worn by full members of the order open any door in the city to them, often accompanied by a warm welcome.

The Order of St. Jethra

The Hospital of St. Jethra the Martyred is operated by the Order of St. Jethra, a religious order dedicated to the goddess Solanus. More than a thousand beds lie within the walls of the hospital, and the Order of St. Jethra treat all manner of sickness from wounds to curses. They are skilled healers who wield mundane and mystical cures with equal aplomb. People from across Akados and even at times lands beyond, come to the city of Reme seeking care and cure, and the Order of St. Jethra is happy to provide it.

The order charges no fees for medical care, even in the most extreme of cases. They do, however, accept donations and expect patients of wealthier backgrounds to donate generously. Most patients donate something, even if it is a few coppers or a chicken. Income is also generated through priests teaching at the collegium, regular tithes to the temple, and a twice-annual collection of a small percentage of the taxes collected by the city.

* Even magical healing requires the right ingredients, and we need those as well as certain rare herbs for our more mundane cures. Blue maiden mushrooms grow only in certain parts of the Deepfells, but these are needed to prevent infections arising from disorders of the liver. We are willing to pay per pound gathered, but they must be carefully harvested and dried lest they lose their potency.

* A sickness has fallen upon the city of Vazarath, and we are sending four members of the order to tend to the afflicted. As our order is forbidden from violence even in self-defense, we need mercenaries to escort and protect our healers. Yes, going into a plague-ridden region and protecting defenseless healers is a lot to ask, but I would counter, what price on your soul if you refuse?

* The things adventuring does to the body, you are fools to risk so much, fools or brave beyond measure. Have you considered the benefits of precautionary action? No? Well, we can offer the protections you need against poison and disease. The ingredients are rare and expansive, and we do need these for other patients, but if you could be kind and generous, so would we.

CHAPTERHOUSE OF THE SOLARI TEMPLARS

The preeminent martial order of the faith of Solanus, the Solari Templars maintain their headquarters and chapterhouse in the high altar of Solanus. Dedicated to serving their goddess's righteous causes, the Solari see themselves as the most elite of holy warriors. Their numbers are in decline, but they are still a powerful force in the grand duchy.

Bearing their goddess's symbol of a blazing sun on an open palm, the small order of knights (there remain only 100 knights, plus 200 squires and lay brethren) is very active. Rarely are more than a dozen at the high altar at a time, and those are the aged, wounded, and ill who spend their time training the next generation. The remainder of the order rides the grand duchy in much the same manner as the Knights of St. Longus; indeed, it is not unusual for a troop of the Mithraic knights to have one or two Solari Templars accompanying them.

* For the glory of Solanus, we ride; for the healing of wounds physical and spiritual, we ride; for the defense of civilization and all we hold dear, we ride. Do you ride with us?

* Much has been lost in the centuries of disfavor, and not just the ephemeral notion of political power. Great relics were carried into hated lands and left by those who died fighting to bring light to darkness. We are too few to fulfill our duties and recover these, but for a small sum would you lend your arms to our cause?

* Our numbers may be small, but we are no less strong because of this. Still, the loss of any one knight of Solanus is a grievous injury. Perhaps if you could help us to find our missing brethren, Solanus herself will smile upon you.

7. LORD MAYOR'S MANOR

Dame Sura Sosii, the current lord mayor of the city of Reme, manages the city from the complex of residences and offices that make up the manor of the lord mayor. When Iltobarus took power, he balked at appointing a member of the Sosii family to such a high position, especially one who would allow her to fill the lower offices of the grand duchy with her people. However, when he took the throne, he was advised to keep her in place as a means of maintaining stability, as thanks for her loyalty during the short-lived civil war and due to her reputation for avoiding the corruption common to her family.

Only some of this was true. Iltobarus' first cadre of advisors was made up of people who had been at court for decades, and nearly all were in the pay of the Sosii. Lord Mayor Sura did support Iltobarus during the civil war by sending money and supplies to his camp. She has long been the lord mayor of the city of Reme, having held the position for nearly 20 years when reappointed by the grand duke. However, she is far from innocent.

Nevertheless, her corruption at least has the benefit of caution. Lord Mayor Sura has filled half of the offices she oversees with friends, family, and others loyal to her. The rest, however, are granted on a strict basis of merit and without regard for whether the applicants come from Foerdewaith or Loreclannic backgrounds. This tends to conceal the fact that the lord mayor is building a strong powerbase by granting a large number of positions based solely on considerations of her own power and that of the Sosii family.

While this has allowed the Sosii to amass an amount of power within the city, the meritocratic side of the equation has had the intended benefit to the city. A great number of commoners fill the lower ranks in the lord mayor's offices, though even here these are nearly all from the merchant houses and guilds that make up the lord mayor's council.

8. TEMPLE OF MITHRAS

The temple of Mithras is a veritable fortress, as befits the temple of a god of soldiers. Mithras has been popular in the urban and village communities of the grand duchy since its founding, and is not unpopular with the Loreclans, but is just not a deity whose worship particularly caught on. The temple is open only to soldiers and their families, and many parts are closed to any who haven't proven themselves in battle. Families are permitted into the outer sanctuary and the training wards, but they cannot pass the great bronze doors leading to the inner and more sacred provinces of the temple.

The Hill of Mithras was established, much like the Great Rise of Solanus, as a holy area long before the city ever reached its edges. The center of the hill is used for tournaments, drills, and other military operations requiring ample space, and is open for use by any martial organization, not just the knights and priesthood of the temple. Around these great fields are a number of freestanding buildings and stalls of many kinds that are far less packed than the rest of the city's wards. Smiths, vendors, and other small businesses catering either to soldiers or spectators flourish on the hill, along with some temple outbuildings and residences of retired soldiers who have served the temple. However, the temple has not, unlike the temple of Solanus, opened its provinces for the ordinary residence of citizens.

Like any solid temple of Mithras, it is built to withstand a siege and was incorporated into the city walls when they were expanded to the river's western banks. The outer walls are three feet thick and 15 feet high, broken by towers at five corners and a sturdy barbican gate. The outer ward just inside these walls is a maze of shorter walls that delineate practice wards, meditation areas, small gardens, and smaller shrines. All these walls are at least a foot thick and 10 feet high, and the entrances can be closed off with iron-studded doors. An attackers who breach the outer wall face a long hard fight as they try to clear all these smaller spaces and find a route to the main temple.

The main temple itself is built like a keep, but with shell-like protrusions along its walls that allow archers to fire into the open-air spaces of the outer wards. The four corner towers of the temple sit juxtaposed to the towers of the outer wall, thus allowing crossfire to reach those below, or even to turn on a tower that has fallen. The northwest tower connects to the outer walls of the castle via a high bridge that can be collapsed with a few sharp blows to the right stone.

Inside the temple keep are three sanctuaries, barracks that can house 1,000 men-at-arms, granaries, cisterns, workshops, shrines, and the chapterhouse of the Knights of St. Longus, a martial order of religious knights in the service of Mithras. More so than the patronage of the nobility or the steady loyalty of the soldiery, it is this order that has given the city of Reme's temple of Mithras a reputation that extends far beyond its borders.

In addition to the priests and Knights of St. Longus, the temple in the city of Reme serves as the gathering place for two lay orders of the Mithraic creed, the Order of the Orphans of Mithras and Order of the Bull's Hooves.

Order of the Orphans of Mithras

War leaves more than dead soldiers, it leaves widows and orphans as well. The temples of Mithras are well aware of this, and just as the Bull's Hooves serve as a means of allowing honorable retirement for soldiers, the Orphans of Mithras ensure that should a soldier fall in battle and leave children behind, they will be taken care of. Gathered up by the priesthood and taken to the temples, the Orphans are given a chance at life that many parentless children never get.

It is a hard life, no doubt, for Mithras is a martial god who wishes his followers to be strong, self-reliant, and obedient to their superiors. The Orphans are up before dawn, scrubbing floors, lighting cook fires, and tending to livestock. Their days are filled with exercise, fighting practice, theological lessons, and tutoring in all the arts of war. No mere warriors, the orphans are taught to think as well as fight, and classes cover military history, tactics, and strategy, as well as battlefield medicine and leadership. Those with the right talents are taught the basics of craftwork, some even apprenticed out to spend part of their day with nearby master craftsmen.

Once the Orphans of Mithras reach adulthood they may leave, but some stay on to become priests or lay people at the temple. Graduates make excellent soldiers and more than one great general in history got their start as a crying orphan sleeping on a hard bed in the back of a Mithraic temple. When an orphan leaves the temple, they are given the tools of whatever trade they have learned, most often a suit of armor and a weapon, a small amount of money, and the discipline they need to succeed in life.

The Orphans of Mithras are famed for the grueling training they undergo. Often they are made to endure extremes of heat and cold, go without food and drink, and live with few comforts. They are also taught a philosophy of stoicism and community. What is never withheld from them is love, and they are encouraged to care for each other as the priests care for them. The result is usually people with incredible fortitude, self-control, and confidence.

Most Orphans of Mithras grow up to uphold the values of the god, being honest, loyal, brave, and steadfast. Others learn the wrong lessons and become bloodthirsty, taking after their god's rather gruesome rites and love of battle. A few reject their upbringing and follow a different path.

Order of the Bull's Hooves

At the other end of the spectrum of life are the Bull's Hooves. Bulls figure prominently in Mithraic symbology, and the Hooves are the stout foundation that all else is built on, or at least so the priesthood teaches. Made up of soldiers who suffered grievous wounds in battle and those too old to serve, the Hooves provide the support staff for most Mithraic temples. The temple in the city of Reme is no exception. Some of the Hooves serve as craftsmen who maintain the temple, the priests, and the knights. Others have no other skill than warfare, and failing to be able to pursue that, are sweepers of steps and scrubbers of pots. Many of the Hooves find more than some solace in life at the temple, even if they are constantly on latrine duty. The Hooves still live under martial discipline and those that can, train daily. The priests contend that even those with missing arms or legs can still fight, and they go to great lengths to train and arm the Hooves in case they are needed.

The Knights of St. Longus

Founded 530 years ago by Commander Longus of Mithras, the Knights of St. Longus are a holy order dedicated to protecting the grand duchy and its residents from outside threats. They take no part in civil wars, nor do they rally if another "civilized" nation invades. Indeed, should a neighboring nation invade, the Knights of St. Longus simply fortify their temple and wait out the war. However, they do not consider the humanoid tribes to the north a civilized nation and have, and will again, ride forth to bring them to battle.

Mostly, the Knights of St. Longus pursue two main activities. Members of the order patrol the grand duchy, often alone or with a small entourage of lay people, not all of whom are members of the order. These patrols hunt bandits and monsters, seek out incursions by orcs and other dangerous outsiders, and champion the cause of the common people. They have been known to exert their influence on Loreclannic barons and other nobles who are tyrannical and unjust; this is normally handled by the Loreclans themselves, but in some cases a normal solution would be too slow to rescue commoners from tyranny, and in these cases the order might choose to take matters into their own hands.

When not on patrol, the Knights of St. Longus provide training for adherents of Mithras and the next generation of knights. One cannot join the knights; they certainly do not accept open enrollment, nor do they recruit. All members of the order — be they lay brethren sworn to Mithras or sworn knights and priests — are orphans left behind by one of the many wars waged across Akados. Every year, elder knights go forth from the temple in the city of Reme to visit temples of Mithras across the grand duchy and in lands beyond. At these temples, the local priests gather the war orphans for review by the order. Only one in 10 are chosen; the remainder are brought up by the priesthood (and either join the priesthood or become soldiers). Those chosen are taken to the city of Reme to be trained in the temple. The best of these are ordained as warrior-priests and become knights of the order, while the rest are found some role as lay brethren. The Orphans of Mithras, of course, contribute a significant proportion of the knights' recruits.

The ethos of Mithras exalts solders, but it does not disdain others. The lay brothers are members of the order and must adhere to its strict martial ethics. They are considered valuable and important parts of the larger mission. The order needs smiths, grooms, cooks, stewards, and scribes as much as it needs knights. The Bull's Hooves, an order of lay brethren of the temple of Mithras, serve some of these roles, but the order prefers to rely on its own lay brethren whenever possible.

Newly-anointed knights of the order are not fully knights until they complete their errantry. During this time, the young knight must wander the lands and meet any challenge encountered. For most, the period of errantry lasts for a year and a day, although some feel the need to venture longer than the prescribed period.

9. ACROPOLIS OF THE FOUR WINDS

The Acropolis of the Four Winds is a holy place attached to the temple of Dame Torren on the Island of Heroes. It is a structure of ancient pillars arranged in a square with four major openings. Each of these wide gaps between the pillars has a stone lintel that bears a carven image. These images are a horse (western opening), a hawk (eastern opening), a gaunt woman's screaming face with flowing hair (northern opening), and a beautiful woman with flowing hair (southern opening). The two faces are depictions of Dame Torren herself, and these entrances are never used other than by the priesthood of the goddess during specific ceremonies. Entering the acropolis between the pillars rather than through one of the gates is highly sacrilegious, but temple guards are posted around the acropolis to prevent visitors from making this mistake.

The ashes of Loreclannic heroes are usually released to the winds inside the acropolis, and in some cases the bodies of heroes are cremated here. A wide, scorched stone altar in the center of the open space within the acropolis is used for funeral pyres and for sacrificial purposes.

The temple building adjoining the acropolis is more of an administrative center for the priesthood of Dame Torren, although it does contain the stable of the goddess's two sacred horses and the eyrie of her two sacred hawks.

During extremely high winds, designated priestesses ride in a column through the city, wind-lashed and chanting to the skies. The column is led by the high priestess mounted on one of the two sacred horses, with the second horse beside her, saddled but without a rider. This second horse is reserved for the goddess herself should she deign to join the procession. The column of priestesses carries banners and long poles mounted with ratcheted wheels designed to produce a loud, clicking whir of sound — the eerie noise carries far into the wind and informs the folk of Reme that the priesthood of the goddess is abroad upon the storm.

In gale-force winds, when ships in the harbor of Reme are actually threatened, a cantor stands atop the sacrificial altar in the middle of the acropolis to chant a strange, ululating song into the gale. This is ordinarily a young, hardy person since the chant is required to continue until the wind subsides, even if the storm lasts for days. Long-lasting storms have, in two cases, led to the demise of a cantor who maintained the song — somehow — to the very point of death from exhaustion. The ashes of these two cantors were scattered on the Island of Heroes alongside legendary kings and warriors. The possibility that the goddess herself may have maintained their strength and voices all the way to their deaths is a bit disturbing to some who stumble upon this particular bit of the city's history.

10. LICH'S REST

Lich's Rest is the city's cemetery. The second wall was built so as to enclose it, although this was done solely for the purpose of building the wall to take advantage of the higher ground on which the burial ground sits. In ancient times, the people of the city of Reme followed the Loreclannic custom of cremation, and Lich's Rest still contains great stone slabs for funeral pyres. However, after the arrival of the Foerdewaith, many families began using the Foerdewaith custom of aboveground mausoleums and tombs for burial of their dead. As the city grew, it became popular to inter the departed in graves marked with headstones. Following the Purple Plague, however, cremation once again became the order of the day (and an official ducal order during the plague) and remains the standard practice to this day. As a result, nearly half of Lich's Rest is covered with stacked vaults that allow urns to be placed inside — only a very few are permitted the honor of having their ashes scattered by the temple of Dame Torren onto the Island of Heroes. Many families own private vaults adjacent to the older tombs. Poorer people make do with flimsy wooden vaults that are not much more than shelving, while the poorest dump the ashes of their dead in the river or harbor. The Foerdewaith have generally returned to the ordinary burial of dead, so the Terriers patrol Lich's Rest, ever vigilant for corpse thieves, necromancers, and other dangers. It is not a popular patrol route; even the sewers are far less spooky than Lich's Rest at midnight.

11. LIVONIA'S PARK

Two years ago, a part of the city known as the Cherayl burned to the ground in a three-day fire. Only the combined efforts of the Bandi and Terriers prevented the fire from consuming the entire city, and to this day nearby streets bear the scars of the fire. For the most part, the nearby parts of the city have recovered, but the old neighborhood was a total loss. Iltobarus chose to forbid rebuilding and reimbursed the landowners for their losses, a gesture of generosity no doubt from the mind of the grand duchess.

In place of the aging but genteel neighborhood will be the city of Reme's first planned neighborhood, Livonia's Park. Named after the grand duke's late great-aunt and former resident of the grand duchy's throne, Livonia's Park will be a splendor open to all subjects of the grand duchy, not just the wealthy and powerful. The plans include a large open space for relaxation and pleasure that also provides a respite from the hustle of the city, a museum honoring the history of the grand duchy and great works of art (several former grand dukes and duchesses were patrons of the arts, and the ducal vault is near to bursting with priceless works), shrines to many of the lesser deities worshiped in the city, and a tournament ground to rival the one on the Hill of Mithras.

This is a massive undertaking and requires the expenditure of more wealth, talent, and time than even a prosperous nation can afford. Again, the ever-questing mind of the grand duchess has found solutions to these problems. First, the guilds of the city have been permitted to pay their taxes in work instead of money, provided that they supply all materials and labor. Second, the lord mayor has issued a decree that anyone who comes to the city of Reme and offers themselves as labor on the project will be granted the rights of a citizen of the city after five years labor. These laborers are paid a mere five coppers a day and live in such areas as the Hol-Hebar. Finally, Iltobarus has "requested" that the nobility of the grand duchy, temples, and merchant houses "donate" a certain amount of money to the project. It is not a tax — it is completely voluntary — although the man asking has his own private army and power over the law.

So far, construction has not truly begun, which worries the guilds — for they now owe two years' worth of labor taxes. The hill has been cleared of rubble, and portions have been leveled to make room for the planned buildings. Construction material is being gathered on the hill, and this has added to the work of the Bandi as they must stand constant watches to keep away thieves. The burned-out region is now an open area, dark at night; only the Bandi serve as any sort of guard. Livonia's park might one day be one of the greatest spectacles of the world, but today it is the haunt of criminals, cultists, and others who find the isolation and darkness to be loyal friends.

12. NORTH GATE

The North Gate in the Second Wall is the main entrance into the city of Reme for travelers coming along the Tradeway. The neighborhood straddles the wall and gate, with an inner North Gate neighborhood inside the wall and an Outer North Gate neighborhood beyond it. For some residents, living or working on one side of the gate or another is a point of pride, and this rivalry within the neighborhood can lead to brawls. Both sides exist to serve travelers and provide residences for those working in the many inns, taverns, alehouses, shops, and brothels of the neighborhood.

Inner North Gate is dominated by the Northgate Square, a large paved area at the intersection of the Tradeway and the Street of Stampedes. The area around the square is the heart of North Gate and the oldest part of the neighborhood, having been a caravan gathering point before the building of the Second Wall. Inns such as the Broken Jug, Ducal Arms, and Snarling Face have long histories, and the streets just off the square host establishments such as the Mended Arms, the Green Horse, the Four Corners of the Wind, and Jake's Fancy. These serve less well-off travelers, though none of the Inner North Gate establishments are entirely cheap — or friendly to troublemakers.

Attached to the Bastion of the North Gate is a temple of Vanitthu. This sturdy fortress-temple provides additional protection for the city, and its priests regularly accompany the Bandi on their patrols, occasionally even aiding the Terriers in their role as sewer wardens. While Mithras is more popular in the city, and there is an ongoing feud between the followers of Vanitthu and those of Anumon, the warrior-priests of this grim god are loved for their deeds, if not their theology.

The Outer North Gate is a different story. Only partly patrolled by the Bandi and being somewhat more recent than Inner North Gate, the parts of the neighborhood outside the wall cater to those with less means or those looking for more riotous entertainments. There are also a greater number of businesses serving travelers, such as smithies, livestock dealers, and outfitters. The main stockyards for the city lie in this part of the neighborhood, and there is an outer ring of caravanserais at the very edges of the neighborhood.

Whereas the Inner North Gate has been mostly given some form of order with clear and straight streets, designated zoning, and other aspects of planning, Outer North Gate is a warren of dirt streets, twisting alleys, and taverns sitting next to smithies fronting on narrow streets filled with apartments. The sound and stink from the stockyards tend to pervade the area when the winds are unfavorable.

13. SOUTH GATE

The city's South Gate is considerably less active than the North Gate, and has only two small caravanserais beyond the gates. Most traffic between Reme and Whiterush is carried by sea; very few people taking this road intend to travel its full length. Most of the commerce passing through this gate is purely agricultural; cattle drives from the south are routed around the city to the slaughterhouses north of the city rather than passing through the city proper.

14. UNDERWALL

While not nearly as fashionable as Uphill, the Underwall neighborhood is one of the wealthier neighborhoods in the city of Reme. Lying in the shadow of the Second Wall, Underwall is one of the newer neighborhoods, having been around only for a century or so. Today, most of Underhill is made up of upper middle class townhouses and small estates, with a scattering of offices of various merchant houses.

15. UPHILL

Uphill is the most fashionable neighborhood in the city, save for living on the Island of Heroes itself. The ground here rises slowly toward the hill, which gives the neighborhood its name. In all ways, Uphill tends to copy the noble neighborhood of the Island of Heroes. A residential neighborhood, Uphill is mostly made up of estates belonging to the wealthy merchants, guild masters, and lesser nobles of the city. The streets are wide and tree lined, the Bandi patrol regularly, and at night the place is quiet save for the sounds of a party going on in one lavish residence or another.

16. THE HOUSE OF ORON

One of the three largest merchant houses in the city of Reme and long the second most powerful, the Orons have managed to maintain their position as the Drenwall rose and the Gastone-Shesheks fell. Whereas the Gastone-Shesheks have a reputation for solid dependability and the Drenwall for wild swings of fortune, the Orons have always been the merchant house that others thought of after the other two. Ignored and forgotten in the ferocious scrum of trade and politics, the Orons have been content to go their own way and forge along paths the others do not take.

One of these paths has been in the production, import, and sale of common commodities and low-quality goods. Oron ships do not come back laden with spices and jewels as the Drenwall often do, nor do they provide reliable sources for nearly any luxury good as do the Gastone-Shesheks. An Oron trade ship puts into port with a 1,000 casks of iron nails, three tons of salted herring, and 20 hogsheads of Northlander mead. No one really pays attention to this and there is no fanfare, but the merchant house can sell the nails to the Smith's Guild (who buy these cheap nails so that the Orons don't dump them on the market and undercut the guild pricing), the herring is sold at half the rate that local slat fish is going for, and the Northlander mead is bought up by the castle steward. For the Orons, there is enough gold to cover costs and make a solid profit, and solid profits are the name of the game as far as the House of Oron is concerned. Multiplying solid profits by the hundred or more ships flying the Oron family flag, and the family does quite well for itself.

The House of Oron has never suffered the vast swings in fortune as the Drenwall have; indeed, they have benefited from several failed Drenwall projects by buying up (and later selling back) Drenwall ships, warehouses, and trade contracts. They also do not engage in the shady work the Gastone-Shesheks do — not that the Orons know anything about their rival's criminal connections. For centuries this has been enough for the family. As with all of the great merchant houses, the Oron family maintains factors in ports throughout the world, but they are — or at least have been — primarily a trading family, maintaining fleets of ships and recognizing profit solely from the difference between their buying price and their selling price. They have never chosen to take the risk of venturing into the financing side of commerce: They sell shares in their vessels but do not buy shares in the vessels of other houses; they do not lend money; and they do not invest in real estate beyond their own warehousing needs. This conservative approach, which has made the House of Oron the second-greatest mercantile dynasty in one of the world's greatest mercantile cities, is in the process of changing.

Prisca Oron, the current head of the family, has spent a great deal of time studying the activity of banking houses in Reme and elsewhere. This is not a connection the Orons have traditionally sought, because their conservative approach to trade has allowed them to operate within their cash flow limits for generations. However, it has become clear to Prisca that the family actually holds onto too much cash; cash that could very easily be put to use if the family were to expand from large-scale trade into banking as well.

The family's expansion into banking has been — as with everything the Orons do — cautious and incremental. They initially made loans only to other mercantile houses against hard collateral assets such as warehouses and ships currently in port. They have expanded at this point into loans that carry actual risk, such as financing cargoes carried by other families' ships, but they still stay away from high-risk, high-return ventures. What they have recently begun, however, is a startling innovation: a true "bank" that allows depositors to withdraw money whenever it is desired (with certain limits, of course). In general, if someone "deposits" money with a moneylender for any kind of return, the money is actually being lent to the moneylender and will be returned at the end of the loan period, not before. The Orons have managed to accumulate enough cash that they can allow people to deposit money (with a monthly fee, of course) and withdraw it again at will. It is, in essence, a way for small merchants and tradesmen to secure their money from thieves, but have access to it whenever they need it. Prisca is pleased to note that while the family vault still holds as much cash as before, it is now the foundation for a much-larger network of loans and deposits — with the Oron family making money on loans that were funded entirely by its depositors. As long as the bank's depositors do not suddenly deplete the vault by withdrawing all the money faster than lenders repay it, the family is in a position to make considerable profits from this innovative idea.

House of Oron Adventure Hooks

* This needs to be kept discreet; if you tell anyone, we will react most unkindly. We can't find Prisca Oron. Somehow, she was spirited out of one of our vaults, a vault that was locked from the outside with only her inside. Yes, guards were outside the door; there always are. Naturally, our own people are making their inquiries, but this must be kept quiet. You are not linked to us; you can go places we can't without attracting suspicion.

* We have a loan that has gone unfulfilled. It would be illegal for us to use any form of threat to reclaim the money, but you on the other hand, we don't know you. If for some reason you get the dept repaid, in full mind you, and let us say 10 percent is missing, we certainly wouldn't look for it. Do we have an understanding?

* Baron Lucus Laronius is sending in a large amount of money and other wealth for our bank to hold. Guarding such a large caravan of riches is beyond what our own guards can handle, so a few mercenaries would go a long way toward getting the valuables safely to our vaults.

17. House Drenwall

One of the three major mercantile houses of the city of Reme, the Drenwalls are speculators willing to undertake much greater risks than their rivals. They have a reputation, not undeserved, for supernatural powers — witchcraft and sorcery run in their blood. Whenever a Drenwall deal goes well, a trade fleet returns with holds filled with goods, or even the smallest fortune befalls a member of the family, people look and nod knowingly. Likewise, when misfortune befalls their rivals, tongues wag and gossips hint that the true cause is a curse pronounced by the Drenwall.

This suspicion is not a new thing for the family. The Drenwalls have a higher than normal number of family members who exhibit some form of sorcerous power. Some are outright magic-users, while other just seem to have some sort of luck, and many can conjure up some minor magic such as changing the color of a cloth or lighting a pipe with their fingers. These minor traits make the common folk (and no small number of nobles) speak of demonic blood, witchcraft, and other foul rumors.

Naso Drenwall is the current head of the merchant house. He followed the normal path for leaders of the family and served as a cabin boy on his family's ships before rising to take command first of a trading ship and then an entire fleet. When his grandfather, the head of the family, died, Naso won control of the House of Drenwall in a whirl of internal politics and has managed the Drenwall fortunes for the past 13 years. Under his stewardship, the Drenwalls have gone from the third-ranked merchant house in the city of Reme to the first, displacing the Orons and Gastone-Shesheks along the way.

Naso Drenwall

Naso Drenwall is a middle-aged man whose face and demeanor betray many years spent at sea — unusual characteristics for a powerful warlock. He does not publicly reveal himself as a spellcaster, but his capabilities are an open secret in the business and financial circles of the city. Although all the major mercantile houses avail themselves of hired magic-users, the Drenwalls seem to use their hireling spellcasters more effectively than their rivals — possibly because Naso is simply more familiar with the details of the tasks he puts them to. He is a ruthless leader, although the siblings, cousins, and second cousins who share control of the house all admit that he is fair (within the family, at least) and that he is a genius when it comes to matters of trade.

Drenwall Adventure Hooks

· Olives are going to turn the best profit next year, and we need to corner the market. Don't ask how we know, we know. We purchased some orchards cheap because they are near an area infested by monsters. Your job is to make sure nothing disrupts the crops. Use force if necessary.
· Of course we are hiring guards for our caravans and ships, and you look like just the sort we want. If you are interested, there is extra pay for those willing to take great risks and keep their mouths shut. Where? Oh, you'll be going to the Deepfells…

18. House Gastone-Sheshek

Once the top mercantile house in the city of Reme, the family of Gastone-Sheshek has fallen to third place. Partly and publicly, this is due to the rise of the Drenwalls, who, under the leadership of Naso Drenwall, have managed to capture parts of the Gastone-Sheshek family's market share. The truth is that although the rise of House Drenwall has hurt the Gastone-Shesheks, the real cause for their declining fortunes has been an ongoing war with the Red Thumb thieves' guild.

For most of its history, House Gastone-Sheshek has been most well-known for a slight elven bloodline that often manifests itself with fair skin, delicate features, pointed ears, and their ability to acquire even the rarest of goods at a fair price. In terms of their visible operations, they are primarily a trading house rather than a financing house, investing almost exclusively in ships and trade, but they diversify their risks by selling shares of as much as 50% of many of their ventures, and by carrying cargo for others at normal rates. Due to all of the background transactions behind any particular Gastone-Sheshek venture, it can be difficult to determine exactly who owns what — which is convenient for a house that maintains a strong presence in organized crime.

For a great many years, the money and resources of the Gastone-Sheshek family have been used surreptitiously to operate the largest thieves' guild in the city — at least, until a few years ago. Through their guild, the merchant house sold smuggled goods (brought in on always-honest Gastone-Sheshek ships), organized large-scale thefts (and sold off the proceeds in foreign ports), fixed sporting events, set up brothels, ran illegal loan offices, and suppressed crime in the better parts of town. Their focus on the richer parts of the city, however, led to their downfall, as another guild formed in the Hol-Hebar and the Sujabi neighborhoods. When the Red Thumb first organized, the Gastone-Shesheks ignored them as a band of upstarts that couldn't possibly manage to build any significant kind of operation using only the city's poorest citizens as a resource. By the time the Red Thumb began to take over the smuggling trade, the Gastone-Shesheks were already outnumbered and outmaneuvered.

Then Corva Gastone-Sheshek, the head of the family, died and left as her only heir her young son Marinus. Only three years old when he became the head of the Gastone-Sheshek family, Marinus is now nearly 10. Besides being groomed to one day take the reins, he has little influence. Instead, his uncles Otho and Frugi now run the family business — and do so rather poorly. Even in the best of times, Otho would have struggled to hold the merchant house together, and Frugi is not much more than a rich thug who runs the criminal half of the family. Profits both legal and illicit have fallen, and the shadow war between the two thieves' guilds of the city is starting to attract official notice.

House Gastone-Sheshek
Adventure Hooks

* Her name is Slippery Solin and you need to kill her, publicly, and leave the body for the Bandi to find. Make sure to leave our name out of this.

* Meet me at midnight at the corner of Hill and Sea. Bring some friends if you can, and come armed. Yes, there will be a fight.

* Do you have a problem killing a Bandi master? No? Good, Master Buteo knows too much. Go to his pottery shop, wreck the place, rob it, and leave him dead in the ruins. His apprentices and journeymen, too, if you can. After all, who knows who he has talked to?

19. Fortress of the Bandi
(The Honorable and Courageous Band of Free City-Holders)

Reme has only a small professional town guard that serves as a cadre more than an active force. Most enforcement of the city's law relies on the masters and apprentices of the Honorable and Courageous Band of Free City-Holders. Made up of members of the city's various artisan guilds, the Bandi, as the locals call them, serve as volunteer fire brigades and law enforcement. They also train for military service and can be called out to bolster the grand ducal levies and standing army, but by ancient law may not be deployed more than 25 miles from the city walls.

That they are volunteers does not make them any less effective than the watches of other cities, and as they draw from some of the better-educated commoners in the city, the Bandi are known to have a fairly high level of competence. Every guild member is by default a member of the Bandi, though the youngest apprentices and older masters tend to take a support role in the organization.

The vast majority of the Bandi, as well as the vast number of artisans in the guilds, are journeymen. Adult journeymen serve as the rank-and-file and patrol the city, stand guard on the walls, and make up the bulk of the formations when the Bandi drill or are deployed to war. By law they are required to turn out with uniform, a chain shirt or steel breastplate, helmet, short sword, dagger or dirk, long spear, crossbow or arbalest and 60 bolts, 10-days preserved rations, and a waterskin. Although all journeymen are required to provide themselves with this equipment, in practice they are divided into crossbow and spear formations. It is not unusual for a financially pressed journeyman to sell the equipment they do not use and hope not to be inspected any time soon.

Masters are expected to provide themselves with the same equipment as a journeyman with the addition of a longsword instead of a short sword. It is not required, but it is very common, for masters to carry equipment of better craftsmanship, and between the cost of new equipment and the fees for becoming a master, this can easily bankrupt a person. As a result, many of the younger masters begin their careers in debt to one of the merchant houses of the city. The Bandi elect their officers, though only masters can stand for election. Officers are required to equip themselves with heavier armor such as full plate and a mount. Officers serve five-year terms. An additional 20 masters are elected annually to serve as the Mounted and Unrestricted Band of Trained Free City-Holders, though usually the same 20 are elected year after year until they need to be replaced due to loss or age. These Bandi wear the heaviest armor, equip themselves with lances, and ride warhorses. When backed by a cadre of officers they can form a small, but powerful, mounted formation.

When on patrol in the city, the Bandi are grouped into five-person "vigils." Vigils don their armor and carry crossbows and daggers, but their main weapons are supposed to be short cudgels. Many equip themselves with weaponry not on the Bandis' required equipment list, such as short spears, halberds, battleaxes, and other more exotic weaponry. Each vigil is led by the most senior journeyman who leads three other journeymen and an apprentice. A vigil is tasked with maintaining the peace, investigating disturbances, and keeping an eye out for fires. In the case of serious trouble, the apprentice is sent as a courier to the nearest guardhouse to summon a larger force.

Bandi guardhouses are scattered around the city, and every neighborhood has at least one of these. Each member of the Bandi is required to serve a 24-hour watch every seven days, as well as a two-week stint every year. Many spend their off hours in the guardhouses seeing to their equipment, visiting with friends, and training. A general call at a guardhouse can call out two dozen Bandi. Their weapons and other equipment (aside from swords, which are considered a personal weapon and badge of status) are kept at the guardhouses and allow a force of Bandi to be deployed in minutes. The guardhouses also contain — or are supposed to, at any rate — fire-fighting equipment, basic medical gear (bandages, ointments, and such), and a storehouse of food and water casks. The guardhouses have sturdy doors and stone walls, and can serve as small fortresses if need be.

See the ***Convenient Reference Guide to Reme*** for information about playing a member of the Bandi.

20. Angry Gull

A seedy, rundown, and altogether scurvy-looking tavern, the Angry Gull has a reputation as the nastiest tavern in the city — a reputation it tries to maintain. Tucked between a fishmonger and a ropemaker's shop, the Angry Gull's only signage is a freshly-killed seagull head nailed above the door when the tavern opens at sunset. The regulars know not to show up until the gull stops dripping — not only does this keep blood off their hats, but the staff is usually surly for the first half hour or so.

Inside are six long benches stained with ale, grease, and blood. At the back of the room is a small counter where the proprietor can oversee operations and keep the drunks back from the booze. The room is lit by grim, encrusted lanterns that hang from the ceiling and a large fireplace that serves to cook food, accept rubbish, and keep back the cool salt air.

The staff is composed of Hard-Faced Dana and her three daughters. A former pirate, Dana is a middle-aged woman with stringy hair, three teeth, and a build like a bundle of cables wrapped in too little canvas. She does not suffer fools and gladly knifes anyone who causes her too much trouble before having their body dumped in the harbor. Her tongue is as sharp as her blade, and she regularly insults her customers. Her daughters are much like her, but younger and not yet entirely ground down by the hard life of running a tavern in this neighborhood.

The regular customers are equally rough, and fights are common. Dana does nothing to break these up; they are good for business, since drunken brawls are the Gull's prime attraction and are much less expensive than hiring musicians. Besides, two friends having a drunken brawl and then loudly making up is good for business; they usually stand drinks for the entire tavern if they were drunk enough at the start.

Bill of Fare at the Angry Gull

Food and Drink

Watered down Ale	1 cp
Rum	2 cp
Grog	3 cp
Fish stew with day old bread	1 cp
Bowl of fried corn kernels	1 cp

21. Hol-Hebar

The poorest part of the city, even worse than the Sujabi, the Hol-Hebar is a seasonal neighborhood at best. Lining the west bank of the Remenos River, Hol-Hebar sits outside the city walls. In the spring, the river floods and inundates the neighborhood, in some years completely carrying it away. The floods leave a broad mud flat upon which the residents of Hol-Hebar build their shanties and shacks.

Hol-Hebar is not a good place to live. Mosquitoes are common and reportedly the size of small stirges. Disease is rampant and often blamed on the malarial miasma from the river. The people of Hol-Hebar are poor, often without jobs or other means of support, and there are not any services. Water is drawn from the Remenos, and refuse is dumped right back in. The buildings here are made of scrap, sod, old shipping crates, and a range of scavenged material. The only law is of the strong and cunning, save for when a Terrier patrol comes through and things get quiet fast.

Iltobarus and the lord mayor have concocted several plans to clean up the Hol-Hebar, but so far other matters have been more pressing. Previous rulers have sent their men-at-arms out to burn the place down from time to time. Other attempts to discourage resettlement have only been short-term solutions; as soon as official eyes turn elsewhere, the population of Hol-Hebar returns.

22. The Blue Rooster

Follow the smell of brimstone and look for the garishly painted sign showing a bright red rooster with a large blue appendage that roosters certainly do not have (at least not like that!). Open all hours of the day and night and boasting never to have closed its doors in a hundred years, the Blue Rooster is almost as much a landmark of the city of Reme as the Island of Heroes.

There are taverns and inns in the city catering to specific clienteles or frequented by certain classes of people. Some draw in the roughest of criminals, while others permit only nobility or the very wealthy to enter. The Blue Rooster bars none from its premises, but it especially invites arcanists, magic-users, mages, will-workers, and wonder makers. The use of magic within the common room is not just permitted, it is encouraged, and all of the wait staff are at least minimally gifted in the arcane arts. Mugs of ale drift through the room on invisible wings. Platters for fried food sail past, and both payment and change zip back and forth above the patrons' heads.

In addition to this constant magical sideshow, the Blue Rooster also features a magically stabilized room for storage and can offer out-of-season fruits, vegetables, and meats, as well as exotic extraplanar foodstuffs that would not last long in our reality. They are still serving pieces of the great wyrm Ithklinuatus that was slain nearly two centuries ago.

Private meeting and study rooms are on the second floor and range in size from those able to host a dozen suspicious, feuding mages to rooms for a single student who just wants a quiet place to read. These can be warded against scrying and other means of detection at an additional cost, and the staff mages of the Blue Rooster are happy to make the private rooms suitable to a variety of creatures with exotic environmental needs. In other words, this is a *powerful* place.

Two basement levels are accessible down a long *levitation* shaft. These basements spread out beyond the surface footprint of the Blue Rooster, something that would no doubt discomfit the tavern's neighbors if they knew. The upper basement level offers private workshops to rent. These include standard wizardly laboratories, as well as specialized spaces for alchemical work and summoning. All these rooms are blocked from scrying, and the walls, ceilings, and floors are magically strengthened in case of accident.

The lowest basement level is a well-stocked library of magical and mundane lore. Use of the library is through subscription or a fee, and not even the most loyal patron is permitted to enter the library unattended. Hundreds of volumes are down there, which makes the library of the Blue Rooster one of the largest in the city. People using the library may not take any of the books out of the tavern, but they are welcome to rent a study room or workshop and have their books delivered there.

Food and Drink

Transmutation Spiced Ale ....4 cp
Wizard's Rest Stout ....6 cp
Imported ales, lager, and stouts..1 sp
River Wren Wines ....3 sp
Imported beverages ....6–12 sp
Roast meats with vegetables and bread............................1 sp
Vegetarian plate...2 sp
Dragon steaks with roasted vegetables and spicy mustard ....15 gp
Bring it and We Fry It ....4 sp
Fried Anything (lots of options, changes daily)........................8 sp
Pie of the Day..1 sp
Study Break (hot coffee, fried dough balls, dipping sauces) ...4 cp
Private meals by request...10–500 gp

Rooms and Stabling

Private Study Room ....1 gp/12 hours
Private Meeting Rooms...........................5 gp per person/6 hours
(includes light food and drink)

Standard Wizard's Workshop ....50 gp deposit*, 5 gp/hour
Alchemical Laboratory........................150 gp deposit*, 15gp/hour
Summoning Room 500 gp deposit*.............................50gp/hour
(you-summon-it-you-dismiss-it)

Library Access.........................20 gp deposit* 10gp/hour

* You get only half your deposit back, or none if you damage anything. Students of the Arcanum Collegium pay half rates and deposit and get their full deposit back.

23. The Sujabi

The Sujabi neighborhood has long been among the poorer parts of the city. It is populated by the poorest dockworkers, those without stable employment, crippled workers, destitute families, and a high concentration of the city's criminal element.

Even in the days of the Hyperborean hill-fort that crowned the Island of Heroes, Sujabi has been where the refuse of the city was dumped, a tradition that continues to this day. Many attempts have been made to clean up the neighborhood, and laws have been passed that required all trash to be carted off and dumped elsewhere, but the convenience and habit of Sujabi has won out every time.

Tradition, one of the greatest forces of Rhemish life, has only encouraged the growth of one of the city of Reme's least popular but highly-profitable industries. Tanners have long situated themselves in the Sujabi, where they collect night soil from the many readily-available pools of it. Many residents of Sujabi make their livings collecting urine for use by the Tanner's Guild, which save the tanners from having to do it themselves. Sujabiers maintain their own collection tubs and cisterns, and in turn sell casks of urine to the guild.

Urine collection is just one of a thousand means by which Sujabiers manage to eke by, but the largest business in Sujabi is crime. Crime in the Sujabi even includes the sort of crime a thieves' guild wouldn't involve itself with — the slave trade.

Slavery in the Sujabi Quarter

Many of the realms of the world practice slavery under some concealing name or other, and not all of their needs can be served through conquest or raids. Sujabi is beneath official notice, the people there are beneath social notice, and the dark practice of moving slaves through the city of Reme and onto ships bound for foreign lands can

proceed in safety. This dark business is under the control of one man, the slave master Yorjar Goaj.

Born just another poor resident of Sujabi, Yorjar parlayed his size and strength into becoming the leader of a gang of thugs that extorted money from the urine collectors of the city's dump. When he tried to move up to extorting money from the Tanner's Guild, the Bandi came down on his gang and Yorjar fled the grand duchy. It was while living as a sell-sword that he discovered that slavery was popular in many places … and that there was a market for it.

Yorjar began by hiring on as muscle with a slaving operation. By cruel cunning and violent murder, he evolved into the leader of his own gang of slavers. Although it was profitable, it was also dangerous, and Yorjar wanted something a bit more regular and secure. He returned home to the Sujabi and set about building his network. He acquired slaves from across the grand duchy and parts beyond, employing means such as kidnapping travelers (those who wouldn't be missed), paying off people's debts in exchange for them entering slavery, taking people off the streets of cities (always in the poorer districts and including the Sujabi itself), to funding raids beyond the Wizard's Wall to capture humanoids.

Most of these unfortunates are brought secretly to the Sujabi, where they are kept in underground pens until a ship is ready to transport them to slave-holding nations. While he might move only a hundred or so slaves a month (of which fewer than half survive the voyage to their destinations), the trade is highly profitable. This has allowed Yorjar to build a large (but well-concealed) palace-fortress in the Sujabi and fund legitimate business interests. Moreover, a slaver's network also serves as a good smuggling network, and Yorjar brings in contraband — as well as serving the needs of anyone wishing to enter or leave the grand duchy without drawing notice.

See **Encounter 5** in the ***Convenient Reference Guide to Reme*** for NPC stats, if you need them, for one of Yorjar's slaver gangs, who might be encountered as guards or possibly even collecting a few unfortunates from the Sujabi itself.

24. Hauk Skarpson's Feast Hall

Hauk Skarpson's is a Northlander-style feasting hall that is open to the public. Since their homeland is far away, Northlanders are a rarity in the Crescent Sea. And even though the Northlanders sail far to trade and raid, rich pickings can often be found closer to home. Nevertheless, Northlander trade does bring some of these folk to the city of Reme.

One such is Hauk Skarpson, an enterprising Estenfirder who was willing to try something new and outrageous by Northlander standards. He took passage on ships belonging to a dozen nations, often working for his room and board. After two years of travel, he arrived in the city of Reme. After first visiting the jewelers on Guild Street to sell the gems he acquired troll-hunting in the Andøvan Mountains, Hauk began looking around the city for a building that would allow him to put his plan into operation. He settled on a dilapidated warehouse in an area with a fair amount of street traffic. He tore the building down, which left plenty of room to build a large structure with plenty of open space remaining.

And build a large structure he did. The feast hall is three stories tall, and wide enough to hold 300 people in its main hall, and still has private rooms and quarters for Hauk and his growing family. The ornate building is built to look like a jarl's hall from the Northlands, and a rich jarl at that. All the details are as authentic as Hauk could make them in this faraway land. When he couldn't find someone able to transform his sketches into reality, he built, carved, and painted parts himself.

Hauk Skarpson's Feast Hall is in many ways the closest one can get to the Northlander experience in this distant southland. The interior of the main hall is open, lit by a central fire pit, and decorated with Northlander art showing mighty heroes fighting hordes of foes or battling giants, dragons, and other monsters. The serving staff dresses the part, though fewer than half are actual Northlanders. The bill of fare reflects Northlander tastes.

The feast hall is mostly known for its entertainment, with skaldi (or local minstrels dressed for the part) who spin away the evenings telling tales and singing songs. Every fifth night, the benches are moved aside and some form of live entertainment takes place in the center of the hall. This might be a mock duel between warriors dressed as Northlanders, caged fights with bears (also mock battles — bears are expensive), juggling, feats of strength and agility, and once a display of marksmanship by a Nûklander archer.

The décor and ambiance draw in a fair number of customers, but the real success of the feast hall is the patronage of the grand duke. Hauk built the feast hall as if a great jarl occupied it, and toward that end, a high seat is at one end. Shortly after opening, he let it be known that the high seat is reserved for the grand duke. Hearing this rumor, a curious Iltobarus finally decided, mostly as a lark, to visit the hall and sit in the seat reserved for him. Enchanted by the spectacle and pageantry of the Northlander performance, Iltobarus has returned several times, and this has brought many of the nobles and hangers-on, as well as those hoping to climb the social ladder, to the feast hall. It is a sight to see the finely-dressed wealthy and powerful of the grand duchy eating roasted goat with their hands, all amid a barbaric milieu.

HAUK SKARPSON'S FEAST HALL MENU

FOOD AND DRINK

Ale, and lots of it	1sp
Mead, home brewed at the Feast Hall	2sp
Dragon's Blood (an imported dwarven stout but sold as a true warrior's brew)	5sp
Roast meat (goat, mutton, beef, or pork), vegetables, black bread	1gp
Aurochs cuts (only served on Northlander holidays), vegetables, black bread	5gp
Stewed apples with butter and spices	8sp
Oat cake	2sp
Sweetened ice milk	1gp

ROOMS

Huscarl's room	10gp/ night
Jarl's room	15gp/ night
Hero's room	20gp/ night

25. LANCERS' HALL

The house for the Arcanum Collegium's Order of the Lance, this three-story building presents a gentle and wealthy face to the world. A pair of men-at-arms guards the front door, and another pair patrols the premises or are on watch in case trouble starts. The building itself sits within a small walled garden that fills the entire lot and provides an outdoor venue for the Lance's activities. Down the street is the Island Stables, a high-end livery where most members of the order keep their mounts.

The hall serves as a place for social gatherings and as a headquarters for the order. The main floor is divided into a large study complete with a small library, padded chairs, and a few tables to spread maps out on and a larger common room complete with private dining nooks and a bar. The offices of the order are on the second floor, but a truly opulent ballroom takes up most of the floor. The Order of the Lance's annual ball is second only to the grand duchess's in pedigree and prestige. The third floor has 10 suites for members of the order, though two of these are always kept as the private quarters of the order's grandmaster

and high provender. A large basement houses the kitchens, servants' quarters, larder, and wine cellar. The hall has a staff of a dozen servants who clean, cook, and serve the members and their guests.

Membership in the Order of the Lance is limited to students of the Arcanum Collegium who are of knightly birth (and can prove it — the grandmaster will not hesitate to demand patents of nobility from foreign students). Dues are 100 gold pieces per year, but it is expected that on top of that members will contribute to various funds throughout the year, often totaling 4,000 gold pieces and more if the order has a particularly busy social schedule planned. Members of the order have their student's robes trimmed in cloth of gold to denote their status, and they openly display the order's arms (crossed lances over a diamond) on their clothing and other possessions.

26. ROOST OF THE OWLS

This unassuming building crowded between the Grey Horse Inn and the offices of the Guild of Scribes is the headquarters of the Arcanum Collegium's Order of the Owl. The building's three floors and garret apartments are made of wood and stone, with a sturdy tile roof. There is an obvious main door, but a single door in the back of the building leads out onto a walled garden area. The garden can be reached from the alley behind the Roost, though students coming in after curfew are known to drop down from the roof of the neighboring inn.

The main floor of the Roost is given over to offices for the order and a large study with one of the most exquisite libraries in the grand duchy. Graduated members are free to come and make use of the library for a small fee of 5 gold pieces per visit. A large enchanted globe that can rotate to show any part of the known world dominates the center of the study. Private study areas are available just off the main study. The upper floors provide small but comfortable rooms for members and their guests, as well as the apartments of the order's grandmaster.

The Roost is comfortable, but geared toward study and the arcane arts. Generations of aspiring magic-users and powerful alumni have left their mark upon the building, and not merely the scorch marks of failed experiments and spells gone awry. The Roost does not employ servants; permanent *unseen servants* wait to be summoned for ordinary tasks. Each has its own command word, and one of the games played with new members is to have them try to guess these commands. Between the *unseen servants* and a few cantrips here and there, the Roost is well-kept and its residents well cared for.

Membership in the Order of the Owl is open to any student of the Arcanum Collegium who can pass the entrance exam. As the exam requires the production of some chosen magical effect, those who are not arcanely gifted are kept out of the order. Dues are on the high end, costing 60 gold pieces a year, but this includes access to the order's library. Members of the Owls can be spotted by the purple border on their robes and their badge, a stylized owl's head.

27. QUILL HOUSE

The Order of the Quill, one of the high orders of the students of the Arcanum Collegium, is headquartered here. The residents of this solid, four-story brick building are famed as the most studious of the orders, even more so than the magic-wielding Order of the Owls. The Quills are, for the most part, children of prosperous commoners, mostly guild masters, though children of the merchant houses are also welcome.

Despite the supposedly modest backgrounds of the residents, the interior of Quill House is as richly adorned as the exterior is plain. Funded by guild members for generations on behalf of their children, the hotel has been carved, painted, and decorated to the highest level of quality. It is a practice for each new generation to renovate, remodel, or add to the interior decorations, and many members bring with them the tools and skills they gained from a childhood in the guilds.

The Quills have a reputation for academic excellence. Part of this is the result of their "humble" upbringing: They know how much it costs for them to attend the collegium and what is expected of them during their studies and afterward. It is also the culture of the order to be diligent and hardworking. Quills wear their badge (a pair of crossed quills on a blue field) with pride, and many further adorn this badge with symbols of the tools of their parents' trade.

28. The Pit of the Lizards

Known for hosting wild parties and the most likely of the collegium's orders to be involved in brawls, the Order of the Lizard has its headquarters in a freestanding street-house with vacant lots to either side. For years, the former owners of these lots complained bitterly about the Lizards; no one wanted to have a business or residence next door to the notorious house known as the Pit of the Lizards. Eventually, the Lizards simply purchased the neighboring lots and demolished the buildings. These lots remain empty, though it is not unusual to find some outdoor activity going on at all hours of the night. During the Harvest Festival, the order hosts the largest tent-covered beer hall in the city on its neighboring lots, and festivities tend to spill over into the streets and nearby market squares.

The Pit is not dilapidated, but the activities of the order tend to be rough on the building, so it is always in need of repair or currently under repair. Only two stories tall, the building has fewer amenities than can be found at the houses of the other high orders. The first floor is largely one large common room that bears a striking resemblance to a taproom. Private rooms for members — including the grandmaster's suite — are upstairs. The order employs a small, rotating cadre of servants who have a tendency to quit frequently.

Membership in the Order of the Lizard is open to any student of the collegium, but they must maintain a good academic record. The members of the order are surprisingly good at their studies, and the usual festive atmosphere tends to quiet down during examinations. The Lizards are known by the green tassels on their robes and by their badge, a rather surprised-looking dragon.

29. Fallenhouse

Home of the Order of the Rook, the Fallenhouse is a small estate just outside the walls of the city. While it might seem odd for one of the high orders of students from the Arcanum Collegium to live outside the city walls, it suits the Rooks' purposes rather well. True, if the city were to be attacked, the Rooks would be in trouble, but when was the city last attacked? Lying outside of the city proper also places the Rooks beyond the patrol routes of the Bandi, and this is the true reason they live outside the walls. That, and it makes it easier to slip in and out of the city as opposed to already being there when trouble brews — and for the Rooks, trouble always brews.

Mostly composed of younger children of Loreclannic knights who managed to get into the collegium based on heritage as well as merit, the Rooks are academically poor compared to the other orders. Their families have just enough wealth and power to get their children into the collegium, and having a collegium education is a large social boon. Everyone who is anyone has one, don't you know. That the Rooks gain little from their education other than that they attended the collegium is of little account; they attended, and that is it. Few of the Rooks actually graduate.

The Fallenhouse itself is a walled manor that more often than not is in some form of disrepair. The Rooks pride themselves on their pranks and hard-partying life. Pranks are most often performed on each other, but the Rooks target the other high orders on a regular basis. Their greatest prank, and one that each new generation of Rooks seeks to top, was to release thousands of rats into the city, all of which had been painted bright colors. The resulting havoc nearly shut the entire city down for hours.

The Terriers were not amused.

30. The Kujuk (Gate)

The Kujuk is the least important of Reme's gates, giving out upon the Western Reme Road (which essentially disappears within the city gates). The stretch of road between Reme and Whiterush is characterized by hundreds of trails leading to the interior, most of which terminate near coastal towns. Merchants in these coastal towns purchase goods from the interior and then ship them by sea to Reme or Whiterush to avoid the long and arduous trip down the road itself. The other main use of the road is for moving herds of cattle from the interior; the small coastal markets cannot absorb the price of large herds. Travelers are warned to stay clear when dust rises like a cloud over the road, for this indicates the approach of as many as a thousand head of plains cattle, essentially wild, that can stampede on a moment's notice.

31. The Ice Cult

All is not safe and pretty in the city of Reme. There are political factions vying for control of the city, nobles hoping to gain some advantage over their fellows, and criminals that prowl the night. The Bandi do a good job of keeping the peace, and the grand duke and duchess are becoming skilled at manipulating the political factions and nobles into stalemating each other. Yet there are threats that the Bandi and ducal couples might prove unable to face. A cold cancer is growing at the heart of the city, and thus in the heart of the grand duchy. A cult of the demon god Althunak has formed and hopes to soon tighten the icy grip of its dread master around Reme.

Winters along the Crescent Sea are mild — the land is not locked in the grip of snow and ice during the colder months — which allows the grand duchy to remain fertile and growing. These factors are not ones the cults of Althunak tend to favor. Indeed, their usual aim is to tip the scales of winter and savagery in places such as the Northlands or the Far North. Yet the warmer lands to the south are in many ways more offensive to the cult, and Reme is a prominent example.

The cult of Althunak in the city of Reme calls itself the Retinue of Snow and Frost. An individual by the (possibly false) name of Sven the Gaunt is the cult's high priest. Its members include several of the Loreclannic barons of the court, a number of Loreclannic knights, and a few scions of the merchant houses. These members all have different motivations for joining the cult, and not all of them actually realize the nature of the cult's activities.

The secret temple of the Retinue of Snow and Frost is hidden beneath a disused warehouse. The Gastone-Sheshek family nominally owns the warehouse, but Fidialus Gastone-Sheshek, a cult member in good standing, has made sure the family accounts have "forgotten" the ownership. The cult does not meet regularly, save for on feast days of Althunak (each new moon in the winter and the hibernal solstice).

Aside from the terrible feasts (Althunak is a demon-god of cannibalism) and the dreadful orgies (the better to entice jaded and decadent nobles), the cult offers many advantages. The members work to aid each other in their political and financial intrigues. There is also mystical power to be gained from the worship of the Lord of Ice and Snow, not the least of which is access to demons that can provide information, end rivals, and perform other tasks.

See **Encounter 6** in the ***Convenient Reference Guide to Reme*** for NPC stats, if you need them, for Sven the Gaunt and a group of the ice cultists.

The growing Retinue of Ice and Snow built a small temple for itself hidden beneath a warehouse in the dock ward. This allows them to stay out of sight, as well as to bring people and goods in through the docks. The intrigues of nobles are well known, and if any of the folk who frequent the docks on lonely nights have taken note of passing nobles in voluminous cloaks, they no doubt attribute it to some clandestine plot or love trysts. Perhaps the nobles are just slumming.

32. HALL OF THE TERRIERS

Officially known as the Guild of Rat-Catchers and Sewer Wardens, the Terriers are the only guild not invited to join the Bandi. Formed by Grand Duke Augustus IV as an unnamed band of rat hunters and sewer wardens, the Terriers were granted guild status following their heroic actions during the Purple Plaque, when the source of the plague was determined to be a thieves' guild run by wererats. Despite this high honor, the other guilds and the merchant houses have never truly accepted the Terriers into their midst. Terriers just aren't their sort of people.

Largely a hereditary guild, the Terriers do accept new members, although not everyone wants to prowl the city's waste dumps, back alleys, and sewers in search of rats and fouler vermin. Supported by a combination of an annual ducal grant and fees for their service, the Terriers are actually one of the better-funded guilds in the city. Rat removal might only run a copper piece per rat, but a city the size of Reme has a lot of rats. It adds up.

Despite this wealth, the Terriers are still much the same as they have ever been: scraggy, bedraggled, poorly educated, and reeking of trash and sewage. Despite their appearance, on the whole they are courageous and honest, heroes in their own right. Often crude and rough-edged in their social ways, the Terriers are also very insular, prideful, and pugnacious, factors that have added to their ostracism by the city's elites. However, Iltobarus and the lord mayor have shown themselves to be much more accepting of the Guild of Rat-Catchers and Sewer Wardens than the guilds, and meet with their grand master and even invite leading members to balls, feasts, and other social affairs at the castle.

The Terriers are organized like other guilds, with a grandmaster to oversee operations, ranks of masters, journeymen, and apprentices beneath her, and several families that tend to dominate guild politics. The current guild master, Sasha Streets, is of the prominent Streets family of Terriers. Her great-great-grandfather is the Terrier who drove a half-pike through the heart of the Rat King to end the Purple Plague. A woman in her late 60s, Grandmaster Streets appreciates the duke's attempts to lend respectability to the guild, but knows that it is a lost cause. The Terriers are more than just rough around the edges — generations of social isolation has made them a people of their own, unique in the city.

Joining the Terriers is relatively easy. Present yourself at the guild house, bring a letter from the temple of Mithras stating you are a person of good character, and pay the guild fee of 100 gold pieces. Members must provide themselves with the standard equipment of the Terriers: a long pole, a basket to carry rats, a suit of armor, and a hand weapon. Even those with magical aptitude must provide a suit of armor; extra armor and equipment is kept at the guild house and loaned out to Terriers as needed. A feisty dog, trained cat, or clever monkey is optional, but many Terriers have several, and more are available at the guild house.

See the *Convenient Reference Guide to Reme* for information about playing a member of the Terriers.

While rat-catching takes up most of the Terriers' work, they also patrol the city's ancient and expansive sewer network, the garbage dumps outside of the city, the granaries, and the back alleys of the city's poorer quarters. During harvest season, the guild contracts out groups of Terriers to protect the harvest as it is brought in. Many of the estates near the city also hire Terriers to guard their granaries. The Bandi are supposed to serve as a city watch, but those notables are well known to ignore areas such as the Hol-Hebar and the Sujabi, along with other dangerous pockets found in the city's tangle of streets and alleyways. The Terriers serve as the de facto watch in these areas and often mediate disputes between the poorer citizens of the city.

From time to time, other cities in the grand duchy — and even municipalities as far away as Bard's Gate — contract with the city of Reme to have a group of Terriers take care of a particularly bad infestation or clean out sewers overrun by monsters, smugglers, and other threats. These assignments are highly prized by the guild and can bring fame, adventure, and a great deal of money to those dispatched in such service.

TERRIER ADVENTURE HOOKS

* Things live in the sewers that even a Terrier finds too much. We'll pay a fair rate for you to go down and clear out a nest of, well, things. A squad of Terriers will go with you as guides.

* We are sending a squad of Terriers to Bard's Gate for the harvest patrol. They shouldn't arrive tired, wounded, or dead, so you lot need to go with them and make sure they get there safe and sound. We catch rats, not battle bandits in the woods.

* Ten gold coins to the person who can wrestle this huge rat we found in the sewers and win! Side bets welcome! First come, first fight!

33. FIELD OF THE SIRKAN PASHTARS

The Loreclans of the city produce a number of skilled pashtars, the mediators and advocates who act on behalf of multiple Loreclans at a time. However, pashtars drift between the plains and the city depending on whether they are mediating between plains' Loreclans or representing them in the ducal court. The Sirkan pashtars are those with druidic powers (or those who follow druidism), most of whom were born on the plains, and many of whom dislike the clutter and bustle of the close-in city streets. The Field of the Sirkan Pashtars is an open area studded with traditional tents of the plains' Loreclans, where the city invites these pashtars to reside while they are representing Loreclans in the duke's court. The area is open to any pashtar, of course, and many of them stay here to avoid the cost of city life, but the druidic Sirkans pashtars make up more than half the population here.

The Field of the Sirkan Pashtars is a good place to begin adventures with a druidic flavor, which is quite different on the open plains of Reme than in the forested areas where most druids are assumed to live.

34. THE QUOJO

The large area known as the Quojo is the redoubt of the city's upper-middle class. Wealthy journeymen, up-and-coming merchants, petty nobles, and more than a few retired adventurers have their houses here. The architecture harkens to an earlier time in the city's history, for many of these houses were built before the walls were extended. The houses are small, rectangular, and made of a mixture of stone, timber, and adobe. They present a bare face to the streets, with only a small, reinforced door allowing entry. Inside these walls is usually a small courtyard ringed by rooms that open into it or onto a balcony that runs around the interior. Nearly all of the older homes of the Quojo have their own wells, and many have subterranean cellars and cisterns. Rumors abound that the many cellars, basements, and cisterns somehow connect through tunnels, both natural and artificial. This rumor is, as one might suspect, entirely true.

35. HALL OF THE RED THUMB

Recent upstarts in the world of crime, the Red Thumb rose from a brawling dockyard gang to become the city of Reme's preeminent thieves' guild, displacing the Gastone-Sheshek family as the unchallenged leaders of the city's criminals. Originally just one of the many street gangs that form and break up every year, the Red Thumb once controlled only one of the city's docks. They practiced the usual crimes of small-time hoodlums: extortion, armed robbery, and malicious loitering.

If not for its leader, the Red Thumb would have followed the same path as its street rivals, the Blue Ferries, Sons of Halwark, or the Salt Street Revenants. They would have formed in a local power vacuum, battled with their neighboring rivals, risen to power, and then fallen to infighting, deaths, imprisonments, and other calamities that await Reme's minor criminality. Instead, when Kria Fell-Minded took control of the gang, she set it on a radically different trajectory than that of a normal dockyard gang. A veteran adventurer with years of experience outside of the city, Kria was a far more dangerous opponent than most of the small dockyard gangs had ever encountered, and she undertook a mixed policy of violence and assimilation.

Within two years of Kria's leadership, the Red Thumb wiped out or absorbed virtually all of the city's other dockyard gangs. It then reached tendrils out to other neighborhoods and took over crime in the Hol-Hebar. A tense truce was made in the Sujabi with Yorjar Goaj and his slaving ring — the Red Thumb had no interest in slaves, but it had a great deal of interest in preventing potential rivals in the heart of their power. The Red Thumb's methods were brutally efficient and highly secretive, at least as far as the authorities were concerned. Few cared what happened in the poorer parts of town, and when petty criminals began to appear in the alleys, sewers, and even floating in the Remenos and harbor, the Bandi approved; they thought someone was cleaning up the city for them. As far as the Gastone-Sheshek were concerned, this had no effect on them; they were far more worried about Goaj's growing smuggling operation.

After a few years of violence and another two consolidating their gains, the Red Thumb was ready to move on to their next conquest. Kria had contacts from her adventuring days that put her in touch with thieves' guilds in other cities. This allowed her to hire "consultants" to teach her street thugs more subtle approaches. They used these skills to strike directly at the rich and powerful with a series of daring burglaries.

At the same time, the Red Thumb turned its more brutal tactics against the Gastone-Sheshek family's crime network. They broke up gambling dens, intercepted smuggled goods, and made sure that the shopkeepers protected by the Gastone-Shesheks' extortion network switched alliances. Debtors to the Gastone-Shesheks found their debts cleared, but now they were indebted to the Red Thumb. The merchant house's legitimate businesses were also targeted: warehouses burned down; ships were stolen right out of the harbor; and in one brutal event, a foreign merchant negotiating a deal with the Gastone-Shesheks was murdered in broad daylight.

The Gastone-Shesheks were taken by surprise and slow to react. The family's power was damaged by the initial onslaught, but they still had wealth far in excess of the Red Thumb, despite their rival's almost total control of dockyard thefts. Reprisals began as soon as the merchant house learned that the Red Thumb was responsible. These led to counter-reprisals, which in turn drew further attacks. Today, the two criminal networks are locked in a death struggle, but the Red Thumb is stronger by far, and the Gastone-Shesheks are losing the war to retain control of crime in Reme.

RED THUMB ADVENTURE HOOKS

* A boat will be on the Remenos in two nights. Meet it before it gets to the Hol-Hebar, kill everyone on board, and bring the chest on the boat to me. You can keep the rest.

* We have to make a move on Goaj and his people. Go to the Yellow Dog tavern, pick a fight with one of his men, and make sure you kill them.

* Burn this warehouse belonging to the Gastone-Shesheks. The warehouse next door is vacant, so try starting the fire there and make sure it spreads. No one goes to that one except some jaded nobles doing who knows what.

See **Encounter 7** in the ***Convenient Reference Guide to Reme*** for NPC stats, if you need them, for a group of Red Thumb members.

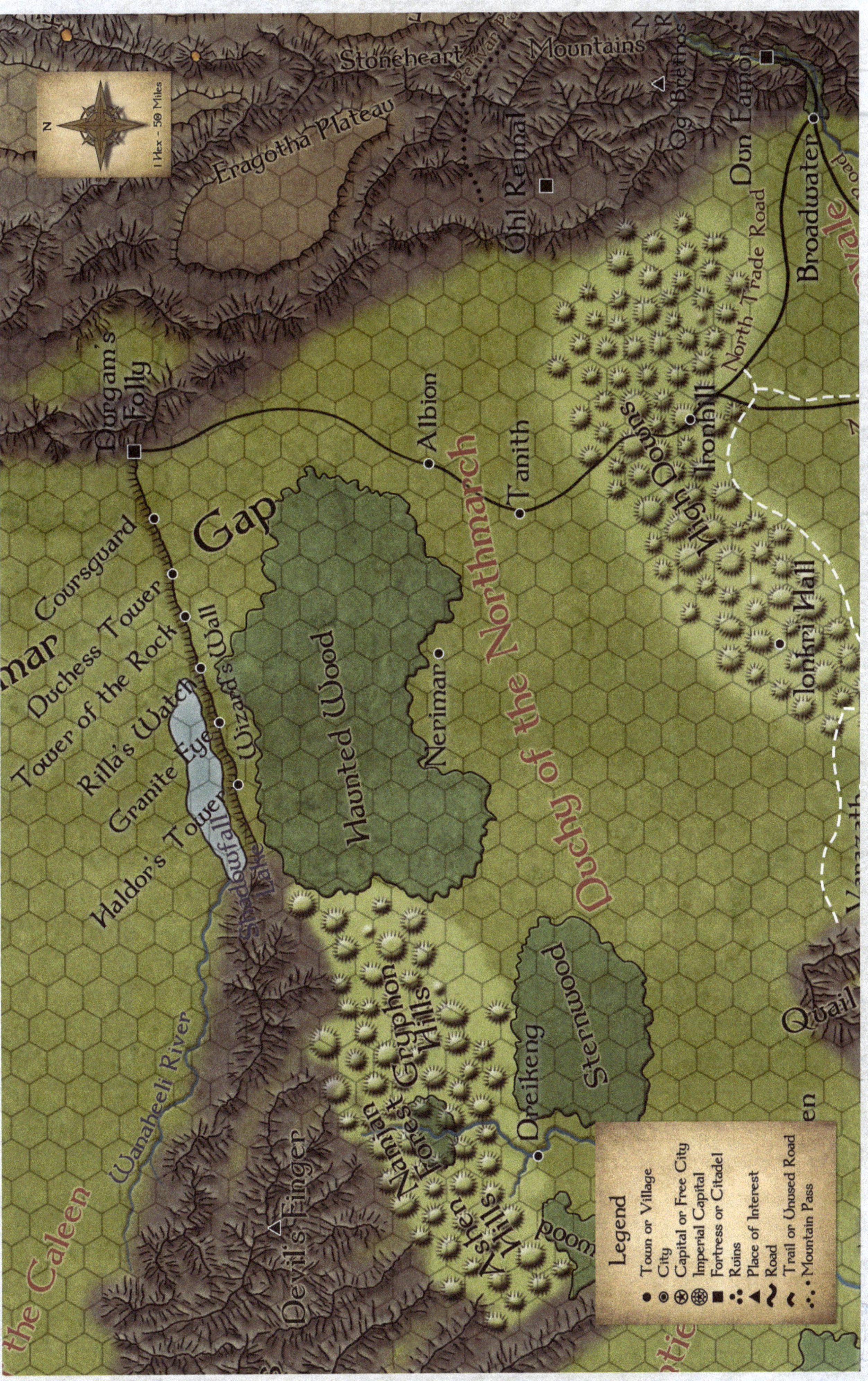

N
1 Hex = 50 Miles
Stoneheart Mountains
Eragotha Plateau
Pelican Pass
Og Brehtos
Dun Eamon
Broadwater
avale
Ohl Remal
North Trade Road
Dorgam's Folly
Albion
High Downs
Ironhall
Gap
Tanith
Jonkri Hall
Coursguard
Duchess Tower
Tower of the Rock
Wizard's Wall
Haunted Wood
Nerimar
Duchy of the Northmarch
Rilla's Watch
Granite Eye
Valdor's Tower
Shadowfallen Dale
Gryphon Hills
Sternwood
Dreikeng
Quail
Wanebeeli River
Namian Forest
Ashen Hills
poom
en
Devil's Finger
the Caleen
ntie
Legend
Town or Village
City
Capital or Free City
Imperial Capital
Fortress or Citadel
Ruins
Place of Interest
Road
Trail or Unused Road
Mountain Pass

Alignment: Lawful Good
Capital: Ironhill (15,658; Foerdewaith 5,200, gnome 1,522, half-elf 440, human Loreclan ethnicity 7,311, halfling 660, hill dwarf 525)
Notable Settlements: Chalktown (200), Dreikeng (500), Gauldark (200), Nerimar (1,583), Riverside (800), Royal Bluff (300)
Ruler: Duchess Candrella Iskadar
Government: Feudal
Population: 120,000–135,000 depending on the season (Foerdewaith 50,000, half-elf 11,500, Loreclans up to 60,000, other human mixed ethnicity 11,000, halfling 5,000, gnome (High Downs) 8,000, wood elf (Haunted Wood) 3,000, hill dwarf 800, other humanoid 2,000
Monstrous: Hobgoblins (Deepfells), goblins, centaurs, gnolls (the Frontier), trolls, creatures of shadow (Haunted Wood), orcs (Ashen Hills), kobolds (High Downs), dryad (Eisenwood, Haunted Wood), bugbears, ogres, ettercap (Haunted Wood), ankheg, banshee, basilisk, chimera, cockatrice, peryton, treants (Haunted Wood), cyclops, manticores (the Frontier), owlbears (Haunted Wood, Sternwood)
Languages: Common, Kirkut (among some Loreclannic visitors from the deep plains), Elven
Religion: Solanus, Dame Torren, Mithras (Ironhill); Kamien, Freya, Telophus, Ceres (countryside), Halatra, Solanus, Dame Torren (Loreclans)
Resources: Cattle, sheep, iron, chalk, timber
Currency: Reme
Technology Level: Medieval
Demonym/Adjectival Demonym: Northmarchers

OVERVIEW

For most of Reme's history, the Northmarches constituted the effective frontier of the grand duchy. Though lands beyond have been claimed over the centuries, this march has always been the last line of defense, the farthest reach of homeland that must be protected at all costs. Those crossing the windblown plains occasionally stumble across bones or rusted weapons or armor half-buried in the thin soil, remains of ancient battlefields where the legions and Loreclans of Reme met humanoids and darker enemies from beyond the Crynnomar Gap or hobgoblin armies from the Deepfells. Fortunately, few such forces have threatened the lands of the grand duke for many centuries now, though a watchful eye is still maintained in Durgam's Folly and in watchtowers on the Wizard's Wall overlooking the Haunted Steppes.

The land here is lightly populated, with little agriculture possible. Horses and cattle graze on the plains, however, and several of the plains' Loreclans range over the Northmarches on a seasonal basis. Iron and chalk are profitably mined from the High Downs.

On official maps, the Northmarches include the Frontier and the Haunted Wood, but the duchess ignores both, since any effort to civilize those lands would cost more in lives and treasure than it could ever conceivably be worth.

The few settlements, other than the capital of Ironhill, are largely trading posts for trappers, cattle drives, and prospectors or logging towns along the forest edges. The folk dwelling here are hardy, proud of their self-sufficiency, and often suspicious of those from the south. The duchess also maintains the military outposts along Wizard's Wall, including the fortress of Durgam's Folly, and fields a substantial standing army that patrols the outskirts of the Haunted Wood and the Gryphon Hills to protect against incursions of humanoids and other threats. The army is well supplied with light cavalry from the Loreclans, and very little gets past these watchful eyes.

HISTORY AND PEOPLE

A considerable part of the area now known as the Northmarches of Reme was initially held by the elves as part of the Green Realm, although a substantial portion of it has always been open plains.

Legends of the Green Realm hold that this region was once home to the goddess Shalraei, whose presence blessed the kingdom of Alathanar and the wild elves of the Alathi tribe. Only whispered echoes of those early days survive, including stories about battles with demons, fallen gods, and the hordes of shadow. In those days, the goddess stood beside her children and helped them repel even the fiercest horrors.

As centuries passed, the goddess's power infused itself into the forest itself. In the Age of the Gods, she departed the material realm, but left the forest to the Alathi, who continued to care for and nurture it as they transformed it into one of the spiritual centers of the old elven kingdoms. Here, the elves say, the greatest druids of forgotten ages came to commune with a land that still held the life energies of Shalraei, making it far greener, lusher, and more spiritually powerful than any other. The Alathi elves maintained good relations with the rock gnomes of the High Downs and the Thistlehill gnomes of the Namjan region, though gnomes were forbidden from settling in or even entering forests directly under the Alathis' control.

The realm of Alathanar had fallen to evil magic and civil war by the time the Hyperborean legions reached the edge of the forest, but the invaders were nevertheless overextended and held at bay for a time. Unfortunately, the last days of elven dominion were rapidly passing: In the late 600s I.R., humanoids from the Great Steppes threw themselves against the Green Realm in ever-increasing numbers. In one of many tragic events of the day, the elves were forced to abandon Alathanar and withdraw north into the Crynnomar Gap.

Land-hungry and with little concern for the region's spiritual importance, the imperator of Remenos sent his legions and Loreclan auxiliaries north, felling trees to build roads, fortresses, and towns. By 725 I.R., most of the forest had been replaced by vast grasslands, and its timeless beauty was lost forever. Disheartened, the elves did not try to retake their old holy land, but instead left it to the human invaders. A few remnants of the old world remained in the shadowy depths of the Haunted Forest where the corrupted Alathi persisted — and in fact persist to this day.

The newly-minted province of Northmarch grew over the next few centuries as purely nomadic Loreclans settled into villages or semi-nomadic permanent camps in ever-increasing numbers. In the High Downs they encountered the old kingdom of the rock gnomes. Though well past their prime, the gnomish kingdom continued to exert a claim on the downs, with dozens of small settlements scattered across the area. The spoiling of Alathanar had indeed been an egregious act, but the Hyperboreans balked at outright genocide, and the gnomes were allowed to remain. Gnomish laborers began to work in Ironhill and other human settlements, and gnomish traders provided chalk to the resource-hungry Hyperboreans. The empire did not officially annex the gnomish lands or demand fealty, but as the generations passed, human influence grew to a point that Hyperborean dominance was inescapable. The gnomes continue to live in the region to this day — officially independent but effectively subjects of the Grand Duchy of Reme.

Elsewhere, the vast plains of the Frontier seemed ideal land for settlement, but to the Hyperboreans' intense frustration, various humanoid tribes as well as the great nomadic centaur nation known as the Vaeltaia already occupied the region. Tense from the start, relations between the indigenous centaurs and the intruding humans grew over the years, finally culminating in the Frontier War of 1013 I.R. when a Hyperborean legion marched into the Frontier determined to put the unruly centaurs in their place. In this case, the Hyperboreans forgot the lessons learned on the Rhemish plains in the early days of Reme's history. Primarily infantry with a contingent of heavy cavalry, the Hyperboreans were quickly outmaneuvered on the open plains, surrounded, and shot to pieces by centaur archers. The Loreclannic knights were likewise frustrated, goaded into fruitless charges against a phenomenon they had never before encountered: foes who moved faster than they were able to ride. A handful of legionnaires limped back into the Northmarches, protected by the legion's few Loreclannic light cavalry auxiliaries, and in a rare display of pragmatism, the Hyperboreans made peace with the centaurs and agreed to build no further settlements in exchange for the Vaeltaia's symbolic acceptance of imperial authority in the region.

Many believed that the Northmarches would one day become one of the central provinces of a powerful empire, and plans were made for large cities, paved roads, and elaborate palaces. These dreams proved elusive and were in the end shattered by the arrival of the hobgoblins of the Deepfells, who beginning in 1548 I.R. shattered and routed all Hyperborean legions sent against them. The plains' Loreclans fought a rearguard action as they retreated, inflicting horrendous casualties upon the horde, but the sheer numbers of the hobgoblins allowed them to take control of the plains. By 1557 I.R., nearly the whole of the Northmarch fell and was now part of the brutal Deepfells' kingdom. The single exception was the defiant citadel of Durgam's Folly, which held out against the invaders while drawing a tenuous and frequently-interrupted flow of supplies through the treacherous trails and passes of the Stoneheart Mountains.

In the years that followed, the Deepfells hobgoblins slaughtered or enslaved most of the surviving Northmarchers and destroyed many of the cities and palaces the Remans had built. The hobgoblins' grim, warlike state and its occupation of the Northmarches lasted until 1572 I.R. when Grand Duke Borell led the victorious army that smashed the Deepfells' forces and vanquished the hobgoblins' leader, the demigod Kakobovia. The liberation of the battered but still undefeated garrison at Durgam's Folly in 1573 I.R. officially ended the war and returned the Northlands to Hyperborean-Reman control.

The province's old potential was never again realized, as grassland and forest reclaimed the Northmarch's abandoned towns and old palaces. Occupied elsewhere, the Hyperboreans did little to rebuild the region and left it to nomads, villagers, and various humanoid tribes. Decades grew into centuries, and the province withstood various crises and disasters, with its people largely fending for themselves.

Threats — humanoid raiders, marauding monsters, and desperate bandits — arose from the depths of the Haunted Wood, the Ashen Hills, and of course from north of the Crynnomar Gap. As poverty spread across the march, communities began to compete for scarce resources, often giving rise to open conflict. The hobgoblins of the Deepfells, defeated but not driven out, continued to raid in small groups and caused significant damage and even on occasion defeated the ill-equipped second-line Hyperborean legions sent against them.

Inevitably, with the waning of Hyperborean power, local Rhemish leaders began to assert their authority. When at last the Hyperboreans left in the late 25th century I.R., Reme became an independent nation and a semblance of order returned to the Northmarches. Rhemish garrisons helped to control raiding and banditry, and some old fortresses were restored and new ones were built — particularly the citadel of Durgam's Folly, which protected the regions south of Crynnomar Gap against attack from the north. The Northmarches were still wild and relatively unsettled, but in time they grew into a more peaceful place, once more attracting settlers.

When Grand Duke Altharus Oersi III agreed to peaceful annexation by the rising overkingdom of Foere, the Grand Duchy of Reme became an official royal vassal and the Northmarches were incorporated as a province.

The adoption of the Foerdewaith Prince Cale, and his ascension to the title of grand duke shortly thereafter, had more of an effect in the Northmarches than in any other part of Reme — except, possibly, in the city itself.

To the north of Reme lay the Great Steppes — and to the Foerdewaith eyes of Grand Duke Prince Cale and his advisors, this area was unsettled and open to colonization. Only a handful of "primitive" humanoids and nomads lay in Foere's path to empire, and the Northmarches soon became a vital steppingstone in the process of conquering and incorporating the vast northern plains. The first of what came to be called the Caleen Colonies was established along the northern edge of the Deepfells in 2861 I.R., and slowly the Foerdewaith began to make their way farther north.

The era of the Great Colonization was a good one for the Northmarches. From Cale's ascension through the 2920s I.R., a constant flow of settlers passed through the land, stopping at growing caravansaries and trade cities, spending gold, and sometimes even choosing to settle in the marches rather than face the hardships of colonizing the harsh plains farther north.

After its initial successes, however, the Great Colonization met with resistance, for the inhabitants of the Great Steppes were not as sparse nor as helpless as they had initially seemed. Beyond the range of Foerdewaith and Loreclannic scouts, the humanoids of the region regrouped along the shores of Lake Hali and grew strong. When the wave of colonization finally reached Lake Hali in 2931 I.R., they encountered well-organized and aggressive humanoid forces that quickly pushed them back and besieged the Caleen Colonies.

While Grand Duke Cale sent urgent requests for aid to his brother in Courghais, the humanoids maintained pressure on the colonists but made little headway. In 2947 I.R. however, the situation grew incalculably worse. Possibly sensing the colonists' vulnerability and thirsty for mortal souls, dark forces of shadow stirred deep in the Lost Mountains and descended, leading still more hordes of humanoids. These were the Scaedugenga — the shadow walkers of ancient legend — unleashed against the already beleaguered Caleen Colonists. Lights flared in the night as the Shadow Horde moved south, burning colonies as they went.

A desperate Grand Duke Cale oversaw the recruitment of a substantial, if largely inexperienced, force dubbed the Caleen Legion that stood against the humanoids but then proved unable to stem the tide against the Shadow Horde. Cale himself perished in battle, and the Caleen Legion was scattered, leaving the Northmarches all but defenseless.

What followed was one of the most celebrated and mysterious events in Foere's history. Fully alert to the danger, the overking sent his legions north while also sending out a call throughout the kingdom for magical aid against the horde. The task seemed desperate, for the ancient stories of the elves' battle with the shadow walkers — long dismissed as fairy tales — had turned out to be all too real. While human steel and bravery might delay the foe, they were no match for the shadow walkers and their terrifying powers. Fearful and all but resigned to defeat, the legions marched out of Durgam's Folly to face the oncoming foe.

It was then that two figures from the mists of legend responded to the overking's call and returned in their people's hour of greatest need. The archmagi Margon and Alycthron appeared before the outnumbered legions and cast an ancient ritual to raise the land in a vast and towering escarpment that forever sealed the Crynnomar Gap and stopped the Shadow Horde's advance. In the face of these legendary magics, the horde stopped its advance and eventually turned back.

With his armies unexpectedly saved, the overking stationed garrisons along the wall and withdrew his legions. The triumph was bittersweet, and some even refused to call it a victory, for the colonists of the north were cut off from their homeland, and the northern steppes were forever locked away. Never again would the people of Foere — or of Reme — cross the Crynnomar Gap into what was now known as the Haunted Steppes.

Today, the Northmarches remain Reme's wild frontier — sparsely populated and still popularly believed to be untamed and dangerous. The folk that dwell here do so for a variety of reasons. The Loreclans have always lived here and see it as their home, hard won through centuries of struggle. Some residents are hardy settlers of Foerdewaith ancestry, determined to "tame" a "savage" land, much to the chagrin of those who live there. Others simply want no part of the intrigue and corruption of the "civilized" lands. Still others seek out the Northmarches for their freedom and the adventures that this largely unexplored region still holds. All of these factors combine to make Northmarchers a tough and independent sort, almost as distrustful of each other as they are of outsiders.

Significant divisions exist between the Northmarchers. The inhabitants of Ironhill, mostly of Foerdewaith ancestry, see the region as a place to be conquered, full of dangerous inhabitants and monsters, as well as provincial villagers and nomads whom many city-dwellers hold in utter contempt. For their part, the folk of the Loreclans put little faith in urban Northmarchers and go their own way, disdainful of outside attempts to "civilize" them.

Townsfolk — that is to say, the inhabitants of settlements such as Tanith and Albion — are somewhat more pragmatic since they have significant populations of Loreclannic background and deal frequently with settled and semi-nomadic Loreclans. There is a tendency even among the urban Loreclan-folk to consider farmers, ranchers, and even semi-nomadic Loreclans to be a bit bumpkinish and unsophisticated. This prejudice is by no means universal, and it is usually hidden behind a mask of politeness in any case, as the town and countryfolk need each other for survival, especially in times of need or in the event of external attack.

While the Northmarchers tend to be distrustful of outsiders, especially those hailing from large cities or the kingdoms of the east such as Foere, there is nevertheless a grudging acceptance of those who wish to come here, based upon the locals' traditional independence. Unless a stranger is overtly wicked, greedy, or arrogant, Northmarchers provide aid, assistance, food, and shelter, albeit with a grumbling acquiescence. They are a taciturn people, insular and slow to trust, but are at heart generous and fair.

Despite their provincial attitudes, Northmarchers tend to be loyal Rhemish. Hostility and outright anger may be directed at nobles and the "fancified" inhabitants of other duchies, but in the end, nearly all Northmarchers are proud of their Rhemish heritage and defend the land against external threats. This is actually unsurprising, as the Northmarches have always been an important part of Rhemish defense, and have suffered under the yoke of foreign intruders many times, leaving them dependent upon the ducal army and other duchies for their survival.

Northmarchers of Foerdewaith ancestry share the land with the nomadic Loreclans, many of whom spend the summer months on the plains of Northmarch. Despite the violent history of both peoples, this arrangement has endured for so long that it is considered a normal part of life in the Northmarches, to the point that many merchants and villagers actually look forward to the seasonal arrival, for the nomads are skilled traders and bring with them livestock, clothing, animal skins, and leather goods for sale, and in exchange purchase tools, metal, weapons, chalk and timber. The Loreclans graze their herds on the green grasslands and interact with the more settled Northmarchers in vast encampments. Conflicts over grazing lands sometimes erupt between visiting Loreclans, but pashtars from both town and camp are usually able to prevent bloodshed.

A healthy population of halflings lives in the Northmarch's towns, and several small halfling villages with populations of a few dozen to several hundred can be found throughout the duchy. Unlike most human Northmarchers, these halflings are welcoming and friendly, like their fellows elsewhere in Akados. Halfling archers and scouts are often important members of local militias, and halfling messengers mounted on sturdy ponies are frequently employed to carry messages and important goods throughout the duchy.

The duchy is home to others besides humans. Dwarven miners in the western Stoneheart Mountains dig for iron, tin, and copper, while gnomish workers are the prime source of chalk that is used in local construction and sold elsewhere in the grand duchy. Dwarven and gnomish merchants venture into human settlements, especially Ironhill, to buy and sell. Both groups are traditionally skilled at engineering and construction, and some are employed in Ironhill to assist with public works, fortifications, and building. Recently, dwarven engineers and gnomish laborers assisted with the repair and renovation of the fortress at Durgam's Folly.

The gnomes have inhabited the High Downs for millennia. Today they remain officially autonomous and continue to exercise their old social order, with the ancient royal Clan Granith at its head. While today's gnomish homeland is only a shadow of its former self — a collection of small communities devoted mostly to farming, animal husbandry, and chalk mining — a few retain the ambition to return the kingdom to its old status. A handful of distant Granith relatives in Castorhage, or others with claims to the gnomish crown, have called for a return to the Downs and a restoration of the kingdom. Exactly how this would sit with the grand duchy remains to be seen, and so far the great restoration of gnomish glory remains the pipedream of the powerless and deluded.

RELIGION

Despite the fact that the ducal capital of Ironhill is more deeply influenced by Foerdewaith culture than most places in Reme, its temples are mostly dedicated to faiths common elsewhere in the duchy. Duchess Candrella Iskadar is a faithful follower of Solanus and graces the temple with her presence on holy days. For the remainder of the time, the duchess' spiritual needs are seen to by High Priest Religar, an old and wise gentleman who speaks multiple languages and has much knowledge of the kingdom's history and politics.

In the countryside and small villages north of the High Downs, more traditional Hyperborean gods are still worshipped. While Solanus is popular, locals generally reserve their greatest devotion for Kamien, Telophus, and Freya. A few settlers brought their gods with them — Tanith boasts the only temple to Arialee in Reme.

TRADE AND COMMERCE

Reme sees the Northmarches as a buffer between them and the dangers of the north, and so the province receives little real economic support from the remainder of the grand duchy. As a result, the Northmarches are largely self-sufficient and host only a relatively small trickle of trade with the outside world. Northmarcher livestock, iron from the western slopes of the Stoneheart Mountains, and chalk from the High Downs all make their way along trade routes to the rest of the grand duchy and to places such as Foere, Waymarch, Ysser, and Bard's Gate, earning much-needed gold and silver. An equally small but vital trickle of trade returns, bringing textiles, grains, manufactured goods, and a variety of foodstuffs back to Reme.

It is really internal commerce that keeps the Northmarches alive, however, with the farms and ranches of the plains trading with towns and cities. The nomadic Loreclans provide an especially vital link to the other duchies as well, for their yearly migration route takes them from the Northmarches in the summer to the grand duchy during the spring and fall, and to their winter camps in the Waymarch, then back again. Skilled merchants, the semi-nomadic Loreclans trade as they go, obtaining goods they need and items they know will be needed in their upcoming destinations. This vital trade connection helps keep those of Loreclannic and Foerdewaith ancestry at peace, for each group sees the other as an important part of their economic survival.

LOYALTIES AND DIPLOMACY

While Northmarch is a loyal member of the Grand Duchy of Reme, its people feel little real kinship with the rest of the realm. Independent, insular, and distrustful, the Northmarchers see their duchy as a neglected corner of Reme generally left to its own devices and seen as little more than a buffer state. The presence of Rhemish troops is seen as both blessing and curse, for even the most distrustful of Northmarchers knows that without the grand duchy's aid, their state would be at the mercy of banditry, raiders, and even darker forces such as the shadow creatures of the Haunted Wood and the fierce humanoid tribes of the north.

The city of Ironhill, separated from the remainder of the duchy by the High Downs, represents a very different society and people. Populated mostly by city-dwelling Foerdewaith, most of whom have never ventured into the northern regions, Ironhill is the only part of the Northmarches that most outsiders see. Here, the duchess and her court hold sway and govern from palaces and official buildings much like those in the remainder of Reme. Her stated goal is to see that the duchy is brought into the modern world, with the old roads, cities, and fortresses rebuilt.

GOVERNMENT

Rhemish rule in the Northmarches is minimal out of necessity, for beyond the various military garrisons sparsely posted throughout the duchy, the grand duchy exercises little real authority. Fortunately for Grand Duke Iltobarus, Northmarchers maintain a strong sense of Rhemish identity despite their isolation and distrust of outsiders.

A hereditary duchy, the Northmarches are currently ruled by Duchess Candrella, the fifth ruler in the Iskadar line. While she is ambitious and wishes to see the Northmarch become a fully-integrated part of the grand duchy with new roads, palaces, fortresses and cities (she has familiarized herself with the region's history and longs for the old days before the Deepfells invasion), Candrella is also realistic and knows that such changes cannot take place within her own lifetime. With little in the way of support from a grand duke who has numerous other priorities, Candrella must content herself with less ambitious projects such as building a paved, raised road through the High Downs and providing some much-needed repairs to the walls of Durgam's Folly.

The Iskadar family is old and politically savvy. Candrella's father, Duke Stephan, taught her every one of his family's tricks, all of which came into play with the ascension of Grand Duke Iltobarus. Candrella managed to steer a safe course through treacherous political waters and maintained her family's power and position even in the face of potentially catastrophic change. That Iskadar survived and even prospered during the tumultuous days of Iltobarus' rise is testament to the family's resilience and Candrella's instinctive diplomatic skill.

Today she realizes that despite its wildness and the occasional humanoid invasion, the Northmarches are nevertheless free of the dynastic struggles and civil conflicts that affect other parts of the duchy, such as the adjoining Westmarches. In place of troublesome noble houses such as the Merciers and the Brodcheks, the Northmarches have marauding orcs and hobgoblins, and to some extent Candrella is grateful for this.

Despite the duchy's relative political stability, there are those who suspect that Candrella's seeming loyalty and compliance with the grand duke's authority is nothing but a cunning disguise, and that she secretly still supports the House of Decian's claim to the grand ducal crown. After all, they claim, the Decians were responsible for the Iskadars' past prosperity and were always loyal allies of the old grand duke. They suggest that perhaps she still supports the old rulers and might yet play a role in their return.

While there are no known heirs to the Decian legacy, and related families are too far removed to claim the grand duchy, rumors continue to circulate that there might be a hidden pretender who might yet rise to challenge the "usurper" Iltobarus. For her part, Candrella claims to find such rumors amusing, or in extreme cases, downright treasonous, and has moved to quickly squelch suggestions that she is anything but a loyal supporter of the current grand duke.

MILITARY

After a long history of war and conquest, the Northmarches are seen as an important defense against foreign invasion. In the past, the region was well garrisoned by Hyperborean legions and mercenaries, but with the raising of the Wizard's Wall, threats from the north have lessened, and the defense of the Northmarch has fallen to local militia and those troops raised directly by Duchess Candrella. The Loreclans — at least the semi-nomadic and purely nomadic ones — are capable of ferocious combat, but their tactic in the face of overwhelming odds is to retreat and then return, giving up ground until the attackers are trapped and vulnerable in the plains. For a ruler responsible for protecting permanent settlements, villages, and towns, simply giving up ground is not an option. Thus, the duchy's primary defense is more traditional and raised from the settled people of the countryside. These militia companies are raised by individual settlements and vary greatly in quality and capabilities — some are well-trained and equipped, while others are simply local peasants or farmers armed with spears or improvised agricultural implements.

Militias are commanded by local nobles — in the Foerdewaith sense, not the Loreclannic baronial system — by mercenaries paid by the duchy or by regular army officers trained in the southern duchies. Once more, these commanders vary significantly in quality and experience, but those in regions that are regularly subjected to raids and attacks tend to be more competent, and the militia somewhat more skilled. Roads are often patrolled by hired sell-swords from groups like the Wheelwrights and the Road Agents, who are called upon to take up the slack when local authorities aren't able to do so.

The largest group of regular Rhemish soldiery, Durgam's Legion, is garrisoned at the northern fortress of Durgam's Folly (see below) at the eastern edge of the Wizard's Wall. Originally intended to defend the northern provinces against attack through Crynnomar Gap, the fortress has fallen into disrepair, though it and its garrison are frequently tested in raids by humanoids (and worse) from both mountain and forest.

MAJOR THREATS

Historically threatened by the might of the Deepfells hobgoblins, humanoids, nomads, and the terrible Shadow Horde, the Northmarches are familiar with facing dangerous foes. Though currently no major force threatens the duchy, lesser powers collectively represent a significant threat to the Northmarches' security.

Though their power was broken long ago, the hobgoblins of the Deepfells persist, surviving today as fragmented petty kingdoms that sometimes band together in an alliance and raid into the lowlands. These attacks are intended to capture slaves and plunder and not occupy territory, but they take a significant toll nonetheless, leaving burned towns, ravaged farmlands, and the bodies of slain Northmarchers and livestock in their wake. Those captured alive face a terrible fate; they are sold to other humanoid tribes or dragged back to be worked to death in the dark tunnels under the Deepfells beyond light and hope of rescue.

In response to the threat represented by the Deepfells kingdoms, Duchess Candrella Iskadar is taking steps to keep the hobgoblins divided and dispatched elite agents to plant evidence and provoke continued conflict lest the hobgoblins unite and once more threaten the Northmarches. To this end, her diplomats made tentative contact with the Stoneaxe dwarves, and these normally-insular people have responded cautiously, providing some aid and guidance to the Northmarchers' efforts.

Other humanoids occasionally raid into the Northmarches, with the most prominent being the bizarre orcs of the Ashen Hills. Divided into rival tribes, the orcs fight each other as much as outsiders, but their thirst for blood and plunder is such that they gather and surge south, attacking human settlements and centaur tribesfolk with equal ferocity.

Between the humanoid threat and the scourge of even more fearsome monsters — trolls, owlbears, worgs, ettercap outbreaks of giant insects, and even fiendish outsiders such as demons and devils that inexplicably plague regions bordering the Haunted Wood — local militias often have their hands full and sometimes are forced to call for assistance from adventurers, mercenaries, or the ragged warriors of Durgam's Legion.

WILDERNESS AND ADVENTURES

The Northmarch has never been truly settled in any kind of modern sense. Even in the old days of the Hyperborean and Foerdewaith kingdoms when walled settlements, noble estates, and paved roads were constructed, the land was still largely wild or held by the purely-nomadic "deep plains" Loreclans. In the early days, this fact actually attracted settlers both wealthy and common who wished to explore and tame an "empty" land. That the Northmarches were not truly empty, and that there were others who lived there, held little importance to these individuals, but their dreams were shattered in a series of wars and disasters, leaving today's Northmarches in a similarly unpopulated state.

Most of the region is rolling grassland where once the sacred trees of Alathanar grew and were tended by the land's original elven inhabitants. The axes of the Hyperboreans destroyed the land's peaceful beauty and now leagues of golden-green grass sway in the wind instead of quiet, ancient trees and their shepherds. The grasslands are home to Loreclans and some elven clans who make camp in the High Downs during colder months, then wander the region as the weather improves. These elven tribes are quite friendly with the Loreclans, and there is virtually no conflict between the groups, even though they share the same land. Unlike most humans, the elves are free to roam through Loreclannic territory without being treated as intruders.

Occasional visitors to the plains are orc and goblin raiders who emerge from the forests and surrounding hills or mountains to make war on Rhemish settlements. Their lairs are distant from the duchy and well-guarded, but sometimes their offenses are so egregious that the Northmarchers are compelled to follow, hunt them down, and inflict bloody revenge. Adventurers and mercenaries such as the Wheelwrights and the Road Agents are often employed in such pursuits.

As civilization has ebbed and flowed over the centuries, some remnants of old glory can still be found here in the form of ancient elven cairns, underground temple complexes, and weathered ruins where sacred forests once stood. The elven remains are usually avoided by the Northmarchers, who consider them cursed, and in many cases they are correct in this assumption, as old magic and strange energies still linger in such places.

Human ruins from the Hyperborean and later eras are also to be found, though these are less hazardous, at least from an arcane standpoint. A few rough stretches of paved road remain, along with the shells of villages, old estates, and military citadels. Those few that are still in shape can serve as temporary homes for bandits, humanoid bands, or even travelers forced to seek shelter.

Towns are few and far between, and all but absent in the empty plains of the Frontier. In these areas, close to the Sternwood, the Ashen Hills, and the Deepfells, travel is especially dangerous, for goblin and hobgoblins are frequently encountered, along with dangerous predators and monsters who seek prey beyond the forest.

Legends still linger about the fearsome Shadow Horde. When the horde re-emerged to destroy Foere's Great Colonization movement, its victims realized that the old stories of the elven wars against the shadow were not exaggerations or fairy tales after all. Only the intervention of the mythic archmagi Margon and Alycthron to raise the Wizard's Wall saved the Northmarches, and the lands of the grand duchy beyond, from the horde's shadowy dominion, but even the most optimistic and heroic tales warn that the horde was only driven off and not permanently defeated. Wisps of the old horde still linger in the duchy. Many fear that they will one day return in force, and not even the mighty magics of the Wizard's Wall can stop them.

The exact nature of the Shadow Horde is not widely understood, especially by the provincial Northmarchers, who only know of them from stories told to frighten children. Those who venture into the Haunted Wood in search of answers, adventure, or treasure often do not return, and those who do are usually changed for the worse by the experience. The inhabitants of Nerimar have the most experience with the shadowy things of the wood, but their stories vary and it is hard to determine exactly how much of a threat they truly represent. The creatures commonly called "shadows" are found in the depths of the forest, but stories tell of demons, hounds, flying things, and even dragons composed of shadows and possessed of a burning hatred for mortal creatures.

Use the **Plains (General) Encounter Table** for random encounters in the Northmarches.

LOCATIONS

ALBION

Alignment: Neutral Good
Ruler: Mayor Jorgin
Government: Feudal
Population: 2,406 (Loreclans 1,210, Foerdewaith 653, gnome 351, half-elf 62, halfling 130)
Languages: Common, Rheman, some Kirkut speakers
Religion: Solanus, Freya
Resources: Grain, livestock, timber
Technology Level: Medieval

Albion is a small village north of the High Downs on the road from Ironhill to Durgam's Folly. Living relatively near the eastern eaves of the Haunted Wood, locals make their way with some logging and trapping in the forest, and providing for those on the road heading south to the ducal capital or north to the Wizard's Wall. The level-headed Mayor Jorgin was appointed to his position by the Earl of Tanith, whose domain nominally includes Albion, though villagers see little of their lord other than the annual tax collectors. Of late, a wizard from Reme settled in the area and built a tower outside of town.

This location has been the site of several settlements, including an early Hyperborean village and a major stopover during the Great Colonization. Both settlements ended up destroyed, however — the first by the Deepfells hobgoblin and the second by forces of the Shadow Horde raiding south of the Crynnomar Gap before the raising of the Wizard's Wall.

The town also boasts the Wayward Inn and Stables, the Northmarches' best-known inn outside of Ironhill. Owned by the rock gnome Barenos Deepminer, the inn is almost a small settlement in itself, with accommodations for more than 100 travelers, their wagons, carts, and animals. A small squad of 20 hired mercenaries protects the inn and also serves as the core of the town militia in case of humanoid or bandit attack.

Most locals worship Solanus and village priest Gerald Cor tends a small church near the center of town. He provides healing, potions, and food to those in need and does not charge for such services, though contributions to the church are always welcome. Elsewhere, villagers maintain shrines and pray to other gods, with Freya being the most popular of these.

Surrounded by wheat farms and horse ranches, Albion produces enough of a surplus to trade with the rest of the duchy, but this relative prosperity is a bit of a double-edged sword, as it draws attention from various dangerous groups. Goblin raids, while not a daily event, are nevertheless a familiar event, with humanoid bands throwing themselves at outlying farms or even raiding into the town itself — killing, burning and looting. The town militia can be called up and in extremity totals more than 600 individuals. All able-bodied adults are expected to participate in Albion's militia and most do so with great devotion, making some members the equal of or even superior to regular Rhemish soldiery.

Other challenges may call for further reinforcement, for the settlement's proximity to the Haunted Wood has at times drawn things far worse than marauding goblins and greedy bandits. Monsters such as ettins, ettercaps, and undead have been encountered in the forest, and sometimes even emerge from its shadows by night to fall upon travelers, farmers, or even townsfolk. While Albion's militia can sometimes deal with these incursions, the town is frequently forced to call on outside assistance from adventurers, mercenaries, or the ducal authorities in Ironhill. Worse still, some more remote farmers claim that they have seen creatures of shadow lurking near the edge of the woods, leading some to wonder whether the ancient Shadow Horde or its descendants may be returning. If this were to happen, Albion would be among the horde's first victims.

ASHEN HILLS

This area of rocky, largely barren hills east of the Deepfells contains no know veins of precious ores, though some of the gray stone here can be quarried for use in building. Tribes of orcs roam these hills. In addition, it is said that an ancient complex of tunnels — possibly dug by a prehuman race — can be found deep in these hills and can be followed to a secret valley containing a magnificent temple.

The Ashen Hills are beyond the control of Reme and described in the chapter "Beyond the Borders."

Use the specific **Ashen Hills Encounter Table** for random encounters here.

Durgam's Folly

Alignment: Lawful Neutral
Ruler: Captain Eyrik Tulah
Government: Military
Population: 2,500 military, 250 civilian (human)
Languages: Common
Religion: Mithras
Technology Level: Medieval

The fortress of Durgam's Folly stands against the ramparts of the Stoneheart Mountains on the eastern flank of the Wizard's Wall. It is home to a significant body of regular Reman troops from the central duchies, with more than 2,000 infantry and 500 cavalry standing watch over the northern borders. Some coin-counting Reman officials believe that even this is too much, for the Wizard's Wall has served to guard the northern frontier for many years, allowing the grand duchy to limit access to those nomads selected by a lottery that is held every 50 years.

Distance and the myopia of rulership appear to be behind these attitudes, as the fortress continues to serve its purpose of fending off attacks from the Haunted Wood, the Stoneheart Mountains, and elsewhere, while periodically sending expeditions south to counter raids on towns such as Tanith and Albion. These battles are largely unheralded however, and news of the garrison's sacrifices and heroism rarely reach the rest of the grand duchy. In its centuries of existence, Durgam's Folly has never fallen to enemy attack.

Hyperborean Captain Durgam Volmsmer constructed the citadel in the 750s I.R. Its name was something of a joke, as a number of imperial skeptics questioned the need for a fortress in such a remote location. There was reason for such doubts, as the full extent of the dangers that lay beyond the Crynnomar Gap had yet to be experienced. It was in 1550 I.R. that the Deepfells hobgoblins drove the Hyperboreans from the area, leaving Durgam's Folly isolated and seemingly doomed.

What followed was nothing short of a miracle, for the beleaguered warriors in the citadel held out, withstanding sieges and assaults for years as supplies and reinforcements made their way north through the treacherous Stoneheart Mountains and to Durgam's Folly. This tiny spark of Hyperborea remained for 22 years until Duke Borrell's victorious legions finally liberated it.

Though the citadel was repaired and reinforced, the Northmarches remained an imperial backwater, passing to the control of the independent grand duchy, then the Kingdom of Foere. The marches returned to importance in the 2920s I.R. as Grand Duke Prince Cale's ambitions led to the Great Colonization, and thousands of settlers moved north to settle the Great Steppes. Durgam's Folly became an important stopover and also provided troops to defend and escort the settlers. Though banditry and attacks by nomads and humanoids did occur, they were comparatively minor detours on Prince Cale's road to greatness. When the Shadow Horde awoke and swept away the shocked Remans, Durgam's Folly was again at war — the last bastion between the Northmarches and utter destruction.

The soldiers of Durgam's Folly — now proudly calling themselves Durgam's Legion — sortied forth again and again to face fates far worse than death and defeat. When Prince Cale himself fell at Crynnomar Gap in 2947 I.R., the survivors fled to the Folly. Soon, the ancient citadel would once more be under siege, and this time there was little hope that it could hold out against the tide of shadows.

Only a miracle could save Durgam's Legion and the survivors of Cale's doomed campaign. And so it was that a miracle did occur, as legendary spellcasters from Hyperborea's past returned to save the duchy. The Wizard's Wall rose to halt the horde's advance, and both Durgam's Folly and the Northmarches were saved.

Once more the citadel was left to fall into obscurity, and as Foerdewaith authority faded to be replaced by a newly-independent duchy, Durgam's Folly grew shabbier and in greater disrepair. Durgam's Legion remained, however — scruffier, dirtier, and more disreputable perhaps, with many legionnaires sent there as punishment for incompetence and insubordination, or as an alternative to execution or prison. Yet the pride of the legion remained, carried on by a cohort of old officers who had seen much and done more.

Today, some effort is being made to restore the citadel as dwarf engineers and gnome laborers have been sent from Ironhill to improve or repair its walls and facilities. The legion still marches to protect villagers and travelers as they face off against continued raids by goblins, bandits, giants, and their old enemies, the hobgoblins of the Deepfells, still dangerous even centuries after their rise.

Captain Eyrik, a grizzled veteran of many fights against raiders and humanoids, currently commands the citadel. He ended up there after a petty dispute with a superior officer grew into a major rivalry and ended in a duel, with Eyrik standing over his opponent's corpse, bloody sword in hand. Rather than face imprisonment or execution, Eyrik accepted command of Durgam's Folly and gained his soldiers' loyalty (and even affection) with his gruff but evenhanded administration. Every warrior on the walls knows that Eyrik is one of them and would never send his troops to face a danger that he would not face himself. Durgam's Legion continues to stand — ragged and battered, forgotten by most, but known to the folk that they defend.

Reference Sources

The Siege of Durgam's Folly

Golden Oak

Alignment: Chaotic Good
Ruler: Elder Verithrien Shadowleaf
Government: Elder and council
Population: 2,439 (wood elf)
Languages: Elvish, Sylvan
Religion: Shalraei
Resources: Furs, timber, fruit
Technology Level: Medieval

This relatively small village represents the last real remnant of the Alathi's greatness — a settlement founded in the wake of the terrible civil war in which the usurper-king Taloran was defeated. The Alathi's victory was costly, and they lacked the power to fully vanquish the shadow magic that Taloran unleashed. Golden Oak was founded as a place of refuge, where the remains of Alathi sorcery and divine magic could be used to keep the people safe. The Third Exodus further reduced the population of the Haunted Wood, and now only Golden Oak and a handful of tiny settlements remain.

At the center of the village is the great emerald-leafed, golden tree that gives the settlement its name. Raised by one last great spell from the sorcerers of House Shadowleaf and their druidic counsel, the tree is the center of life in the village, its rich branches extending over the other structures like a shield. Elsewhere the Alathi, who once crafted their dwellings from the very living rocks and trees of the forest, built more conventional huts and houses.

When she finally passed on to the next plane of existence, a saddened and weary Queen Aurea abolished the monarchy and granted authority to the elders of the region's various communities and tribes. For many years, House Shadowleaf has seen to affairs in this part of the forest, ruling with wisdom and grace. The lurking threat of the nearby Shadowhold has sometimes cast a shadow over the small community, but its people remain steadfast and determined to resist the shadow's influence.

Reference Sources

Curse of Shadowhold

Gryphon Hills

This low range of hills lies north of the Sternwood. It is the subject of many legends and stories, but as of today is largely unexplored and unsettled by the folk of the Northmarch. Rugged and rocky, with a few patches of grass and shrubby trees, the hills have an air of antiquity that is almost hostile. Those few who visit them find the hills oppressive and gloomy, even on bright days, and the occasional ring of standing stones that crowns a peak or weathered monument tucked away in sheltered ravines adds to the atmosphere of mystery and hidden menace.

Inaccessible at the best of times, the Gryphon Hills are further isolated in the cold months when snow piles high and blocks roads and passes. Heavy rains visit the region in spring, sometimes causing flash floods or mudslides, while the summers are oppressively hot. Mundane creatures such as antelope, coyote, wild pigs and sheep, puma, and even bears can be found in the hills, but stories are told of other more frightening creatures such as owlbears, bulettes, leucrotta, and shadow-infused monstrosities similar to those found in the Haunted Wood and Namjan Forest.

The history of the hills is very old and fragmentary. From the weathered monuments, it's clear that the region is quite ancient and has been inhabited for a very long time — likely from well before the coming of humans to Akados. Elven stories suggest that the hills were once a stronghold for the prehistoric serpent folk who occupied various regions of the world and experimented with frightening and powerful magic and technology.

Use the **Hills (General) Encounter Table** for the Gryphon Hills.

Reference Sources
The Six Spheres of Zaihhess

Crynnomar Gap

The Crynnomar Gap is the 500-mile pass between the Deepfells on the west and the Stoneheart Mountains on the east, constituting the border between the lands of Reme and the Haunted Steppes of the north. Through this gap, dark armies of humanoids and worse have poured south several times in the long-ago past, seeking to conquer the lands of the elves and humans. Since 2947 I.R., the gap has been sealed off by the Wizard's Wall.

Haunted Wood

The Haunted Wood is a vast forest crossing northern stretches of the Duchy of the Northmarches from the Deepfells almost to the foothills of the Stoneheart Mountains. This woodland has always been considered fey and strange, and it is believed that large portions of it currently lie under a shadowy curse. It was never actually a part of the Great Akadonian Forest that once swathed much of the continent, always having been separated by the Green Mountains and chalky High Downs to the south. Tribes of reclusive wood elves still live in this forest but are largely confined to the settlement of Golden Oak as a consequence of the shadowy curse that besets the woodland.

The wood connected to the Namjan Forest on the border of the Ashen Hills 5,000 years ago. It was then the domain of the elven kingdom of Alathanar, home of the Alathi tribe. These elves, who worshipped the goddess Shalraei, were advanced in arcane knowledge and lived in homes melded from the living trees and rocks of the forest. It is said that a king among these elves turned to dark powers, which led to a civil war that ultimately destroyed the kingdom. Since that time, the elven presence in these northern forests has diminished (particularly after the wild elves departed to the west in the Third Elven Exodus), and the shadow increased. The forest gradually shrank over the years until it is now completely isolated from the Namjan to the west.

Somewhere in the Haunted Wood can be found the ruins of Shadowhold, the stronghold of the dark elven king.

Use the **Forest Encounter Table** for random encounters in the Haunted Wood.

High Downs

The High Downs are a natural chalky highland area of central Reme between the Green Mountains and the Stoneheart Mountains. It is considered to be the southern boundary of the Duchy of the Northmarches, and is technically a separate kingdom, with the exception of the road and the area around Ironhill.

Further detail on the High Downs is provided in the chapter "Beyond the Borders," although for all intents and purposes, the High Downs are controlled by Reme.

Use the specific **High Downs Encounter Table** for travel in the High Downs.

Ionkri Hall

This gnomish town sits in a valley in the western High Downs, surrounded by a high wall that seems to have been made of a single seamless block of stone. Visitors are allowed into the mercantile quarter inside the main gate where shops, taverns, and inns cater to traders and travelers. Only gnomes may enter the rest of the town, which is said to include homes aboveground as well as dwellings below. Several mines are located a few miles to the north and west of Ionkri Hall, and carts are regularly seen traveling the road to and from the town.

Ironhill

Alignment: Neutral Good
Ruler: Mayor Ingal Stellan and Duchess Candrella Iskadar
Government: Chartered city; feudal
Population: 56,194 (Loreclans 24,677, Foerdewaith 21,481, gnome 3,890, hill dwarf 2,111, mountain dwarf 1,841, halfling 1,041, half-elf 912, high elf 219, other humanoid 22)
Languages: Common, Rhemish
Religion: Solanus, Dame Torren, Mithras, Vanitthu
Technology Level: Medieval

The capital of the Duchy of the Northmarches is heavily fortified, its walls and other defenses built with the aid of hill dwarves and designed to withstand attack from any foe no matter how strong. The scene of the final battle against the demigod Kakobovia in 1573 I.R., the city has grown significantly since then and is the only real urban center in the Northmarches. The ducal palace is the center of political power in the region, and temples of Solanus and Dame Torren have both been expanded recently to house larger congregations.

History

Like many major cities throughout Akados, Ironhill began life as an outpost of the growing Hyperborean Empire. For many years, Ironhill — a fortress with a small associated settlement — represented one of the Hyperboreans' most remote settlements, among the High Downs on the northernmost fringe of the empire.

With the withdrawal of elven forces in the early 700s I.R., Ironhill was founded as a staging area for the Hyperboreans' assault on the old forest. The rock gnomes of the High Downs, who had been defending themselves against outside incursion for many years, noted the new settlement with alarm, but were unable to prevent it, preferring instead to negotiate treaties with the Hyperboreans to establish their territories and rights. For their part, the Hyperboreans were more focused on the forests and steppes to the north and allowed the gnomes to retain their kingdom.

As time passed, Ironhill benefitted from the colonization boom that followed, growing significantly in size and political influence. For several centuries Ironhill prospered as the settlement and development of the Northmarches continued. The gnomes remained technically independent, but even then the growing influence of human civilization was rapidly reducing their effective autonomy.

The Deepfells invasions of the mid-1500s I.R. brought all that to an abrupt end, and within a few years Ironhill swelled with refugees, straining the city's resources and leading to widespread deprivation. Slums and dangerous camps surrounded the walls as crime and disease grew. Priests of Solanus tried to stem the tide of sickness and poverty, but they were quickly overwhelmed. It was not until the climactic Battle of Ironhill in 1573 I.R. when Grand Duke Borell I defeated the demon-god Kakobovia and broke the back of the Deepfells hobgoblins that the crisis finally began to lessen.

Time passed and Ironhill slowly returned to a semblance of normalcy, though her population declined sharply. The rise of the Kingdom of Foere and Reme's agreement to join the kingdom triggered another wave of settlement and prosperity, this time directed toward the vastness of the northern steppes. Ironhill served as an important departure point, and once more the population grew, though many temporary inhabitants spent only a few weeks or months there before moving on. Caravansaries and other services flourished, many outside the city walls.

While the ultimate goal of the Great Colonization was the Caleen Colonies along the northern flank of the Deepfells, many Foerdewaith colonists chose to remain in the Northmarches, and the province began to once more develop. Ironhill became a base for transit to and supply for these new settlements. However, even as the city's fortunes were again on the rise, disaster struck once more in the form of a threat even greater than the Deepfells' invasion: the Shadow Horde had come. In a matter of years they had swept away Foerdewaith-Rhemish armies and were on the march. Prince Cale fell in battle in 2947 I.R., and a new wave of refugees fled south, again overwhelming the city. The epic raising of the Wizard's Wall ended the immediate threat and dispersed the Shadow Horde, but the days of prosperity and settlement were over, seemingly for good.

It took several more decades for Ironhill to recover from the catastrophe, as some refugees remained in the city and others departed southward. Only a handful chose to resettle the Northmarches, leaving the region to return to its status as a ducal backwater, and Ironhill to its position as the capital of a wild and largely undeveloped duchy.

GOVERNMENT

Originally a Hyperborean stronghold, Ironhill grew into a secure, walled enclave and the leading city of the Northmarches. Once controlled by a military governor, the city now has a more conventional governmental structure, as decreed when Reme was absorbed into the kingdom of Foere. Today, the town is governed by a mayor appointed by the duchess, and the mayor is assisted by a city council, usually made up of merchants, nobles, and other influential citizens. One seat on the council is reserved for the high priest of Solanus and another for the highest-ranking priest of Dame Torren. A representative of the High Downs' gnomes is also allowed to sit on the council but cannot vote. While the mayor and the council make policy and govern the city itself, the duchess can overrule any of their decisions.

Needless to say, Duchess Candrella Iskadar represents the real power in Ironhill. Despite her ambitions for the duchy, she is pragmatic and unlikely to intervene where her attention isn't welcome. For the most part, she allows Mayor Ingall Stellan and the city council to govern the city as they see fit and rarely intervenes, saving her energy for the administration of her duchy.

LOCATIONS IN THE CITY

TEMPLE OF DAME TORREN

Dame Torren is the city's other patron deity and her high priest is Druos Callifan, a middle-aged cleric with a good heart and little stomach for municipal matters. Though he has an official seat on the Ironhill city council, Druos usually sends a priest to act as his proxy and to vote the same way as Solanus' priestess Andrega.

The temple itself is somewhat more modest than that of Solanus, with a single great hall and priests' quarters in addition to the open-air sacred precinct, but it also has an attached school, library, orphanage, and public spaces, with several pleasant gardens that are open to the public that are used for weddings, christenings, funerals, and even picnics in the pleasant days of late spring and early summer. The temple of Dame Torren is often the destination of visiting Loreclans.

TEMPLE OF MITHRAS

Though Mithras is not generally well known in the Northmarches, playing second fiddle to Dame Torren and Solanus, his worship in the more Foerdewaith-influenced capital is very popular. Mithras' temple in Ironwood is a simple, stone affair that dates back to the Hyperborean period. Though it has been rebuilt and extensively renovated over the centuries, many of its original features remain and are frequently the subject of study by scholars and historians. Father Landro tends to Mithras' worshippers here, holding weekly and holy day services. A large wooden shelter also provides beds and meals for the poor.

DUCAL PALACE

Located on the heights at the center of the city, the palace is built out from the old Hyperborean citadel. It has been extensively expanded and improved over the years, but it still has many very old rooms and passages, many disused and in poor repair. Duchess Candrella of course occupies the best-maintained and most comfortable areas, while ducal guards, advisors, courtiers, and arcanists are stationed nearby.

Repair teams, assisted by gnomish and dwarven workers and engineers, are always working in the palace, though in some areas the task may be more than even a small army of repair workers can handle. Rumors persist of sealed subterranean passages that may date back to wild elven days or earlier, and some workers are known to have abruptly quit the project, departing for their homes and leaving lucrative contracts behind. Rumor has it that these workers encountered something beneath the palace that was sufficiently disturbing that it forced them to flee, but so far no one has been able to confirm these rumors for certain.

TEMPLE OF SOLANUS

The leading deity of the Northmarches, Solanus is the good and merciful goddess of the sun and healing. The official ducal Temple of Solanus has grown steadily over the years along with the city's population and influence. Located near the westernmost wall in the area known commonly as the Holy Quarter, the temple boasts a single, soaring dome and two smaller domes, with a main hall that accommodates 1,000 worshippers at a time.

The cleric Andrega de Solanus wears the white robes of a high priestess and oversees a dozen lower-ranking priests and countless red-robe acolytes. She is an old woman who has served here for nearly 40 years, and the temple is buzzing with rumors of who is to replace her when she retires or passes on. Andrega remains in the position out of a deep sense of duty and in the knowledge that she is responsible for an especially valuable and possibly dangerous item.

The vault beneath the temple contains a number of treasures valuable to the church, but the most notable of these is a great black gem struck from the crown of the demigod Kakobovia by Duke Borrell himself. The gem displayed a number of dire properties — it appeared to drain the energy and life force from nearby living creatures, enhanced the magical properties of evil creatures, and seemed to inspire malign thoughts in the weak-minded. In addition, it appeared to enhance the natural combat properties of any armor or weapon to which it was attached. Worse still, it seemed to be possessed of a malign intelligence and often managed to get itself displaced or lost, in what some believed was a purposeful attempt to "escape" from captivity and make its way into the hands of another powerful evil master.

The gem, known as Kakobovia's Stone, has been kept in a heavily-secured casket that is locked behind iron doors in the undertemple vault. Few know of the stone and its powers beyond High Priestess Andrega and a few trusted advisors. Andrega herself believes there is good reason for this; though the duchess and the folk of Reme are basically good, Andrega wonders whether the gem's powers are simply irresistible, and that there are those who might want to use it for their own purposes. Long study has convinced her that the gem contains some essence of Kakobovia or some other powerful demon or god's consciousness and even in the hands of a well-meaning individual, it could cause untold harm. Though she believes that the gem needs to be destroyed, it has thus far resisted all such attempts, and Andrega has yet to find a successor whom she can trust with its secret.

Temple of Vanitthu

The temple of Vanitthu is found in the western part of the city and is one of the largest temples to the God of the Steadfast Guard in all of Akados. It is a huge, two-tiered tower with siege engines ringing the top of the lower tier. Basements below the tower contain quantities of food and cisterns filled with water. The interior of the tower's bottom tier is a labyrinthine warren containing practice features such as the top of a city wall, various intersections of city "streets," stairs of various widths, and all manner of other defensive structures that can be used to train guards. Given that most of these are in large rooms separated by steel doors, an attempt by attackers to fight through the bizarre mix of defenses in the lower tier would be tantamount to suicide.

The Citadel

The old central fortress has long since been converted into a palace for the dukes and duchesses, and in any event is in poor repair. The newer military citadel located along the north wall near the city gates was built by the Foerdewaith and expanded on by the grand duchy. It currently houses more than 1,500 Rhemish troops — 300 archers, 600 infantry, 300 cavalry, and 300 halfling scouts — a fortress second only to the northern stronghold at Durgam's Folly. The garrison can also call on small numbers of Loreclannic cavalry, but Ironhill's location in the High Downs means that few, if any, Loreclans will be near enough to respond.

The garrison is under the capable command of General Mara Polos, a veteran from the grand duchy assigned here several years ago. The posting was something of a reward for good services, as the general desired a quiet posting where she could relax with her family and prepare for retirement. The Northmarches seemed to fit the bill, and the garrison has had few major challenges since she took command.

General Polos' service has proved somewhat more eventful than she might have liked, but she has served well and kept the Ironhill garrison well trained and equipped. Ordinarily, the army sees to the security of the city and sometimes escorts caravans, settlers, and merchants north through the High Downs and into the plains beyond. They are kept on their toes, however, as humanoid raids, banditry, and marauding monsters are more common in the Northmarches than elsewhere in the grand duchy.

Recent alarming reports from Nerimar suggest that shadow creatures have begun to stir in the woods, necessitating General Polos to dispatch a few companies of troops to safeguard the community and investigate the rumors. Some of her officers have been calling for regular patrols into the Frontier to stem the rising tide of goblins and bandit activity.

Gnomish Quarter

The gnomes have inhabited this region longer than humans, and the first Hyperborean settlers made wary but ultimately friendly contact with them in the High Downs soon after Ironhill's founding. The gnomes of the Downs technically retained their independent status, but for all intents and purposes are now under Rhemish authority. Ironhill's growth attracted many gnomes who work as tinkers, merchants, artisans, and laborers and live together in a southern neighborhood with narrow, winding streets and gnome-sized buildings. The community's leader is Tybalt Shortstone, the wealthiest gnome in Ironhill, whose family owns the most successful chalk mining concern in the downs. Tybalt is a vain and petty gnome who insists on decorum and adherence to old gnomish social mores and practices. He enjoys hosting dinner parties and holiday celebrations in his mansion, and finds it amusing to invite important humans, forcing them to stoop in the diminutive rooms and hallways as they socialize.

The Gilded Chicken

An oddly-named but quite popular inn near the center of town with easy access to various important parts of the city, the Chicken has stood here for nearly 200 years, always owned and operated by the Macale family, who claim descent from the original Hyperborean settlers. The Chicken provides food and drink for almost every budget, as well as small but neat rooms that are popular with adventurers, merchants, and travelers. The current innkeeper is Kas Macale, a tall man with a dry sense of humor and a closely-guarded book of recipes handed down from and added to generation after generation. Other local cooks have tried to steal his recipes, but so far none has succeeded. Kas is aided by his wife Marbelle and his six children, who are a rich source of gossip and insider information about the inn and its various clients.

Duke Borrell's Victory

Widely considered to be Ironhill's finest inn, Duke Borrell's Victory — locally simply called "the Victory" — is named in memory of the Battle of Ironhill at which the Deepfells hobgoblins were decisively defeated. Sir Gracis Merl, the Victory's owner, is a retired Rhemish knight of Foerdewaith ancestry who built the inn 10 years ago and used his significant personal fortune to hire skilled cooks and staff from as far away as Endhome and Bard's Gate. When he brought specialty chefs from the Ammuyad Caliphate and offered a unique menu of dishes from across Akados and beyond, Sir Gracis' institution became popular with nobles, first in Ironhill and then elsewhere in the grand duchy. As visitors began to filter into Ironhill from even greater distances, Sir Gracis expanded the inn to include luxurious accommodations, stables, baths, a library, and even workrooms for arcane spellcasters. While these facilities are indeed impressive, they have proven to be quite costly, leaving Sir Gracis to contemplate how to further improve his income. He has been planning to send an expedition to far Xha'en to seek out new recipes and ingredients, and possibly to persuade one of the land's master chefs to venture to the Northmarches to work for him. In addition, chief chef Vashir has been running low on many of his most prized herbs and spices, and has sought out merchants and adventurers to locate replacements — this is not as trivial a task as it sounds, as many of these ingredients are to be found in particularly distant and dangerous areas, including the far north, the deep caverns hidden far below ground, or in some cases, on distant planes.

KHELED'KHADUIN

This cold, narrow river flows through the forested depths of Ebonmark Vale, rushing down from its source on the mountain Runha'mor then vanishing into the depths at the southern end of the valley.

Nerimar

Alignment: Neutral
Ruler: Mayor Ganik Athranos
Government: Democratic
Population: 1,583 (Foerdewaith 1,133, gnome 144, human mixed ethnicity 218, halfling 88)
Languages: Common
Religion: Solanus, Freya
Resources: Timber
Technology Level: Medieval

Nerimar, with a population of approximately 1,500, is a frontier town located a day's march south of the Haunted Wood. It is a bustling trade hub, the last stop before passing into the western wilderness. The residents are a rough-and-tumble sort, mainly trappers and loggers, who are overseen by a mayor who appoints a small city council and is democratically elected every two years. The current mayor is Ganik Athranos, who also owns the leading local inn, the Wizard's Wall.

Given its location near the Haunted Wood and in a region also frequently plagued by bandits and humanoid raiders, Nerimar is surrounded by a strong palisade that is closed and secured each night. Foresters, hunters, and adventurers use the town as a base for their expeditions into the woods, and though some vanish in its shadowy depths, others may return with timber, game, or even plunder. Though the forest's fearsome reputation is growing, Nerimar remains an island of relative security, having survived many attacks and raids over the years.

History

Nerimar has been here in one form or another for a very long time. The town was founded during the initial Hyperborean push into the elven kingdom of Alathanar around 800 I.R. It was a rough frontier town that functioned as a base for foresters, hunters, and a garrison of Hyperborean troops. The humanoids who had driven out the wild elves proved a challenge for the new settlement, and Nerimar weathered numerous assaults before the empire finally solidified its control of the Northmarches.

Located so near to the Haunted Wood and the Ashen Hills meant that the settlement had to be well prepared, for the area proved resistant to Hyperborean influence, and when the empire finally withdrew, the briefly-independent state of Reme proved even less capable of holding the forest. Troop levels were cut, forcing Nerimar to see to much of its own defense. Sell-swords and adventurers were engaged to assist in the task as humanoids and organized outlaws sought to take advantage of the settlement's perceived weakness. It was not until the Kingdom of Foere finally took control of the grand duchy that the folk of Nerimar were provided some respite as Foerdewaith and Rhemish troops arrived to reinforce the garrison and patrol approaches to the Haunted Wood.

Today, Nerimar remains wary, and though it is not immune to attention from the area's denizens, their attacks are far fewer than they once were. Foresters, rangers, hunters, and others set out from the town, and a steady flow of merchants and Loreclannic traders come and go. Rhemish soldiers and the veteran city militia also regularly patrol the surrounding lands to keep them clear of potential threats.

Nevertheless, a persistent darkness pervades the heart of the town, believed by many to be due to an ancient curse visited upon the old, corrupt leaders of the Alathi tribe. Darkness seems to seep into the town from the nearby forests and hills, distant though they are. Visitors to Nerimar complain of sleeplessness and fatigue, and of bad dreams during what little sleep they can manage. While crime is not unusually high in Nerimar, it is unusually violent as assault and murder are quite common. Serial murder and homicidal madness occur at a much higher rate than in the rest of the grand duchy. Though Mayor Athranos continually tries to squelch rumors, presenting his town as a pleasant and prosperous place, it is known that unexplained disappearances are on the rise, as are rumors of demon worship and dark magic going on behind closed doors or in the dead of night. Many suspect that the mayor is not truly in charge, and that another power actually controls the city. Who or what this other power or organization might be is anyone's guess, however. Those who believe in this conspiracy agree on one thing however: It is neither good nor friendly.

Locations in the Town

City Palisade

The city walls around Nerimar are wood rather than stone, but they are a sturdy and imposing barrier nevertheless, and while Nerimar is no military citadel, it is more than capable of defending itself.

Merchant Hall

Most trade activity takes place in this large, two-story structure with a long central atrium. Originally built to house the small merchants who worked out of the town, it has been expanded, and its various spaces are occupied by local sellers and tradesfolk. The shops here range from floorspace where sellers offer fruits, meat, fish, and other foodstuffs to the large and spacious confines of Mellak's General Merchandise, which has become the go-to spot for adventurers and offers clothing, camping supplies, ammunition, dried rations, maps, lanterns, rope, poles, and even basic weapons and armor. Most merchants in the town can be found in the hall. Those who wish to sell here must wait until another merchant leaves, which has led to a serious shortage of space and caused a few newer sellers to build shops within the town itself.

Gardens

In the past, Nerimar often came under siege by goblins, bandits, hobgoblins, orcs, or other hostile local denizens. During those desperate times, the town was forced to fend for itself as it waited for relief, or for the enemy to give up and depart. A large space near the center of the town was designated as a massive community garden where locals could grow vegetables and grains for local consumption and to help ward off the threat of starvation. Anything grown here was harvested and donated to the city, and officials divided the crop up equally among Nerimar's townsfolk. In times of peace, the area serves as a community growing space, with villagers reserving their own plots and keeping anything they grow.

Theater

Nerimar is not without its cultural attractions, and the mayors have always encouraged art and performance to keep citizens entertained and also to potentially draw outside tourism from the nearby Loreclans and beyond, for theater is a favored hobby and entertainment of all the Loreclans. The Nerimar Theater is a surprisingly aesthetic building constructed from pink granite hauled from stone quarries far to the south. It features a theater in the round surrounded by a wide gallery where audiences can stand, and beyond that raised stadium tiers with seating (for a somewhat higher price). Luxury boxes are reserved for the mayor and guests. Overall, the theater can seat more than 800, and shows here are often sold out. Recent performances by the Foerdewaith royal opera troupe presented *The Tragedy of Prince Cale* to rave reviews, and the grand duke of Reme himself was in attendance when Reme's poet laureate Sanya Otrena read her epic chronicle of the Hyperborean age. Famed playwright Elias Trem presented early versions of some plays here and considers it one of the best venues for audience response. Several of his plays were extensively rewritten and gained considerable success after early presentations in Nerimar.

The Wizard's Wall Inn

The affluent Mayor Ganik Athranos is also owner of Nerimar's most successful and best-known inn. The Wizard's Wall Inn is a sprawling three-story structure first built over a century ago and extensively renovated and added to over the years. Here, anyone with the coin can dine on rich fare and sleep in luxury with their every need catered to by an efficient staff. Innkeeper Ganik realizes that all sorts of folk pass through his town, however, and there is fare and accommodation for those of many different levels of affluence. A single block of sleeping and dining rooms is reserved for adventurers, for example, with comfortable but basic facilities. A marble bath house was built two years ago and attracts the wealthy, while nearby wooden shower and sauna facilities are available without cost to guests of all levels.

Though Ganik is proud of his establishment, and probably has its very prosperity to thank for his political success, he is nevertheless concerned about his reputation, quickly hushing up any negative news or rumors about the Wizard's Wall. In the past, this has meant hushing up stories of fights or killings, paying off victims, bribing the town guard, and similar unethical but petty acts. In recent years, however, a number of disturbing incidents have proven harder to cover up, including the death of a tax official of the grand duchy who was in town on official ducal business. Two other guests broke into the man's room and stabbed him repeatedly but professed no knowledge of the event, claiming that they had been plagued by terrible but forgotten nightmares. Ganik eventually mollified the grand duchy, and the incident was largely forgotten, but similar events have continued to occur, both at the inn and in the town in general.

Armory of the Militia

Nerimar's militia has traditionally been one of the best in the Northmarches due to the town's history of siege and assault. Today's militia is slightly less capable than in the past due to the reduction in attacks and regular patrols by regular Reman troops, but they are still an effective fighting force. The armory contains weapons, armor, and ammunition, and includes a drilling yard and stables. All able-bodied citizens of the town are required to serve at least one month out of each year, and at any time up to 100 militia members are here honing their skills and engaging in mock-combat in preparation for the next crisis.

Reference Sources
Curse of Shadowhold

Runya'mor

Located at the northern end of Ebonmark Vale, the mountain of Runya'mor (Shadow Peak) dominates the land below. Cold springs form the headwaters of the river Kheled'khaduin that tumbles down into the vale below. The mountain itself contains the drow city of Blackflame, the first true drow settlement built here centuries ago. It is also studded with hidden entrances to the city, each secured and guarded.

Shadowhold

The ruins of an old Alathi guard post and citadel, Shadowhold is said to be an especially evil place still plagued by the curses and perils of the past. Today, the ruins are shunned, and some believe that the shadow has returned, stretching its tentacles out to the Alathi to cause nightmares, dire visions, and madness. The Alathi themselves do not wish to return to the hold, but instead strengthened magical wards surrounding it and Golden Oak. These wards are far weaker than those commanded by the ancient Alathi, and the shadow that may or may not be confined to the hold might easily grow powerful enough to overcome them. Once more the Alathi are considering recruiting outsiders to investigate.

Sternwood

The Sternwood Forest is a thick mass of old-growth timber that dates back to the old days of the elven kingdom of Alathanar. Like the nearby Haunted Wood, the Sternwood escaped the axes of the early Hyperboreans and was left alone due to its inaccessibility and rumors of dark forces deep within its gloomy depths. Today, the Sternwood has a very bad reputation because of the many people that have of late disappeared in its vicinity. The most accepted cause is the presence of a particularly ferocious and well-organized pack of wolves. Others believe that a band of thieves and refugees use the forest as a hiding place, and some even think that some terrible monster inhabits the forest. Others go so far as to suggest that the forest harbors a demented wizard of considerable power who is sending his minions to capture victims for foul experiments.

Those who have delved into the forest and returned alive have found it full of typical creatures, with occasional odd creatures such as gigantic boars, cave bears, and worgs. A handful of witnesses claims that the deeper parts of the forest contain shambling undead — zombies, walking skeletons, and the like, and that these creatures seem compelled to attack intelligent living victims. These stories are not widely believed, for the folk of the Frontier tend to be stern, no-nonsense types who prefer to fight flesh-and-blood enemies such as orcs and hobgoblins and put little faith in tales of faeries and walking corpses.

Use the **Forest Encounter Table** for random encounters in the Sternwood.

Reference Sources
The Six Spheres of Zaihhess

The Old Oak

A shaded glade whose grasses bear a reddish tinge lies deep in the Sternwood. An oak tree of ancient mien and great proportions stands in the middle of this glade. Other oaks might reach 30 or even 40 feet in height, but this one towers above the neighboring trees at a magnificent 75 feet. The canopy of the Old Oak can be seen from miles away sticking out above the other trees of the Sternwood. Its age is unrecognizable, but some of the crude carvings on its trunk date to the era of the Hyperboreans. Other carvings have been made, none too deeply of course, and the Old Oak bears these as a person might bear a tattoo, as memories of the past and personal artwork.

The Old Oak has been the center of cultist and druidic activity for as long as people have traveled the Sternwood. It belongs to no deity or cult, for the Old Oak is its own being. When people bring it gifts or spill the hot blood of sacrifices beneath its boughs, it accepts these as its due, for the Old Oak is a king of the forest, and a king must have its subjects.

The current worshippers at the roots of the Old Oak are a band of druidic schismatics that have broken from the other circles found in the grand duchy to follow their own course. To them, the Old Oak is a deity in flesh — well, bark and bough — a living god who grants them boons in return for their service. They gather in the glade on nights of the crescent moon and sing paeans of praise, dance sacred dances, and slit the throats of deer, sheep, and men. For its part, the Old Oak grants the things it can, refuses those requests it cannot, and lets its roots drink hungrily of the bloody feast.

See the ***Convenient Reference Guide to Reme*** for more information on the followers of the Old Oak.

Tanith

Alignment: Neutral Good
Ruler: Count Sir Silas Novar
Government: Ducal county
Population: 1,251 (Foerdewaith 766, gnome 103, Loreclans 356, halfling 26)
Languages: Common
Religion: Solanus, Arialee
Resources: Grain, livestock, iron, copper
Technology Level: Medieval

The second largest town in this region of the Northmarches, Tanith lies close by the Stoneheart Mountains. It is an important trade center for iron and copper from the dwarven mines to the east and a stopover point for troops going to and coming from the fortress at Durgam's Folly.

Tanith is a ducal territory with a hereditary governor who bears the official title of count. The current count is Sir Silas Novar, a young knight forced to take the office only two years ago when his father perished while fighting marauding hill giants.

Sir Silas has taken up residence at the family estate, a small castle and attached residence on the west side of town, with his servants and 50 veteran guardsmen, who are well-trained and often called upon to aid the village militia.

The villagers themselves are descendants of a handful of Foerdewaith colonists who returned here after the defeat of the Shadow Horde. Though most pay some homage to Solanus, they are far more devoted to the goddess Arialee, who is generally not worshipped anywhere else in the duchy. A small temple to the goddess tended by the priestess Michaela is the only temple of Arialee in the entire grand duchy.

Tanith is located to the east of its sister-town of Albion and consequently does not face quite as many threats. Goblins and mounted bandits sometimes attack the town or try to plunder outlying farms, and mountain creatures — usually giants and ogres — sometimes descend from the Stonehearts, particularly in winter. Sir Silas' own father, Count Marcus, fell in battle against a hill giant raid two years ago, and Silas himself still nurses a desire for revenge against his father's killers.

Wayland's Fane

This pale marble temple has stood here for countless millennia and serves as the center for worship of Wayland the Smith, an ancient god of the old elves. Here, priests and priestesses tend to the Crystal Anvil, an object hewn from the living land and set here immovably. The anvil once allowed direct conversation with Wayland, but today it serves primarily as a conduit to Wayland's home plane, drawing incredible amounts of divine and arcane energies here that the elves of the vale can use to cast spells and perform rituals that are all but impossible elsewhere in Akados. The fane has sufficient space to house almost every citizen of the vale and is accessible to any of them at any time if they wish to consult with the priests, worship, pray, or otherwise commune with their god.

Wizard's Wall

The Wizard's Wall is a vast cliff escarpment more than 500 miles in length that runs across the Crynnomar Gap between the Deepfells to the west and the Stoneheart Mountains on the east. For well over half a millennium, it has been an impenetrable barrier protecting the Northmarches of the Grand Duchy of Reme from the Haunted Steppes to the north.

Approaching the wall from the Northmarches, the land slopes gently upward, almost imperceptibly, until it suddenly drops in sheer cliffs to a base on the Haunted Steppes, as much as 1,000 feet below. Near its eastern end at the base of the escarpment, the shallow, swampy Shadowfall Lake formed from the waters now collecting from the redirected Wanaheeli River. The face of the escarpment is effectively impassible, the rock of its vertical walls brittle and likely to crumble in the hands of any who might try to climb them. Attempts to pass the wall on the west are thwarted by the sharp crags and high peaks of the Deepfells, while the fortress known as Durgam's Folly guards the only known trail through the Stonehearts at its eastern end. More than just a physical obstacle, the stony precipice holds power over the unseen as well, barring passage by dark spirits from the steppe seeking to cross into the southern lands.

After the destruction of the Caleen Colonies in the Haunted Steppes in 2947 I.R., the wall was raised through the use of ancient and powerful magics by the archmagi Margon and Alycthron, blocking what otherwise would have been an unstoppable invasion of Reme by hordes of humanoids and shadow walkers from the Lost Mountains far to the north.

In the long years since, Reme has kept a watch on the Haunted Steppes beyond Wizard's Wall. In addition to the permanent garrison at Durgam's Folly, the Duchy of the Northmarches maintains a number of watchtowers along the top of the escarpment. Troops are regularly shifted among these watchtowers, Durgam's Folly, and other assignments in the Northmarches, including patrols of the outskirts of the Haunted Wood and the Gryphon Hills. While some smaller towers are not always manned, the six largest host permanent contingents of soldiers charged with watching over the plains beyond. From the west, these six are called Haldor's Tower, Granite Eye, Rilla's Watch, the Tower of the Rock, the Duchess Tower, and Coursguard.

Namjan Forest
Grü...
Ashen Hills
Dreikeng...
Eisenwood
Sten...
The Frontier
Aciier River
N
1 Hex = 50 Miles
Harrowfar
Tree of the True Heart
Tanner's Green
Tower of...
Legend
Town or Village
City
Capital or Free City
Imperial Capital
Fortress or Citadel
Ruins
Place of Interest
Road
Trail or Unused Road
Mountain Pass

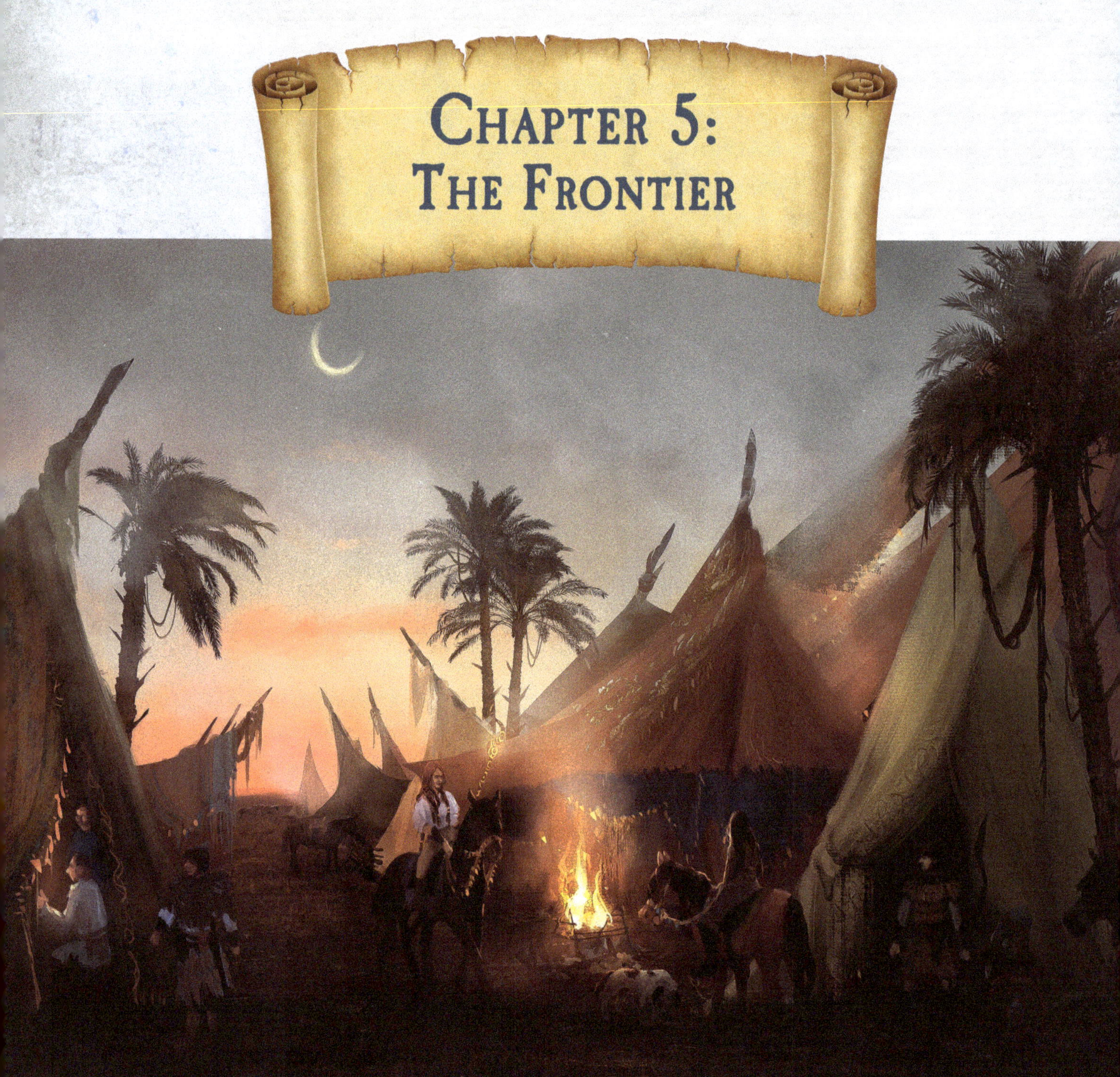

OVERVIEW

Alignment: Chaotic Good
Capital: Harrowfar (1,172)
Notable Settlements: Riverside (800), Tanner's Green (300)
Government: None
Population: 12,500 (centaurs 10,250, Foerdewaith 500, Loreclans 950, gnome 200, halfling 200, half-elf 300, wood elf 100)
Monstrous: Goblins, hobgoblins, cockatrices, giant boars, ankheg, griffons, chimera, bulettes, pegasus
Languages: Common (Northmarchers), Sylvan (centaurs)
Religion: Shalraei, Halatra
Resources: Timber, wild game, leather
Currency: Barter (centaurs), Rhemish
Technology Level: Iron Age (centaurs), Medieval (Rhemish)

General Information

Borders and Lands

The region known as the Frontier includes the Aciier River Valley and the lands to the west, with its southern border not far north of Tanner's Green. It is bordered to the north by the Ashen Hills (see "Beyond the Borders") and the Deepfells. The Endless Hills are also claimed by Reme, but human rule over the hills themselves is nonexistent. This region is at a higher altitude than the lower plateaus of the Northmarch — colder and less forgiving — and rising higher as it approaches the hills and mountains.

Although the lands called the Frontier are considered a part of the Duchy of the Northmarches of Reme, in truth it is wild and outside the control of the grand duke and his vassals. The land is higher, the climate is generally cold, particularly in the winter, and is not favorable at all for crops. Flora and fauna are both hardy, with herds of elk, buffalo, and caribou migrating with the seasons.

The nomadic Vaeltaia centaurs scratch out a hard living here, moving from place to place following the seasons and the game that they require for survival. Old treaties with the centaurs limited settlement, but today small farms are dotted throughout the territory, with occasional cottages of trappers, woodcutters, and hunters. There are also a few communal farms of religious fanatics who believe that someday these lands will become fertile, with well-cultivated fields. To the extent there is an economy here, there is money to be made from timber and the fur trade.

Travel through the Frontier is a challenge, for in addition to the centaurs' opposition, both the climate and the harsh landscape are major factors in why neither the Hyperboreans nor the Rhemish Loreclans were able to make much headway in colonizing the area. Winters are harshest near the Endless Hills, and heavy snow is common and persistent. Snow is less prevalent in the region of the Green Mountains where the Vaeltaia make their winter camps. Spring heralds heavy rain and wind, but summers are generally mild, and the land is surprisingly beautiful, with great swaths of green grass and wildflowers swaying beneath the sun. The cold clamps down on the Frontier in the mid- to late fall, leading once more into the harsh and unforgiving winter.

History and People

The centaurs don't have a written language but pass stories down from generation to generation. Their oral history speaks of their earliest days and the blessings of a goddess who dwelled nearby — these are probably memories of the goddess Shalraei, who once lived with her people in the wild elves' kingdom of Alathanar. A nature goddess, Shalraei held all her children sacred and was equally protective and benevolent to the centaurs, though the wild elves effectively erased them from their own stories, focusing in typical elven fashion on themselves and their relationship with the gods.

Those days were good for the centaurs, for their goddess's blessings made the land rich with game and forage, and her priestesses commanded mighty divine magics that could change the weather and make the land bloom. Like the gnomes of the High Downs, the centaurs were forbidden entry into the forest, they but traded with the elves nonetheless. The land grew harsher and colder with the goddess's departure and the isolation of the wild elves, who withdrew into their forests and broke off contact with the plains. The centaurs, who once lived in a virtual paradise, were forced to scrape and struggle for survival, migrating from one end of the plains to the other with the changing of seasons and the migration of game.

The Wanderers — as the migrating centaurs came to be known — suffered at the hands of the humanoids who emerged from the mountains and woods to ravage Alathanar in the late 600s I.R. With the humanoids' defeat, the Hyperboreans stepped into the vacuum, claiming the Frontier as part of the Northmarches. Human settlers ventured into the region heedless of its original owners, and tensions began to rise, culminating in the brief Frontier War of 1013 I.R. in which an entire Hyperborean legion was surrounded and all but destroyed by the nimble and elusive centaur archers and lancers. The Wanderers accepted Hyperborean authority in the region in exchange for limitations on new human settlements. The existing human towns remained, and tensions remained high for many years until the coming of the Deepfells Horde in 1548 I.R.

At last the centaurs and the humans had a common enemy, though the Wanderers' brave stand against the invaders remains virtually unknown in the Northmarches. As the hobgoblins and their allies pressed eastward toward the heart of the Northmarches, the centaurs harried and raided, falling on stragglers, destroying supplies, committing acts of sabotage and murder, slowing the enemy's pace, and requiring Kakobovia to detach more troops to guard his rear and flanks.

Outwardly, the centaurs' actions did little to stop the hobgoblin advance, and the Hyperboreans were badly beaten in several battles before the Deepfells' forces at last advanced into the High Downs to threaten the city of Ironhill. Though the northern fortress of Durgam's Folly held out against the Deepfells' tide, theirs was an act of suicidal defiance, for the Northmarches would be lost if Ironhill fell.

Chieftainess Nyma gathered her priestesses and war-leaders into a final, desperate council. Their campaign against the hobgoblins had been costly, for many brave centaurs had given their lives in the struggle. The humans, she told them, were on the verge of defeat, and if their capital fell, it would only be a matter of time before Kakobovia turned his attention to the Frontier. Even the most optimistic of her advisors acknowledged that the nation could not endure long against the full might of the Deepfells. Though relations with the Hyperboreans had never been good, the centaurs knew that the humans were infinitely preferable to the warlike and ruthless hobgoblins. Their only chance was to attack the divided enemy to buy time and resources for the beleaguered humans.

A new threat arose when a hobgoblin army began marching south across the plains to join in the assault on Ironhill. Combined with the existing enemy forces, this would create an all-but-irresistible force that would overcome even the most determined defense. Nyma and her war-chiefs decided to confront the enemy directly on the plains using old tactics that had proved so effective during the Frontier War generations previously.

No human chronicle tells of the battle that follows, and no bard sings of the centaurs' sacrifice. But during the Battle of the Plains, a host of centaurs — swift and mobile, but armed with the most primitive of weapons — faced an armored horde of fanatics who saw retreat as blasphemy and death in battle as the greatest of achievements. Some centaurs still bore flint-tipped lances and arrows. Others carried clubs and slings. Yet they defended their homeland and threw themselves at the enemy with raw determination and courage.

Things did not go as easily as they had against the Hyperboreans. The hobgoblins had allies: giants and ogres who could shrug off arrows and sling bolts; ferocious white worgs that could gut an adult centaur with a single bite; and goblin slave-troops that surrounded their masters' formations like clouds of flies. Yet in a series of running battles over nearly a week, the centaurs managed to not merely slow the advancing horde but to stop it entirely in its tracks.

Tactically, the struggle was a draw, for though they inflicted significant casualties, the centaurs suffered as well. Nyma lost a dozen experienced war-chiefs and was herself wounded in multiple encounters with hobgoblins, worgs, and ogres. Yet the Wanderers succeeded in their goal — the horde was unable to reinforce their fellows at the gates of Ironhill, which allowed the Hyperboreans to smash the hobgoblin army, vanquishing both them and their demonic leader.

As word of the defeat reached them, the hobgoblins fell back in unaccustomed dismay, their iron resolve finally broken. They retreated back to the Deepfells, and within a few years Kakobovia's empire shattered into competing kingdoms, leaving the Frontier and the

Northmarches safe from invasion — at least for the time being.

The following years proved good and bad for the centaurs. They remained relatively secure in their homeland, migrating with the seasons, and relations with the handful of human settlements improved as all grew accustomed to the new reality. With the departure of the Hyperboreans, the old treaties were no longer enforceable and more humans began to venture into the Frontier. New settlements such as Riverside were founded, but the Grand Duchy of Reme approached the Wanderers in the same fashion that they viewed the fully-nomadic Loreclans, which led to fewer conflicts and, in a few cases, even outright friendship between centaur and human.

The Frontier remained dangerous, and the old days of peace and divinely-blessed prosperity were over. Goblins, orcs, and hobgoblins still raided out of the hills and mountains. Banditry grew worse as human outlaws found their way to the lawless Frontier and preyed upon their own people and the centaurs. Though the Northmarchers remained unaware of the vital role the centaurs played in driving out the Deepfells' invaders, they now began to work with the Wanderers, sometimes even coordinating defensive operations.

The Wanderers are fewer than they were, but they are Reman subjects in name only, unlike the gnomes of the High Downs, whose independence is largely illusory. They still roam the frontier, from the Green Mountains to the Endless Hills and back, and they still conduct themselves in the old ways. How much longer this can continue as the humans reconsider pacifying and settling the Frontier remains to be seen, but for now the Wanderers remain a proud people, peaceful and gentle in all things save the defense of their own land. Each year they traverse the region, following the herds of buffalo and caribou native to the Frontier.

RELIGION

As the descendants of Rhemish and Hyperborean settlers, the current population of Northmarchers follows the same religious traditions as their ancestors. They are a tough and independent breed given to hostility and unwilling to help outsiders. The generous nature of many other settlements is absent among most settlers since they feel isolated from the Northmarch and the grand duchy, whom they feel have little to no interest in their welfare. Some particularly old families follow Mithras, and several small villages have quite ancient Mithraic shrines that are still tended by the elderly and the particularly faithful. In these days, however, the faiths of Kamien and Ceres are popular, with many following along with more traditional Rhemish deities such as Solanus and Dame Torren. The region is particularly starved for priests and religious officials, and some communities have banded together to build common worship facilities. Halatra, a major deity of the plains east of the Aciier River, is not as well known here in the cold highlands where wild horses are uncommon.

There is a darkness abroad in the Frontier as well, for by its very isolation the region offers privacy and security to those who might attract unwanted attention elsewhere. One of the most common rumors in the area is that a secret cult of the death god Zaihhess still exists and thrives in secret, performing rites and sacrifices unknown to ordinary god-fearing folk. The truth of these rumors is not known, but mysterious disappearances do occur, and some of the more superstitious or conspiracy-minded individuals may attribute these vanishings to the work of a secretive cult.

The Wanderers still revere their old goddess Shalraei, though they acknowledge that the ancient times when she dwelled in the material world are long past. She remains in her celestial realm, however, and still visits her people with blessings. Her priesthood is entirely female, and these blessed individuals are sworn to faithfully care for their tribe in her name, providing healing to the sick and wounded, comfort to the dying, guidance to children, and advice to adults. Some priestesses are chosen simply for their wisdom, while others practice druidic or divine magic.

TRADE AND COMMERCE

In the distant past, the centaurs traded with the wild elves for food, timber, and metal implements. Trade slowed to a mere trickle during the tense days of the Hyperborean Empire but has begun to grow once more as humans begin to venture back into the Frontier.

The Rhemish settlers of the Frontier generally produce only enough to support themselves, and any surplus is either stored or traded to each other or the centaurs. Timber, fish, animal hides, and leather are produced here, along with hardy winter wheats and other sturdier crops. Loreclan humans and centaurs hunt the buffalo and caribou herds, but so far few conflicts over resources have occurred. The Loreclans have only a few settlements here, and these are usually no more than summer grazing pastures.

The centaurs provide a number of resources, including their own crafts and artwork, game, pelts, and skins, finished leather goods. In exchange, they receive tools, weapons, textiles, and cultivated foodstuffs. Trade remains a small but significant part of the centaurs' economy, and the growing interaction with humans is seen by many as a sign that relations between the two nations are improving.

LOYALTIES AND DIPLOMACY

The Frontier Rhemish have little time or consideration for diplomacy, preferring instead to stick together and largely shun the greater world beyond their borders. Stern and often outright unfriendly, the Frontier folk would probably make particularly bad diplomats in any event. They view their own rulers with disdain, but will be as polite as they can be when visited, knowing that the grand duchy holds considerable influence in the area.

The Wanderers are loyal to their own nation, and its interests supersede all others. This is not to say that they are insular or hostile, however — at worst they are wary and distrustful of the humans who appear to have designs on their homeland. That in the past both the Hyperboreans and Foerdewaith have shown this to be true makes their wariness more than justified, but as more Northmarchers and outside adventurers make their way into the Frontier, it is becoming clear that accommodations must be made by both sides.

While the Vaeltaia do not maintain official diplomatic relations with others, they have been visited by Reman officials and are open to negotiation with local humans over grazing rights, land ownership, and other matters. Not aggressive or openly antagonistic toward the humans, the centaurs are well aware of past conflicts, and view the Rhemish (especially the Loreclans) as the lesser evil when dealing with such threats as the hobgoblins and the creatures of shadow. At least, some elder centaurs say, the humans will talk, even if every word they say can be interpreted a dozen ways. The slippery and somewhat duplicitous humans (in the Wanderers' view) are at least open to discussion, while orcs, goblins, and hobgoblins want only to rob and kill.

Relations with local humans, who are largely independent of Rhemish authority in any case, have fared slightly better, for a sense of shared hardship and challenge sometimes grows when centaur and human stand together against an enemy raid, or combine forces to track down marauding bandits. The two cultures and economies are radically different and may never be fully reconciled, but at least today there is peace, and the two sides are willing to talk.

GOVERNMENT

The Frontier is ostensibly part of the Northmarches and subject to the authority of the grand duke in Reme, but one would never know this from the attitude of the average inhabitant. With no real government or ruler, the folk of the Frontier consider themselves to be largely independent of outside authority and free to go about their business as they choose. The token presence of Rhemish troops doesn't change this, for the folk of the Frontier are well used to seeing to their own defenses. Visiting Rhemish are treated with stiff courtesy, while those from beyond Reme would face open hostility and refusal of the most basic hospitality.

The Vaeltaia are matriarchal and ruled by a chieftainess who is chosen from among senior females. A good chieftainess is expected to leave other centaurs to their own devices and interfere only in cases of serious disagreement or crisis, and is always advised by an informal council of elders, both male and female. Disputes between individuals are usually settled by families, usually after a meeting of elder members. Should they prove unable to solve a dispute, the matter is brought to the chieftainess, who is expected to devote both time and wisdom to the solution. Her judgement is final, however, and cannot be overruled even if her elders disagree. As may be expected, conflicts rarely rise to this level, and when they do, it is usually a matter of importance to the entire Vaeltaian people.

MILITARY

A small number of regular Rhemish soldiers are quartered at Harrowfar and in a few small garrisons around the Frontier. Elsewhere, local militias and nobles provide their own protection, such as at the Owl Tower that guards Dreikeng and surrounding areas from raids by the Ashen Hills orcs and other humanoids. The people of the Frontier place little faith in the grand duchy's soldiers and have learned to defend themselves against outside threats. They employ a wide range of weapons and armor, from improvised farm implements to heirloom weapons that have defended the Frontier for generations. These local warriors' skills vary widely too, and humanoid raids may end up destroying numerous homesteads and costing many lives before they are finally stopped. Beleaguered villagers have been known to approach the centaurs for assistance or to go so far as to recruit mercenaries and adventurers to aid in the defense of their communities.

All centaurs are skilled in athletic endeavors and highly trained in weapons for hunting and warfare. Their favored weapons are the spear, the bow, and the sling. Most centaurs fight unarmored, though some high-ranking nobles and influential individuals have taken to wearing leather or metal armor in battle. Small but powerful groups of armored centaurs can be mustered for war and act as a potent counter to the charges of enemy knights and heavy cavalry.

Until recently, many centaurs still fought with flint-tipped spears and arrows, but contact with the Rhemish and advances in forging and smithing have replaced these with stronger and more reliable iron and even steel weapons. Though the centaurs' material culture is somewhat less advanced than that of their human neighbors, they are a potent fighting force.

The centaurs continue to practice the mobile hit-and-run tactics that have served them so well over the centuries. Invaders find themselves beset by swarms of centaur archers who surround slower enemy formations with a circle of archers and slingers in a formation that they call the Iron Wheel. Attempts to counterattack are met with swift retreat in all directions, so that even if enemy cavalry manages to catch one or two centaurs, the remainder can quickly come back together and resume the attack. The speed of the centaurs has proven effective even against Loreclannic light cavalry.

MAJOR THREATS

The Frontier stands at a crossroads of various dangers and is constantly under threat from outside foes such as the bizarre orcs of the Ashen Hills, the hobgoblins of the Deepfells, ogres and giants from the Green Mountains, and various other wild humanoid groups. So far, the townsfolk and villagers of the Frontier have managed to stand against these dangers, but in every case at least a few homesteads are burned or villages pillaged. The Rhemish military, present only in small numbers, may be effective against minor raids and banditry, but in the face of large-scale raids or invasion, the Frontier is essentially on its own.

Neither the human settlers nor the Vaeltaia centaurs have forgotten the many tales of invasion and destruction by the Deepfells or the humanoids who ravaged the old Alathanar kingdom. The centaurs, in particular, are well aware of the true story of the Deepfells incursion and imagine the terrible fate that would have befallen them had the hobgoblins triumphed. That the hobgoblins survived and still live on, dominating the Deepfells, has not been forgotten, and the possibility that the shattered rival kingdoms may someday again unite to threaten the outside world is a constant fear. Both humans and centaurs see the other as a lesser evil and are beginning to come to the conclusion that they are the only mutual allies available. Common danger may yet lead to common cause.

REFERENCE SOURCES
The Six Spheres of Zaihhess

LOCATIONS IN THE FRONTIER

Use the encounter tables for the High Plains of the Rhemish Frontier west of the Aciier River (listed as **High Plains Encounter Table**) and the **Plains (General) Encounter Table** for travel east of the Aciier.

ACIIER RIVER

This river runs from its source in the Ashen Hills, past Dreikeng and between the Eisenwood and the Sternwood, and thence around the Green Mountains into the fields of the Westmarch, until it reaches the Quail River some distance north of Eckland. Logs of Eisenwood red cedar are shipped by barge down the Aciier for sale in the markets to the south.

Use the **River (General) Encounter Table** for travel on or along the Aciier River.

THE DEEPFELLS

The Deepfells are fully described in the chapter "Beyond the Borders."

Use the **Mountains Encounter Table** for the Deepfells if the characters are foolishly wandering around in this area.

DREIKENG

Alignment: Neutral Good
Ruler: None
Government: Council
Population: 512 (Foerdewaith 181, Loreclans 256, dwarf 50, half-elf 21, half orc 4)
Languages: Common
Religion: Solanus, Dame Torren
Resources: Timber, trapping
Technology Level: Medieval

Dreikeng is a village of about 500 souls (the vast majority being humans, with a small number of dwarves, half-elves, and half-orcs) which is, for the most part, dedicated to woodcutting, hunting, trapping, and manufacturing. Located on the Aciier River, it is governed by a council of three local merchants.

REFERENCE SOURCES
The Six Spheres of Zaihhess

Officially part of the Westmarch, the Endless Hills are wild, well beyond Reme's control, and contain a near-zero human population (other than Harrowfar, which is usually considered to be Northmarch territory). Hot in summer and cold in winter, the Endless Hills are arid, rugged, and covered in coarse grasses that are interrupted here and there by seasonal streams and stands of hardy oak, juniper, and cottonwood. Farming is nearly impossible due to the terrible soil quality and unpredictability of water sources.

Hyenas, both dire and ordinary, roam the hills alongside a hyena subspecies unknown anywhere else in Akados. Officially categorized by scholars as the "western hill hyena," they grow long, shaggy coats in winter, and both their black-and-tan coloration and their subtly more canine body and skull shape mean they are often mistaken for stray or wild dogs until they begin their signature hyena yipping and "laughter."

The western hill hyena is slightly larger on average than other known hyena subspecies in Akados, and the females are significantly larger still, generalizations that remain true for the dire varieties as well. Despite their large size, however, their prey tends to be rodents, birds, reptiles, and large insects. The Endless Hills are too sparse of vegetation to provide for extensive herds, but the hyenas do hunt larger prey when they can get it.

As is often the case with hyenas, gnoll tribes also reside in this region, with appearances very similar to the local hyenas. All documented cases of interaction with these tribes have shown them to be insular and hostile, dangerous to travelers and would-be settlers. In the distant past, these gnoll populations are recorded to have been far more numerous and powerful, threatening the elves of the Westwood and raiding nearby human settlements. But if this was the case, the Endless Hills must have been much more hospitable once to support such a large population. It is unknown what might have happened to alter the hills' environment, and one scholar of gnoll behavior postulated that whatever damaged the soil and plant-life of the Endless Hills could also be what caused the gnolls to begin raiding their elf and human neighbors in such force. Now that their population is so much lower, they are able to subsist once more on what is available nearby, and they rarely leave the Endless Hills.

The elves of the Green Warden Nations to the south tell one legend of the hills where a hyena goddess was banished here from a divine plane for some unknown crime. She was pregnant when she arrived, however, and gave birth to the first western hill hyenas and their dire kin. She loved her hyena children and cared for them, and as she atoned for her unknown crime, she also blessed the land that had become her home so that her children would always prosper there. She knew that one day she would be allowed to go home to her godly plane, and she wanted her descendants to be happy without her after she left.

Time went by, and her sentence continued. She met an elven sorcerer, and they fell in love. At first, other elves persecuted them for their love, but eventually they accepted the couple. Their children were the first western hill gnolls, and they were good, kind, and wise, always friends to the elves, and everyone in the region prospered as neighbors. Eventually, the goddess' sentence was served and she returned home, but her blessings remained, and her people were still happy and good.

Then the humans came.

They came by ship from the west, the legend claims, unlike every known history of Akados; most scholars assume at least this portion of the legend is based on misunderstanding rather than fact. Whatever the case, however, these humans came en masse, with powerful wizards leading them and helping them cross the Deepfells into the Great Forest that still stood in those days. Immediately upon their arrival, they began to cut and burn the forest for the sheer delight of watching the trees die and the birds and beasts flee in terror before them.

The elves and gnolls allied to protect the natural world, and soon the humans realized that their forces were insufficient for their foul conquest. They turned instead to terrible magics. Learning that a divine blessing lay upon the Endless Hills, they worked a hideous blood-rite to twist that blessing upon itself, corrupting all the hearts and the lands that the blessing touched. Overnight, the gnolls became evil and bloodthirsty and turned on their elven allies. The elves were able to fight them off, as well as the foul humans, and the humans were driven away, back to the sea, but the gnolls remained, and did not return to their former selves.

The elves appealed to the hyena goddess, offering her many rites and prayers until she spoke to them in their dreams. She did not understand why her children had changed. She kept trying to cleanse them with her blessing, but nothing seemed to help. When the elves explained what the human wizards had done, and that she must therefore withdraw her blessing in order to save her children, she remembered the way the elves had treated her when she first fell in love with one of their kind, and she believed these elves were trying to trick her into abandoning her children.

Time moves differently for a goddess, and especially so in the divine realms. Thus, it was many centuries before the hyena goddess was finally convinced of the truth of the elves' tale. She did withdraw her blessing, but it was too late. The land and the hyenas returned to normal, but the gnolls' hearts had adapted to the poison and could never become good or wise again. Devastated, the goddess turned her back on her former home in the mortal world. With her blessing removed, the weight of her sorrow was enough to stunt all growth in the hills forever more.

To this day, the gnolls remain wicked and cruel, but the elves hope that one day the goddess will return to her children and help them to heal. In the meantime, they say, there is nothing to be done but to fight them off when they attack, as they always will.

It is unknown if any part of this legend has any relation to actual history, but the gnolls of the Endless Hills do worship a hyena goddess called Heepirauru, which the Westwood elves say means "Plentiful Mother" in the gnoll tongue of the Endless Hills.

Use the **Endless Hills Encounter Table** for travel in the Endless Hills.

REFERENCE SOURCES

Demonheart

THE STRANGENESS

The Endless Hills are not, of course, endless, yet their name has the same meaning in both Common and Elven, and even in the gnoll tongue spoken by the native residents. The reason for this lies in the region known simply as "the Strangeness." No one knows where the Strangeness came from or what purpose it serves, or even how long it has been there, though the elves say longer than living memory, even for them.

Though always located in the same general section of the hills — far in the west, where the Endless Hills border the Impassible Peaks — the anomaly does move around somewhat from north to south, and it also changes slightly in size and shape, though it is usually a rough circle less than 10 miles in diameter. It is most easily noted by its lack of wildlife, as birds, insects, and other natural creatures give the area a wide berth. The gnolls native to the Endless Hills follow suit as well, whenever possible.

The region is not discernible by sight or sound, other than its emptiness, but elven rangers say that the air along the edges moves strangely, and that creatures who navigate primarily by scent or by touch seem to dislike the place instinctively, even beyond being disturbed by its stillness and quiet. For whatever reason, the Strangeness does not radiate a magical aura of any kind.

Other than these subtle clues, the Strangeness looks much like any other section of the Endless Hills. Walking into it by accident is easy to do. Walking out is less easy, and that in itself is exactly what makes it strange. When people travel through the Strangeness, everything seems normal — at first — but eventually even unskilled trackers notice that they are walking in circles, passing the same landmarks over and over.

This continues to happen regardless of one's navigation skills, because the hills themselves are either somehow teleporting people without them noticing, or bending and folding themselves together in impossible ways, also without anyone noticing. Either way, the hills inside the Strangeness are quite genuinely endless. A party could wander forever and never reach anything but the same 10-mile stretch of hills, over, and over, and over. Magnetic compasses can give a clue to where the borders of the Strangeness lie, however, as they will tend to spin for a second or two in the moment of crossing from one end of the anomaly to the other, even if no other signs are observable.

Of course, since animals avoid the place, few parties could really wander forever. Most will die of starvation, even if they are able to find water in the arid hills, because so few of the plants are edible, and there is nothing to hunt inside the Strangeness. People who die in the Strangeness leave no corpse, for reasons no one understands. They know only that the Strangeness itself is not strewn with the bodies of its victims, nor do the corpses reappear somewhere else in the Endless Hills. Perhaps the bodies are transported to another plane, or perhaps the Strangeness consumes them somehow as its fuel.

There are two known ways out of the Strangeness, more if you have a powerful mage along. Several of the most powerful known magical spells can be used to break the enchantment of the Strangeness, but for-less-experienced mages or those unable to cast magic, only two routes exist.

The Path of Shadow

The elves of the Westwood call the first route "The Path of Shadow." This route is difficult to find and very perilous. First, find a large object that casts a shadow. The Strangeness always includes at least one. Sometimes this is a thorny bramble bush or a large boulder, or perhaps a small cluster of scraggly trees. Sit within this object's shadow so that your own body casts no clear outline on the ground. If the day is too cloudy for a clear shadow, you must simply guess and hope, but it is very important to have something solid between every part of your body and the sun, especially as it is setting.

When the sun dips low in the sky, you must close your eyes and keep them closed no matter what you hear, until the sun dips completely below the mountains. If your shadow is properly hidden, you will hear strange whispers and hissings around you, and you may feel eerie breezes across your flesh as if something is moving past you, very close. If you open your eyes before the sun is gone, you will see nothing, the sounds and sensations will stop, and you will have lost your chance to find the Path of Shadow until the next sunset. If no sounds occur, your shadow was not entirely hidden; you will have to try again at the next sunset.

If your shadow is hidden and your eyes remain closed until the sun is entirely down behind the mountains, when you open your eyes you will be on the path. Most things around you will look the same, but not everything. Shadows on the Path of Shadow are the wrong size and shape for the things that cast them and have a tendency to move of their own accord or whisper and chuckle when you're not looking at them. Depth and distance are difficult to gauge, and it is possible to encounter hostile creatures from the Plane of Shadow.

Once you arrive on the Path of Shadow, the only thing left to do is to walk once more to the edge of the Strangeness. This time, instead of space folding itself, or whatever the Strangeness normally does to transport its prisoners, the anomaly becomes a gateway that transports you into the Plane of Shadow.

You are now outside the Strangeness, but how you get home from the shadow plane is a whole new problem.

The Path of Blood

The Path of Blood, as the elves call it, is both easier and more terrible than the Path of Shadow. First, you must pinpoint one of the edges of the anomaly. Any edge will do. Magnetic compasses are useful here, as described, or sometimes a smear of old blood can reveal where someone else used the path of blood before you.

At the exact edge of the Strangeness, you must spill fresh blood upon the ground in a quantity sufficient to create a path across the border. There must be enough blood that no part of your feet or shoes touch any ground not covered in newly-spilled blood at the moment of crossing the edge. For most medium-sized humanoids, a carefully-spilled pint or two will do. If the blood is sufficient in quantity and freshness, and appropriately located at the Strangeness' edge, simply stepping across it should free you to re-enter a world where distance does not wrap around on itself.

Spilled blood from a thinking creature remains sufficiently fresh for this purpose for approximately three minutes after leaving a living body. Blood from animals loses potency within one minute or less. If multiple people attempt to use the same blood path, any non-blood-soaked dirt tracked onto the blood path by a previous crosser must also be soaked in blood before the next person may cross.

The most difficult part of the Path of Blood is trusting that you have successfully escaped and continuing to walk away from the Strangeness as far and as fast as you can get. Only the canniest wilderness experts are likely to be able to tell for certain that they are free upon the first step outside the anomaly. Nothing will look, feel, sound, or smell any different yet, since animals do give the place a wide berth. It will take miles of walking for most people to be absolutely certain that they are free.

And, of course, if something goes wrong — if the blood isn't quite fresh, or one's shoes touch bare dirt while stepping across, for example — it may be many miles before you realize you need at least another full pint of fresh blood before you can try again.

Eisenwood Forest

The Eisenwood Forest is regularly logged for its famous red cedars. The reddish wood is used to build most of the structures in the surrounding area, and is sent on rafts via the Aciier River to the markets of the grand duchy for sale. Largely free of the grim legends and tales of curses associated with the nearby Sternwood and Haunted Wood, the Eisenwood is a surprisingly pleasant place with very little in the way of outright hostile inhabitants. Many animals also call the Eisenwood Forest home, including deer, squirrels, and the like, with the occasional dire boar falling prey to the hunters, and vice versa. A few travelers have encountered giant spiders, and some stories tell of occasional incursions by goblins, but for the most part the forest is one of the safer locations in the entirety of the Northmarches.

Use the **Forest Encounter Table** for encounters in the Eisenwood.

Reference Sources
The Six Spheres of Zaihhess

Gauldark

Gauldark is home to about 200 residents, principally humans and a few refugees — often half-orcs. For the better part of the year it is almost vacant as many inhabitants are not married and spend their time in the forests, woodcutting, hunting, and trapping. Only during winter, when the inclement weather forces the people to find shelter, is the hamlet full of "suffocating life" as the villagers say. The town contains an outpost of the local thieves' guild that is known as the Silver Crown Society, a shrine to the god Bablukar, and The Stuffed Bear, a tavern that despite the name has a stuffed boar instead.

Alignment: Neutral

Ruler: Mayor Saum Sivr

Government: Mayor and council

Population: 200 (human Loreclannic ethnicity 110, elf 22, half-orc 68)

Languages: Common
Religion: Bablukar
Resources: Subsistence only, basic needs
Technology Level: Mostly Dark Ages, with occasional Medieval elements

HARROWFAR

Alignment: Neutral
Ruler: Mayor Alijah Drusk
Government: Informal democracy, chartered by the grand duke
Population: 1,172 (Foerdewaith 237, Loreclans 304, elf 231, dwarf 165, halfling 127, gnome 85, half-orc 14, other 9)
Languages: Common, Elvish
Religion: Solanus
Resources: Subsistence only, basic needs
Technology Level: Mostly Dark Ages, with occasional Medieval elements

Though ostensibly the capital of the Rhemish Frontier and thus under the jurisdiction of the Northmarches, the town of Harrowfar is located at the eastern edge of the Endless Hills, which are often also considered to be Westmarch territory. This confusion is, itself, indicative of the region surrounding Harrowfar, as no real control over these lands is maintained or presumed by any authority in Reme, though Harrowfar's mayor does occasionally receive instructions from the duchess of the Northmarches, the duke of the Westmarches, or from the grand duke directly. When she's lucky, these instructions do not contradict one another.

A rough border town, Harrowfar boasts steel-reinforced wooden palisades along with other defenses against the hostile gnoll tribes of the hills. Harrowfar's full-time professional guard is unusually large for the town's size and often provides protection for other settlers and travelers in the region. This guard force was originally funded by the grand duke as part of his sponsorship of the Harrowfar settling expedition. Some years later, Harrowfar was officially declared "settled" and thus theoretically no longer in need of public funding. By this time, however, the large guard force had become integral to survival for the settlers in the dangerous conditions of this wild region.

These days, all full citizens of Harrowfar must pay a tax to fund the town defense, and settlers outside Harrowfar may voluntarily pay for guard protection as well, which many choose to do. In this way, Harrowfar is able to pay its guards and to sustain itself, but only barely. In the last four years there has only been enough excess food for the barest of emergency preparation, and said preparation has come to be needed in all four years. Only Mayor Drusk's expert planning and management have kept Harrowfar from disaster.

All adult citizens of Harrowfar are welcome to participate in town hall meetings for all major decision-making, which is accomplished via specially-carved wooden tokens placed in one of two boxes to cast one's vote. Mayor Drusk is known to be fair and practical, with little patience for excuses or stupidity. Other than the guard, Harrowfar's only significant source of outside income is from its two competing inns, which primarily cater to would-be settlers on their way out west or monster-hunters heading out to the wilderness for bounty.

NAMJAN FOREST

This is an old growth forest of northern Reme that was once connected to Haunted Wood but has receded to where they are almost entirely separated by the Ashen Hills. Though it is not widely known by the folk of the Northmarches, this region was once at the heart of the territory controlled by the Ancient One — the sorcerer-warlord Dyraxl Uhl-Kal-Totten — who sought to conquer and enslave the Alathi elves, but was killed in a sorcerous explosion as the Alathi laid siege to his fortress. The fortress was blasted to bits along with its master (at least that is how the stories tell it), but its stones and foundations remain, buried beneath the land. The Namjan's inhabitants continue to shun the region — with good reason. It is said that shadow creatures still stalk the area, and that some remnants of the ancient sorcerer's magic still linger and affect those who come into contact with it.

Despite its isolation, the Namjan supports a small population of humans in the village of Stillwater and the gnomish settlement of Thistlehill who live by fishing, mining, farming, and occasionally by trading with one another. The Alathi elves venture here infrequently to trade or to pursue raiders. Besides these visitors, the only folk who visit Namjan are orcish raiders from the Ashen Hills, sturdy adventurers from the Northmarches, or occasionally hostile hobgoblins out of the Deepfells. Both gnomes and humans have become skilled at self-defense and recruit adventurers should they be available and willing to help.

Use the **Forest Encounter Table** for characters traveling in the Namjan Forest.

REFERENCE SOURCES

Namjan Forest, the Fehlween River, Stillwater, and Thistlehill are described in the adventure *The Darkening of Namjan Forest* in *Quests of Doom*, published by **Frog God Games**.

LOCATIONS WITHIN THE NAMJAN FOREST

FEHLWEEN RIVER

This river flows energetically from the Deepfells but grows broader and more placid as it makes its way south. The Fehlween plays an important role for the village of Stillwater as it provides fish and transportation. Some local tales tell of diminutive fey communities that exist in backwaters or ponds near the Fehlween, but these are mostly dismissed as fairy tales told to amuse children.

STILLWATER

This tiny human settlement lies along the banks of the Fehlween River and is home to perhaps 200 souls. Though technically under the governance of the Duchy of the Northmarches, the folk of Stillwater have little contact with the outside world beyond their mutually beneficial relationship with the gnomes of Thistlehill. The close proximity of the ruins of Dyraxl Uhl-Kal-Totten's ancient shadow fortress hangs heavily over Stillwater, for though the shadow-sorcerer was vanquished thousands of years ago, the remains of his magics have only grown and festered, even buried as they are beneath tons of earth. Some believe that buried artifacts, old enchantments, and even the creatures of the shadow plane still linger in the area, sometimes reaching out to ensnare the unwary.

THISTLEHILL

Thistlehill is a small settlement in the Namjan Forest. About 500 gnomes live here, the descendants of an old gnomish kingdom that occupied the Namjan in the distant past. The arrival of the sorcerer-warlord Dyraxl Uhl-Kal-Totten heralded the doom of the gnomish realm, for the Ancient One quickly conquered or corrupted nearby settlements and set up the Namjan Forest as the center of his power. Intending to spread out and conquer the neighboring elven realm of Alathanar, Dyraxl was foiled by the Alathi elves who, aided by the last surviving free gnomes, laid siege to his fortress and defeated him.

The gnomes never recovered from the disaster and today only Thistlehill and a small handful of other settlements remain in the area. Like Stillwater, Thistlehill is officially part of the Duchy of the Northmarches, but ducal officials rarely if ever visit the place, leaving the gnomes to live more or less as they choose. The lingering remains of Dyraxl's shadow-empire still plague the community: creatures of shadow sometimes lurk in the forest, strange visions are visited upon sensitive or artistic minds, madness sometimes affects entire families, and lone travelers sometimes vanish without trace. Nonetheless, the gnomes of Thistlehill continue to follow the old ways and delve for the rare sunbreath quartz, which they trade with the humans of Stillwater and the elves of the Haunted Wood. Rare human traders from the Northmarches sometimes make their way into this distant region to trade for quartz as well.

SUNBREATH QUARTZ

Sunbreath quartz appears identical to clear quartz except when exposed to light over several hours. After such time, sunbreath quartz glows naturally and produces illumination equal to a candle for 12 hours. The emitted light is always a pale yellow glow similar to sunlight regardless of the origin of the absorbed illumination. This property makes it valuable to tailors who adorn clothing with sunbreath quartz, as well as jewelers who use the glowing stones in their creations. Sunbreath quartz can also be "charged" with magical light to create an effective weapon against creatures affected by bright light. A single sunbreath quartz crystal is worth 25 gp.

RIVERSIDE

Located on the eastern shore of the Aciier River, the settlement of Riverside has been growing in importance in recent years as an important offshipping point for red cedar from the Eisenwood Forest. It has grown from a small hamlet of fewer than 100 souls to a thriving village with a population of nearly 800. Riverside is notable also for its large population of gnomes and halflings, both of whom have become vital to the log-shipping business. Currently, they outnumber the humans, with more than 300 gnomes and 200 halflings forming the backbone of the industry. They maneuver the massive timber rafts that drift downstream from Dreikeng and offload the logs for transport or cutting in a number of newly-constructed lumber mills. The gnomes and halflings' small statures, combined with their surprising strength and nimbleness, makes them excellent log wranglers, and more are bound for the town, drawn by the promise of good pay. Already conditions are crowded, and new workers are being housed in tents and improvised shelters.

Before Riverside's rise to prominence, there were no facilities to offload timber along this stretch of the Aciier. Logs had to be transported all the way to Westmarch and milled in Eckland or other mill towns along the Quail River. Demand for lumber in Varazath, Ironhill, and other growing settlements grew however, and the long route from Westmarch became less economic. Port facilities and docks were built in the small town of Riverside, and within a few years, a significant amount of timber was being offloaded. To further enhance the location's value, several Northmarch concerns built sawmills where the red cedar could be cut and turned into lumber that could be shipped directly west.

The increased trade and Riverside's growing prosperity have made it and the lumber trains heading west into prominent targets for raids by bandits and humanoids, so the town's defenses have been bolstered and the militia expanded. Adventurers and Road Agency sell-swords have been engaged to help guard the lumber shipments as well.

Riverside's population is now exploding as gold and silver flow. This sleepy river village now has all the characteristics of a boom town, including a burgeoning trade in liquor, drugs, prostitution, and crime of all sorts. The local authorities under the guidance of the overburdened and underequipped Mayor Duras Teller have grown more desperate and concerned that their town's expansion is out of control. Requests for assistance from Ironhill and from the Grand Duchy of Reme have so far had little response save for the assignment of a few squads of regular Reman soldiery. Feeling overwhelmed, the city leaders have begun to impose taxes and fees on all transactions in town in the hopes of raising enough to hire their own law enforcement, and a call has gone out for qualified individuals to visit Riverside and see what they can do to help.

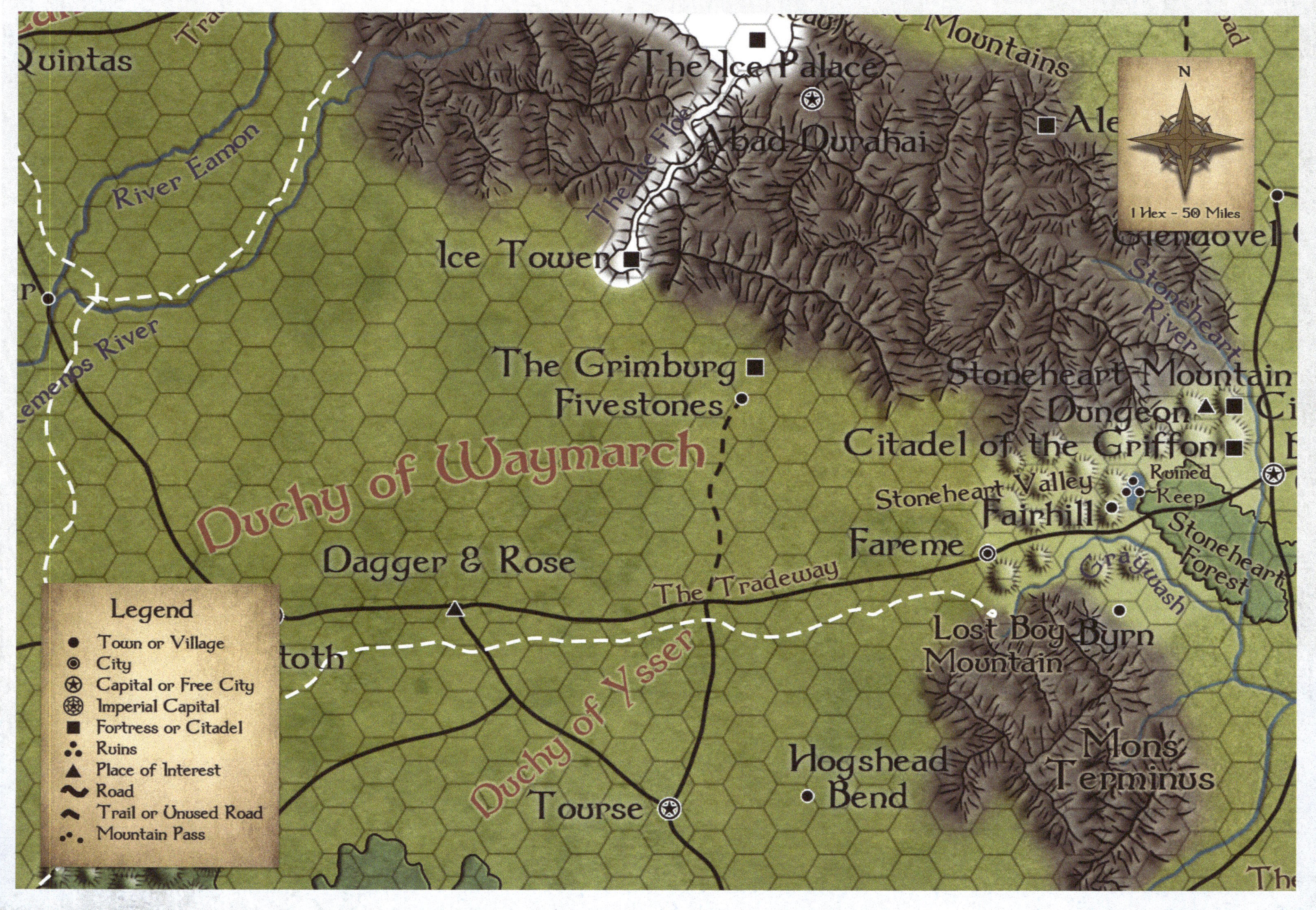
Quintas
Tra
River Eamon
Lemenos River
The Ice Palace
Mountains
Abad Durahai
The Ice Floe
Ale
N
1 Hex ~ 50 Miles
Ice Tower
Glendovel
Stoneheart River
The Grimburg
Fivestones
Stoneheart Mountain
Dungeon
Ci
Citadel of the Griffon
Duchy of Waymarch
Stoneheart Valley
Fairhill
Ruined
Keep
Stoneheart
Forest
Dagger & Rose
Fareme
Graywash
The Tradeway
Legend
Town or Village
City
Capital or Free City
Imperial Capital
Fortress or Citadel
Ruins
Place of Interest
Road
Trail or Unused Road
Mountain Pass
toth
Duchy of Ysser
Lost Boy Burn
Mountain
Hogshead
Bend
Tourse
Mons
Terminus
The

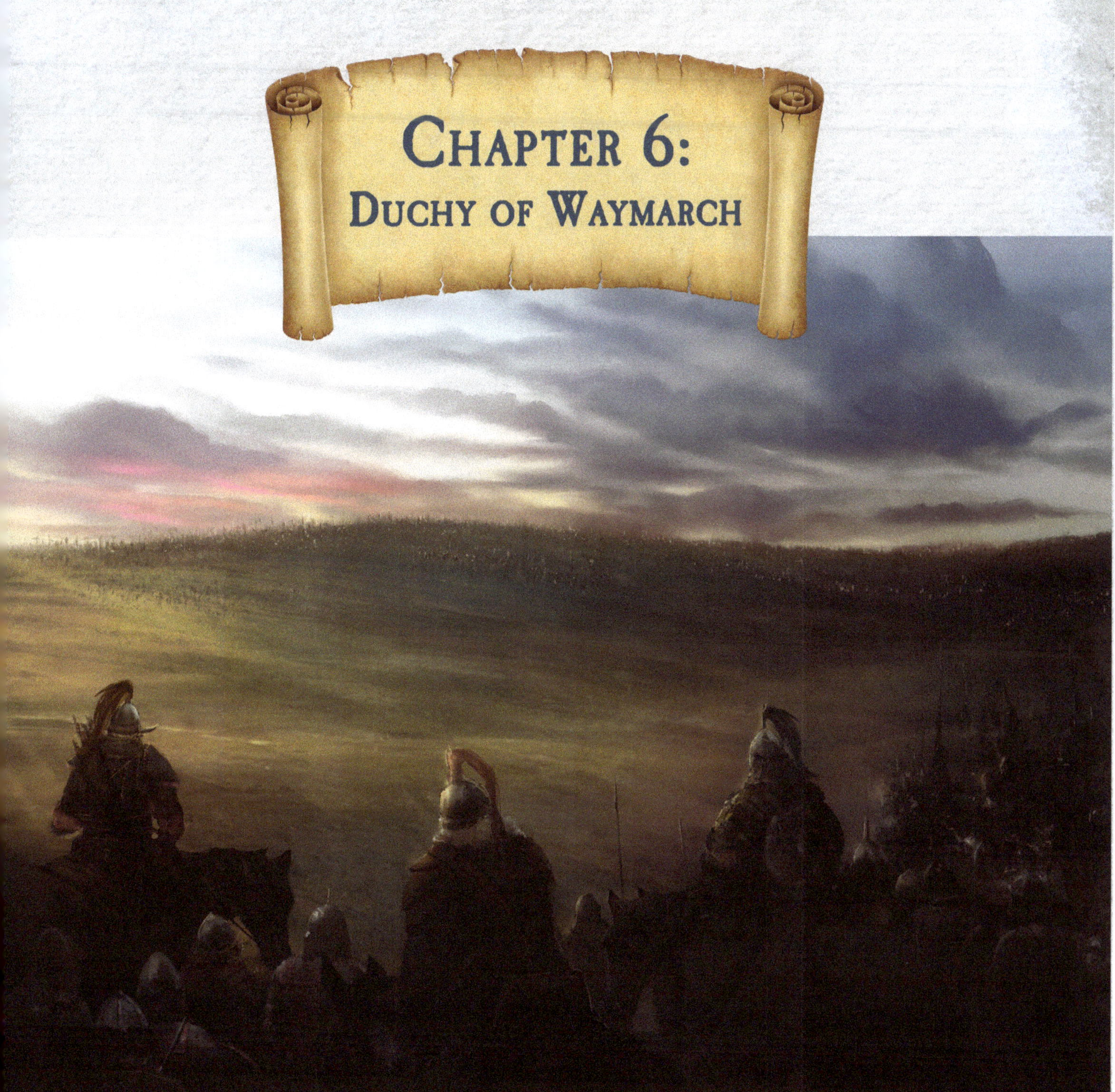

CHAPTER 6: DUCHY OF WAYMARCH

OVERVIEW

Alignment: Lawful Good
Ruler: Lucius Qellinroque, Harmost of Panetoth, Duke of the Waymarch, Voice of the Grand Duke in the East
Government: Feudal
Population: 3,752,500 (Foerdewaith 1,330,100, human [Plainsfolk] 975,300, human mixed ethnicity [other] 799,700, halfling 267,100, half-elf 133,400, mountain dwarf 111,600, hill dwarf 102,800, high elf 31,200, other humanoid 1,300)
Languages: Common, Elven
Religion: Mithras and Mitra (primary), Quell (secondary as patron of duke's house)
Resources: Horses, cattle, military
Currency: Rhemish
Technology Level: Medieval
Demonym/Adjectival Demonym: Waymark, Waymarch

The vast lands of the Duchy of Waymarch are mostly made up of rolling grassland with limited water other than a few lakes where water from spring rainstorms and winter snowmelt collects. No major rivers cross the Waymarch plains, so water shortages are common in summer. As a result, the plains are excellent for raising horses, sheep, and certain cattle, but make for poor farmland.

The region of the Waymarch has, since Hyperborean times, been governed by a military administrator called a harmost who is based in Panetoth, the regional capital, and is always assigned to the Loreclannic ducal family that actually controlled most of the Loreclans of the region. When Reme became a grand duchy, the position of harmost was made hereditary and also given the title of "duke" in the common tongue. This combination of harmost of Panetoth and duke of Waymarch survives to this day.

Lucius Qellinroque of the House of Qellinroque ("Rock of Quell") is the current duke. He is the great grandson of Duke Borell, who was named for the famous Grand Duke Borell I of Reme who defeated the forces of the Hobgoblin Kingdom of the Deepfells in 1573 I.R.

Under the charter granted by the grand duke to their dukes, Waymarch is required to keep a large military force for the protection of the grand duchy, but with its limited resources has historically not had the income required to support such an expense. In the last century, the dukes of Waymarch hit upon a solution to their persistent lack of income. The city of Bard's Gate to the east was growing ever richer in coin, but not in the military presence necessary to defend its extensive assets. With the blessing of the grand dukes, Waymarch began a tradition of hiring out their forces to the City of Lyres as mercenary troops. Such soldiers are permitted to serve only in regions geographically adjacent to the grand duchy in case a military emergency arises that causes them to be recalled home. This requirement is technically met because the lands controlled by Bard's Gate adjoin those of the Waymarch, even if the troops hired by the city are often deployed to posts as far away as the Binjerin River Valley in the Gulf of Akados or even deep into the Sundered Kingdoms.

BORDERS AND LANDS

The Duchy of Waymarch is made up of a vast grassland descending from where Eamonvale and the River Eamon form a border with Northmarch and the protectorate of Reme, of which it is a border territory. The western reach extends the length of the river to within a few hundred miles of the city of Reme itself. The eastern border of Waymarch begins at Fareme at the very edge of the Stoneheart Valley. The southern border extends roughly 50 miles north of Tirwatch Keep across to the Lost Boy Mountain, south of which stands their primary regional rival, the Duchy of Ysser.

Waymarch is a major producer of sheep, cattle, and horses, with herds found throughout the prairie, semi-nomadic Loreclannic encampments, and on permanent ranches that dot the plains. Farming in wheat and barley takes place in more settled areas near the towns and cities. Weather and a lack of major water sources have an impact on herds and agriculture. Significant winds blow across the plains of Waymarch, and spring brings hail-hurling thunderstorms and devastating tornados.

Waymarch is renowned throughout the Grand Duchy of Reme for its brave cavalry whose knights have seen frequent combat against monstrous incursions from the Stoneheart Mountains. Unlike most of Reme, Waymarch produces heavy cavalry in the Foerdewaith style as well as the light Loreclan cavalry found in the rest of Reme. More recently, they served a term of service in the Suzerainty of Bard's Gate where they saw significant combat. This warrior spirit is reinforced with jousting tourneys that are the official sport of the realm — both Foerdewaith and Loreclannic style. The military and political alliances are a financial boon for Waymarch, allowing it to meet its tax obligations to the grand duchy in the form of coin, wheat, meat, wool, leather, and linens.

HISTORY AND PEOPLE

Waymarch is one of the three marches of the Grand Duchy of Reme and was established when Reme declared its independence. Like Northmarch and Westmarch, the duke of Waymarch swears his allegiance to the grand duke in Reme, though like his cousins in Northmarch and Westmarch he also lays at least some remote ancestral claims to the throne of the grand duchy itself.

Waymarch is predominantly made up of Foerdewaith stock, though large populations of Loreclans in the region deal and trade there, with large groups of purely-nomadic Loreclans gathering throughout the year in Eamonvale in the north for their turn at managing the Corral of Broadwater. A number of semi-nomadic Loreclans visit Panetoth in early summer to trade horses for the duke's cavalry and to pasture herds in the areas outlying the city.

Waymarch's capital is in Panetoth where Lucius Qellinroque, the duke of Waymarch, administers his lands and Loreclans on behalf of the grand duke in Reme. Other cities in his domain include Yalendir and Fareme. The earl of Eamonvale serves in semi-autonomy and pays tribute to the duke in Waymarch and the grand duke in Reme as well.

Most of the folk of Waymarch are of Foerdewaith extraction, particularly in Panetoth and the other towns and cities of the March. In the plains, however, are nomadic Loreclans that migrate throughout Waymarch, Reme, and the Northmarches each year. These Loreclans are distant descendants of Shattered Folk of the Haunted Steppe. Every 50 years, Loreclannic families among the Shattered Folk beyond the Crynnomar Gap are permitted to petition for a right to settle in the Rhemish plains, and a lottery is held to determine who may immigrate. Those permitted to settle often join existing Loreclans in the plains of Reme, but some occasionally form new clans when they are directly granted a piece of ancestral territory — this usually happens only when the duke declares an existing Loreclan for elimination for egregious violation of ancestral tradition. There is a good chance that at some point in the near future a Shattered-Folk Loreclan might replace the Quick Knives. Some of the prominent Loreclans currently in the plains of Waymarch include the Grass Sailors, the Quick Knives, the Stone Faces, the Thunder Riders, the Stone Walkers, and Beast Takers.

RELIGION

The worship of Mithras (in the cities), Solanus, Kamien, and Dame Torren is common in the Waymarch as in the rest of Reme. Devotion to Freya is also common in the countryside, and Sefagreth has followers in many of the towns and inns along the Tradeway.

TRADE AND COMMERCE

Waymarch is essential to the protection of nearly 3,000 miles of roadway from Bard's Gate in the east to Reme in the west. The duchy further patrols the road from the capital city of Panetoth to the trade city of Broadwater. These roads serve as arteries of commerce for the entire Duchy of Reme and are of vast economic and territorial importance. Large volumes of cattle, sheep, horses, grains, wool, linen, and cotton are hauled along the Tradeway, and finished goods are brought in from the port of Reme and the broad river-markets of Bard's Gate.

To this end, several cavalry waystations dot the road, and dozens of riders are tasked with patrolling and repairing the long tracts of the Tradeway so that commerce can keep moving at a steady clip.

For such a large duchy, Waymarch produces surprisingly little in the way of commodities for trade elsewhere. The horses of the plains are renowned and can fetch good prices in town and city markets. As the Tradeway passes through Waymarch, revenue is obtained from some taxes and other fees, and many are those who make their living catering to the needs of those traveling both east and west. Few make Panetoth or other points in Waymarch their final destination, although goods are often traded from one merchant to another in order to shorten the length of travel. As a result, the largest commodity sold by the March is now the military service contracted out to Bard's Gate.

LOYALTIES AND DIPLOMACY

Waymarch is one of the three great duchies of the Grand Duchy of Reme. Duke Qellinroque is part of the line of ascension to the throne in Reme. Although he is quite a distance from the throne, he recognizes the lucrative position he wields as the leader of the Loreclans and of the duchy's more settled Foerdewaith citizens. Qellinroque is perhaps the wealthiest of the March dukes due to alliances with Bard's Gate and tribute for guardianship of the road from Broadwater.

Waymarch's enemies are most frequently those of monstrous and supernatural nature, though it is currently engaged in a slow-burning rivalry with the Duchy of Ysser to the south. Ysser would like nothing more than to catch Waymarch unaware and seize control of a vast tract of the Tradeway so it could divert trade from Bard's Gate to its own markets. With the fall of Foere, Ysser is in a state of turmoil at the moment, but while this prevents it from any large-scale assault, it also leaves barons at the border free to engage in depredations. Many of the border barons (possibly backed by the realm of Ysser itself) hire out bandits and have made contact with tribes of orcs and trolls to keep the Waymarch cavalry away from its job protecting the Tradeway. In a sense, the fall of Foere has indirectly caused a significant amount of banditry along Waymarch's portion of the Tradeway.

GOVERNMENT

The government of Waymarch is a mix of relatively egalitarian Loreclannic feudalism on the plains, with the more "standard" Foerdewaith style of feudalism in more settled areas. Loreclans owe fealty to the duke on a loose basis of entire clans led by Loreclannic barons, whereas the non-Loreclannic settlements have more of a hierarchy and owe a higher and more complex set of feudal duties to their liege lords.

The cities and townships of Waymarch are administered by various lords, earls, and nobles who are cousins of Lucius and trusted by him due to tours of military service either in his own lands or in the service of the grand duke in Reme. The notable exception is the earl of Eamonvale who is descended from the Angus family that earned royal title and sovereignty from Reme centuries ago.

Lucius Qellinroque is the fourth of his line to hold the title of duke of Waymarch. He has been forced to be a creative administrator of his demesne, always looking for sources of revenue to help pay for his feudal obligations to the grand duke in Reme. So far, by hiring out a substantial portion of his military to Bard's Gate, he has managed to keep local coffers full and his vassals happy.

MILITARY

Under its ancestral obligations to the grand duke of Reme, Waymarch is required to maintain a sizable military presence for the defense of the grand duchy. Of course, many of the soldiers of Waymarch are abroad at any one time in the service of Bard's Gate. They could be recalled were an emergency to arise, but given the distances, it would take time before the bulk could make it back to Rhemish territory.

The Waymarch cavalry is considered the premier force of mounted warriors in Central Akados, for its mixed units of both light and heavy cavalry operating in tandem. Riding warhorses bred by the Loreclans of the Plainsfolk, the heavy cavalry of Waymarch, are renowned for their bravery. The cavalry is typically accoutered in chainmail hauberk, steel shield, steel cap, and longsword. In the east and hill country, their horses are adorned with the silks of Waymarch, chequered with their own noble colors. In the central prairies of their homeland, however, the proud horses of the heavy cavalry are stripped to merely harness and saddle, and the fine, billowing cloaks are stowed in favor of speed and utilitarian purpose. The light cavalry, mostly Loreclannic, wears leather armor and fights with shortbow and lance.

Many of the heavy knights of the Waymarch are granted title and deed to a square mile of land somewhere along the Tradeway or the Northern Trade Road that they may homestead or sell upon their retirement from the cavalry and their entry into semi-civilian life. This incentive means little to the Loreclannic cavalry, who in any case do not serve anything like the lifelong career of the knights. They are usually paid in gold, horses, cattle, or other commodities that are useful in the wide plains.

Those denizens of Waymarch who are not from wealthy families often serve a term of service as footmen and archers for the realm. It is a well-known adage that cavalry can take ground, but holding it requires infantry. These troops form a solid cadre whose work includes defending the waystations on the frontier and operating in the foothills and forests where the cavalry is less useful. Many of these units serve in Bard's Gate and other permanent settlements of the realm where the Loreclannic tactic of retreating until enemy supply lines break is not an option. As "mere" infantry, their lot is not as prestigious as the cavalry — though the money they earn is not insignificant.

Waymarch's military is led directly by Duke Lucius Qellinroque, a renowned horseman in the Foerdewaith style, and not one to shy away from the jousting pitch, though his advisors always counsel against it. Duke Lucius has been known to enter events in Fareme and Yalendir as a black knight to keep his skills top notch against contestants who are not pulling any punches.

Directly beneath the duke is General Eadith Dupond, the Grey Lady, his wisest and bravest general. General Dupond rose through the ranks of horsemen and gained fame for bravery in battle when she led a squadron of her best troops into the southern Stoneheart Mountains, where they did battle against Carrakeer the Butcher, a perversely evil mountain giant with ogre and troll thralls. Dupond, a captain at the time, managed to defeat the foes while only losing five of the 24 troops, clerics, and war wizards under her command. Carrakeer's head was brought down from the mountain and his skull was given as tribute to her commander, who gave it in turn to the duke of Waymarch. Rather than sending the skull to Reme for inclusion in the Avenue of Eternal Warning, the duke chose to keep it in a trophy case in Castle Qellinroque — after all, the skull of a giant would be an inordinately large cobblestone.

Dupond's bravery and tactical prowess made her a hero of the realm and brought her to the attention of the duke. She was sent to the Arcanum Collegium in Reme where she could hone her knowledge of warfare and tactics. As a result of her history, Dupond has Duke Qellinroque's complete support.

Scout units of the March are typically made up of six to 10 Loreclannic knights led by an officer they elect. Infantry units, which are ordinarily of Foerdewaith background, include two dozen troops armed with polearms and another dozen armed with bows. Larger forces are created by combining these smaller units into greater fighting forces. If a call goes forth throughout the realm, the cavalry can be recalled to Panetoth at a rate of 50 miles per day with foot soldiers capable of only 20 miles per day with a full load across the paved roads of the land.

Roughly half of Waymarch's military is serving a term of service in the Suzerainty of Bard's Gate. This pact of protection helps finance Waymarch's tithe to Reme and has made Panetoth a wealthy city in the middle of an arid plain.

Wilderness and Adventure

Adventure abounds on the edges of Waymarch, especially in areas of the Stoneheart Mountains, and along the border with Ysser. Further, solo riders and small parties are the frequent target of attacks by bandits, especially in the region of the Dagger & Rose where Black Jack Cutter's gang is known to thwart the riders of the duke of Waymarch at every turn.

Foreigners have been known to run afoul of the Loreclans dwelling in the lands off the main roadways as they inadvertently insult customs or trespass upon land deemed to belong to the riders of the tall grass.

Weather has its own dangers, as the region can be very hot and dry over the summer months, draining wells of their capacity and making the grass susceptible to wildfires. In the winter, blizzards blow in from the northwest, and tornadic activity is not uncommon in the broad prairie during the spring months.

Use the **Plains (General) Encounter Table** when traveling the plains of the Waymarch.

Major Threats

There are few major threats to Waymarch, other than the risk of severe drought, which occurs once a decade or so. It is on good terms with all of its neighbors, and though a substantial portion of its military is in the east in service to Bard's Gate, there are no true military challengers on its horizon. That being said, were the instability of the former eastern provinces of Foere to worsen, there might end up being deeper involvement by the March than either it or the grand duke may desire.

Locations in Waymarch

Crossroads Center

Alignment: Lawful Neutral
Ruler: Sir Barraud
Government: Feudal
Population: 120–150 permanent residents, mostly military and Plainsfolk. Up to 100 caravan visitors.
Languages: Common
Religion: Mithras
Resources: Trade, grains, horses, cattle, hides and skins
Technology Level: Medieval
Located where the Tradeway crosses the Tourse Road to the south and Fivestone Trail to the north, this cavalry fort and waystation sits in the midst of the tallgrass prairie, baking in the summer and freezing cold in the winter.

Appearance

A sheer-sided earthwork and sod rampart fort rises 50 feet from among a sparse collection of wheat fields, sod houses, and elk skin tents. The fort is topped with a three-story limestone keep and sits at the northwestern edge of the crossroad. Its one entrance faces the exact point of the cross. A drainage ditch filled with sharpened stakes surrounds the rampart, which has a simple wooden bridge and gate allowing entry. Hitched and unhitched wagons line the sides of the Tradeway where drovers and travelers cook meals and tend to their wagons and animals.

Travelers heading east encamp along the southern side of the road, and those heading west on the north. Various tents are plotted out here so that the drovers and their guards can take their rest as wind and weather permits. The grasslands surrounding the fort are kept short thanks to the grazing of horses and oxen used in the transport of goods along the Tradeway.

Description

Located on the Tradeway 10 day's travel between Fareme to the east and the Dagger & Rose Inn to the west, one finds Crossroads Center, an earthen rampart known as Fort Sod and its small waystation, which awaits weary travelers. Crossroads is a significant stop for overland trade heading between Reme, Fareme, and eventually Bard's Gate. It is also the most direct route from Tourse in the Duchy of Ysser, a fact not lost on the duke of Ysser and Duloth's Wheelwright's Guild, who have their own plans for the region. It is of further importance as well, as the northern trail leaving the waystation is the only well-cut trail leading to Five Stones and the Grimburg to the north.

Due to its strategic significance and proximity to the Duchy of Ysser, Crossroads Center is more fully garrisoned than other earthen cavalry forts of the region. The garrison consists of a complement of five Loreclannic scouts and 50 heavy cavalry troops who ride out in patrols of six, typically accompanied by an officer and either a cleric of Mithras or a journeyman wizard recruited from the Tower of Ravens or the Compass Tower in Panetoth. These patrols work on a rotation so that three patrols are out at any given time on the eastern and western Tradeway and on the south road to Ysser. The remaining patrols perform guard duty within view of the keep, and the final patrol is rested. Two dozen archers command the rampart in three shifts.

See **Encounters 8** and **9** in the **Convenient Reference Guide to Reme** for military units of the Waymarch.

Fort Sod

The rampart garrison is sunken on the inside, which provides some relief from the constant prairie winds. Troop barracks are actually cut into the inside walls of the rampart in similar fashion to the construction of the Red Elk Inn on the south side of the Tradeway.

Inside the earthworks are the wooden and turf stables for the cavalry and a three-story Limestone Keep where the officers and their commander keep their headquarters. Riders sleep in the first floor with officers, priests, and wizards sharing rooms on the second and third floors along with Sir Barraud, who keeps his own private quarters there. Ballistae are set at the four corners of the fort and command a view of the prairie surrounding the fort.

The Red Elk Inn

The Red Elk Inn serves the needs of travelers stopping at Crossroads Center. The inn sits atop a smaller manmade hill just opposite Fort Sod on the south side of the road. It is built from a combination of local limestone bedrock and turf, and reinforced with timbers brought at great expense from the region of Fairhill. The drinking hall sits atop the hill, and the rooms as such are turf-house caves carved into the sides of the manmade hill. Six rooms are dug into these caves that are accessed from the outside by a door. Each of the rooms is large enough to sleep four adult humans. The rooms are pleasant and cheery (especially in the case of halflings), with wood paneling and floors; they are prized by caravan masters and wealthy travelers as a "civilized" alternative to sleeping in tents next to draft animals and smelly employees.

The Red Elk is managed by Gauther Weems, an old, one-legged campaigner who spent his career in the saddle of the Waymarch cavalry. Gauther has a special place in his heart for the riders who call the Crossroads Center home for their six-month tours, and he does his best to keep the morale of the troops high and the comfort of travelers at a premium.

Gauther is known to pay a decent rate for fresh meat, and he works deals with various traders to offer a wide selection of rum, whisky, wine, and rare cheeses for his higher-paying guests. Prices vary by rarity, though his fine wines and spirits typically cost 2 sp a glass per 500 miles of distance from Crossroads Center that the beverage was vinted or distilled.

The Red Elk offers a wheated ale grown and brewed by local settlers for 1 sp per mug.

A frequent visitor to the Red Elk is Matteo Linus, who presents himself as an antiquities collector, but is actually a spy for the Duchy of Ysser. Linus is a representative of Yorwich Imports of Panetoth and uses this administrative position to send information about goings-on in Fareme, Panetoth, and Crossroads to the duke in Tourse.

SWITCHGRASS FORGE

The Switchgrass Forge is buried in a hollow dug into the side of the hill fort. The forge descends roughly 50 feet into the hill and is at a depth such that the smith's midnight hammering does not keep the guardians of the Crossroads Center from their slumber when he begins hammering iron and steel in the wee hours of the morning.

The reason for the late night smithwork is simple. The Prairie Forge is run by Megren Limans, a deep gnome from Grimburg who took to the blacksmith trade in Crossroads and in fact helped in the design of the turf structure. Megren serves as a line of communication with the guardians of Grimburg and Fort Sod, allowing Sir Barraud to communicate with the reclusive deep folk who dwell there when necessary.

Megren has a disdain for sunlight and therefore takes his orders after sunset — and as often completes the work by dawn before retiring. When forced to travel in daylight, he covers himself head to toe in white linen and wears smoked black goggles to protect his eyes from the unblinking glare of the prairie sun.

Megren is an expert blacksmith and can forge most weapons in a few days. His rates are 20% higher than ordinary prices due to rarity of materials and the fact that he is the only available smith for 50 miles in any direction. He spends the majority of his time crafting shoes for the cavalry's horses and repairing weapons and armor.

The entry to his shop is trapped to collapse the tunnel into his forge in the event that enemies attack the Sod Fort. Megren would simply tunnel his way out of the shop if this should ever take place.

BEAST TAKERS' CAMP

The Beast Taker Loreclan has a semi-permanent camp on the plains to the northeast of Fort Sod. The camp consists of a dozen earthen lodges occupied by roughly 60 Beast Takers, though there are seldom more than 30 within the camp at any given time. The folk who remain in the camp are typically young or elderly, with a dozen of the younger warriors tasked with defense of the campsite. The rest are off on the prairie hunting game to bring back to the fort.

The folk who remain at the camp prepare and tan hides, prepare furs, and craft fine leather goods that they sell to caravan masters passing through the waystation of Crossroads Center.

See Encounter 10 in the Convenient Reference Guide to Reme for a Loreclan encampment.

ALLIANCES

Sir Barraud employs plainsfolk from the Beast Taker Loreclan to supply additional meat for the garrison, which is provided in fresh venison or other wild game. The Beast Takers also serve as paid rangers and scouts for Crossroads Center and keep an eye on the borders of the Waymarch frontier while the cavalry serves the primary function of guarding the established roads. The rest of the Loreclan, another 300 or so, are scattered in small pasturage camps deeper into the plains.

THREATS

The biggest threat to Crossroads Center is that it would be dominated in an invasion by the Duchy of Ysser and used as a staging ground for their armies to close the Tradeway and shave off the western half of Waymarch for their own uses. Ysser assumes that it could quickly overrun Fareme and block any aid from Bard's Gate or Panetoth indefinitely. At the very worst, they could do extensive economic damage to Waymarch and contest Reme for control of the territory. This threat is relatively minimal given the ongoing collapse of the Kingdoms of Foere, but the border between Ysser and Reme has become unstable given Ysser's increasing inability to control its border barons.

Another hidden threat to Crossroads Center is located 750 miles to the north in the Ice Tower of Kal-Tior where the mad warlock draws ever closer to the prison of Grimburg.

THE DAGGER & ROSE

The Dagger & Rose is a traveler's inn and tavern located 250 miles west of Crossroads Center and 200 miles west of the capital of Waymarch in Panetoth. The tavern is located at the intersection of the Tradeway and the King's Road in a dusty part of the prairie noted as the home of a wild gang of bandits known as the Highwaymen, a group that has grown in power over recent months.

The inn is managed by Tamalaine of Portia, an elf — possibly of noble birth —who is said to have originally hailed from Arendia. She opened the Dagger & Rose 60 years ago and gained a reputation for bravery when a gang of bandits invaded her establishment and used it as their headquarters. Tamalaine is said to have escaped and returned with a band of 50 mercenaries who chased the bandits from her inn; she hung the leader's head from the palisade wall.

The inn is very expensive, and for that reason larger caravans tend to camp outside of its walls, which allows only wealthy merchants a respite in soft feather beds under fine sheets and with good liquor to drink. Visitors are tended by the Famille Monfrad, mercenaries and servants whose family have been with Tamalaine for decades.

The Monfrad clan, trappers and rangers who have lived in these parts for hundreds of years, built the tavern for Tamalaine 60 years ago and then later sent family members to work there. Throughout its history, the Dagger has seen all manner of travelers come through its gates, ranging from humble young aristocrats with barely a gold sovereign to their names to princes fleeing incognito to escape death at the hands of assassins.

HIGHWAYMEN

A band of highwaymen and their leader Black Jack Cutter have haunted this region of the prairie for decades. They have consistently managed to outsmart and stay one step ahead of the Waymarch Cavalry and other mercenaries the duke of Waymarch hires on an almost annual basis to clear them out. The Highwaymen are clever bandits and avoid large or heavily-guarded caravans. They instead set their sights on small groups of travelers and poorly-guarded carriages. They seemingly know how to target the wealthiest marks, often leaving their prey penniless and sunburned alongside the Tradeway.

See Encounter 11 in the Convenient Reference Guide to Reme for the Highwaymen.

FAREME

Alignment: Neutral
Ruler: Lord Ostric Kensalius
Government: Feudal
Population: 3,500 (Foerdewaith 1,730, Loreclans 1,120, halfling 212, half-elf 121, gnome 105, hill dwarf 212); swells to 10,000 during caravan season.
Languages: Common
Resources: Cattle, horses
Notable NPCs: Roelf Flupken, Local Wheelwright Guild Chapter Boss
Religion: Mithras, Sefagreth
Technology Level: Medieval

General Information

Fareme is a trade town on the eastern edge of Waymarch that borders the Suzerainty of Bard's Gate. Fareme is a fortified town where mercenaries of Waymarch leased to Bard's Gate are deployed and cycled through their tours of duty before returning to their homes in the prairies, cities, or towns of Duke Lucius' holding. For many travelers heading into the west for the first time, it is their first actual step into the Duchy of Waymarch and by proxy the Grand Duchy of Reme. Due to the town's military and trade activity, it is far busier than most towns of its size.

Fareme is the first major travel stop of the Tradeway after leaving Bard's Gate, a major waystop and resupply depot for caravans traveling east or west between the lands of Reme and Bard's Gate and beyond. The outskirts of the town are surrounded with privately-owned grazing land and stockyards where local landsmen charge travelers a competitive fee for access to water and pasture, to cattle and caravan animals, and to feed and drink before they continue their trek along the Tradeway between the two largest cities of east-central Akados.

Fareme is under the strong protection of the duchy, with a substantial cavalry garrison. The city is designed to accommodate the many travelers who fill the streets during caravan season, and includes inns, pastures, paddocks, and a market with a constantly shifting array of wares. Many of the inns have signboards out front where advertisements are posted by those seeking guards, adventurers, or others.

Locations

The Great Jousting Pitch

Jousting is sport loved by the folk of the prairie and town alike, as the Waymarch cavalry is considered the crème of the Rhemish land forces. The Jousting Pitch of Fareme is part of the jousting circuit organized to test the mettle of the Waymarch Cavalry and to keep their skills about them in the event of incursions from the monstrous forces of the Stoneheart Mountains. Locals bet on the champions, with winners moving on to competitions in Quintas and Yalendir before they eventually make their way to the Royal Pitch in Panetoth. Jousts are held on a monthly basis with the best knights of horse invited to participate.

Prairie Fire Theater

The Prairie Fire Theater is a raucous and popular tavern-theater near the town's center. It is frequented by locals looking to rub elbows and hear stories shared by travelers on the road so that they can catch firsthand news of the outside world. The Prairie Fire has a small stage that features live entertainment, and often has touring acts from the Bard's College of Bard's Gate performing oratory, dance, and the rustic fiddle and string bass that is popular among the Foerdewaith settlers of the grasslands. For travelers from the east, the Prairie Fire offers the chance to see Loreclannic theater for the first time as well — acting is a favored entertainment among the Loreclans and a highly developed artform.

Admission to the Prairie Fire Theater is 2 sp at the door with ale and spirits for sale in the range of 1–5 sp each.

Temple of Mithras

The temple of Mithras, like many others, is built around a hidden underground cistern near the town's center. Separate from the public well, this water supply is kept pure by the steady work of the high priest and his acolytes, who ensure there is enough water to provide basic sustenance during the dry season and who purify the water from cattle runoff during the rainy season. In fact, protecting the precious water supply is the mission of Mitra's priesthood in the grasslands of Waymarch from Fareme to Panetoth.

The rector of the temple of Mithras is a middle-aged cleric named Aubree. He is served by a dozen lesser priest and acolytes who operate a common school where they see to the early religious and basic education of young people before they become old enough to take on chores and adult work.

The temple provides several other services for a tithe to the temple's coffers. These services include blessing cattle, horses, and caravans; selling vials of holy water, potions of healing, and other such draughts; and scribing lesser scrolls for use by clerics who share their faith.

See **Encounter 12** in the **Convenient Reference Guide to Reme** if you need stats for the population of the Temple of Mithras.

Thunder Head Bar

A painted sign featuring Gromm riding atop a black cloud hangs outside this rough-and-ready tavern not far from the western gate. The Thunder Head Bar is a coarser establishment than most and employs a team of four menacing bouncers to keep the peace, especially on nights when rival caravan teams roll through town. To cut down on the general brawling, Baern the Broad, the Thunder Head's owner, devised bare-knuckle brawling events specifically on weekends.

These fights take place in a sand pit dug in the center of the bar and feature one-on-one competition. The fights are often brutal affairs punctuated by the slapping sounds of heavy fists slamming into sweaty flesh. Bettors surround the fighters and wager handfuls of gold and silver on their chosen warrior. A street dwarf named Osr Manslayer, a distant cousin of Thayco of Bard's Gate, frequently sets the line on the fighters, marking off wagers on a blackboard.

Thunder Head imports Brin Zweischer Ale, which it sells for 1 sp per mug, and serves the local wheat beer and rye whiskey for 2 sp per cup each.

Baern's cooks roast whole sides of beef over hot coals on a massive iron spit. The steers are skinned and split down the middle, their spines removed. They are then rubbed heavily with salt and wild herbs. The resultant tender, smoked beef is served with a hunk of bread and slices of cheese and mushroom.

Baern is a thick-necked, bald-headed Northman with a grizzled beard and scarred face who arrived like many of his fellows some decades ago. He was captured by Loreclan of the Thunder Riders who eventually adopted him after he fought alongside them for many years. He finally settled in Fareme, where he opened the Thunder Head Bar.

Trailblazer's Inn

This inn located in the town's center is rustic but comfortable. Two stories tall, with 20 rooms to rent and a large common room, the Trailblazer is a hub of sorts for caravan masters who want to hire reliable guards and drivers for the long trek to Reme. Travelers looking to book passage with a caravan are most likely to find a caravan master with need for their particular set of skills here.

Trailblazer's Inn sells a heavily hopped "Panetoth Tradeway Pale Ale" that is popular with the younger clientele. The ale is kegged in Panetoth in beechwood kegs and gains its various flavors as it sloshes about on its cross-country journey.

Other popular dishes are its braised mutton chops for 5 sp, or barley with onions and feta cheese for 1 sp per bowl.

Rooms are 1 sp a night for double occupancy. A gold piece a week includes all meals and a hot bath.

Wind Keep

The banner of Waymarch floats bravely over this fortress, which is topped by three high towers. Two of the towers are affixed with windmill sails that make use of the natural wind of the prairie; the castle grinds its own grains and limestone fertilizer. Wind Keep is built atop a hill that overlooks the city to the south and has a long, fortified causeway that leads directly into the town's south side.

The fortress itself is made from locally quarried limestone and serves as the home of Lord Ostric Kensalius, cousin to the Vinewoods of Bard's Gate. The keep is attached to a large stable where the cavalry warhorses are bedded when not grazing on the pastureland reserved for them. The small castle earns its name from the ever-present winds blowing across the wide veldt of the Waymarch. The wind may blow as lightly as a gentle breeze, and in some seasons as a harsh gale, but it never ceases.

The keep is home to 100 members of the Waymarch Cavalry. Twenty squires and grooms attend them, and 200 footmen who man the walls of the town are billeted here as well.

Half of the cavalry is out in 25 man patrols on the Tradeway at any given time, while the remainder stay within a half day of the town as a warning to nearby bandits to keep their distance.

See **Encounters 8** and **9** in the **Convenient Reference Guide to Reme** for information about encounters with the Waymarch military.

GUILDS AND ORGANIZATIONS

BROKERAGE LEAGUE

The Brokerage League, or the "Brokers," is a confederation of traders who work in setting the trade-price for commodities that make their way through the towns and cities of the west. They set prices based on drought conditions, dangers on the road from bandits or other monstrous and sorcerous forces, and political and social issues that impact the price of grain, cattle, fruits, and metal shipped along the Tradeway.

The Brokerage League has close affiliations with the temple of Sefagreth.

The Brokers are headquartered in Reme, but have chapters in the markets of the major towns and cities along the Tradeway route where they estimate time of shipping and additional costs associated with trade. This allows for speculation and creates another form of revenue for the grand duchy.

The Brokers keep a hall between the stockyards and the marketplace where their various client members can keep an eye on the comings and goings of trade goods and estimate their condition and value.

Most of the members of the league are lesser nobles who send deputized proxy traders and clerks, and who arrive in the markets only during big trading sessions such as annual cattle drives or when various crops come into season.

THE ROAD AGENCY

This mercenary band headquartered in Panetoth keeps a barracks in Fareme. The band is made up largely of former soldiers of Waymarch and foreign soldiers who served their duty in Reme or Bard's Gate. The Road Agency is the most organized and sophisticated gang of sellswords to ply the great Tradeway.

The local recruiter for the Road Agency is Roussea du Fitte, a former Rhemish infantry captain of pure Foerdewaith ancestry. Entry to the Road Agents costs a 10 gp initiation fee and requires completion of the agency's training regimen. Recruits are expected to participate in armed and unarmed duels to prove success at arms against the company quartermaster. Additional time spent drilling with other members of the outfit to practice the fundamentals of squad tactics and defensive fighting are also expected. The agency handles individual contracts and pays bonuses to its members based on their performance of duty and the success of their protection of client merchandise and well-being.

The Road Agency of Fareme is currently at odds with the Wheelwrights International, for they see the Wheelwrights as quite blatantly making a move on their business. There is truth to this, as ultimately the Road Agency is in the protection racket, something that Duloth and his lieutenants have more than a passing knowledge of.

Things have not developed into outright war between the organizations, for the Wheelwrights are quick to bribe anyone they can and blackmail those they cannot.

WHEELWRIGHTS

A larger-than-normal brick structure bearing the spoked wheel of the Wheelwrights Guild is prominently located on the western end of the city plaza. The building serves as the headquarters of Fareme's branch of the Wheelwrights Guild International, a chapter of the Wheelwrights of Bard's Gate. From here, Duloth's agents offer their negotiating muscle to drovers and wagon-masters while keeping an eye on local politics and gathering information about the quality and value of goods coming through Fareme on their way into Bard's Gate.

Fareme's chapterhouse is overseen by Roelf Flupken, who has about as much of Duloth's trust as Duloth has for any of his lieutenants. Roelf has 20 Wheelwright enforcers at his command and an unknown number of associates who can be called up at a moment's notice, ready to crack skulls and block roadways.

Like all workings of the Wheelwrights, corruption is merely a scratch beneath the surface. The Wheelwrights offer their assistance in fencing and smuggling operations for the right price. They commonly employ bandits to help them acquire more exotic items to auction at the Black Market of Bard's Gate long before they arrive along the Tradeway from that august city.

See **Encounters 13** and **14** in the **Convenient Reference Guide to Reme** for information about encounters with Wheelwright enforcers and caravans.

FIVESTONES

Alignment: Neutral
Government: Elder Council
Population: 235 (Human, Rock Gnome)
Languages: Common, Rhemish, Gnomish
Ruler: Grandie Hoek the Elder
Resources: Sheep, woolens, cheese, barley, ale
Technology Level: Lower Medieval

A partial ring of five standing stones of what was once a circle of seven stands here. A small, pastoral village is built among the stones themselves. The strange but idyllic tableau is punctuated by the vast Stoneheart Mountains to the north and the more immediate outcropping of a giant stone fortress perhaps two dozen miles in the distance.

The village is the site of an ancient Neolithic settlement that served to supply the Stoneface Clan of nearby Grimburg and has existed since before the march of Oerson. The settlement has changed occupants many times in its thousands of years of existence, though each set of residents seems to take on the same occupation as those who dwelt here before.

The village is currently a mix of human and rock gnome villagers who conduct trade with the distant Tradeway and provide supplies to the Stoneface Clan. They do not know the purpose of Grimburg but the village is rife with rumors that have circulated for thousands of years.

A seldom-used cart track leads south to Crossroads Center from Fivestone, and the immensity of the fortress of Grimburg can be seen from the northeast of the village.

NOTABLE LOCATIONS

STONE TAP TAVERN

Activity in Fivestone centers around the Stone Tap Tavern. The tavern is built from slabs of rock and is sunken about 5 feet below the ground, which gives it a cavern-like feel. Local cream stout ale is served here with goat cheese, ground mutton on bread, and potato stew.

The Stone Tap is typically where the village elder Grandie Hoek can be found and questioned, though he has a bit of a taste for whiskey and few answers. Cups of whiskey are 5 sp and cups of dark ale are 1 sp.

The whiskey and ale are distilled and brewed in the hills about a mile from the village (so the scent of mash doesn't choke the residents).

SHRINE OF THE EARTH SPIRIT

This shrine depicts a Neolithic representation of the earth spirit of the Stoneheart Mountains. It is vaguely humanoid, and its massive arms hold mountains over its head. The locals leave gifts of flowers and grain at the shrine, and these mysteriously vanish in the early morning hours.

THE STANDING STONES

The remaining five standing stones are 30 feet tall, with the two fallen stones lying in opposite directions from one another. The villagers believe these stones collapsed when the archmagi Margon and Alycthron raised the Wizard's Wall, and count it to the time the great crack appeared in Grimburg. Many of the glyphs that once covered the stones have weathered with time. The stones themselves are covered in lichen near their tops, and like many of the domed stone structures of the village, are covered with thick green moss near the base.

Known for Fivestone Whiskey and Fivestone Ale, this cottage distillery/brewery is located a mile from town. The distillery is run by Elwishir Opal — a rock gnome who knows a thing or two about making good ales and spirits — and his rather large family who dwell in a tunnel system they discovered shortly after arriving in Fivestone. Elwishir's brews have grown in popularity, and they can be found as far away as the tavern shelves of Panetoth.

Elwishir's ale is a smooth cream stout. Whiskey is made from a portion of the initial vatted beer that is then distilled and triple casked using virgin casks, cherrywood casks, and charcoaled oak casks. He takes pride in his work, and bottles only a hundred or so bottles of Fivestone Whiskey per year, making it a very expensive but highly agreeable beverage.

The Grimburg

Alignment: Lawful Neutral
Government: Feudal Military Garrison
Population: 500 Deep Gnome Guardians, The Stonefaces
Languages: Common, Gnome
Ruler: Orator Dezzinim Xrach
Resources: Unknown, gems, silver
Technology Level: Medieval

This massive stone fortress predates the arrival of the Hyperboreans. A very visible part of the landscape of northern Waymarch, the fortress is often mistaken as just another huge block of stone rising from the rolling green foothills of the Stoneheart Mountains until one takes a closer look and sees a massive patch of stone, concrete, and cold-wrought-iron stapling pins running up one side of the huge rock. A closer look at the fortress reveals observation holes and arrow slits that are cleverly hidden into the crevasses of the stone.

The fortress itself is seemingly constructed from a solid piece of granite that emerges from the natural bedrock here. The only entrance is a massive, concealed gate that is always guarded by surly, heavily-armed and armored deep gnomes. The gnomes are not talkative and deny any relation to the deep gnomes of Alesardin.

It is rare that anyone is allowed entry into this fortress and even rarer for anyone to come out. The villagers of Fivestones meet with the Deep Gnomes of the Grimburg once per month when the gate is opened the width of a single armored gnome. The Grimburgers then pass sacks of silver to the villagers in exchange for salted meat, small casks of whiskey, and woven woolens.

Known to only a few is that the Grimburg is a planar prison for holding the most dangerous and powerful of extraplanar fugitives, fiends, and godlings. Its interior gives access to many dimensional gates and cells. It has been manned by the Stoneface Clan of deep gnomes who were given their charge at the end of the Age of Strife, roughly 14,000 years ago, by the elemental Lord Mocham — who infused it with a portion of his power to enable it to hold its prisoners. It has had no verified escapes, with one possible exception. When the Wizard's Wall was raised in 2947 I.R. — when Alycthron and Margon called on the spirits of the Haunted Steppe and Stoneheart and Deepfells mountains to move the very foundations of Akados itself — in that moment of siphoning of power, a great crack appeared in the wall of the fortress. It has since been repaired, but rumors persist that one unidentified prisoner was able to make his/her/its escape. The Stonefaces deny any such assertion.

Since that time, observers of the earth spirit in the Stoneheart Mountain Dungeon have noticed that it seems to grieve deeply.

The fortress itself is currently administrated by a deep gnome called Orator Dezzinim Xrach. Xrach has sensed the presence of an outside evil that seeks to invade the fortress and has put his guardsmen on watch for treachery from both within and without. His fears are not unfounded, as the Ice Tower of Kal-Tior creeps ever nearer to the Grimburg at the behest of the Arch-Fiend Perfidium, who seeks to free the Frost-Angel of Kainus from her long imprisonment.

The Ice Tower of Kal-Tior

Standing at the head of a great glacial flow that has broken free from the Stoneheart Ice Plateau is the Accursed Ice Tower of Kal-Tior. The tower serves as home and siege tower of Kal-Tior the warlock, herald of Count Perfidium of Kainus, a high prince in the Court of the Nine Hells.

The tower itself is guarded by a nest of soulless ice goblins and a tribe of frost giants who pledged their allegiance to Count Perfidium in exchange for riches and the promise of an unending age of winters where they may feast upon the flesh of weaker beings and fill their halls to the ceiling with jewels and gold.

The flow of the tower moves slowly but surely now that it has nearly reached the plains of Waymarch. From here, Kal-Tior turns the direction of his infernal tower toward Grimgate. Once there, he intends to freeze the gnomish prison vault solid, smash it to pieces, and free those held within.

The tower's movements are controlled by blood sacrifice and thus far its progression has been moved by the sacrifice of ice gnomes and the capture and destruction of smaller Loreclans of the Plainsfolk that ride the grasslands of Waymarch south of Eamonvale.

The last few hundred miles are going to require greater and greater sacrifices, and Kal-Tior has called upon his master for the assistance of ice devils, more frost giants, and any other help that can be offered to begin his assault on the Grimburg.

The Ice Floe and Deceiver's Pass

The floe that erupted from melt caused by the incursion of the Ice Palace of Perfidium into the mortal realm precipitated an outflow of icy waters from the hell itself. Sailing like a jagged vessel of pure ice upon this floe came Kal-Tior's Tower with Kal-Tior himself as harbinger of his master's frozen torments.

This narrow pass is the only natural ascent to the summit of the Stoneheart Glacier. The pass is 250 miles of treacherous terrain, currently clogged with ice from the unholy ice floe. It has become a hellish trek haunted by spirits escaped from the underworld, frost men, yetis, ice worms, and other horrors. The trek is further exacerbated by natural hazards such as jagged fissures and flesh-freezing, hell-borne winds.

Stoneheart Glacier and Shengotha Plateau

One of the highest and coldest spots in east-central Akados is the great Stoneheart Glacier that sits within the Shengotha Plateau. Comprising a land mass of more than 60,000 square miles, it features a glacier whose depth is estimated at close to 500 feet. The glacier is surrounded by high peaks, and the elevation of the plateau itself is 6,000 feet.

The plateau has existed since long beyond the memory of humankind, and was named by dwarves who once dwelt here before calamity collapsed their ancient kingdom in the center of the Stoneheart Mountains. It is whispered that they were swallowed whole into the hells, pulled down by the weight of their greed and their betrayal of the elves of the east.

The Shengotha Plateau is difficult to access from the towering mountains that surround it, other than by climbing up the frozen floe from the Ice Tower of Kal-Tior through Deceiver's Pass.

Ice Palace of Perfidium

The Ice Palace of Perfidium is a planar incursion from Kainus, a realm of the Underworlds, into the material plane of the Lost Lands. Entry to the palace is indeed a step into a passage to Hell itself. The incursion was created through the summoning rituals of Kal-Tior as he called upon the strength of his patron, Count Perfidium. There, on the spot of a collapsed ancient dwarven empire, Kal-Tior sacrificed more than 600 members of an ice gnome tribe upon the ancient glacier. Their blood was mixed with the icy, interplanar waters, and caused a thunderous crack heard as far away as Reme and Bard's Gate.

The rent in the fabric of reality allowed a mirror duplicate of Perfidium's palace to break into the mortal plane. The palace itself is guarded by a contingent of ice devils, white dragons in service of Perfidium, ice mephits, frost giants, winter wolves, and an army of ice goblins formed from the soulless husks of the ice gnomes who once called the Shengotha Plateau their home.

The palace sits upon a vent of Hell itself and is both cold as ice and boiling with hellfire at the same time, giving the region around it an unholy glow. The palace appears in the form of a stack of massive snowflakes with crystalline edges of indescribable beauty silhouetted against the sulfurous nightmare glow of the infernal realms.

During the deepest, coldest months of the year, Count Perfidium can gate a powerful avatar of himself onto the Shengotha Plateau and occupy the mirror throne. It is at this time that his servant Kal-Tior is at his most powerful.

Count Perfidium is sworn to free his ancient mistress from her prison in Grimburg and has influenced Kal-Tior to do his bidding in executing Perfidium's ancient quest.

Panetoth

Alignment: Lawful Neutral
Ruler: Lucius Qellinroque, Harmost of Panetoth, Duke of Waymarch, Voice of the Grand Duke in the East
Government: Feudal
Population: 82,419 (Foerdewaith 47,297, Loreclans 20,617, human [Plainsfolk] 11,241, hill dwarf 1,256, mountain dwarf 941, halfling 777, half-elf 199, high elf 91)
Languages: Common, Rhemish, Kirkut, Dwarven
Religion: Mithras, Sefagreth, Vanitthu, Quell (House Qellinroque)
Resources: Trade, horses, mercenaries
Technology Level: Medieval

Panetoth is the capital and regional administrative center that oversees Waymarch and houses its main garrison as well as the ducal palace. Patrols of the Waymarch and the absence of many soldiers in service to Bard's Gate means that the military encampments on the plains north of the city are never full. The city is also a key trading center, for it sits on the Tradeway, the main road from Reme to the center of the Kingdom of Foere, and other points east. The temple of Mithras in the city protects the dwindling water supply every summer from contamination to prevent outbreaks of dysentery and cholera.

Rising from the prairie on the crossroads of the Tradeway between Freegate and Reme, and the North Trade Road to Ironhill, Panetoth is a fortress city. It serves as the capital of the Waymarch and is the ancestral home of the Qellinroque family, which claims its long ancestry to Borell I, the heroic duke of Reme itself. Panetoth is a wealthy city whose duke earns a financial boon from tributes provided by Eamonvale and in payment from the city of Bard's Gate for its protection.

Panetoth is also a center for horse trade — the six nearest Loreclans, with representatives from others, gather for a great rendezvous in the plains to the north of the city in the early summer months where they trade yearling horses to the duke for his renowned cavalry. It is not unusual for the grand duke in Reme to visit during this time, renewing oaths and pacts of peace and loyalty between the Loreclannic nations of the grasslands and the Foerdewaith overlords.

Description

Panetoth is built atop a bluff overlooking the prairie and is surrounded by an earthwork that itself is fitted with a 20-foot-tall limestone slab wall that is dotted with guard towers. Rising from the northwestern edge of the city is a limestone bluff upon which sits Castle Qellinroque, the palace of the duke of Waymarch. The city itself is surrounded by fields of wheat and barley. Several pastures are dedicated to herds of cattle and sheep awaiting market. Several horse and cattle corrals are located outside the walls, and beyond these are large pastures used by visiting Loreclans for their own horses and cattle.

Three gates enter the city. The west gate is referred to as Reme Gate, while the east gate is known as the Prairie Gate. Yalendir Gate is to the north and sets a path upon the Northern Trade Road.

Panetoth is a bustling city that receives road trade in goods from Yalendir, Broadwater, Dun Eamon, Quintas, Bard's Gate, Reme, and far-off Ironhill, as well as lesser trade from its rival Tourse, capital of the Duchy of Ysser to the south. Inside the city, the buildings are mostly brick with thatch roofs. Buildings in the wealthier districts closer to Castle Qellinroque are faced with a veneer of marble from Eamonvale, which gives the upper-class sections of the city the impression of being made of greater stuff than they actually are.

City Layout

Panetoth is divided into six major subsections, including the semi-permanent Loreclannic encampments outside the walls.

Outer Lawns

The Outer Lawns is rolling pastureland located outside of the Prairie Gate. This is where Loreclans set up their camps during annual visits to trade horses with the duke of Waymarch. Typically, 30 to 50 colorful leather tents are pitched outside the Prairie Gate on the Outer Lawns at any given time. A variety of Loreclans populate the camp, though the Thunder Riders and the Quick Knives seldom share camp with one another. Indeed, the Quick Knives are shunned by most of the other local Loreclans at this point, and the city is clear that they are not welcome here either.

Prairie Gate

Prairie Gate opens to the east of the city and is considered by most to be — essentially — a foreign quarter where adventurers and mercenaries lodge. The gatehouse structure built along the East Gate is meant to be imposing since it faces any threats that would enter the capital from the east. A recruiting office for the armies of Waymarch is located here, where foreign-born mercenaries are given the opportunity to serve among the ranks of the Waymarch mercenary forces.

The Prairie Gate district itself is the rougher side of the city, though the presence of diligent guardsmen who keep an eye on things tends to keep things under control. When there are feuding Loreclans present at the same time, the guard is especially alert, and they may even pay a few visitors to help keep an eye out for potential violence.

The Prairie Gate itself is a small military encampment in and of itself. It has stables and outfitting for 150 cavalry and 100 men-at-arms within its solid, well-defended towers. Ballistae and catapults dot the outer walls, and watchtowers afford a defensive rampart facing to the east.

Central Market

The center of the city to the southeast of the limestone bluff is the Central Market district. It is here that many taverns and auction houses operate. It is also the home of much of the city's shopping and dining opportunities.

Castle District and Yalendir Gate

The Castle District encompasses the Bluff, the military barracks, the palace, Yalendir Gate, and the wealthy neighborhoods that border the Bluff.

The district outside of the military fort and palace complex is a walled neighborhood known as the Castle District where individual manor houses dot the hill surrounding the bluff and the troop headquarters. These houses have broad, well-watered gardens with individual fountains or wells. This is where the upper crust of society dwells. Many are Foerdewaith gentry, or officers of the cavalry and army who keep a home here in the city. Well-trained patrols walk the streets of this gate community to keep any would-be thieves at bay.

Yalendir Gate stands at the far end of the district and serves as the passage to Waymarch's northern territories. It has barracks for 50 cavalry, 50 men-at-arms, and 50 archers. This gate is typically fully staffed at any time, with troop rotations coming from the castle itself.

South City

South City has no gate and is at the bottom of the hill and rock that form the city of Panetoth. It is a place where wagon drovers and cattle crews are usually hired. Several warehouses and workhouses are found here where products are manufactured and stockpiled (or stashed as contraband). South City is now largely the domain of the Brims, as the Ebon Union have withdrawn deeper into the far reaches of the duchy and farther away from the Red Thumb and its headquarters in Reme. Buildings here are two to three stories in height and become more-ramshackle and poorer the closer they get to the Prairie Gate and nicer and more well kept the closer they get to the Reme Gate district.

Reme Gate and Gatehouse

This district is made up of middle class and upper middle-class homes and the establishments that cater to them. Its gate is the least restrictive of the gates in the city and is the least defended, though cavalry patrols enter and leave on a daily basis, intent on keeping any bandit menace at bay. This area is where many of the tradesmen who do the actual day-to-day work in the city reside.

The towers and barracks of the Reme Gatehouse are capable of accommodating 100 men-at-arms, a contingent of 50 Waymarch cavalry, and 50 archers. That said, there are seldom more than half that number in the Reme Gatehouse at any given time.

Government Buildings

Castle Qellinroque

Castle Qellinroque is located in the Castle District of the city. The 20-foot-tall parapet-topped stone wall surrounds the 300-foot-tall limestone-and-chert bluff near the north-central part of the city. The curtain wall surrounding the bluff is fortified with six towers topped with siege weapons and manned by lookouts who observe the streets below and the plains beyond. The bluff itself is dotted with fine manor houses that are themselves surrounded by their own walls.

Atop the bluff is a palace structure bristling with towers, a shrine to the god Quell, and the Great Hall of Lucius, duke of Waymarch. A grand, winding road flanked with guardhouses is cut into the bluff and affords a twisting rise to the top of the palace while the lower half of the bluff has been carved into a military structure with barracks, stables, and marshalling grounds. The ducal family's allegiance to Quell — a sea god — in the middle of a landlocked province is considered somewhat bizarre, but it is a longstanding tradition of the family.

Military Barracks

The barracks occupies the lower half of the hollowed-out central bluff and is home to 100 Waymarch knights, 200 Loreclannic Knights, 300 footmen, and 500 archers (see **Encounters 8** and **9** in the ***Convenient Reference Guide to Reme*** for information about encounters with the Waymarch military). One hundred members of the cavalry are on the road at any given time patrolling the roadways north, east, and west to ensure that no bandits harass the Tradeway within 100 miles of the city.

The Grey Lady, General Eadith Dupond, has her residence overlooking the marshalling courtyard, and her staff keeps offices below the residence. When not overseeing training of the troops, Dupond often travels to various garrisons for inspections.

Ducal Palace

Atop the bluff stands the ducal palace where Duke Lucius and his wife Miriam host guests and dignitaries. A special suite within his palace is reserved exclusively for the grand duke of Reme when he makes official state visits, and is otherwise closed to all.

The palace walls are covered in paintings of various heroes of the Waymarch, including paintings of Borell I, an ancestor of Duke Qellinroque, who battled against the demon fiend Kakobovia in the ancient history of the grand duchy. The floors are paved in marble brought down from the Stoneheart Mountains and lined with statues made in Reme, Eamonvale, and Bard's Gate that depict heroes and ancestors of the noble family.

The duke's personal guard is on hand to ensure that potential assassins are kept away. Magical defenses wrought by the wizards of the Compass Tower are active — in various ways — throughout the duke's residence as well. These include wards, alarms, and some outright deadly magical traps. The duke pays the Compass Tower handsomely for their protection and is protected more personally by two clerics of Quell, his patron god, who supervise a small church within the palace grounds.

Tower of Law and Order

This 100-foot-tall, hollow, square, block structure topped with the sigils of Mitra and Vanitthu is located in the Prairie Gate District. It serves as common courthouse, prison, and headquarters of the city watch. There are 200 members of the watch billeted here, with 100 members found in some guard rotation outside of the structure, 25 serving as jail guards, and another roughly 25 that can be expected to be off duty due to sickness, injuries, or general leave.

Captain Benedict Enretre commands the guard. Enretre is short, bald, and thick of shoulder and neck. He earned the appointment through nepotism and is largely disliked by the veterans of the watch due to his boisterous commands and lack of actual experience. That said, he is very strict with the prisoners in his care and instructs guardsmen to "crack heads" in the event of any insurrection that would otherwise mar the general peace of the citizenry of Panetoth.

Cases of lesser crimes are heard in the courtyard on a daily basis, with 100 members of the public allowed in to observe the proceedings. A cleric of Vanitthu or Mithras and an appointed magistrate of Duke Qellinroque hear the trial and pass judgement on the accused. Trials are typically brief. Evidence is offered by the arresting officers, and a rebuttal is afforded to the accused. The cleric and magistrate then discuss the case and offer their sentence or acquittal.

The accused is held in a prison wagon during trial and, if they are found guilty, they are immediately taken to imprisonment in the Tower of Law and Order to serve their sentence — or are executed on the spot. A large gallows stands here, to the consternation of most criminals, and those guilty of capital crimes are executed to the cheers and jeers of the audience when sentence is passed.

The jail itself has two common cell areas for short term imprisonment such as disturbing the peace, assault, and petty theft. Individual cells for up to 100 prisoners held in long-term confinement are located on the upper stories of the tower, and the guard barracks are on the lower floors. There are typically 50–100 prisoners in the jail at any given time. A large stone-floored "yard" opens in the center of the prison where long-term prisoners are allowed 30 minutes of time away from their cells per day.

The duke, for his part, visits the prison twice per year to consider pleas for pardon and to make sure that the conditions in the prison have not slipped into cruelty or laxity. He allows neither the starvation of prisoners, nor torture — although the Rhemish idea of what fails to constitute torture is no more pleasant than it is anywhere else in the world.

Mayor's Manor

Located on the bluffs within the walled Castle District is the home of Mayor Cressian Laflev. Cressian is a second cousin of the duke and is charged with making sure that the city's public works are in order. He also serves as a liaison between the nobility and the citizenry of the city. Mayor Laflev was appointed to his title and is good at his job. He is detail-oriented to the point of obsession and sees that the streets remain in good condition — considering the traffic into the central markets. Laflev is approachable and runs the city out of the city hall built on the edge of the Central Market district.

City Hall

Located on the north side of the market is a brick, marble, and timber structure used as the meeting place for the planning and implementation of business strategy for the city. Lately, the local populace has begun to demand an overhaul of the city's sewer system, an issue that is being addressed by the duke and the mayor.

A city council made up of shop owners, local trade houses, and neighboring ranchers (including representatives of the semi-nomadic Loreclans with pastures near the city) meet here once per month. Situations that become unsolvable between the mayor and the citizens are brought to the duke in his palace, where Lucius decides how to address such matters.

Notable Inns and Taverns

Inn-at-the-End-of-the-Road

Located in South City, the Inn-at-the-End-of-the-Road stands near the juncture at the very end of the Northern Tradeway Road, not far from the southern wall of the city. The inn stands off a bit from the road and is equipped with stables to accommodate as many as two dozen horses and has 30 rooms to rent — plus a private banquet hall. This hall is often reserved by caravan masters who are set to begin a trek to either Reme or Bard's Gate.

Rooms at the inn are 5 sp per day or 2 gp per week; they include breakfast and a hot bath. The inn is otherwise "nothing fancy," which is what the owner Tremain Florissant likes. Warm, clean, and reliable is his motto. Tremain is a retired caravan master who seeks to provide his old comrades of the trail with the sorts of amenities he would have enjoyed on his many years driving the road.

The inn is a good place to hire professional guards for long treks along the Tradeway. Typically, these guards are veterans who have been personally vetted by Tremain. They are familiar with the road and its dangers, know where to find the best watering holes and places for beasts of burden and cattle to graze without danger of wolves or worse threats.

Sir Beefheart's Chevalier Tavern

Sir Beefheart's Chevalier Tavern is an upscale bawdy-house and tavern located in the Reme Gate district. The name of the tavern plays on the legendary exploits of Sir Beefheart the Brave, a mirthful hero who failed his way through many an adventure on the way to becoming a Knight of the Marches, decorated by the grand duke of Reme himself. It is unsure whether the bawdy and brave tales actually took place or if they are the creations of Squire Duvalier, who followed Beefheart on his wild adventures throughout the west-central portion of the continent where they battled dragons, matched wits with seductive vampires, and in general managed to be in every major battle that took place along the Marches of Reme nearly 200 years ago. No one particularly cares, since it is an absolutely ripping yarn.

The walls of the tavern are painted with highly detailed frescoes of Beefheart's encounters, and the various rooms of the tavern are named after Beefheart's exploits. For example, the main bar itself is called "Metroxius's Tongue" and is carved in the undulating shape of a long dragon's tongue and polished in brilliant cherrywood as a reference to an alleged encounter between Sir Beefheart and the green dragon Metroxius. According to the story, Beefheart somehow convinced the dragon to cease its assaults on travelers along the Tradeway.

The Chevalier Tavern is popular among veteran officers and wealthy foreign merchants looking for something a little more scandalous to do in Panetoth, without the danger of ever actually getting into any trouble.

Bouncers dress in pink and burgundy hosiery with velvet doublets, and carry truncheons in case anything gets too wild. Other staff members are dressed in costumes befitting the various characters in the Beefheart stories.

Sir Beefheart's Chevalier Tavern is owned and operated by Bertram Aeverart, an entertainer and spy who uses his position to gather information that he sells to wealthy friends in Reme and more unsavory friends in Tourse. Bertram often plies patrons with free drinks or private entertainment if he thinks they have information he might find valuable.

The Western Winds Tavern

This tavern and gaming house in the Central Market area caters to the various wagon drovers and cattlemen who ply their trade across Waymarch and the greater Duchy of Reme as a whole. The tavern is a bit more rustic and affordable than some of the others in the city and is known for serving delicious fresh-cut steaks that have been dry-aged in the tavern's special meat cellar, then roasted over pecan logs. These steaks are often served with roasted oats, rich whole wheat bread, and baked potatoes with butter and sour cream.

Cards, dice games, and other games of chance are played in a side parlor from the main hall. The parlor has open windows and is on the north side of the building where it can catch the breeze spring through fall — the better to draw the thick smoke of dwarven tobacco from the room.

Western Winds is managed by Boudein Isenbrant who has run the place since inheriting the family business. Western Winds has been owned by the Isenbrants for three generations, and Boudein's grandfather was a trailblazer and cattle drover who stumbled across a small fortune more than 100 years ago.

Recently, Boudein has had run-ins with the Wheelwrights Guild, who like the aesthetic of his family-owned operation and see the gambling parlor as a potential for criminal enterprise. This has brought the attention of the Brims, who are pressuring Boudein to hire them on as muscle and protection. Boudein would rather not deal with either, and may seek alternative means soon to relieve himself of the criminal element that keeps sniffing round his door.

Wild Rye Estate

Wild Rye Estate is an upscale inn by Panetoth's standards. The estate is located in the Castle District of the city and features a manor house and several outbuildings arranged to form a gated courtyard. The estate was once owned by a wealthy noble family, but was converted to an inn when the cattle owners were bankrupted by a drought that starved out their herd a century ago. A private investor took over the property and turned its various rooms and outbuildings into full-service geared toward wealthy visitors, essentially a resort.

The main house features a dining hall and ballroom located in the main building. The dining hall serves a seven-course meal, and the ballroom features a 12-piece orchestra of minstrels when hosting dances on the weekends. These dances are frequented by local socialites who are interested in meeting travelers from other duchies and across Akados.

Dozens of rooms are available to rent in the main house, with the majority of the rooms located on the second and third floors with balconies overlooking the courtyard, with staff and owners dwelling on the ground floor.

The outbuildings that once housed servants' quarters for the various staff of the Inn now serve as private "houses" for folk who wish to enjoy the amenities of the Wild Rye Estate without having to share walls with their neighbors. The outbuildings typically feature two to three rooms, including a parlor and two sleeping chambers.

The Bawdy Centaur

This slum dive in South City is a popular stop for those looking for something a little "different" in their lives. Many assume that the Centaur is a hangout for newly-arrived members of the Red Thumb from Reme, or that it may be a safehouse for the survivors of the Ebon Union or the Gavestones. In fact, it is none of these things. It is simply a wilder-than-usual bar that attracts young clientele and foreigners looking to meet up with unusual friends and let their hair down.

Grobel Slate, a famously lecherous dwarf, runs the place, having named it after bawdy stories he heard during service as a Road Agent before settling in Panetoth. He has a more or less anything-goes attitude so long as any blood that is spilled is in the alley out back. Gambling and ribaldry abound here, and Grobel has hired a handful of disparate mercenaries to serve as guards who make sure that things don't get too out of hand within the four walls of his establishment.

The upstairs of the inn has short-term rooms for rent that are more private than the curtained booths and broad benches of the common rooms below.

The Bawdy Centaur offers a wide range of amenities, beverages, and supplements but sells no food. For that, patrons must go elsewhere.

Tradeway Brewers

This halfling-run establishment has begun making its mark throughout the plains as a decent thirst quencher. Tradeway Ale is a bittersweet, crisp ale with hints of pine and sweet-grass. It is strong in locally sourced hops that are grown in specialty farms by Bucheron Bijous, owner of the brewery and his extended family. The brewery itself is found in the south side of the Central Market. The brewery employs two dozen halflings within the city who are easily recognized for their smart breeches, neatly-waxed hair, coiffured sideburns, and knowledge of all things involved in the brewing process. The ale itself is not very popular in Panetoth itself but seems to be the only brew that doesn't spoil during overland trips along the Tradeway. Dwarves claim that this is because the ale is already spoiled when it comes out of the vat. Be that as it may, Bucheron and the Bijou family are newly wealthy for their invention and are among a class of Panetothans that are rapidly moving up the social ladder.

Tradeway Ale

Tradeway Ale has not yet managed to develop a market among the denizens of Bard's Gate. Some suggest it is due to more sophisticated palates of the east. More likely it is due to the stranglehold that Brin Zweischer and Stoneheart Mountain Distilleries hold over the Bard's Gate's market. Whatever the reason, the halflings of Panetoth who have developed this bitter yet interesting flavor have gained some traction in Fareme and as far south as Tourse, where the bitterness seems in keeping with the rulers of Ysser.

Shops and Amenities

Sword of Borell

The Sword of Borell is a smithy and weapons-shop located near the Central Market. Named after one of the brave founders of the duchy, the signboard features a Foerdewaith knight on a rampant horse with a gleaming sword in his outstretched hand

Owned by Garrund Croix, the Sword of Borell is generally considered to be the best sword smithy in the Waymarch. Garrund Croix is always on the lookout for interesting bones to craft his steel with and pays handsomely for them. The bones are needed to infuse phosphorous in the steel so that it has the proper amount of flexibility. Some folk have taken to bringing in the femur of a long lost relative to have a sword made from it. Croix is happy to encourage this bizarre fashion until it dies away for some other craze.

Garrund's swords are of a finer cut than the swords wielded by the armies of Waymarch, as he pays special attention to detail. For that, they are prized by officers and adventurers. Swords crafted here tend to be of finer quality and as such are sold for 20% over market price.

Breastplates by Beatrix

Beatrix Lafvour, a young lady renowned for the quality of breastplates and armor she sells, runs this shop located in the Central Market. Many locals compare her armor to the quality of work that comes out of Eamonvale, as it should, since most of it indeed comes from Eamonvale through Beatrix's second profession as a fence for the Brims and their associates. This gang has found a perfect spot on the Eamon River south of Yalendir where they raid shipments of weapons and armor destined for Reme.

Beatrix is a smith of slightly better than rudimentary skill and magical means who uses the combination of techniques to remove the maker's mark from Eamonvale-constructed gear and replace it with her own.

The Hedge Apple's Bite

This Central Market shop is renowned for hundreds of miles around for its finely-crafted bows made from the hedge apple tree. These trees are renowned for their exceptionally strong and springy wood, which has been prized for centuries by the plainsfolk and Foerdewaith archers who have used them to great effect. The staves that the bows are made from are harvested at the edge of the Haunted Wood by members of the Beast Taker Loreclan and are traded to Noa Taigol, a high elf who has dwelt in Panetoth for over a century. Noa and her husband, Valeitian, a half-elf, are most often engaged in crafting bows to order for the duke's own archers. The pair finishes roughly 10 longbows per week and take special orders only if they are not previously under contract.

The pair's children are engaged in the crafting of arrows, though they buy their arrowheads from a local smith who offers them a bulk deal. It is the bows that truly draw customers here.

Yorwich Imports

Yorwich Imports is located near the caravan corrals in South City and ships large quantities of goods into and out of the city. Typically, they ship flaxseed oil, bolts of linen cloth, wool, and cotton grown in the large farms surrounding the city. Yorwich throws a lot of money around and has been invited to banquets at Castle Qellinroque.

Yorwich is an operative for the duke of Ysser and uses his trade connections to record troop movements, numbers, and training through the numbers of items that he sends to Fareme. The items are counted by Matteo Linus at Crossroads Center. A method of sending their messages has been adopted by which a certain number of bolts of linen represent archers and bottles of flaxseed oil represent cavalry numbers. Bolts of wool or cotton indicate which sides of the duchy troops are concentrated in at any given time.

Dame's Gowns

This dress shop is located in the upscale Castle District and sells dresses made of cotton, linen, silk, and woolens. The shop earns its name from the common affectation used to refer to the duchess of Waymarch. The gowns are worn by wealthier middle-class members of the community (as most of the working-class folk make their own clothes). The gowns are made by Valmont Corsean, a charming, mustachioed tailor with a flamboyant streak who has an eye for dressing up the ladies of the city. He imports silk from Reme for the highest-priced gowns that adorn the bodies of the courtiers in Qellinroque Castle. Corsean often hires Loreclan members to stitch beadwork into the cloth rather than using embroidery — a tradition in Reme that is slowly spreading into Foerdewaith fashions as well.

Wheelwrights Outpost

The Wheelwrights of Panetoth outpost is located in the Prairie Gate District. It is detailed below in the **Guilds and Organizations** section.

Panetoth Road Agency Headquarters

The headquarters of the Panetoth Road Agency is in the southwest side of the Central Market district. They are more thoroughly detailed below under **Guilds and Organizations**.

The Brokerage House

This large auction house sitting on the north end of Central Market is managed by members of the Brokerage League. The current chapter president is Lord Molay De Huhe. His operation is guarded by two dozen veteran knights in the service of the Brokerage League who ensure that the auctions are not robbed and that the league gets its cut of every deal contracted within their hall. Although the Brokerage House is not the only auction house in the city, it is by far the best connected. A percentage of their profits is shared with Duke Lucian, who allows their

guild to proceed under charter. Molay is frequently invited to counsel the duke in times of financial crisis or when trade disputes arise.

Guilds and Organizations

Wheelwrights Outpost

The reach of the Wheelwrights Guild extends only so far, and the Wheelwrights Outpost in Panetoth is the end of the road for the Bard's Gate-based organization in the Waymarch, though spies working on behalf of Duloth and his benefactors are indeed known to operate in the city of Reme for individual transactions. The Wheelwrights outpost is found in the Prairie Gate district, where they have already begun organizing drovers with their popular sales pitch of strength in numbers.

See **Encounters 13** and **14** in the *Convenient Reference Guide to Reme* for information about encounters with Wheelwright enforcers and caravans.

The Brokerage League

The Brokerage League is a group of traders, marketeers, auctioneers, and speculators who drive the markets in the major cities of the prairie. In Panetoth, the league representative is Lord Molay De Huhe, who advises the duke of Waymarch and the high priest of Sefagreth on investments and trade.

The Brims

The Brims are a local organized crime outfit descended from bandits who bought property and construction interests in the city. They found themselves in their current position due to the collapse of the Ebon Union's hold on the west.

The Brims earned their name from wide-brimmed hats cattle drivers wear out on the plains; they have adopted an exaggerated version of the hat that they wear in the city to denote their allegiances. They engage in thievery, banditry, strong-arm protection, and rackets of all kinds. The Brims keep their activities just out of sight of Duke Qellinroque and the mayor, and make sure that the majority of their earnings come from legitimate (albeit expensive) construction contracts overseen by Baron Faasha Hubert.

The Brims operate a different form of thievery than the Red Thumb, who have recently arrived in Panetoth and have an uneasy truce with them. The Red Thumb, for its part, recognizes the danger of confrontation with the "blunter" type of operation that the Brims manage and are instead interested in buying an interest in the Brims' operation — so they can eventually facilitate a hostile takeover. Baron Faasha is aware of the scheme and plans to tentatively agree to the alliance so that he can gather intelligence before executing the Thumb's operatives in Panetoth. He believes that a strong message to Reme should be enough to dissuade further incursions by the outside operation.

Panetoth Road Agency

Vice Commander Dunard Falcone is the acting head of the Road Agents. A lesser lord in his own right, he plays a double role of overseeing protection of caravans heading to Reme and Fareme as well as navigating complex political waters of the Duchy of Reme. He reminds the outfit to avoid situations where they would run afoul of the duke's official troops and orders them to aid the forces of Waymarch when called upon to do so.

Despite this, it has not been unheard of for units of the Road Agents to work against the interests of the grand duke when it comes to the defense of their clients or when an opportunity to enrich their outfit presents itself. This is because, ultimately, the Road Agency is mired in the protection racket. They offer bodyguard services for a fee, and it has long been suspected that they may indeed also create some of the threats that their services are hired to prevent.

The road agency has 50–100 mercenaries operating in the city at any given time, giving Dunard the largest private force within the city, a fact that is not lost on Duke Lucius Qellinroque.

See **Encounter 15** in the *Convenient Reference Guide to Reme* for information about encounters with guards from the Road Agency.

Temples

Temple of Mithras

The temple of Mithras, located in the Central Market, features motifs of huge, carved, marble lion-headed archons, and statues of sacrificial bulls adorn the high marble colonnades. A reflecting pool stands in the center of the colonnade. A staircase is built under the pool and leads to the true underground temple where the clerics keep their quarters and the grand cistern holds the blessed waters that stave off disease and dehydration for the denizens of the city of the great grassland march.

Bishop Roquelair the Rain Maker is the reigning high priest of this temple and is frequently found in the court of Qellinroque offering advice to the duke on matters of state and religion. Like the other temples of Mithras in the region, the chief concern is the production and protection of local water supplies due to the ongoing arid climate. Roquelair and his holy Purifiers see to the health, healing, and prevention of disease in the city. They charge the duke a tithe for the service, which he is more than willing to pay.

The great cistern holds enough water to protect the denizens of the city from siege for months.

See **Encounter 12** in the *Convenient Reference Guide to Reme* for information about priesthoods of Mithras.

Temple of Sefagreth

This temple, like many others throughout Akados, serves a dual purpose as a place of worship for the god of trade and as a secure banking location where merchant confederations store a portion of their wealth (with a small tithe in the name of the god). The temple of Sefagreth is located in the Castle District, where proximity to the army and hired guards affords it a greater amount of protection from would-be thieves.

The gardens of the outer temple are patrolled by guard dogs and a platoon of armored guards who are shielded against charms by the clerics of Sefagreth. The upper levels of the temple house the banking center and altar of Sefagreth and High Auditor Maxim Crysios' private chambers. Crysios is attended by four guarantors and 10 acolytes who handle the occasional deposits and withdrawals.

The vaults below the temple hold tens of thousands of gold pieces' worth of gold and jewels. The vault is allegedly guarded by deadly traps and terrifying beasts. The truth of this is unknown: No thieves are known to have successfully pierced the screen of protection surrounding the temple.

High Auditor Maxim Crysios has four audits who serve under his accounting. See **Encounter 16** in the *Convenient Reference Guide to Reme* for information about an audit of Sefagreth.

Temple Services: The temple of Sefagreth offers the deposit protection of valuables in increments of 1,000 gp of value. Like traditional banks, they offer loans with an expectation of 5%–10% interest on the value of the note. This is all bonded and scribed by the guarantors, who are allowed to handle loans of up to 5,000 gp in value. Loans of greater value must be bonded by Maxim Crysios himself.

Temple of Vanitthu

This fortress-temple is located in the Reme Gate district of Panetoth, where it receives a decent number of worshippers from the folk who live there. The temple of Vanitthu is popularized by the military of Waymarch and the nobles of Reme, and counts members of the Qellinroque family in its ranks. The temple is built in an austere fortress-like fashion not dissimilar to the temple in Bard's Gate. Officers of the Waymarch cavalry are known to donate silver to the temple in Panetoth on behalf of their troops before leaving on military expedition. On their return, they sacrifice the seized weapons of their foes upon the Altar of the Steadfast Guard.

Chaplain Kaisla the Bold is high priestess of the temple of Panetoth. A steely-eyed warrior priestess, she expects absolute bravery in deed and word from the guardians who serve under her. Kaisla's clerics frequently patrol with the soldiers of Waymarch and are expected to lead from the front, affording advice in defensive strategy and bolstering the bravery of troops. She has initiated an order of the Knights of Vanitthu in Panetoth and anointed Ser Jarroth as their paladin watchman.

Two dozen acolytes (guardians) serve under Chaplain Kaisla and two lieutenant chaplains are directly under Kaisla's command. See **Encounter 17** in the *Convenient Reference Guide to Reme* for priesthoods of Vanitthu.

Temple Services: The temple of Vanitthu offers blessings (and potions) associated with strength, bravery, and protection for sale or tithe. Heroes who perish in the performance of great deeds of bravery are brought back to life to serve again another day; this is a rare occurrence, however, and is costly in sacrifices to the deity.

The Compass Tower

The Compass Tower is the headquarters of the Wizard's Guild of Panetoth, which is located in the Reme Gate section of the city. The Compass Tower is allied with the Dominion Arcane in Bard's Gate and the Arcanum Collegium of Reme. Despite its arrangements with other guilds, the Compass tower is an independent consortium of wizards and sorcerers who gather at the ancient tower to further the study of academic and natural magic.

The magical tower is one of the tallest structures in Panetoth, standing over 300 feet tall. Portions of it rotate to point to both the polar north and south as well as magnetic north and south, giving precision directions that can be seen for a dozen miles outside of the city. The tower is built upon naturally occurring ley lines that enhance the power of spells cast within the tower itself.

The tower currently teaches three specific schools of magic as well as the power of pure unifying magic itself that has no particular school. There are roughly 20–30 students enrolled in the Compass Tower's program at any given time. Many of the students have their tuition paid by the duke himself and must work off the value of their training in a four-year term of service to Waymarch's military.

Lord Marracin the Diviner is the current chancellor of the Compass Tower. The most powerful wizard in the Waymarch, Marracin is an advisor to the court of Qellinroque and uses his keen powers of divination to interpret possible decisions and outcomes on behalf of the duke. This power helped Qellinroque negotiate the troubled times that led to the ascension of the current grand duke of Reme and allowed him to maintain his position and further his standing when many other nobles found themselves left outside the corridors of power.

Beneath the rank of the busy chancellor, actual teaching is supervised by Cloette Herriot, head matron of the schools of evocation and abjuration in the Compass Tower. She personally trains many of the wizards who go on to serve Duke Qellinroque, advising them in spells designed for maximum martial effect. Cloette has a history of adventure and has served the duke of Waymarch in battling against incursions of ogres and giants that sometimes rumble their way into the area. She was a member of the company led by the Grey Lady Eadith Dupond in her assault on Rolab the Glutton.

Rolphe Fennic heads the school of enchantment and illusion. His first love being the stage, Rolphe turned away from the entertainer's life to take a position in the Compass Tower. Rolphe is still known to perform at the Royal Theater, providing illusory backdrops and weaving his magic into performances so that the audience is fully rapt by the story that unfolds on stage, feeling that they too are a part of the show.

See **Encounter 18** in the *Convenient Reference Guide to Reme* for the inhabitants of the Compass Tower.

Ducal Theater of Panetoth

Located in the Reme Gate region of the city, this large, cathedral-like structure is a center for arts and entertainment in Panetoth. Though Panetoth is considered a military city, the culture that its soldiers collect during their service in Bard's Gate has brought with it a taste for fine entertainment, and theater has always been a passion among the Loreclans. The theater is the center of a thriving entertainment district that has just recently begun to grow around the Ducal Theater. Touring performances from Bard's Gate and Reme make their way to the theater a few times a year, and local talent has begun to put on its own performances. Typically, the local fare is in the retelling of Borell's ancient victories or operatic war stories. Loreclannic theater troupes perform tales from the plains and short performances from Reme and Bard's Gate.

The theater is managed by Grecian Calais, a local bard who is studied in the school of entertainment. He spends much of his time writing epic operettas popular with the Foerdewaith and the Loreclans.

Jousting Lists of Panetoth

Located between the Central Market and the Castle District are the Lists of Panetoth. Jousting is by far the most popular sport in Waymarch, both in the Foerdewaith heavy-armor style and in the light-armored Loreclannic style. It is seen as a means for the vanguard cavalry of Waymarch to practice their techniques and demonstrate their skill to the local populace (who bet heavily on their favored knights).

The jousting pitch holds competitions one day per week, with major month-long tourneys held in the early spring and late fall. The tourneys are held in conjunction with holy feasts of Vanitthu and Mithras.

The duke of Waymarch attends all three days of the matches during the Feast of Mithras and affords his colors to the overall champion of the tourney. This champion may wear the house colors of Qellinroque until they are defeated or abdicate their championship status, thereby leaving the colors open to new contenders. Abdication has happened in the past when former champions have died in battle against invaders from the Stoneheart Mountains or during border skirmishes with the Duchy of Ysser.

The Plains

Most of the Waymarch, along with the northern extant of the royal domain of the grand duke, consists of vast plains of rolling hills covered by grasses and sedges. Across these plains ride the Loreclans, the mostly-nomadic, horse-riding folk native to Reme. In the Waymarch, the largest Loreclans include the Grass Sailors, the Quick Knives, the Stone Faces, the Thunder Riders, the Stone Walkers, and the Beast Takers. With the exception of the Quick Knives, there are interrelations among all of the local Loreclans.

Superb horsemen and virtually unmatched light cavalry, the Plainsfolk are also great traders, able to carry the goods of Reme much more quickly than traditional caravans, although in smaller quantities.

Use the **Plains (General) Encounter Table** for random encounters on the Plains of the Waymarch.

Loreclans of the Waymarch Grasslands

Grass Sailors

The Grass Sailors are known for their endless treks across the great flowing prairie. Their name is loosely translated from "Those who cross the prairie as if blown by the wind." They keep premade defensive promontories for their Loreclan in the foothills of the High Downs, and hidden among outcroppings and arroyos of the prairie that are unseen to the untrained eye.

Grass Sailors cover more ground than any other Loreclan in the vast grasslands of Reme. In Waymarch, they are renowned for their knowledge of hidden water sources and are said to be able to find a rich, spring-fed well of fresh water even in the deepest drought.

Grass Sailors tend to be friendly with all other Loreclans save the Quick Knives, whom they deeply distrust, and indeed are known to fight brief and bloody battles with them on occasion. They are suspicious of activities in the southwestern Stoneheart Mountains and have begun to shun the area near there, traveling no farther north into that region than where Crossroads Center rests.

Quick Knives

The Quick Knives are an example of a Loreclan that has stretched tradition to the breaking point and beyond. The Quick Knives are the most infamous and problematic of the Plainsfolk Loreclans in the Waymarch. Purely nomadic, the Quick Knives tend to roam the areas between the plains of the Northmarches and the River Eamon, though their members are known to hire themselves out as caravan guardians, meaning bands of their warriors are found as far west as the City of Reme and as far east as Bard's Gate, where they have been spotted in Tent City.

They are disliked and disdained by Loreclans with adjoining territories, as they have been known to raid for horses and plunder — activities that are in many cases permitted under Loreclannic tradition, but certainly not with the frequency of the Quick Knives' depredations. The Quick Knives have legendary tempers. They tend to shave the sides and back of their head, leaving only a long crop on top to grow. This is threaded with porcupine quills collected along the banks of the Eamon River to form great headdresses that further their horrific visage when they paint their bodies with rouge and greasepaint before heading into battle. The Quick Knives are careful not to raid villages and towns, for this falls immediately and squarely outside Loreclannic tradition and would be dealt with swiftly by the duke. Their favored deity is Bowbe, though it is believed that some subsets may have taken to worshipping fiends of the underworld. It is very likely that the Loreclan of the Quick Knives will be eradicated in the near future once nearby Loreclans finally join against them with the support of the duke — unless they retreat beyond the borders of Reme, as many renegade clans do.

Flint Faces

The Flint Faces are a dour people; other Loreclans unsettled by their refusal to show emotion in commerce, battle, or ceremony gave them their name. They have no battle cries, sing no songs, and are seldom seen to smile. They further do not inscribe any sigil upon their leather and wood shields. Their adornment is always of a utilitarian, though finely crafted, nature. They follow Dame Torren and Halatra. It is said that the Flint Faces point their lodges facing north to commemorate the ancient homeland beyond the Crynnomar Gap, for the Flint Faces are a Loreclan that was allowed into Reme centuries ago from these northern lands. They secretly spend a part of each year carving solemn faces into the ridges of the Green Mountains facing the direction of the Wizard's Wall. Why they have done this for centuries is unknown to most. Members of their Loreclan spend moon cycles tending the corral in Eamonvale for their share of profits that were negotiated for them with the earls of Dun Eamon, passing through Waymarch, and stopping at Yalendir or Quintas on their trek across the prairie. This is a well-traveled Loreclan whose lore includes pathways across the territory of a number of other Loreclans in between the Green Mountains and Eamonvale. The Flint Faces are semi-nomadic, with pasturelands near the Green Mountains and Eamonvale.

Thunder Riders

The Thunder Riders are a proud and boisterous Loreclan of hard-drinking, hard-fighting warriors who work among the Foerdewaith as mercenary bodyguards and spears for hire. They tie strings of hollowed gourds to the saddles of their horses to create a thunderous wave of sound across the prairie when they charge into battle, thus earning them their name.

Thunder Riders worship Gromm the Thunderer. They paint their bodies with black greasepaint highlighted with white lightning bolts down their bodies and paint lightning bolts on the legs and faces of their horses before riding into battle.

Thunder Riders are most commonly encountered in the northern prairies of the Waymarch. They are intense rivals of the Quick Knives, whom they compete with for mercenary jobs guarding caravans. They have been known to raid one another's villages when the opportunity presents itself, which leads to bloody feuds that often pashtars fail to mediate. The duke's patience has been severely tried by constant appeals from the Quick Knives and — more commonly — the Thunder Riders.

The Star Walkers

Star Walkers are master navigators; their title is derived from the plainsfolks' words for "Those who walk by the night sky." It is a mark of respect for their celestial knowledge, although some Loreclans consider them to have their heads in the clouds too often. They are the most scholarly of the Waymarch Loreclans. Star Walkers follow the trail of the constellations and provide warnings of oncoming weather, such as predicting droughts or preparing their folk for seasons where more tornadoes or snow may be expected than others and moving their campsites accordingly.

Their Loreclan has practitioners of animistic druidic traditions and counts various skin-changers among its shamans and Loreclannic knights. The Star Walkers are further filled with knowledge of arcane magic, following a non-traditional school of arcane study. Students of the Arcanum Collegium have been known to seek Star Walkers for knowledge not recorded in the dusty tomes of their august institution.

Beast Takers

The Beast Takers are the greatest huntsmen of the Waymarch plains; while they see their name as a point of honor, the other Loreclans refer to them as such because they feel they take more game than necessary. They are superior trackers, archers, and leather craftsmen.

Beast Takers are respectful of Star Walkers and Grass Sailors, but dislike the Thunder Riders and are in a state of feud with the Quick Knives. They typically range the southern duchy where they provide wild game to various outposts and trade horses with the knights of the garrisons of Waymarch. In late summer, they make a pilgrimage to the cooler regions just south of the High Downs. On their way, they generally spend some time at the corral of Dun Eamon.

THE TRADEWAY

This major trade road runs all the way from the city of Reme in the west, past Bard's Gate, and to Freegate on the coast of the Sinnar Sea. Some merchant companies that exist solely for the caravan run on this road. A typical caravan takes roughly one year to travel the entire length, with seasonal stopovers in Panetoth, Fareme/Bard's Gate, and Arendia.

Use the **Road Encounters Table** for random encounters on the Tradeway.

Tree of the True Heart
Westwood
Elkbow River
Tower of Jhedophar
West Fortress
City of Cats
Windreft
Carnival Village
Khaztrecht
Quail Valley
Varazath
N
1 Hex = 50 Miles
Green
Mountains
City of the Lost
Quail River
Western Akadian Forest
Wessem Forswen
Shining Temple
Eckland
Caer D
Dunavenwo
Duchy of Westmarch
Bones
Hollow Mountain
Kemresen
Ontheliavn River
Knife's Edge Ridge
Glondarr
Baronswood
Martyn's Bay
Martyn's Nest
Seaside
Western Reme Road
Fenria
Gilboat
Legend
Town or Village
City
Capital or Free City
Imperial Capital
Fortress or Citadel
Ruins
Place of Interest
Road
Trail or Unused Road
Mountain Pass

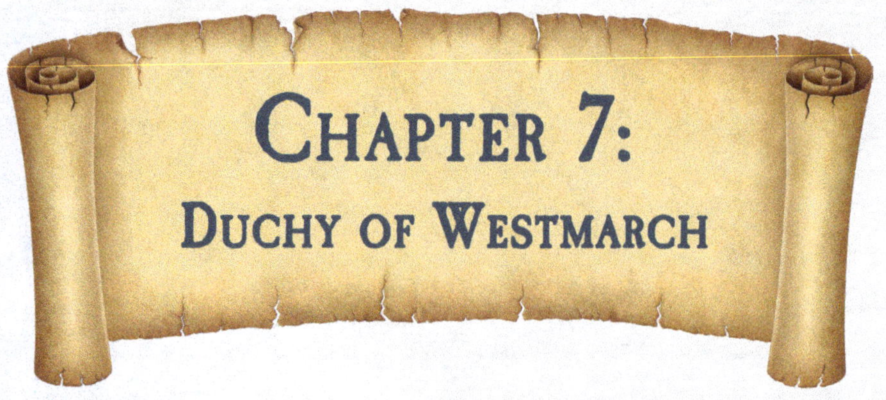

Chapter 7:
Duchy of Westmarch

Overview

Alignment: Neutral
Ruler: Duke Wylan Rogers
Capital: Eckland
Government: Feudal
Population: 1,224,789 (Foerdewaith 470,839, Loreclans 604,844, halfling 79,065, half-elf 45,209, hill dwarf 11,176, mountain dwarf 8,211, high elf 3,890, other humanoid 1,555)
Monstrous: Orcs, hobgoblins
Languages: Common, Rhemish, Elven
Religion: Quell, Mithras, Dame Torren, Halatra (plains)
Resources: Cattle, grains, fish, pearls, emeralds
Currency: Rhemish
Technology Level: Medieval
Demonym/Adjectival Demonym: Westmark, Westmarch

The Duchy of the Westmarches has been a problem for the grand dukes of Reme for generations. At least four of the leading families of the March have fought among themselves for as long as they can recall over slights that no one remembers. These families each have the support of more than one Loreclan, and the pashtars have not been able to broker any sort of mediated peace among them. As a result, this region has been plagued with infighting that finally degraded over the last several decades into regular eruptions of outright civil war. Various grand dukes mediated or interfered in various ways — but without lasting success. Every tenuous peace was eventually followed by new acts of ever-escalating retribution for claimed or perceived wrongdoing.

Two years ago, Grand Duke Iltobarus brokered another new peace when he elevated Wylan Rogers to the ducal seat at Eckland. Duke Wylan — of Foerdewaith ancestry but backed by a number of influential Loreclannic pashtars — managed to pacify his opponents and restore order to the duchy once more, but much traditional strife lurks under the surface still, and few believe yet that the Westmarches are likely to see a lasting peace.

Most of the population of the Westmarches lives in the southern and eastern sections of the duchy, with a more Foerdewaith-type feudal structure closer to the city. The farther north and west one goes, the wilder the land becomes and the more Loreclannic the culture becomes. Warring groups of allied Loreclannic barons have each staked out less-populated territories in the Westmarch wilderness, with the full intention of disobeying the peace imposed by the new grand duke, as soon as they see a clear opportunity to do so.

History and People

Kept impoverished by constant internal conflict, the people of the Westmarches are mostly simple folk, and their nobility (both Foerdewaith and Loreclannic) are considered a bit on the boorish and backwater side by the high society of the grand duke's court. Culturally, Westmarchers are more passionately mercurial than the average Reman; their traditional local foods are creamier, richer, and larger of portions than typical for the rest of Reme.

The Westmarches were first settled by Hyperboreans and conquered by the Remish urban Loreclans during the generations of expansion of the city of Reme (then Remenos). The geography of the Westmarches is in several places ill-suited to large populations, being often poor or rocky of soil and prone to unpredictable flooding nearly everywhere else. For this reason, when the Hyperboreans began to withdraw from the Reme region, the Westmarches fell deeper into disorganized squabbling than did most other settled areas in Reme. The oldest, most powerful Loreclannic and Hyperborean families in the Westmarches began during this era as bandit lords, and a long tradition of competitive raiding between these communities sprang up.

Though eastern Westmarch lands never descended entirely back to wilderness, as did parts of the Northmarches, the authority of the Reman grand duke remained ever tenuous among the Westmarch families, and the assembly of a ducal "nation" of Loreclans never managed to take hold in the Westmarches as well as it did under the dukes of the Northmarches and the Waymarch. For this reason, the Westmarch nobility has a status of "count," not often seen in other Rhemish territory, to designate Loreclannic or Foerdewaith leaders who hold the allegiance of settlements and cities in a layer of Rhemish feudalism below the duke. In consequence, the feudal hierarchy is more layered, and the duke less powerful, than in other dukedoms of Reme where Loreclannic barons are directly loyal to the duke, with only an informal layer of mediating pashtars in between.

For many generations, the best solution Reme's leaders could muster was to appoint dukes or duchesses of the Westmarches since there was no single, dominant Loreclan to step into that role as a single ducal "family." The appointed dukes were relatively powerless mediators, whose primary role was to maintain order in the west at all costs, and to do so without uniting the local Loreclannic baronies against them. Some of these appointees — the ones relying most heavily on pashtars and the least heavily on troops — were more successful than others, but over time the traditions surrounding the maintenance of the duke's palace and other positions of authority in Eckland crept slowly in favor of the Brodchek family, until they were able to influence ducal policy in Brodchek favor, much to the distress of the Harrings, Fenrith-Draguls, and especially the Merciers.

Eventually, without the awareness of the grand duke or his appointed figurehead, the duke, the Westmarches ran almost entirely at Brodchek whims, almost as if the Brodchek family were an underground criminal organization. The Harrings and Merciers petitioned the duke to repair matters, only to find that he had little authority to do so, while the grand duke, due to misinformation from Brodchek-tampered sources, accused both the Harring and Mercier families of inventing slights out of bitterness over their long rivalry. At that point, the Harrings and Merciers, with their allied Loreclans and feudal infantry, temporarily put aside their own differences and lay siege to the Brodchek family fortress. The Brodchek heir, Lady Fiah, was slain soon thereafter by Count Mercier's own brother in a short but bloody Brodchek sortie she led out among the Mercier and Harring forces.

Though that particular conflict was forcibly ended by the grand duke's own soldiery after a mere few weeks, peace in the Westmarches has been a rare and fleeting thing ever since. Alliances, power balances, and motivations have shifted to and fro, with the Harrings switching loyalties now and again or waging side conflicts with the Fenrith-Draguls, but at the core of it all, the Merciers and Brodcheks have been constantly at one another's throats since Lady Fiah's death more than 20 years ago.

Finally, less than four years ago, the duke of the Westmarches was murdered in his bed. The Brodcheks blamed the Merciers and Fenrith-Draguls for the murder, the Harrings and Merciers both blamed the Brodcheks, and the Fenrith-Draguls blamed the Harrings. Law enforcement fell into chaos, and Grand Duke Iltobarus was forced to take a direct hand in restoring order.

Changing the old laws that hampered the power of the Westmark dukes and duchesses, a finally fed-up Iltobarus appointed one of his trusted generals, one Wylan Rogers, as duke, and granted him nearly total autonomy to bring the Westmarches to heel by any means necessary. A charmingly rustic sort of man with a booming voice and a deceptively quick blade, Wylan is popular with the pashtars, the Loreclans, and much of the Foerdewaith nobility as a fair choice of leader to unite the duchy. Duke Wylan has managed to manipulate, intimidate, and otherwise browbeat the various warring factions into settling down, at least for the time being. He did track down the old duke's killer, but the woman turned out to be a hired assassin and escaped custody before her employer was ever revealed. All of the warring families continue to suspect one another in the assassination, though Duke Wylan has intimated that he believes the assassin to have been hired by a foreign power in order to destabilize the region. It is unknown whether this is his sincere suspicion or a ruse to discourage further infighting.

Whatever the case, Duke Wylan and Grand Duke Iltobarus have convinced Lusea Mercier, the Mercier count's eldest daughter, to wed young Relm Brodchek, the current Brodchek earl's heir and Lady Fiah's nephew. Relm and Lusea are both attractive, healthy, intelligent youths, and seem dedicated to bringing their families together in peace, but their marriage has been off to a rocky start since Lusea gave birth a mere eight months after the wedding, and some are now saying she was far too eager to wed a boy she barely knew, from a family she was raised to despise. A herald of the Mercier house apparently fled under suspicion of scandal not long before the marriage as well. Though known for his naive idealism, Relm Brodchek does seem to suspect that Lusea's child isn't his, and many begin to worry that this peace-bringing marriage may in the end inspire the opposite.

As for the Harrings and Fenrith-Draguls, both have always prided themselves on greater subtlety than the Merciers and Brodcheks, so while they all say publicly that they support the new duke's peace efforts, no one knows for certain what Count Harring or Countess Fenrith may be plotting behind the scenes.

Duke Wylan has, however, drastically rearranged the governance of the Westmarches in the name of fairness and balance between the families, and has temporarily outlawed the maintenance of a standing militia outside his own command, save for small forces of household or town guards, and these only with case-by-case permission. In this regard, Wylan Rogers' peace in the Westmarches is different from any ever tried before, because his first step was to persuade the four families' military commanders and win the hearts of their soldiers. Having inspired the common-born soldiery with impassioned-yet-folksy oratory about the joy and prosperity of peacetime, Duke Wylan has cut off the prime troublemakers from the majority of their power to keep fighting.

All suspect that the four families (and perhaps other, lesser nobles in the duchy) secretly retain more loyal troops than they are legally allowed, and no one believes that decades of war can be brushed aside with one simple wedding. But Duke Wylan is wildly popular with the common people, and as long as he also wields all of the duchy's major military might, it seems likely that the long war may be over. Of course, if Wylan Rogers remains unable to discover who hired the last duke's assassin, he may not be able to keep the ducal seat long enough to seal a lasting peace in the Westmarches. The former duke's murderer must be found before a new assassin is sent for Duke Wylan.

RELIGION

The Westmarches are, in general, not very interested in religion. They worship any gods that seem appropriate, without much thought given to theology or scripture. That said, the most popular deities in the duchy are Freya, Mithras, and Solanus, and all three are used as excuses for grand festivals, dances, feasts, and frivolity, whenever anyone can drum up any rationale for celebrating. The Loreclans, for their part, worship Solanus, Dame Torren, and Halatra. Priests in the Westmarches are usually imported from elsewhere in Reme, and Westmarch churches and temples are almost always underfunded, save during festival time.

Notable exceptions to this trend include all who make their living from the sea along the southern coast. Here, worship is taken very seriously, especially worship of "the Sea God" (known elsewhere as Quell, though few in the Westmarches speak his name aloud out of respect). The most popular temple in the Westmarches is the Sea Temple in Martyn's Nest, and the head priest there is sometimes consulted by Westmarch rulers.

Another exception to typical Westmarch secularism is the cult of St. Sophia, a rural phenomenon in the Caer Dire and Dunavenwood regions, sprung up around a grisly old tale that some claim was the original foundation of the yet-ongoing feud between the Harrings and the Fenrith-Draguls. The cult centers upon reverence for an ancient oak tree believed to be, in some way, the reincarnation of the brutally murdered Sophia Westmarche Dunaven, the last lady to marry into the now-defunct Dunaven noble family. Practice seems to mostly center around defense of the tree itself.

A recent schism in the cult has formed two branches: one is led by Jon Oakborn, sheriff of the Wood Wards, and the other by Sara of Westmarche, prophetess of the Riders of Westmarche. Westmarche claims direct descent from St. Sophia herself, though this should be impossible. The Harring family (who contain the remnants of the old Westmarche family and have inherited the old Westmarche holdings) have yet to comment on Sara's claims, but the Fenrith-Draguls, who long ago captured the loyalty of most of the old Dunaven Loreclans together with their direct landholdings, have officially decried her as a charlatan. Worship of St. Sophia is expressly forbidden on Fenrith-Dragul lands.

TRADE AND COMMERCE

Trade is finally returning to the Westmarch along with the peace established by the new duke. The port of Martyn's Nest sees seaborne traffic from around the Crescent Sea, most of which comes for the pearls obtained in the nearby coastal waters and for the emeralds mined from the Green Mountains and cut by the Gemcutters Guild based in the port. Cattle ranching can be found in the southern and western portions of the duchy, with sparser Loreclan herds occupying the rest of the duchy.

Internal strife has held back the commerce of much of the Westmarches, which tends toward a barter economy among the commoners and a fixation among the nobility with siege weaponry and countermeasures.

The exception to this, and the source of most of the duchy's revenue, is the Westmarch coastline — especially Martyn's Nest. Enriched by sea trade of many varieties, including goods from the growing Tycho Free States, and being also Reme's second-largest port city, Martyn's Nest is a wealthy and stylish city largely untouched by the duchy's decades of civil war. Martyn's Nest's market district is also known far and wide for its wondrous gemcutters guildhall, considered among the greatest architectural works of the Crescent Sea.

Other major revenue sources in the Westmarches come from livestock in the west, out beyond most of the fighting, and the emerald mines in the Green Mountains. Duke Wylan is working hard to restore the prosperity of the Duke's Market in Eckland, and merchants and farmers in the region have reported increasing profits each year since his appointment. The duke's third daughter, Emna, is known to be fond of numbers and of analytical projection, and has been serving as Duke Wylan's chief financial adviser, to apparently excellent effect thus far.

LOYALTIES AND DIPLOMACY

Despite their internal squabbling (or perhaps because of it), Westmarchers traditionally take great pride in being part of the Grand Duchy of Reme. Most call themselves Rhemish before Westmarcher, and consider their culture and traditions to be "true Rhemish heritage." As such, Westmarch forces can always be counted on for Reme's defense, and more so than ever now that Wylan Rogers has claimed all of the Westmarches' armies for himself and enjoys the friendship he does with Grand Duke Iltobarus. In general, the Westmarches' loyalties are Reme's loyalties, and all Westmarch diplomacy takes place through or under the direction of the grand duke.

That said, rumor has been circling of late of a young girl living as a ward under the protection of the countess of Aciier out in the outer marches between the Green Mountains and the Westwood who looks very much like the supposedly-childless former grand duke and duchess. Though the few remnants of the Decian family (the former line of the grand dukes) lost their claim to the grand ducal line long ago, it is said that emissaries from their ancestral lands in the north have been seen snooping about the western Westmarches, perhaps seeking the truth of these rumors. For her part, Aciier's countess claims absolute loyalty to Iltobarus and the new Calvian grand ducal line, and as Aciier has traditionally refused to involve itself in typical Westmarch squabbles, the Aciier family is in high favor with Duke Wylan. Only time will tell if treachery or revolution might be brewing in the Westmarch countryside.

GOVERNMENT

Duke Rogers is in large part taking full control of the levers of power within Westmarch. He has appointed trusted friends and advisors to all of the positions of authority within the duchy, and so far, the vast majority of them appear competent and trustworthy. But he has a long way to go before he can claim to have excised all the decay and corruption that has taken deep root from decades of internal strife.

Wylan Rogers was an admiral in the Rhemish navy before a sea hag's curse (the precise nature of which he does not disclose) forced him to change careers to the army some years before his appointment as duke of the Westmarches. Fortunately for himself and his family, he has exceled at both military and civilian leadership on land, nearly as well as he did at sea. He served in the Westmarches as a general of cavalry, which put him into contact with the Westmarch Loreclans, and befriended a number of the region's most influential pashtars. These connections have stood him in good stead now that he is the duke, since a number of Loreclans originally loyal to the region's various counts have transferred their loyalty to him personally in his capacity as duke. No doubt this is due to his popularity among the pashtars, but it is also the more traditional Rhemish structure of government, and tradition is always a strong factor in decisions made by the Loreclans. His wife and eight daughters report that while he still speaks wistfully of his years upon the waves, he seems happier with his current position and spends a great deal of time with his family — another characteristic that weighs in his favor among the Loreclans.

Wylan Rogers is the first duke of the Westmarches in several centuries to have total feudal power in the region, with little check on his authority barring decrees from the grand duke himself. Traditionally, the duke of the Westmarches has not been an inherited position, as part of the constant dance to keep any one Westmarch family from gaining enough power to start trouble with the others. However, given Duke Wylan's unusual level of authority, some have postulated that if he succeeds at keeping the peace in the Westmarches, perhaps his family will be gifted the ducal seat in perpetuity as a reward. Should this happen, he will be succeeded by his eldest daughter Vyla, who currently serves as her father's chief tactical advisor and is making quite a name for herself throughout the Westmarches. Her military style is clever and inventive, and she takes great care to avoid loss of life in all conflicts, wherever possible. The duke saw to it that his children's education included pashtar tutors, and Vyla's use of light cavalry certainly shows the influence of Loreclannic battle-theory in addition to the more traditional Foerdewaith use of infantry and heavy cavalry. She has even experimented with mixed units in the same manner as the Waymarch cavalry operate.

MILITARY

The Westmarch land military, currently centrally controlled by the duke, has primarily served as a peacekeeping force. It is used to guard the countryside against bandits and monsters, as well as to minimize opportunities for feuding noble families to pick fresh fights with one another. In addition, all noble households are permitted a small personal guard for their own security, and a few towns without ducal barracks are permitted to organize semi-professional guard militias. Ducal barracks dot the outer Westmarch borders and are common in all major Westmarch cities as well as most larger towns, so the duke's own forces keep most of the region safe for travel and trade.

More popular in the Westmarches than the army, at least in the south, is the Rhemish navy, which is made up disproportionately of Westmarch-born sailors. The Westmarch coast is very well defended by the Rhemish armada, and many a Westmark aristocrat has served for a time as a naval officer during younger years.

MAJOR THREATS

The most obvious ongoing threat to the Westmarches is the internal feuding among its powerful families. While all the family heads currently claim that their differences are settled and that they are dedicated to peace, no one believes — even if the leaders are sincere — that every member of every family is of the same mind. Young hotheads seeking excitement or bitter old veterans with a grudge might yet find excuses to renew the violence.

Between the Brodcheks and Merciers, even if young Relm and Lusea are devoted to their alliance and able to resolve their marital issues privately, it is said that the older soldiers in both families are likely to dismiss the young couple's dedication to peace should the Brodcheks uncover any sort of hard evidence that Lusea was already pregnant when she married Relm. As for the Harrings and Fenrith-Draguls, the new schism in the cult of St. Sophia could potentially be spun into a renewal of the two families' ancient property disputes, depending on how the Harring count ultimately chooses to respond to the claims of Sara of Westmarche.

The Westmarches do face other threats, however, both internal and external, including the usual coastal pirates, wilderness bandits, and occasional monstrous incursions. No one yet knows, either, who paid for the assassination of the last duke, and no one knows whether Duke Wylan or his family might be in danger still. If the perpetrator was a foreigner, as the duke claims to believe, what foreign body is seeking to destabilize western Reme and why? Castorhage is the prime suspect, but the details remain unclear even if this should turn out to be true. Castorhagi officials deny all such allegations as absurd, of course. The assassin in question is being tracked by an elite team of the grand duke's own choosing, it is said, but her identity has not been made public, and if her employer should find a way to silence her before she is recaptured, it may prove difficult to ever discover said employer's motives.

It should also be noted that the Green Mountains have been found to contain some of the realm's least-guarded entrances to the continent-spanning Under Realms. Should the denizens of the Under Realms ever feel the time is right to emerge in force against the nation of Reme, it is not believed that quiet Quail Valley or the inhabitants of the surrounding mountains are likely to be able to prevent the drow or other creatures of the Under Realms from gaining a strong foothold there and using the Green Mountains as their base of operations for a larger campaign. Preventing such an incursion is a more important priority for the Westmarches than any may yet realize.

WILDERNESS AND ADVENTURES

Though nominally a part of the Westmarches, the Westwood, Endless Hills, Windreft, and much of the Green Mountains are only sparsely settled. Indeed, only east of the Windreft and south of the Green Mountains are the Westmarches truly organized into farms, villages, and cities with maintained roads between. Even the foothills just east of the southernmost tail of the Green Mountains are primarily wild lands inhabited by a diverse blend of species, monstrous and otherwise. The Loreclans of this area are sparse, with large territories and small populations.

Banditry and raids are common, especially from species on less friendly terms with the legal authorities of Reme, such as orcs, hobgoblins, trolls, and others.

Use the **Plains (General) Encounter Table** for random encounters on the Plains of the Westmarches.

REFERENCE SOURCES

The Book of Taverns, *A Family Affair*, *Town of Glory*, *Demonheart*, *Razor Coast*

LOCATIONS IN THE WESTMARCHES

ACIIER RIVER

ORIGIN IN THE FRONTIER

The Aciier River runs from a source in the Ashen Hills and is fed by several tributaries with sources in the Deepfells, all joining not far north of Dreikeng in the Northmarches Frontier. It merges with the placid Fehlween as it passes between the Eisenwood and Sternwood, and from there wends its course through much of the Westmarches, all the way to its junction with the Quail, just north of Eckland.

An unpredictable and flood-prone river, the Aciier is nevertheless the best trade transport available for the sparse populations and often-isolated communities past which it runs. Up near Dreikeng, the river is tamer, and better suited to the barges by which Eisenwood red cedar logs are shipped to market from that region. About 50 miles north of where the flow first rounds the northwesternmost spur of the Green Mountains, the watercourse has a tendency toward flash flooding, unreadable and variable depths and speeds, and even course changes from season to season after the floods recede. Much of the river's banks are mud or even swamp, sometimes for more than a mile in either direction.

DOWNRIVER IN THE WESTMARCH REGION

Aciier river pilots are some of the best in the world, especially those who operate in the Westmarches' Aciier province. Most of these are apprenticed for years in the town of West Fortress, where the Aciier rushes past three low, wide granite tors, making life near the river slightly less uncertain there than it is for most of the Aciier's length. West Fortress journeyman and master pilots often make their way to Dreikeng in the north or to Silverlight or even Eckland in the south to wait for craft that need an Aciier-specialized pilot. Even the best river pilots from elsewhere in the world have trouble reading the Aciier's many terrible moods, so it's always advisable to hire someone with training for the unique conditions and subtle cues one needs to recognize in order to know when and whether any given stretch of the Aciier is safe to travel upon.

Sometimes, even in peak trade seasons when the river is at its least disagreeable, certain stretches become impassible with any degree of safety. This may be due to recent rockslides down the Green Mountains (especially in the Windreft), submerged logs or even boulders from recent flooding, the occasional giant electric catfish, or the relative likelihood of an imminent flash flood. For this reason, Aciier river barges are usually designed with flat bottoms and attachable wheels for ease of portage, and little mini-forts dot the banks ahead of many of the river's worst problem stretches, with extendable ramps, hauling stays, or other useful emplacements to help maneuver a craft up onto stable ground for portaging. In bad seasons, some heavier barges travel with an accompanying livestock barge so that mules or oxen can do most of the portage work, where necessary.

In the lower Aciier province, south of West Fortress and just north of the Windreft, the river's course is the most changeable from year to year. In some years, the water even splits into two or more narrower rivers here after a flood recedes. Such years are particularly hazardous for river travel, with higher than average likelihood of giant electric catfish or even catoblepas encounters. In addition, choosing which fork of the river to take is one of the many Aciier-unique problems for which Aciier pilot-apprentices study in order to avoid hull damage or worse.

The Windreft is perhaps the most hazardous stretch of all, though less so since the constant fighting has ceased there due to the end of the Westmarch civil war. Even without the threat of becoming collateral damage in a pitched battle, however, the Windreft stretch of the river is also prone to rockslides from the mountains, roc attacks in the autumn, other dangerous creatures wandering down from the Green Mountains or up from the Green Warden Forest, or simple bandits. The river's course is deep cut and predictable here, but can be extremely swift at times, and recently submerged detritus from rockslides is not always visible in the Aciier's typically muddy waters. Choosing the center, north, or south "lanes" of the river's flow can be the difference between life and death here. Aciier pilots are trained to choose the safest routes through this stretch, both for hull integrity and to avoid more active threats.

Passed the Windreft, the Aciier quiets down somewhat, though it's still inadvisable to travel it in winter due to the chance of flooding. River traffic is heaviest in this section, however, so it remains wise to know the local etiquette for passing other barges or for having the bascule bridge raised at Kemresen, if necessary.

Use the **River (General) Encounter Table** for random encounters on the Aciier.

REFERENCE SOURCES

The Six Spheres of Zaihhess

Baronswood

This impassible coastal forest covers the Baronswood Peninsula between Martyn's Bay and the Bay of Biscone. Reme's Forest Coast Road runs around the Baronswood along the shore, then through Martyn's Nest and the other surrounding coastal towns, so passage is possible in that way. Many travelers also choose to pass from Martyn's Bay to the Bay of Biscone by boat as well. Since the impenetrability of the Baronswood does not interfere with transport or shipping, few have seen the value in cutting a way through the wood itself, and the forest remains largely untouched.

The wood was named generations ago when it was part of the land belonging to the then-baron of the Martyn's Nest region. This was the noble family's private hunting area, the legend says, complete with the grandest, most decadent hunting lodge ever built. None can prove, however, whether this tale was ever true, as none living in the region today can remember a time when the Baronswood forest was safe to cross. If the ruins of a hunting lodge can indeed be found inside, none alive today has ever laid eyes upon it — at least, no human has.

Some do enter the edges of the wood, particularly to view the giant crystals that grow on the Baronswood peninsula, and local guides know well how far it is to safely enter among the trees. Any of them will warn travelers, of course, that even the edges of the forest are deadly at night. Adventurers seeking to pierce the wood's heart are always strongly dissuaded from such an endeavor by any locals who learn of the expedition. Everyone in the region knows that all who attempt to cross through the Baronswood are never heard from again, and no one knows for certain why. Certainly nothing comes out of it to prey upon townsfolk or ships, at least so far as anyone can prove.

Rumor has it, however, that the green dragon Aureensaador makes her home in this wood, and sometimes, when ships are lost at sea — especially those craft carrying a large haul of fresh fish — people blame the disappearance on dragon attack. Whether or not a dragon claims these woods as her home, however, it cannot be denied that for some decades now, those who step too far in under its branches never leave. The most famous example of this came early in the Westmarch civil war when Baron Gummel, in an act that ultimately cost him his lands and title, boxed in a fleeing band of routed Brodchek soldiers and forced them to retreat into the Baronswood. Not one of the band ever emerged, out of — some say — hundreds of troops. Granted, Loreclannic stories often choose to exaggerate numbers to achieve the proper poetic effect.

Adding to the Baronswood's aura of mystery, a very old chronicle of the region was uncovered a few years back, from where it had lain hidden for centuries in a vault a thousand miles away in another country. A Waymarch merchant purchased it, brought it back to Reme, and gave it to Duke Wylan as a gift. This chronicle, so rumor says, describes an ancient palace of crystal in the southeastern Baronswood that was grown magically by elves and fashioned centuries before the Baronswood region was cut off from the Great Akadonian Forest. This palace is rumored to contain treasures unimaginable, ancient magics, and powerful secrets. It is also said to either be or be somehow connected to the popular old legend of the former baron's grand hunting lodge, though the unearthed chronicle implies nothing of the kind.

Boats in the Bay of Biscone, too, are now claiming to see the most beautiful flashes of crystal through the trees whenever the sun shines in under their branches at dawn. To this, the objective reply is that giant crystals grow naturally in the Baronswood. It means nothing of great import than some are well-positioned to catch the dawn light. Many folk are enthralled by the possibility of an ancient elven palace, however, and despite the locals' fear and respect for the wood, sentiment in favor of an expedition to find this palace of crystal is growing, not only in and around Martyn's Nest, but perhaps more so in Eckland, where rumors about the crystal palace seem far more immediate than rumors about unknown forest perils.

Use the **Forest Encounter Table** for random encounters in Baronswood.

Caer Dire

Alignment: Chaotic Neutral
Ruler: Brazzer Mandragore
Government: Autocracy
Population: 583 (ogre 276, goblin 154, human [mostly Foerdewaith] 139, half-orc 14)
Languages: Common, Giant, Goblin
Religion: Ancestor reverence (ogres and goblins), St. Sophia (humans)
Resources: Ogre- and goblin-style alcoholic beverages and foodstuffs
Technology Level: Medieval (to many visitors' surprise)

Centuries ago, a bizarre and grotesque tragedy ended with a practice quintain housed in the top of the abandoned Caer Dunaven castle tower and the shameful end of the once-noble Dunaven house. The castle fell into ruin within a few generations, but the quintain's tower remains to this day, and this is the central structure of the approximately 50-mile-radius region now known as Caer Dire.

Though these lands were given, at the time, to the then-Foerdewaith Dragul family, and though Caer Dire technically remains within the territory of the surviving Rhemish branch-family of Fenrith-Dragul, it has been centuries since anyone has made a real attempt to bring order to the region. Countess Fenrith, like her predecessors, relies instead upon the rangers known as the Wood Wards to maintain these wildlands and keep their monstrous inhabitants from terrorizing anyone outside this little realm that has been all but officially granted to the monsters.

Thus, the land technically belongs to Countess Fenrith, and the Wood Wards are technically her servants. In reality, however, the Fenrith-Draguls ignore the place and can be quite superstitious about even visiting. They make no attempts to enforce the same laws in Caer Dire that they do in other parts of their county, and they give little instruction to the Wood Wards, who are left to their own devices.

Nor do the Wood Wards really constitute an authority in the region. They are a major force for order and safety, to be sure, but the only part of Caer Dire that they currently claim for their own is the very top floor of the ancient Quintain's Tower, a roofless solar housing five oak trees. One of the trees is gigantic, as old as the terrible legend that left the surrounding castle in ruins.

Instead, the de facto ruler and authority in Caer Dire is an ogre mage named Brazzer Mandragore. Brazzer acts as a mediator between the three competing ogre tribes that inhabit the region and maintains close relations as well with a local goblin king, the Wood Wards, and other humans in the area. An avid brewer of questionable beverages, Brazzer has turned all but the top floor solar of the Quintain's Tower into a public house that serves primarily ogre and goblin fare to a primarily ogre and goblin clientele.

The monstrous denizens of Caer Dire are allowed to remain there in peace, not only because of the understanding (and, indeed, shared living space) between Brazzer and the Wood Wards, but also because the ogres and goblins of Caer Dire serve a very useful purpose to the surrounding human communities: They are constantly at war with the marauding orc and hobgoblin tribes of the southeastern Green Mountains.

Some believe ogre and goblin nature to be such that, if they ever lacked orcish and hobgoblin enemies to keep them busy, they would quickly turn on the surrounding humans, and the truce between Brazzer and the Wood Wards would immediately fail. Others believe that the harmony between humans, goblins, and ogres in Caer Dire is a sign that perhaps ogres and goblins are as diverse, soulful, and capable of goodness as any human, elf, dwarf, etc. Only time will tell the Caer Dire ogres' true nature, but for now, Caer Dire remains a strange little slice of peaceful inter-species coexistence.

Of course, "peace" is a relative term here. The three local ogre tribes (Warhammer, Steel Ring, and Black Iron) often "disagree" violently, which is why Brazzer's mediation between them is so important. Additionally, a schism has recently developed in the Wood Wards' odd local religion. The Wood Wards have long worshiped the giant oak tree in their solar, addressing it as Saint Sophia and believing it to be a kind of reincarnation of Sophia Dunaven, whose grisly murder marked both the end of the Dunaven line and, supposedly, the founding of the Wood Wards.

A young seeress calling herself Sara of Westmarche — Westmarche being Sophia Dunaven's maiden name, another now-mostly-defunct Foerdewaith noble line — claims (impossibly) to be the direct descendant of St. Sophia. Many of the human villagers in the Caer Dire region, as well as some of the Wood Wards, have been moved by Sara's visions and have chosen to follow her. The rest of the Wood Wards decried her as a fraud and refuse to give her access to the tree she claims is her ancestor.

Sara and her "Riders of Westmarche" live essentially as bandits, plaguing the Wood Wards and passersby. However, her message of change and renewal resonates with those Caer Dire residents dissatisfied with their current lot, and while some see her as a common brigand, others put her on a pedestal as a revolutionary and savior. The ogres don't much care, as long as Sara's riders continue to aid them in their fight against the orcs and hobgoblins, which they do.

All told, these various conflicts make Caer Dire an exceedingly dangerous place to live or to travel, and most give it a wide berth if they can. The grand duke and the duke of the Westmarches continue to tolerate Countess Fenrith's hands-off approach to the region, so long as its various conflicts remain confined to the Caer Dire area claimed by Brazzer Mandragore. Rumor has it that the Fenrith-Dragul countess has long been laying plans to clean up the whole place so that she can act quickly and cleanly should either of her lieges ever change their minds. Of course, any interference by the Fenrith-Draguls in Caer Dire could reignite the old embers of the family's long feud with the Harrings, which could in turn not only set back whatever plans the countess might have, but also revive the Westmarches' recently ended civil war.

Reference Sources

The Book of Taverns

The Carnival at the End of the World

A small dirt track, remarkably well-maintained despite being barely larger than a game trail, can be found in the rocky central-western foothills of the Green Mountains. It is not marked, but folk in surrounding villages roll their eyes if asked about it and explain that it leads to "the Carnival."

The Carnival, they say, is a group of crazy people, or maybe a cult, that just sit around in the mountains year in and year out having a party. Most aren't clear on the details of how these people survive with so carefree a lifestyle, but some admit that it would be a fun place to visit if it weren't so hard to get to.

The dirt trail is 15 miles long, switchbacking its way up into the mountains. It remains well-kept along the whole route, with stairs cut into the rock face where necessary, or laid across the path in wood. The trail never widens to more than two feet at most, and even with the stairs and switchbacks it remains very steep. There are no good places to stop and camp or hunt along the way, though there are a few streams clear enough for replenishing water supplies.

A very small valley with a little pond fed by a tinkling mountain stream lies at the end of the trail, just over the top of a ridge. This is the only good campsite on the whole trail, being large enough for perhaps 30 people to pitch tents, and many such tents or semi-permanent shelters are already here, such that it almost resembles a village. People of many species lounge here, engaged in activities as diverse as swimming or fishing in the pond, playing music together, repairing tents or clothing, and generally behaving as if they live there. If asked, however, they explain that they are not the Carnival. The Carnival, they say, isn't here right now.

If you want to see the Carnival, they say, you'll have to wait with them for it to arrive. It appears two to four times a year on moonless nights. It stays for a few hours or a few days, and then it vanishes again. That's why they live here. Its arrivals and departures can't be predicted, so if they don't wait for it, they'll miss it. So they stay here, and they wait.

The Village

This is Carnival Village. According to those living in the foothills below, this is the Carnival—it's all there is. These people are just crazy. The inhabitants of Carnival Village, however, insist that no, they are only waiting for the Carnival to arrive, but it is absolutely worth it to wait! They are very friendly, welcoming, and generous.

They live by fishing and trapping, supplemented by actual clerics of the Carnival who are able to summon a bit of food and heal the sick. Occasionally, someone visits with supplies of various kinds, which they apparently donate voluntarily to the cause. Usually such people stay for a few days of revelry before departing, but some stay longer. If attacked, the villagers are surprisingly well-defended, as a few of their number are retired adventurers of impressive power, and other villagers are actually rather dangerous monsters, including a pair of satyrs with pipes as well as a cyclops and a handful of stone giants who visit almost daily. They all seem to live together in blithe harmony, barring the occasional housemate-like disagreement over dishes or other chores.

Carnival Village varies in size depending on the time of year. In the spring and fall, usually about 15 people are living there, not including the giants. In summer, the campsite is at full capacity, and the village is noisy with splashing from the pond, impromptu concerts on the nearby rocks, the occasional barking dog, and other benevolent chaos. In especially busy years, some of the overflow campers temporarily move in with the cyclops and stone giants a few miles to the north. In winter, the village can dwindle to just the satyrs and five to eight others, all either clerics of the Carnival or powerful retired adventurers. These residents cram themselves together into the village's one permanent structure — a tiny cabin — and pool their resources to survive whatever terrible weather conditions may come their way until spring.

Even in the summer, children are rarely found in Carnival Village, and the villagers don't recommend bringing them. They swear that the Carnival is a good place, wonderful even, but that it's difficult to supervise children there, and that many at the Carnival will be intoxicated. A few might admit that the Deeper Carnival might be dangerous to children, but the residents of Carnival Village seem loathe to speak of the Deeper Carnival, explaining that it's hard to understand until you see it for yourself. They just encourage people not to bring kids.

The Cliff

The cliff stands about 100 feet away from the village, up and over a ridge and around a few boulders. The villagers are always happy to show anyone the way. It is a small, natural rock shelf on the mountainside, with a sheer rock face beside it. This sheer rock face is, they say, the cliff. It's about three feet high. Anyone climbing up it (very easy) sees another small natural rock shelf, and nothing more.

The villagers explain only that the cliff is known as the End of the World, and that it will all make sense if the Carnival arrives. They keep

a guard posted beside the cliff every night, regardless of weather, just in case the Carnival happens to appear. In the worst snowstorms, everyone in the village works together to survive keeping watch on the cliff.

If the Carnival does arrive (which it may in fact do), it is easy to tell it is there by looking at the cliff. When the Carnival is present, the cliff appears to go from three feet high to an infinitely high rock wall that stretches into the sky farther than the eye can follow. It is absolutely sheer, with no natural hand- or footholds.

When the cliff appears this way, the villagers become very excited and spread the news at the tops of their voices, whooping and laughing and running to the cliff. As fast as they can, they run up to it and leap, or boost each other up, all of them apparently flying up into the air faster than the swiftest eagle could dive. They disappear up the cliff face out of sight.

If asked before they jump, villagers assure newcomers that the cliff is still just the cliff. It only looks tall. They encourage anyone who wishes to do so just to climb it, as if it is still just as easy as it was before. When you reach the top, they say, you will find the Carnival. If asked how the cliff is the End of the World, they still only say, "You'll see." They assure all and sundry that it is perfectly safe. They seem very happy.

Anyone who attempts to climb the cliff as if it is still just three feet tall succeeds. Anyone who treats it as if it is a genuinely tall cliff finds it to be a basically impossible climb. Anyone who tries to fly up the full height of the altered cliff finds it to go on as high as one can possibly fly, with no end in sight, apparently forever. The only way to scale the cliff is to trust that it is three feet tall and to treat it as if it is easy. Anyone who chooses to attempt this succeeds, as long as they could ascend the cliff by themselves under normal circumstances. Animals cannot understand the trick of the cliff, but they can be boosted or lifted up as long as the person helping them understands the trick.

Ascending the cliff feels exactly like ascending three feet, despite how it looks to the people on the rock shelf below. At the top of the cliff, though, one can now see the Carnival.

The Carnival

Despite what the people in the foothills believe, the Carnival is very much real, though no one understands clearly quite what it is. The residents of Carnival Village are correct that it arrives on some moonless nights, determined apparently as randomly as moonless nights themselves seem to be in Akados. Approximately one in every four moonless nights will bring the Carnival. It can come for two or more moonless nights in a row, or none at all for over a year. When the Carnival arrives, it stays for at least half the night, and usually longer than two nights, though rarely over a week. Its departure seems as random as its arrival.

The ledge the Carnival sits on grows to accommodate its otherworldly new occupants, as large as is needed. In appearance, the Carnival contains elements from every carnival in every universe. Everyone observing it recognizes it as a carnival and sees familiar elements (stalls, games, attractions, etc.) from carnivals they have visited in the past. Everyone also sees elements that confuse or awe them, utterly alien sights, sounds, and smells from times and places so far away they are beyond imagining.

Some attractions are a bit dangerous to humans, but those running the booths seem to always know who should and shouldn't partake of a given delight. They give ample and appropriate warning as needed. Some attractions are, indeed, a bit scary or sexy for children, and intoxicants are widely available to all. The music is loud and rhythmic, somewhat trance-inducing, but pleasantly so for most people. It is always night at the Carnival, and the weather is always pleasant.

The Carnival is crowded with people, and occasional animals, from what seem to be a thousand different worlds. Visitors and booth-attendants range through every conceivable species and beyond, throughout time and space. All visitors are courteous, or at worst the drunken equivalent of courteous. Most of them ignore those who enter from Akados, save to be blandly polite (or drunk) and hurry on their way

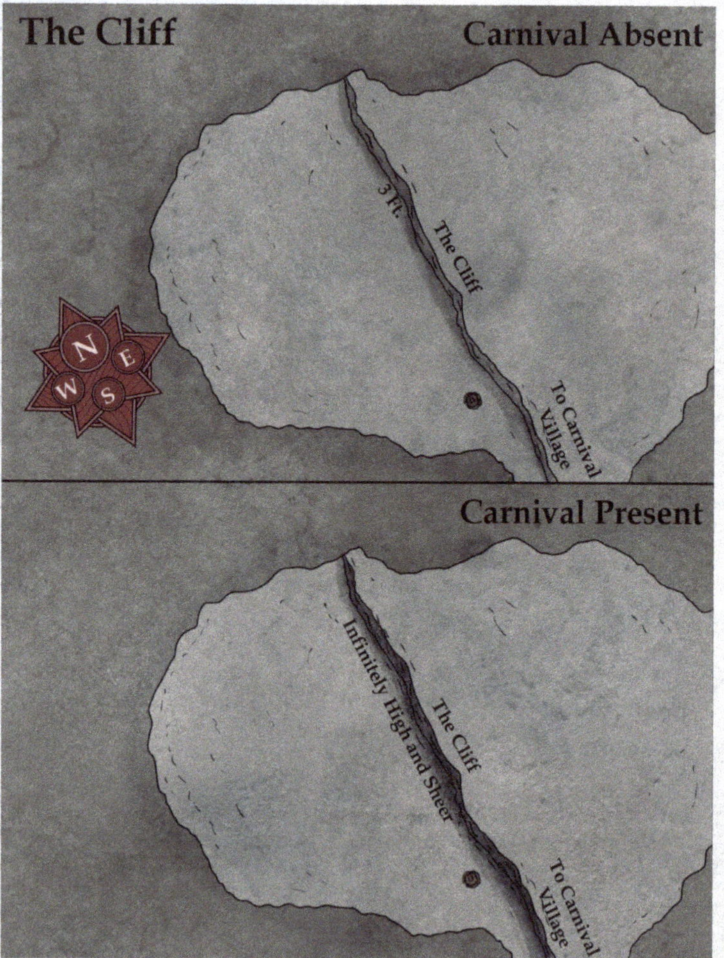

The Carnival Above

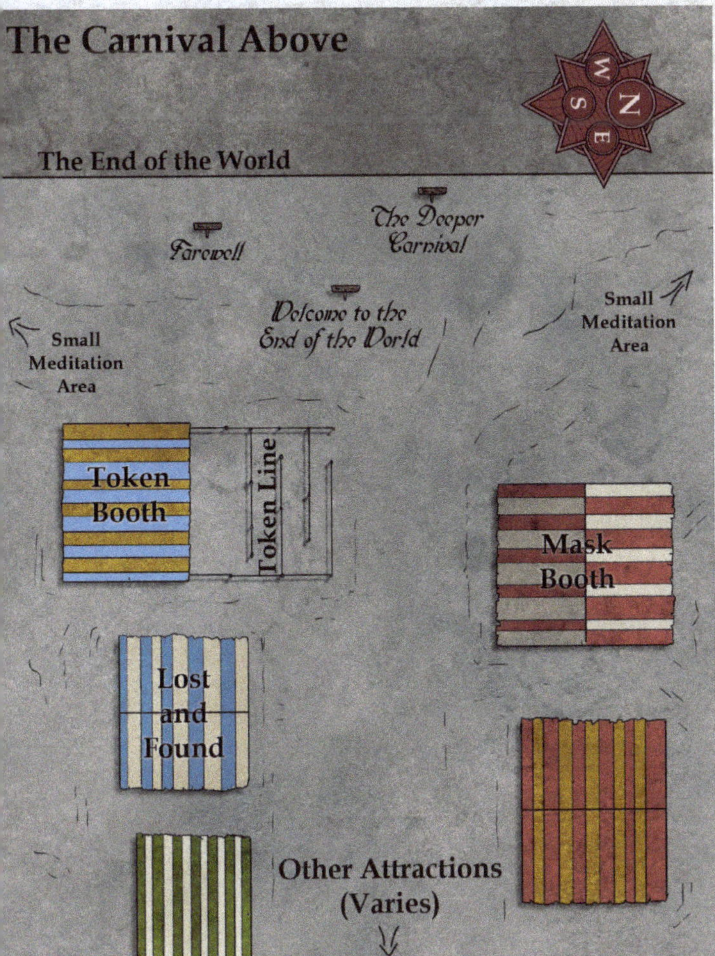

to some other attraction. Booth attendants are cheerful and eager to be helpful, but they will not leave their booths, and they encourage visitors to explore on their own.

Most of the Carnival-visitors from outside Akados wear masks, as do most of the booth attendants. These can be simple or elaborate, and beautiful, scary, or neither. Some cover the full face, some only the eyes or only the mouth and nose. Some masks don't seem to have eyeholes. Some have the "wrong" number of eyeholes or eyeholes in the wrong places. No one is required to wear a mask. Most just do.

Most booth attendants have humanoid bodies and are of medium size, with rare exceptions. Visitors range in size from tiny or smaller up to huge, and can come in all manner of bizarre body shapes, though most are basically humanoid. Extra appendages or horns are the most typical variations from the humanoid species common in Akados. Many have fur, feathers, or scales. Everyone is fully dressed (unless one enters the sexier tents, of course), but clothing styles and quality varies as widely as do the content of the booths.

If anyone becomes violent, or otherwise disturbs the peace and fun of the Carnival, the Carnival has powerful bouncers that escort the offenders to the End of the World and drop them off the edge. Anyone who brings an animal to the Carnival is held responsible for its behavior as well and is thrown out along with the pet if a disturbance occurs.

No one from Carnival Village has ever seen the bouncers defeated, though that doesn't necessarily mean it is impossible. No one is sure what would happen to the Carnival if it were invaded by someone the bouncers couldn't handle. It has been peaceful and fun in the memories of all present. Some believe, however, that if the bouncers were ever slain, the Blue Man would emerge from the Deeper Carnival to handle the intruders in person. Most who have met the Blue Man shudder at this thought.

The specifics of the Carnival's booths and attractions vary a bit every time the Carnival arrives, so one's favorite stall or game might or might not be present every time the Carnival visits, but there are always so many delights and entertainments, it is hard to be disappointed.

A small number of elements are present in every single visit the Carnival makes to Akados:

The Token Booth

Games, food, and activities at the Carnival cost little wooden tokens. Tokens can be purchased at the token booth, right near the top of the Cliff, for anything one chooses to offer, including but not limited to coin and goods. The token booth attendant gives a seemingly random and utterly inconsistent amount of tokens for all trades offered, but exchanges are non-negotiable. You take what the attendant gives you, or you don't. Sometimes the attendant gives tokens to someone for reciting a joke or a poem, but no one is allowed to hold up the token line (which is always a bit long) to offer a lengthy performance or tell a tale.

Despite the apparent arbitrariness of the token attendant's trades, the attendant never takes sides or plays favorites. Amounts often seem truly random, but do also seem to be somewhat influenced by how much a person cares about the item offered in trade. For example, a child offering up a favorite toy (however frayed and torn) will be courteously warned that the toy will be taken away and never seen again, but if the child still insists on the trade, an awkwardly large bag packed full of tokens may be given in exchange. By contrast, someone offering a brown apple core is unlikely to receive more than one token for it. Nothing will be accepted if it does not belong to the bearer. Stolen goods can be an exception to this only in the case of coin or anything that the former owner does not want back. How the booth attendant knows this is a mystery.

Some pieces of valueless junk are accepted (for one or two tokens) and some are not. It's difficult to tell in advance, other than the following guidelines: Anything dangerous or disruptive (such as stinky or otherwise nauseating) to the rest of the token line is turned away and may summon the bouncers even before reaching the front of the line. Harmless and less-disturbing junk such as banana peels, rusty nails, or an old shoe, or even slightly gross junk such as fingernail clippings or spit may and may not be accepted, at random.

Some wildly inhuman attendees offer truly strange things such as globs of slime or their own tentacles or eyeballs. This never seems to hurt them, and if asked, the attendant assures that "it will grow back." Visitors are discouraged from harming themselves in their offerings, though if anyone insists on offering anything truly valuable, the attendant accepts it, and tokens will be offered. Everyone can choose to take back an offer if the number of tokens it will buy is too few for their tastes. Trades are never forced. One may make only three offers at the front of the line, however, before being sent to the back to wait again.

Two common things that the (often near-destitute) inhabitants of Carnival Village offer for tokens are locks of hair and drops of blood. These are always accepted, for varying amounts of tokens.

The attendant's booth seems to have an infinite number of containers within easy reach and plenty of space for stashing accepted trade items, and an infinite number of tokens to pull from an eternally half-full token box. The token booth looks small and is locked at the back. Attempting to break in by any means summons the bouncers. No one knows what the Carnival does with the objects and substances it collects in trade. They are never seen again.

Most food and drink in the carnival costs 1–4 tokens. Intoxicants cost up to 10 depending on strength of effects. Games and attractions can cost anything from 1–20 tokens depending on the quality of entertainment offered.

The Mask Booth

For anyone wishing to don a mask, there is always a mask booth near the token booth. Masks cost anything from 1–20 tokens. Many residents of Carnival Village have masks in varying states of cleanliness and repair that they bring along with them from previous visits to the Carnival. Unlike most carnivals, these masks are the only souvenirs available for purchase anywhere in the Carnival. Some objects can, however, be won as prizes for games.

There is always a mask to suit anyone who enters the mask booth. Whatever sort of mask one wants is available, in the color one wants, and it always fits comfortably. Cheaper masks are less durable and made with cheap materials. More expensive masks are better and finer-made. The most expensive masks are occasionally enchanted. When one leaves the Carnival, anything purchased inside it, even the wooden tokens, disappears. These masks are the one exception. Anything won as a prize (or brought in with you), however, also remains. Only purchased items disappear, with rare exception.

Lost and Found

Everyone at the Carnival is expected to return found items to the Lost and Found booth. This is a remarkably organized and well-run booth, and is a good place to look for missing children or pets as well as missing objects. Anything found on the ground at the Carnival finds its way here eventually. Even if you decide to keep something you find, if you try to leave the Carnival with it, it disappears from your person and reappears at the Lost and Found booth. The Lost and Found booth attendant always looks human for some reason. Behind the attendant, weird and alien things can be seen lining the shelves, alongside very mundane things such as hats and coin purses.

Lost children are given candy and a place to sit next to the booth (pets are given treats appropriate to their species). If they wish to leave, they may. They can also return later for more candy. Children (or pets) who abuse this are given increasingly healthier treats (fruits, nuts, carrot sticks, etc.) until they stop asking. This does not mean, however, that the Carnival is actually a wonderful place for children. No one ever stops them from wandering off, leaving with strangers or by themselves, or even entering the Deeper Carnival. If anyone tries to hurt them or take them by force, the bouncers intervene, but the Carnival attendants are not babysitters, and they do not force anyone to do anything, ever, even children, unless they hurt others.

The End of the World

The cliff that one ascended to enter the Carnival is labeled, from inside the Carnival, as The End of the World. (The sign always appears to be in the reader's native language.)

And indeed, the cliff now looks like the End of the World.

It is the edge of a precipice as high as the cliff appeared from outside once the Carnival arrived. One can look down forever, down and down and down, and there is nothing. Eventually the face of the cliff disappears into a bed of clouds. The clouds go on forever. The night sky above goes on forever, as if nothing else exists in the universe. Out at the very edge of one's vision, the clouds are so dark that it is difficult to discern a horizon between the black, starry expanse and the clouds below. This holds true to the north, south, and west. To the east is the Carnival.

Many people find the End of the World fascinating and stand and stare out at it in silence for long periods. Well off to either side are rocks on which a few people sit in apparent meditation. Entering those areas causes an instant muting of the noise and distraction of the rest of the Carnival. It is still noticeable as being nearby, but it no longer detracts from one's ability to meditate.

Past the End of the World sign, closer to the cliff edge, two other signs stand side-by-side. One says, "The Deeper Carnival" and the other says, "Farewell." The bouncers drop offending visitors off the Farewell side of the cliff. They fall rapidly, all the way down, and then disappear beneath the clouds. If they scream, it sounds as if they are falling a long, long way.

Other people jump nonchalantly off the cliff on either side of the signs, and no one seems concerned with this in any way. Some who jump off later return as easily as if clambering up an only three-foot cliff.

The End of the World may be an illusion, but it is a very convincing illusion that affects all senses completely, including the sensation of realistic breezes for such a drop. People who are afraid of heights are likely to have difficulty being near it, and even those who know the trick of the cliff tend to find the sight impressive and thought-provoking.

Anyone jumping off (or thrown off) on the Farewell side returns to Akados and to the foot of the cliff near Carnival Village. Beings from other times, planes, or realities do not follow. Apparently, the Farewell cliff always returns departing visitors to wherever they came from. People jumping off the precipice land quickly and comfortably (or fall as long as they think is fun before landing equally comfortably). Those thrown off experience a long and terrifying drop (and may even lose consciousness); when they land, take damage as if they had fallen three feet.

People who leave of their own accord are exactly as sober as they want to be when they arrive home. Those who are tossed out are rendered 100% sober. See the Mask Booth and Lost and Found sections for what happens to items a person carries out of the Carnival. Items traded away at the Token Booth are gone forever.

Those who left willingly may re-enter the Carnival at any time, for as long as it remains connected to Akados. Those who were thrown out may re-enter at any time a) if they were thrown out by mistake, or b) if they have genuinely learned their lessons and will not disrupt the Carnival again. Anyone who fails to meet these criteria find the cliff to be as unscalable as it appears to be, regardless of knowing the trick.

No one is ever thrown into the Deeper Carnival. People choose to

explore there or not, as they wish. Leaping down from the Deeper Carnival side is always a bit scary. Something about the sound of the wind or the feel of the night air is inexplicably eerie — perhaps a bit exciting, and also perhaps a bit wrong. The fall is long, usually just a hair longer than one would prefer.

THE DEEPER CARNIVAL

Everything here is dim and foggy, difficult to see. Distances and shapes are disorienting, and depth perception is unreliable. The ambiance feels somewhat like the inside of a large cavern, but full of humid, muddy-smelling fog. If there are walls and a ceiling, they are invisible in the fog beyond the tents and booths. The attractions in the Deeper Carnival are fewer than the Carnival above. Usually there are only five or six. All are a bit creepy, and three are always the same on every visit: The House of Horrors, the Gladiatorial Ring, and the Blue Man.

Many believe that the Deeper Carnival is the reason the Carnival exists, in some way that no one seems to understand.

Leaving the Deeper Carnival is usually dizzying and disorienting, but is otherwise as easy as entering the Carnival above. The cliff looks its actual height of three feet tall from inside the Deeper Carnival, but may feel strange — too large, too small, too squishy or slimy, or any number of other harmlessly weird things.

THE HOUSE OF HORRORS

The Carnival above often has a nice little haunted house attraction that is scary enough even for adults to find fun but probably only nightmare fuel for small children. It is an ordinary carnival haunted house with a bit of magic for added veracity. The House of Horrors is different. It costs 20 tokens, and each person has a 100% individual experience of mind-altering horror. Most people only ever go to the House of Horrors once and afterward recommend avoiding the place. Some have nightmares for the rest of their lives. They do emerge, however, hale and whole, if shaken. Some even feel they learned something of value. A very rare few go back for more.

Some who enter the House of Horrors experience it as a brief journey, like a haunted house, while some experience it as a longer visit of even hours or days. But for those waiting in line outside, each trip through the House of Horrors takes five minutes. Many people emerge ashen-faced, trembling, or weeping. Many then choose to leave the Carnival entirely. Few discuss what they saw, but for those who do, the horror doesn't always make sense to others and is sometimes difficult to articulate clearly. Some see their own deaths, but it's very individual. No one at the Carnival really understands why this is one of their attractions, but it is always here, and there are always people who pay 20 tokens to experience it at least once.

THE GLADIATORIAL RING

This is a caged fight between two people, with stadium-style seating surrounding the ring on all sides. Seats in the stadium are 15 tokens, and viewers may stay as long as they like. Participating as a contestant pays five tokens per fight. If you win, you may choose to keep fighting if you wish; if you lose, you may not fight again until the next time the Carnival visits this plane. If you win 10 fights, you are given an enchanted item but, again, barred from further participation until the next time the Carnival visits this plane. The prize items awarded are never cursed and always worth at least 1,000 gold. As a prize won in a contest, they can be removed from the Carnival upon departure.

No one is ever barred from watching the fights, but only those capable of consenting are permitted to participate. Before participating, fighters must state clearly that they understand the following:

- The cage cannot be broken or passed through. I will be trapped inside with my opponent.
- I might die, and no one will punish the person who kills me. My corpse and belongings will not be returned to my companions or next of kin.
- I can yield at any time. I will lose if I yield, but the fight will be stopped, and I will be set free.
- If I harm or kill someone who has yielded, I will forfeit the match and be banned from the Carnival forever, and possibly face additional punishment.
- There are no other rules.

Those clearly expressing their understanding of these things may fight. Those who survive the ring are healed before they leave or before their next fights. Those who die are removed from the ring and never seen again. Those who cause harm or death to someone who has yielded are taken by the bouncers to the Blue Man. The ring is magically cleaned of blood between fights, and the enchantments on the cage prevent the audience from being harmed by any form of attack used inside it.

The fights in the Gladiatorial Ring are usually simple fisticuffs and end with minimal blood and no major damage. In most mismatched fights, the weaker fighter yields before things go too far. Deaths in the ring are very rare, and the fights are usually like any sporting event. Usually.

THE BLUE MAN

There is never a line to see the Blue Man. Some believe this to be evidence the Blue Man is a god who is able to interact simultaneously with an infinite number of people. Others believe that no one ever waits outside his tent because no one wants to enter it. Those who have bargained with the Blue Man in the past generally advise against it. "It's never worth what you pay," they say.

The only people ever forcibly brought to the Blue Man's tent are those who violate the few rules of the Gladiatorial Ring. Everyone else enters or leaves of their own will. There is no admission charge. No one remembers ever having seen the Blue Man outside his tent.

The Blue Man's tent is all in blues — patterns and solids, silks and velvets, all manner of opulence and comfort, but everything is blue. It is lit with blue light. The only things in the tent that are not blue are carried in by visitors.

The Blue Man lounges on cushions in the back of the tent, in blue clothing that looks wealthy and a little bit foreign to everyone, but also a little bit different to each person who looks at him. Indeed, everything about his appearance shifts slightly with the perceptions of those viewing him. His skin, hair, eyes, teeth, and tongue are all blue, however. No part of him isn't blue. The whites of his eyes are simply a paler blue, while his pupils are a dark blue. The shade of his hair and skin and irises varies depending on who looks at him, but everything about him is always blue.

Other than that, he looks like a half-elf to most people, only a bit unnaturally large. Some find him attractive or at least surreally beautiful. Some don't. His eyes look wrong to most people, however, hypnotic and disturbing, ancient and alien. Some people find they can't stand for him to look at them and leave his tent quickly, without even exchanging words.

Those who choose to stay are asked, "What do you want?" in their native tongues. He only asks once. If he receives no useful answer, he is courteous, but engages in no small talk and allows the silence to stretch without apparent discomfort, staring at his guest all the while. He does not appear to need to blink, though he does have eyelids, if he chooses to close them.

If asked a substantive question, he asks, "Is that knowledge what you want?" He never offers truly useful information before learning the answer to his first question.

Once he determines what a visitor wants, he asks, "What is it worth to you?"

Everyone who hears him ask this question understands intrinsically and magically, as if through a telepathic suggestion, that the answer must be taken with extreme gravity, and that this isn't like the Token Booth in the Carnival. Careless words here will not go unpunished.

The Blue Man accepts deals that only hurt his visitors in some way. Some believe that it is part of his magic: He can only grant a wish that is worth less than what was paid for it. There is no known limit to what the Blue Man can provide, but the price will always, always be too high. The bargaining is also one-sided. The Blue Man rejects offers that do not satisfy his conditions of suffering, but never makes a counteroffer. He always waits for his visitor to decide what to give him. Once an offer is made that the Blue Man accepts, the visitor receives a new telepathic understanding: "The deal is struck. Whether or not I choose to pay, whether or not I change my mind, I will lose what I have offered and gain what I have asked for."

Most who leave the Blue Man without making a deal feel relieved to have made the right decision and never go back. Most who do make a deal regret it until the day they die, but some are, indeed, foolish enough to go back — if for no other reason than to try to undo the harm they caused with the first bargain.

No one knows of anyone defeating the Blue Man in combat, and some believe that, if he is a god, the Carnival is his divine domain — that in his tent, he is omnipotent and utterly unassailable. Others believe that the Carnival is its own entity and divine in its own right, and that the Blue Man travels with it at its pleasure. He may be powerful, but he can be defeated, or perhaps cast out by the Carnival itself. Either way, no one has yet succeeded at harming him, so far as anyone at the Carnival knows, though some of his "customers" have tried after seeing the results of their deals with him.

Violators of the Gladiatorial Ring who are brought before the Blue Man have a different experience with him. They say only that he stares at them for a long, uncomfortable time, and then they understand in their hearts that some terrible, cosmic justice will befall them for what they have done in the ring. He then waves his hand, and they are taken away to be dropped off the End of the World. After that, they never again see the impossible cliff that means the Carnival has arrived, even when everyone else around them can, and they cannot enter the Carnival by any known means.

As far as anyone knows, all deals struck with the Blue Man come to pass, whether his customers want them to or not, usually within a year of meeting him. Punishments imposed by the Blue Man for crimes committed against the Carnival also take place within a year and tend to be remarkably fitting to the circumstances and severity of the crime. No one knows whether any mortal magics can prevent or counteract the Blue Man's power.

Carnival's End

When the Carnival leaves Akados, living attendees who entered from Akados find themselves on the ledge above the cliff without transition, and without warning. The Carnival can end at any time. Objects left behind in the Carnival, even if they never made it to the Lost and Found, appear beside their owners on the stone ledge (unless they were willingly traded away at the Token Booth).

The Carnival will return when it returns.

City of Cats

Well inside the southern corner of the Westwood stands a large clearing full of Foerdewaith-style homes in a cozy little cluster. It is enough of a settlement to house perhaps a dozen or so families. The local elves find the place eerie and speak of it only in hushed tones. They don't like to visit there, and they seem to be afraid of what will happen if they discuss it openly.

Upon entry, the tiny village appears clean and cheerful, but utterly deserted save for a few housecats. The deeper one steps between the dwellings and the longer one stays, the more cats that arrive. Some of the cats beg for food or attention, while others are more standoffish, but all of the cats follow anyone who enters the village, and more of them arrive all the time.

Inside the houses, everything is tidy and in good repair. All goods and items are simple and humble, inexpensive but reasonably well-made. There is no food or drink anywhere. There are no humanoids of any kind. Everything smells newish and looks comfy. There is no sign of any disturbance. There is no sign of any life, even vermin … nothing except for the cats. The cats continue to follow visitors everywhere they go, and always there are more of them, every time one looks. Eventually, hundreds of cats are crowded around the visitors, just watching visitors, following them, and otherwise acting mostly like ordinary cats.

When visitors leave the village, the crowd of cats following them decreases at the same rate it grew, until only one or two are left, and then none.

As yet, no one has penetrated any more deeply than that into the secrets of the mysterious City of Cats. If the elves know more about its origins or enchantments, or the strange behavior of its feline denizens, they have not yet shared this information with outsiders. No tales have yet been told of anyone staying the night in the village, or sleeping in its beds, or really anything else at all about it, and definitely not of what might happen to someone who harms or kills one of the cats.

If the cats could shed light on the situation, they have thus far remained silent, save for the occasional meow.

City of the Lost

Alignment: Neutral Evil
Ruler: Beirndwenyr, the Lost King
Government: Semi-democratic monarchy
Population: 17,845 (varied and strange, including many half-breeds, mutants, and totally unique beings)
Humanoid: All humanoid species are represented, but half-orcs and half-drow are both more common than usual here
Monstrous: Almost any, especially if size Large or smaller, and comfortable living underground
Languages: Common, Undercommon, many others
Religion: Diverse, though few good-aligned deities are honored
Resources: Mercenaries, assassins, contraband, stolen goods, curses and corrupt magics, some mining
Currency: All coins (exchanged by substance and weight)
Technology Level: Medieval
Demonym/Adjectival Demonym: Lostfolk, Lost

The City of the Lost is a grand and terrible metropolis that has long lain hidden deep within the southeastern Green Mountains. Most of the peoples of the Westmarches and of the rest of Reme and the world beyond have, as yet, never heard of the City of the Lost, but those willing to listen and give credence to the tales of the orc and hobgoblin clans of the Green Mountains know that the City of the Lost has been there for generations at least, and that its activities grow ever more overt and bold as time goes on.

Unless you are a citizen, the City of the Lost can be found only by those who are lost and unwanted. They can arrive alone or in small groups, but they must have lost sight of where they are, and they must be outcasts, exiles, pariahs, criminals, or otherwise reviled by all other communities they have lived in or attempted to join. Those who leave the City of the Lost without becoming citizens or citizens' servants can only rarely find their way back, and citizenship is not easy to obtain.

The orcs and hobgoblins of the region know that those who emerge from the city will either be the strong who are devoted to protecting the Lostfolk secrets and way of life, or they will be the weak who failed to find a place among the lost citizenry. The monstrous denizens of the Green Mountains do business with the former and see the latter as excellent prey, certain to never be missed by anyone, anywhere.

History and People

The City of the Lost was founded just under three centuries ago, or so say the orcs and hobgoblins who claim to have traded with its people. They don't know the details of its founding, but have heard talk of a fallen angel of Vanitthu, a half-dragon wizard, the blood sacrifice of a mighty demon-lord, and a drow sorcerer — or sorceress. The stories vary, as stories do.

The tale goes, however, that a group of powerful misfits and outcasts grew tired of running, fighting, and stealing to stay alive. They decided to found a city for all the unwanted people in the world where they could come together and defend one another, side-by-side. In the course of their quest, however, they realized that such a city would be hated and feared above all other cities and would quickly be conquered and scattered. Thus, they first sought a hidden location and the massive magical means that would be required to maintain an entire city in secrecy for generations.

Whatever ritual they ultimately used, it seems to have worked, as this city lies perilously close to the heart of Reme, yet Grand Duke Iltobarus has been heard in only the last few years to say with conviction that the City of the Lost is a myth — a wild tale being put about by Green Mountains' monsters in an attempt to lure the unwary into their territory to be robbed or enslaved (or eaten).

Whatever the case, one orcish account claims that the people of the City of the Lost practice solid, orcish values, prizing strength above all else and having little use for the weak of body or will. They say that most of the Lostfolk are ugly and twisted of appearance, but what that means to an orc is uncertain. They say that the Lostfolk keep slaves, but they kill any others who call them "slaves"; they insist on calling them "indebted servants." All the free Lostfolk, these captured orcs claim, are improbably strong warriors, smart and fierce and not to be trifled with.

The orcs seem to dislike and fear the Lostfolk, but they seem to respect them very greatly. One claimed to have a half-sister who had become Lostfolk — a human-tainted halfbreed who was driven from the tribe for weakness but later returned as a lost sorceress and razed her home village to the ground. The orc seemed very proud to be related to such a person.

A hobgoblin account from the same region spoke of a culture that prized vengeance and retribution as an important show of strength, with a concept of justice that included punishing all who mistreat the strange and unique people within their communities. This hobgoblin, who was herself born terribly disfigured, claimed to have found the City of the Lost after being driven from her clan as a child. She described being treated much kinder than she had been by her fellow hobgoblins, and worked hard but fed and trained as a warrior, just as she would have been among her own kind.

Upon passing a Test of Adulthood at age six — which she felt was typical for hobgoblin children in the city, showing pride that hobgoblins could pass the test much younger than human children — she was presented with her "receipt of debt" for the investment that had been made in her upbringing. After that, she served her "creditor" in relative contentment, but never distinguished herself enough to make much headway on paying off what she owed. Ultimately, when she lost an arm in battle, her creditor was unwilling to invest in her regeneration, or any further in a crippled warrior. Her debt was sold to a lesser, crueler creditor and she ran away from the city, only to be captured by humans in the Dunavenwood. When asked if she resented her "creditors" or any other aspect of Lostfolk culture, she expressed only that they had treated her more fairly than her own people.

The hobgoblin was illiterate and received very little education among the Lostfolk. She knew nothing of the city's origins or history, or even much of its governance. She did know, however, that the city's ruler was a male drow named Beirndwenyr, who styled himself the Lost King. He was a mighty sorcerer, she was told, with a will of iron and a razor wit. He was the only king the city had ever had, she said, and had been one of the founders, centuries ago. She said the story went that he was raised as a drow priestess but rejected the teachings of the Queen of Spiders and was transformed into a man, though the hobgoblin wasn't clear on the order of events or whether they were true. She knew that drow men were among the more common citizens of the City of the Lost because of their oppression and degradation within drow culture. She also claimed that many citizens were halfbreeds or otherwise of mixed species, and that most citizens were beings she couldn't even identify, though few were larger than ogres or smaller than goblins, and most were at least fundamentally humanoid, even those who came from other planes.

Of the latter, she said many citizens came to the City of the Lost from other worlds, though she didn't know how they found the place. Others, she said, were "freed slaves" brought to the city by force and "granted the opportunity" to work themselves free of debt and become citizens. She wasn't sure this was a good idea, since she said most such creatures (often humans or halflings) were weak and died before they could pay back their "debts" of "freedom."

The hobgoblin was unwilling to guide her captors to the entrance to the City of the Lost, even after her missing arm was regenerated, and she died in human custody in Gilboath, having never produced any proof of her claims.

One interesting note in all this, however, is the stir the City of the Lost is beginning to raise among the dwarves of the Green Mountain region, especially in Gemtown. A very old Gemtown legend speaks of a sister city from long before the forest receded from the Green Mountain foothills and the humans came to settle them. Gemtown's sister city was called Coppertown (or Khazghren in the local dwarven dialect of the time) and was lost to some mysterious disaster more than 3,000 years ago. Dwarven explorers searched for its ruins for generations upon generations but to no avail, and many now believe that Coppertown was never anything but a tale.

Based on orcish and hobgoblin descriptions, however, some dwarven scholars now believe that this City of the Lost may have somehow been founded in the rediscovered ruins of Khazghren. The location is approximately correct, they say, and the descriptions of the high-ceilinged, vaulted architecture and grand elegance of stonework sound dwarven to them, and inconsistent with accounts of smaller brick-and-mortar dwellings constructed into cramped city streets in the poorer Lostfolk neighborhoods. If this King Beirndwenyr simply found an abandoned dwarven city, they say, it makes more sense that it could have grown so large in so few centuries, though they still agree that major magics must have been used to keep it a secret.

Then again, with how hard the dwarves have looked for their sister city's ruins over the centuries, perhaps, they say, some great and terrible magic already enchanted the place when Beirndwenyr found it. They hope they can find some way to penetrate and study the City of the Lost to determine whether it really is built within the ruins of Khazghren, and whether or not it is still possible to solve the mystery of Coppertown's ancient fall. Some dwarves have also begun to ask what relationship, if any, this City of the Lost might have to the strange sounds echoing in the depths of Gemtown's easternmost mines.

Religion

Based upon the many stories told of the City of the Lost among the Green Mountains' monstrous denizens, it can be inferred that most religions are welcome among the Lostfolk, but that good-aligned deities are rarely revered in their culture. Two notably reviled deities among the Lostfolk, however, are apparently the Queen of Spiders and Vanitthu, despite the opposing natures of these two divine beings.

Worship of the Spider Goddess is apparently strongly discouraged by the king, who has been known to spit at the sound of her name. He is said to be condescendingly tolerant of male drow Lostfolk who continue to worship the spider goddess, but to be very harsh with drow women unless they first reject the Queen of Spiders and all her teachings. Many describe Lostfolk culture as largely consistent with the Spider Goddess's teachings, and they say that the king does not realize the extent to which he still conforms to his culture of birth, but few are willing to tell him so to his face, and most worship of the Spider Goddess in the City of the Lost is done in secret, if at all.

As for Vanitthu, he is apparently taught as a kind of foil in Lostfolk mythology, the hypocrite who claims to care about justice and retribution but understands nothing of suffering or the true value of punishing wrongdoers. Portrayed as a bumbling fool who constantly sides with the oppressors over the oppressed while claiming to do the opposite (in some stories due to cowardice or greed, and in other stories due to his own stupidity and misunderstandings), Vanitthu is seen by Lostfolk as the epitome of all that they wish to destroy, both within themselves and the world around them.

Trade and Commerce

The orcs and hobgoblins say the Lostfolk trade openly with the monsters of the Green Mountains. Disguised as ordinary traveling merchants from other parts of Reme, they also trade with the dwarves and even the humans and other communities around them. None of the monsters who has been questioned on the subject has claimed to know whether or not the City of the Lost has trade with the Under Realms or with other planes, but the hobgoblin who claimed to have been raised in the city suspected that such trade did take place. Then again, she tended to ascribe near-divine powers to her king, so her testimony might be suspect.

By all accounts, the City of the Lost produces fine crafts and magic items, powerful warriors or assassins for hire, and also engages in smuggling and the fencing of stolen goods. No products are known to be illegal in the City of the Lost. The Lostfolk do some mining, hunting, and mushroom-farming, but they trade for the majority of their food and textiles, often while pretending to be ordinary human merchants from well-known cities.

Loyalties and Diplomacy

The City of the Lost is not known to engage in traditional diplomacy with any entity, nor to have loyalties to any but their own. Instead of treaties and negotiation, they have long dealt with their neighbors through a combination of impenetrable, magically-augmented secrecy and (in the case of the local orcs and hobgoblins) total military superiority. If, as the local monster populations are beginning to claim, the City of the Lost is preparing to abandon its centuries-long practice of hiding from the authorities of Reme, it is unknown what sort of relationship it intends to pursue with the larger nation surrounding it.

Government

While tales of the city's founding are usually of several misfits banding together — often featuring a servant of Vanitthu who left the "foolish" god's service and struck out in pursuit of a "more just" (more violent) form of retribution for wrongs — there is no evidence today that anyone but King Beirndwenyr remains of the founders, assuming that he ever really was one of their number. Whether the other founders (or all the founders) have died or simply left the city is unknown, but Beirndwenyr holds his throne in an odd combination of sheer magical might and popular acclaim. He is believed to be neither kind nor particularly generous, but residents of the City of the Lost seem to be quite proud of his power and his strange "justice."

Beirndwenyr is said to be exceptionally handsome, almost pretty, frighteningly charming, and to exhibit an odd combination of drow feminine and masculine traits in his speech patterns and body language. He shows no sign of the humility and obedience considered natural among drow males, instead being as proud and arrogant as a high-ranking drow priestess, and every bit as authoritative as well. He is said to be cultured and educated, at least as drow measure such things, but refuses to speak of his past or childhood, even with those closest to him.

As for the rest of Beirndwenyr's government, it is said that all positions must be won in contests appropriate to the positions held, and then the winner must be acclaimed by the people in an unopposed popular vote. In general, the system is believed to be fairly popular, even among those who suffer under it, for reasons not yet well understood.

Military

Because freedom ("from debt") and full citizenship are won largely through either the completion of dangerous missions or what the hobgoblin informant called "sports" (vicious gladiatorial combat, from her description), most Lostfolk full citizens are extremely powerful in combat. In that sense, warriors of the mundane or the magical variety seem to form a kind of unofficial ruling class in the City of the Lost, ensuring that the city is always prepared to defend itself from threats of any kind.

All menial labor is performed by "indebted servants," many of whom are children or in some way disabled. Everyone is trained to fight, however, such that while the lower classes (slaves) do labor to support the elite full-citizen military, even said lower classes will never include helpless non-combatants. Also, because of the dangled promise of future freedom, most of these servants do seem to be loyal to the city — and to King Beirndwenyr — even if not to a particular "creditor."

Nevertheless, however well each individual of the Lostfolk might do in a fight, those who have spoken of their battle tactics do not describe an exceedingly disciplined or well-organized military. It is as yet unknown if any such body exists within the City of the Lost or what sort of command structure it might have if one does exist.

Major Threats

Just as the legend of its founding says, the City of the Lost is likely to be threatened by anyone and everyone around it should it ever lose its veil of secrecy. Even if the Lostfolk have never openly gone to war with their neighbors, they seem to have structured nearly everything about their culture to antagonize and provoke the major powers around them, especially Reme and Reme's Westmarch dwarves, as well as any nearby drow settlements in the Under Realms beneath them. Since the Lostfolk harbor criminals as well, they might even draw the enmity of peoples and governments much farther away.

Perhaps the only beings that might not majorly threaten the City of the Lost are the orcs and hobgoblins with whom they are known to trade, though such folk are hardly celebrated for their loyalty in the face of peril. All in all, it seems unlikely that things will go well for the City of the Lost should their concealing enchantments ever fail. Then again, King Beirndwenyr is supposedly an intelligent elf. If he thinks his "kingdom" can survive without its spells, perhaps he knows something that his neighbors do not.

Of course, if he does, perhaps that unknown power too might constitute a danger to the citizens and servants of the City of the Lost.

Wilderness and Adventures

The City of the Lost is surrounded by wild mountains known to harbor populations of particularly warlike orcs and hobgoblins, as well as whole aeries of rocs. In addition, the mountains themselves are treacherously steep and difficult to traverse, particularly on the southeast arm of the range. What sorts of underground wilderness and adventures might exist in or near the City of the Lost are as yet unknown, but the Green Mountains are thought to be riddled with tunnels to and from the Under Realms, so it is likely that adventure exists around the outer tunnels of the city as well.

Dunavenwood

To the south of Caer Dire, near the southeastern foothills of the Green Mountains, lies a forest known as Dunavenwood. Once, it is said, this wood was the many private orchards and the well-stocked hunting grounds of the Dunaven family. In the 500 years since that line's tragic end, the wood is no longer recognizable as anything that was ever cultivated by humans. It has grown into a wild forest inhabited by all manner of natural creatures, including large herds of the forest buffalo hunted for meat by many in the region. Rocs from the Green

Mountains are also known to hunt in Dunavenwood as part of their autumn migration.

Dunavenwood has long been protected by the Wood Wards of St. Sophia, though in recent generations, especially since the start of the Westmarch civil war, marauding tribes of orcs and hobgoblins have been venturing down the mountains for raids and to make war with the ogres that have claimed nearby Caer Dire as their home. Though the Caer Dire ogres actually help the Wood Ward rangers defend the forest from these invaders, they cannot wholly keep their enemies away. In addition, of course, the ogres pose no small threat of their own, since many are easily provoked, especially by humans who know little of ogre cultural etiquette.

Technically belonging to the Fenrith-Dragul family as part of the Fenrith Earldom, Dunavenwood is also supposedly policed by the countess' soldiers, or rather by the duke's soldiers, as — since the end of the civil war — the noble families are not permitted sufficient troops to defend the countryside on their own. However, troops from the duke or countess are rarely in evidence in Dunavenwood. The Fenrith-Dragul family harbors ill will toward this place that bears the name of their ancient, fallen enemies, and Duke Wylan has his hands full cleaning up his duchy after decades of civil war.

Finally, a competing group of rangers called the Riders of Westmarche claim to protect the Dunavenwood as well, though many would argue that they are in fact bandits that threaten the wood. They do combat the invading orcs and hobgoblins, and are said to aid and defend the homes of forest-dwellers, but the Riders of Westmarche are also often found fighting the Wood Wards or robbing wealthy travelers.

All in all, while Dunavenwood is a fair bit safer to traverse than the ogre-ruled Caer Dire region to the north, it has become a bit of a blood-soaked place in recent years, and unlike the rest of the Westmarches, the Dunavenwood conflicts are ongoing. Worse yet, recent tales have begun to spread that Lord Dunaven's ghost wanders the wood on moonless nights, searching forever in vain for his ruined castle many miles to the north. Such tales do always tend to spread about bloody old legends, so perhaps this one is just a children's story. Then again perhaps not.

Use the **Forest Encounter Table** for random encounters in Dunavenwood.

REFERENCE SOURCES

The Book of Taverns

ECKLAND

Alignment: Neutral Good
Ruler: Duke Wylan Rogers
Government: Feudal
Population: 37,811 (Foerdewaith 24,335, Loreclans 10,093, halfling 1,224, half-elf 1,002, hill dwarf 771, mountain dwarf 330, high elf 41, other humanoid 15)
Languages: Common
Religion: Quell, Vanitthu, Solanus
Resources: Trade, grain, cattle, emeralds
Technology Level: Medieval

Eckland is the capital of the Westmarches and is located at the end of the Western Reme Road on the Quail River. The duke's castle sits on a large peninsula jutting into the middle of the river, which becomes an island when the waters rise during most of the winter and spring each year. Though the majority of Eckland sits on the east bank of the Quail, both banks have docks for barges going upriver toward the Green Mountains and downriver to the Crescent Sea. On the east side are the passenger docks and most of the high-class, expensive mercantile activity, while anything smelly, dirty, or considered low class is handled on the west docks, which are usually downwind of the ducal palace.

As with the rest of the Westmarches, Eckland is firmly under the personal control of the new duke. Wylan Rogers has appointed a city justice to run the majority of operations of the capital, with his daughter Emna as moderator of a newly-founded Eckland Merchants' Council, as well as all new city magistrates and the captain of the city guard. Emna is regarded as a pashtar by the nearby Loreclans as well, which gives her considerable authority. Rogers' second and fourth daughters, Reka and Maeri, have been permitted to found new guilds of Philanthropists and Educators, respectively, and the public works projects and literacy outreach efforts of these two guilds are said to be making great strides in subduing and healing the various lingering pains of the generation-spanning civil war that has so recently been put to rest in the Westmarches.

The major Westmarch markets have traditionally been found here in Eckland, but civil conflict spilling over into Eckland neighborhoods has depressed Eckland's commerce for some time. With Duke Wylan's efforts (and those of his daughters and skilled appointees), this is changing, and Eckland is once again becoming the endpoint for many merchants and traders traveling the Western Reme Road. Though this diverts some business from Martyn's Nest and causes some coastal guilds to grumble about the changes, most agree that river congestion and overall profits are improved by the restoration of Eckland's former prominence.

The lands surrounding the city of Eckland are fertile and well-watered, some of the richest and most productive in all of the Westmarches, and with the Westmarch civil strife now abated, farmers and cattle ranchers are pouring into town to sell their best wares in decades. Eckland has a high percentage of farmers of Foerdewaith ancestry, and two entire settled Loreclans that are entirely urban: the Yaarej and the Fish-Singers.

HISTORY

Though the majority of Eckland was built more recently, with the oldest east bank construction dating back a mere 800 or so years, and the west bank a bare three centuries old, the duke's palace on the Eckland Peninsula shares parts of its foundation with an ancient Hyperborean fort, the name and history of which are long since lost and forgotten.

The fort was first rediscovered by the Fish-Singer Loreclan when, in efforts to found a fishing village along the fertile east bank of the Quail, the settlers were forced to remove an undead monstrosity of some kind (legends disagree as to the being's true nature or origins), which had taken up residence in the fort's abandoned remains. After its defeat, Eckland was founded and grew to be very prosperous. For the first few centuries, the island/peninsula was believed to be haunted, and in the summer and early fall, when the path to the island was dry and clear, the folk of Eckland feared to walk outside at night lest the monsters from the old fort prey upon them.

Under these circumstances, during the interregnum of Foere, a large number of Foerdewaith soldiers and settlers were dispatched to Eckland to subdue the menace, which led eventually to the city's large population of ethnic Foerdewaith.

It is unknown whether real monsters or even bandits ever made the old fort their base of operations after the original undead threat was defeated, but that didn't stop Duchess Winslynne III of Foere from claiming that she and her guard had personally cleansed the peninsula in spring of 3049 I.R. not long after she was tasked with the Civilization of the West by her liege (or, rather, banished from Foere's court, some say, as a punishment for insubordination). Duchess Winslynne, who may, perhaps, have ousted a band of goblins or vagrants from the island, began construction of her new ducal castle there that very summer. When Reme gained its independence from Foere, Eckland and its castle were retained as the ducal seat for the Westmarches.

Always located in a prime position for farming, fishing, and riverboat commerce, Eckland grew in population and importance in the local region and all of Reme, year by year, for generations. For this very reason, however, the ever-squabbling noble families soon set their sights on controlling Eckland's commerce and, indeed, most of the ducal administrative offices behind the scenes. Eckland became a hotbed of scandal and counter-scandal, inter-neighborhood street gang violence, and rampant procedural corruption, all of which slowly stagnated the culture and prosperity of the citizens and further hampered the frustrated dukes and duchesses of the region from improving relations between the various Westmarch aristocratic families. Over time, this ultimately led to near-total control of Eckland — and through Eckland the whole of the Westmarches — by agents of the Brodchek family (patrons of both the city's settled Loreclans), which in turn led the Merciers and Harrings to attack Brodchek Castle in Wessem.

When full civil war broke out after the death in battle of Lady Fiah Brodchek, the same forces of the grand duke that helped to break the siege on Castle Brodchek also helped the duke to seize the majority of Eckland's east bank, but the west bank and other outlying Eckland neighborhoods were plagued by regular violence in the streets for nearly two decades. Some eight years ago, matters became so bad that most non-humans and humans of non-Foerdewaith appearance were driven from the city en masse, along with any Foerdewaith folk who refused to swear fealty to the Harring count at the time. Even the few remaining neighborhoods within ducal control were so strictly guarded and regulated that the city's historical commerce all but ground to a halt, and a children's rhyme began to circulate that ridiculed the duke as a prisoner in his own castle.

> Oh, Eckland's duke sits out on the isle,
> Can't smell the west bank's steaming pile.
> When he goes out, it's a shameful rout.
> Now he tells all his dogs, Let's stay a while!

It is said that the last duke of the Westmarches begged the grand duke not to appoint him, but was unable to dissuade his liege or to acquire the support he would have needed to make a difference for Eckland and the duchy in general. He, too, was a laughingstock, like his predecessors, up until the day four years ago when he was found murdered.

Since Wylan Rogers was named duke, however, and given the grand duke's full authority and support, Eckland's fortunes have changed entirely. The Fish Singer Loreclan shifted its allegiance from the Brodchek family to the duke himself, the ducal court is regaining its former grandeur, and even the west bank and poorer east bank neighborhoods are cleaner and safer than they have been in generations. A small number of the city's exiled Foerdewaith residents are returning, and the exiled Loreclans simply moved back in as soon as they were allowed to do so. Some say the duke is planning a sponsorship program to return the city's population to its former levels and to restore its historic cosmopolitanism by enticing former exiles to return and inviting people of all species to Eckland to help the Westmarches rebuild.

This idea has met with mixed responses from the Westmarch nobility, but Eckland's commonfolk are more in favor. They adore their new duke and his family, and a spirit of community pride is uniting the recently-beleaguered citizenry. Nearly all the duke's ideas are therefore very popular, especially since those already implemented are going so well. Various public projects are keeping everyone employed and flush with coin, and newly-appointed officials — chosen for skill and integrity rather than inter-family politics — are quickly smoothing away the corruption and rot of generations.

It is a wonderful time to live in Eckland, a time of camaraderie and rebuilding, celebration and progress, but many fear that this leap forward can only be too good to be true, and only time will tell whether Duke Wylan can make his changes stick for the long haul.

GOVERNMENT

Under Duke Wylan, the governance of Eckland falls primarily under the authority of Wylan's appointed city justice and four city magistrates, three for the larger east bank (north, east, and south quarters) and one for the west bank. These magistrates orchestrate the smooth interplay of the militia with the various guilds and noble families. In this they are aided by the new Eckland Merchants' Council, formed by popular representation (under the moderation of Wylan's daughter and chief financial advisor, Emna Rogers) to oversee the restoration and improvement of Eckland's commerce.

Laws in Eckland are currently quite strict to ensure the city's fragile peace, but Duke Wylan does his best to keep his security measures from unduly impacting the lives of his citizens. Just last midsummer, the evening curfew was experimentally lifted for the city, and as crime has not since skyrocketed, it is hoped that the law will be permanently repealed. Weapons searches at the city gates have slowly relaxed as well to allow for smoother commercial traffic in and out of the city. Weapons of all kinds remained banned within Eckland's city walls, however, for all but the duke's own military, and punishment by the lash in a public square is the sentence for those convicted of theft, vandalism, assault, unlawful weapons possession, and several other major crimes. Murder is punished by imprisonment in the rumored-to-be-haunted castle dungeon and sometimes by execution.

LOCATIONS IN ECKLAND

DUCAL PALACE

Though the otherwise-buried stone foundations of the ancient Hyperborean fort are visible at the rear of the castle on the north side of the Eckland Peninsula, the rest of the ducal castle is much more palatial than fortified. A high wall extends around the island, and with the Quail River itself for a moat, that wall has always been sufficient to maintain the duke's safety from military assault without additional fortifications. Inside the wall, therefore, the palace is grand and lovely — sturdily built from humble, local materials but graceful of architecture and widely considered romantic of silhouette, especially when the river's waters around it are a-sparkle with winter moonlight.

THE EAST BANK

More than two-thirds of Eckland sits on the east bank of the Quail, straddling the two natural harbors to the north and south of the Eckland Peninsula. The east bank is a steeper rise up from the river than the west bank is, so it's only a few hundred yards from the docks before the houses and shops are all safe and snug atop low, rounded hills. Even in the worst winters, flooding has never been known to reach the hilltop neighborhoods of East Eckland. The same cannot even be said of the duke's castle!

All the wealthiest families in the Westmarches have homes in East Eckland, as do even some aristocrats from other parts of Reme, though more for political reasons than for the climate, as Eckland is wet year-round, gloomy in winter, and humid in summer. Nevertheless, East Eckland architecture is old and stately, and East Eckland artisans are on par with the best in Reme. These are the neighborhoods in which to look for custom enchantments, expensive but well-staffed temples, and all upper-class goods and services.

Here, too, are the Westmark nobility on their best behavior, all of them at least pretending to get along and let bygones be bygones. High society parties in Eckland — when they aren't held at the duke's palace — all take place in the hilltop mansions or on the luxury river yachts. Though peace and harmony are currently in vogue, it should be expected that a certain amount of petty intrigue will continue to take place at all aristocratic Eckland gatherings, most likely for decades to come.

THE EAST DOCKS

The Eckland docks on the east bank of the Quail River are clean, sturdy, orderly, and well-guarded. Docking fees are half price for anyone with a large merchant cargo as part of the ongoing efforts to rebuild Eckland's post-war commerce, but the full-price fees are higher than standard elsewhere in Reme in part to discourage non-merchants from taking up too much docking space, and in part because, being at the end-point of the Western Reme Road and so conveniently located on the barge-friendly Quail, dock space in Eckland has always been in high demand.

The Eckland dock markets are also known as a place to purchase fine-crafted jewelry made from less-expensive materials, as well as lower-grade gemstones, often useful for powdering as spell components or in crafting fine paints and dyes. Finally, Eckland is the best place in Reme to buy freshwater pearls. The quality of Reme's freshwater mussel cultivation is nothing compared to the sea pearls available on the coast, but the freshwater pearls have a charm all their own, and with the help of his wife and daughters, Duke Wylan is working to raise their popularity as romantic gifts for all occasions. Though the duke swears he didn't start it, a rumor has begun to circulate that Quail River pearls will make couples lucky in love. As Relm Brodchek's first gift to Lusea Mercier — on their official introduction before their engagement — was a bracelet of Quail River pearls, the popularity of the rumor may hang on the future fate of Relm and Lusea's marriage.

The Duke's Market

The Duke's Market is a grand fairground located near the outer edge of East Eckland's North Quarter district. It consists of a spacious showroom, several large fields, and a circle around the outside of simple open-air shelters. Traditionally, this space was used for any markets, contest tournaments, spectacles, or public festivals the duke chose to sponsor. The original structures, however, were among the early casualties of the Westmarches' long civil war. First, the showroom was burned to ash, and then the fields and shelters became the grounds for a series of pitched and bloody battles, all of the worst in the Eckland area.

Upon ending the war, one of the duke's first acts was to hold a large mass memorial service for the fallen, followed by a ritual cleansing of the market grounds. He then commissioned the rebuilding of the showroom, larger and grander than before, and filled it with works of art and craft from all over the Westmarches and sometimes other parts of Reme, all either promoting themes of peace and unity or making vivid the grief and horror of violence. This Peace Gallery holds regular auctions of its works, all proceeds of which go to aiding impoverished veterans or families of the fallen. Once a year for the last two years, the duke also hosts an art competition at the peace gallery. The winner is granted a bag of gold, a duke's star (freeing the bearer from all tolls and tariffs in the Westmarches for life), and the winning artwork is displayed in the grand hall of the duke's palace for a year.

The fields and open shelters around the Peace Gallery have been returned to their former purposes, though small memorial shrines dot the market year-round, and many bring offerings of flowers, pretty stones, or small carvings to these shrines in honor of their loved ones lost to war.

The Road Gate

The Eckland city wall's largest gate is the Road Gate on the far eastern edge of the old city. This gate stands at the very end of the Western Reme Road, and in times of peace stands open day and night. However, since the implementation of Eckland weapons' ban, passing through the gate has become a long and tedious process, and often a muddy one as well given Eckland's generally damp weather.

This state of affairs has, in turn, led to an interesting little market springing up outside the gate. The Open Market is a longstanding Eckland tradition wherein farmers and ranchers sell their wares twice a week or more during the spring, summer, and fall, often without bothering to cart things all the way into town, especially if they can't afford market stalls in the high-class east bank neighborhoods. This has long been where the poorer common folk come to trade for fruits, vegetables, eggs, and other simple staples.

Because people need to eat, this tradition persisted even throughout the civil war and was usually mostly immune from the fighting among the upper classes. Since the weapons ban, however, new services have made themselves permanent additions to the open market, including refreshment stands for travelers waiting in line for their weapons inspections, guarded weapons lockers for those willing to pay to house their weapons more securely than the guard-post attendants can guarantee, as well as street entertainers, foot-washers, flower-sellers, and stands hawking cheap trinkets, all hoping to eke a bit of coin from the bored and tired lined up outside the gate.

Duke Wylan encourages this new face of the open market, welcoming anything that might take the edge off the irritation and congestion of his weapons' ban. As much as he wants to encourage commerce and travel to and from Eckland, he does not feel that the city is ready yet to risk a renewed threat of bloodshed in the streets, and most of his people still agree with him, tolerating the aggravation with a smile and a sigh, just glad to finally feel safe in their capital city again.

The West Bank

On the west bank of the Quail River, just across from the rest of Eckland, sits a community that is almost a whole different city from that on the east bank. The west bank began as a series of docks and markets to handle the east bank's overflow and those goods that catered to a less discerning (or less moneyed) crowd than the east bank markets tended to welcome. Simple materials such as sackcloth, low-grade bricks, and straw, as well as any smelly goods the nobility didn't want ruining their afternoon market strolls — such as fertilizers, fresh hides, and alchemical goods — were sold here.

Over time, a shanty town sprang up around the west bank market — and with it a hotbed of criminal activity, especially smuggling. This state of affairs went on for generations until it bit by bit became a full-fledged community, but the core of Eckland's west bank remains to this day the western docks and market, illegal activity included. Neither the aristocracy nor the military is particularly welcome there, nor is the asking of too many questions. Residents seem oddly proud of the west bank's reputation and often call their home Westbank, instead of its official name: Eckland's West Quarter. The West Quarter magistrate is usually referred to by residents as "the mayor," a title some magistrates fondly adopt while others find it insulting.

The current magistrate of the West Quarter is Kaeron Wilming, who served for 15 years as Wylan Rogers' quartermaster in the navy and moved with him to his service in the army. She is a widely-respected administrator, but strict, steely, and more often feared than loved. As the West Quarter is not walled, unlike the east bank, Wilming has found the weapons' ban difficult to fully enforce in her district, and in response cracked down very hard on all West Quarter criminal activity. This has had a mixed reception even among law-abiding west bank residents, and the smugglers are, of course, said to be quietly incensed. Within the last year, Magistrate Wilming has reported that she has begun to receive anonymous death threats, and many wonder whether riots may be brewing along the west bank.

Others, however, say that the upsurge in river traffic since the end of the war has been so good for the smugglers that they don't really mind having to jump through a few extra hoops or grease a few extra palms to get their goods to and fro. In fact, these same folk claim that the criminal element is even somewhat fond of Magistrate Wilming and might even protect her from threats. They're just that relieved that the troublemaking aristocracy are no longer able to gum up the smooth machinery of west bank crime with their petty feuding.

Reference Sources

A Family Affair, Razor Coast

Endless Hills

See "The Frontier" for a description of the Endless Hills, which are technically part of the Westmarch but so remote from the duchy's control that they are more properly described as a part of Reme's frontier region.

Use the specific **Endless Hills Encounter Table** for random encounters in the Endless Hills.

The Kingdom Beneath

Alignment: Unknown
Ruler: Council of Grace
Government: Theocracy
Population: 30,000 or more (unknown species)
Languages: Telepathic communication with any language-capable beings
Religion: The Waking World
Resources: Unknown
Technology Level: Unknown

The Kingdom Beneath is an only-recently-rediscovered land concealed in a series of vast caverns stretching and honeycombing beneath, it would appear, almost the entirety of the Windreft (or so explorers from a nearby tiny town claim). Their tales are contradictory, however, and many do not yet believe them to be true. When asked by Duke Wylan of the Westmarches to produce proof of what they had seen, the explorers seemed (or pretended to seem) surprised to realize that they had no proof at all. These same explorers then supposedly returned to the Kingdom Beneath to seek corroboration of their claims. None has heard from them since their second departure.

According to their original, garbled tale, the Kingdom Beneath (called by its inhabitants "Awakening Grace") is a beautiful land full of glittering crystal, cathedral-like palaces, subterranean towers and spires, enthralling sculpture and music, magical lanterns as bright as the daylight above, and fantastical prismatic plants and creatures. All is harmonious and hospitable, and all citizens are wealthy and happy.

Beyond these details, however, all of the first explorers disagreed in their descriptions. The humans in the group claimed the inhabitants of the kingdom looked human. The elf said they looked like elves. The gnome saw gnomes, and the half-elf saw an entire kingdom of half-elves. Other details of their experiences disagreed as well, such that they emerged from their journey certain that they'd encountered an illusion or trick of some kind, but none of their mages were able to pierce or even fathom the magics to which they had been subjected (other than to confirm the presence of powerful illusion magic). When asked, the kingdom's inhabitants confirmed only that illusions are considered a prized artform among their people, and that of course there are illusions everywhere. The explorers were informed, they said, that it was considered discourteous in the Kingdom Beneath to attempt to pierce illusions.

History

The various peoples living in and around the Windreft have long shared legends of a glorious realm called the Kingdom Beneath. Records of these legends date back as far as recorded history, even among the elves of the Green Warden Forest. Most consider it only a fairytale, and even the oldest elven records treat the place like an ancient legend. Accounts are always vague yet extravagant, and until now none has written about the place as a first-person witness.

It is uncertain at what point the peoples living near the Windreft began once more to take the legend seriously and believe the Kingdom Beneath should be found and explored, but for the last several generations it has become relatively commonplace for adventurers and bored youths

to scour the Windreft wilderness areas for signs of an entrance to the kingdom. As the Windreft is a dangerous region, a number of deaths resulted from such pursuits, though during the long Westmarch civil war, a few deaths here or there were barely noticeable among all the constant warfare.

After Duke Wylan was given the authority and resources to step in and enforce peace in the duchy, Grand Duke Iltobarus himself took an interest in the Windreft, and no one knows for certain just why. He might have any number of reasons, including most obviously the easing of trade-transport through this dangerous corridor. Perhaps he has also received some perfectly mundane tip of a little-known resource to be mined in the area, or any other piece of Windreft-relevant intelligence. If Duke Wylan knows his liege's mind on the issue, he has said nothing to his people, but he has certainly been happy to help with all of the grand duke's projects for the region.

The locals, however, all assume that what the grand duke and duke are after is access to the Kingdom Beneath, and the number of explorers has increased at least one hundred-fold. Many a badger's den or interesting rock formation has been declared an entrance to the kingdom in the last few seasons, only to be discovered to be nothing of the kind.

Some believe that the now-missing explorers are engaged in the same sort of thing, with a liberal sprinkling of con-artistry and imagination mixed in, perhaps in an attempt to trick the duke or grand duke into granting them some sort of reward. When asked for proof, these naysayers insist, of course, that the "explorers" disappeared. If there is no Kingdom Beneath to prove, the best they can hope for is to leave town and wait to be forgotten.

Those who know the explorers in question, however, insist that they are not liars, and that if they were, their story would have been more consistent. No, their friends say, the missing explorers are good people, honest and brave, and if they haven't returned yet, they must have a reason. The longer these explorers remain missing, the more their friends in the region begin to worry for their safety.

According to the tale they told, however, the Kingdom Beneath was sealed to outsiders for thousands of years because the world was not ready for the awakening they offered. It is only, the inhabitants are said to have explained, in the last few years that the stars aligned once more in just the right way to allow them to admit visitors again. As the heavens move further into position, they will even gain the power to leave their magical realm and travel among the surrounding people, offering wisdom and blessings, and ushering in a new paradise beyond mortal imagination.

When asked about their species and origins, according to the explorers who supposedly spoke to them, the people of the Kingdom Beneath claimed to have come to this plane from beyond the stars and beyond time itself, and to themselves be entities beyond mortal comprehension, which they claimed as one of many reasons for their habitual illusions.

Since their arrival in this world, they supposedly say, they have devoted all of their efforts to bringing about a reign of eternal peace and harmony on earth. Thus far, they say, they have been thwarted in their efforts five times, over thousands and thousands of years of building up the resources to make the attempt. They hope that this time they will finally succeed, and they ask for all beings to support them in their endeavors.

Government

The explorers of the Kingdom Beneath were told that the kingdom is governed by divine appointment. All with gifts of prophesy or truth-sight are tested, and the most accurate diviners are appointed to the 77 seats of the seers. The 77 seers, they say, use divine inspiration from the holy Waking World to choose the Council of Grace, which is usually (but not always) nine members. The Council of Grace determines all laws for the kingdom and appoints all other government administrators.

It should be noted that while the people of the Kingdom Beneath call themselves Awakening Grace and are ruled by a council instead of a king, they do not, apparently, object to being called a "kingdom." The explorers who claim to have visited these strange beings say that the inhabitants of the kingdom do speak of a forgotten king. They do not speak the king's name, but they clearly hold him in reverence, almost as some sort of deity. They claim that when the world is fully awakened and ready, the forgotten king will be remembered, and all shall rejoice at his glory.

Locations in the Kingdom Beneath

The Shining Altar

Though the explorers' tales were inconsistent, one feature of the kingdom that all agreed had been present was the Shining Altar. Set on a grand, stepped pillar in the center of the city stood a beautiful crystalline altar. Though the explorers did not claim to have themselves witnessed any religious rituals, they reported that this was where community rituals were held when they occurred, and that from this altar the entire world would one day be transformed in the name of peace and joy.

Different explorers saw different sorts of offerings piled around the Shining Altar, including flowers, gemstones, foodstuffs, and works of art.

The Singing River

Another feature on which the explorers' stories mostly agreed was the Singing River. A sparkling, prismatic river flows through the kingdom, they said, running beneath and parallel to the Aciier river in the world above. The sound of this river was strangely musical, they said, and one explorer postulated that this was due to properties of the shape of the river's underground course, combined with the specific type of crystal that formed the walls of the kingdom's glorious, shimmering caverns. The waters of the Singing River tasted pure and perfect, like the sweetest and cleanest of mountain streams in the world above.

The Forbidden City

The explorers also agreed that one section of the Kingdom Beneath was closed to them. They were told only that visitors were not welcome there, but they agreed that from the outside that it seemed to be the most beautiful and palatial of all the neighborhoods they saw in the entire, crystalline kingdom.

Reference Sources

Town of Glory

Martyn's Nest

Alignment: Neutral Good
Ruler: Council of Ministers
Government: Three duke-appointed district ministers (Vennelitia Shiningtide, Augusthir Megson, and Athlindra Penabi) and their appointed staff
Population: 5,672 (Foerdewaith 2,120, Loreclans 1,737, elf 682, half-elf 567, halfling 341, dwarf 113, gnome 57, half-orc 55). The broader border of Martyn's Nest includes as many as 20,000 individuals.
Languages: Common, Elven, many others
Religion: Quell, Sefagreth
Resources: Fish, pearls, emeralds, mercenaries, shipping, foreign goods
Technology Level: Medieval and renaissance mixed

The size of Martyn's Nest depends entirely upon where one chooses to draw its borders. Many towns dot the western Reme coast, and as Reme's population has grown over the generations, the towns around Martyn's Nest in particular have bled together at the edges to form what some consider to be a single, sprawling town along the entire eastern shore of Martyn's Bay, nearly two-thirds the size of the city of Reme in total.

Officially, however, Martyn's Nest is a modest town on the southern Baronswood Peninsula, just south of the Quail River's shipping-friendly mouth. This is, indeed, the best-organized and best-governed portion of the city, with a population approaching 6,000 permanent residents and perhaps twice that during peak shipping seasons.

At one time, Martyn's Nest was the seat of a prestigious barony, but when the Westmarches' civil war broke out between the Brodcheks and Merciers, Lerwen Gummel, the baron of the Martyn's Bay region, had the poor taste to entangle this important Reman commercial asset in the conflict, siding with the Merciers and perpetrating the infamous Battle of Baronswood in the summer of 3499 I.R. Though forced for the most part to leave the Westmarches' duke to his own devices, the grand duke's advisors all agreed that civil war in Martyn's Nest would be devastating to Reme's security and economy. Thus, the baron was stripped of his lands and title, and his authority was replaced in the port city by a council of ministers.

These ministers successfully, with the help of the Reman navy, maintained Martyn's Nest's neutrality throughout the remainder of the civil strife. Though the first three have now retired with knighthoods for their service to the grand duke, Martyn's Nest remains governed by three appointed ministers. The current three are sworn in service to Duke Wylan Rogers and are generally highly regarded.

The Martyn's Nest market district is additionally known throughout the world for its remarkable gemcutters' guildhall expertly hewn from a giant natural crystal formation, and the mouth of the Quail River is considered one of the region's safest and tamest, even in bad weather, making Martyn's Nest one of the most popular ports of entry for merchants, not just in Reme, but in all the Crescent Sea. Martyn's Nest cannot yet compete for shipping prominence with the city of Reme or Castorhage, but it remains inarguably a major trade hub in the region and a major revenue source for Reme.

Government

The Martyn's Nest Council of Ministers consists of one elf, Vennelitia Shiningtide, and two humans, Augusthir Megson and Athlindra Penabi. Megson takes charge, primarily, of the Dockside District of Martyn's Nest; Penabi controls the high-class Eastlake district across Martyn's Lake; and Shiningtide directs the surrounding communities and natural areas. The Martyn's Nest city guard operates out of a citadel within city walls and is commanded by Captain Brant Viobie.

Locations in Martyn's Nest

Dockside District

For supposedly such a small town, Martyn's Nest has a slum as dangerous as that of any big city. This is the Dockside District. It's safe enough during the day, though the entire neighborhood reeks of rotting fish, and even in daylight it's not wise to wander away from the main thoroughfares or into blind alleys or abandoned warehouses. Nighttime is worse still and is known for regular muggings and turf wars between local gangs of smugglers, small-time pirates, and street youths that some claim are proxies for the supposedly-at-peace feuding noble houses.

The Martyn's Nest guard do what they can to keep crime at a minimum, especially near the all-important commercial neighborhoods, including the central docks themselves, but the rambling streets and rocky hills of the whole Martyn's Nest region lend themselves so well to sneaking, hiding, and other clandestine activities, that previous barons and now the Council of Ministers have all despaired of ever cleaning up the place.

The guard are, however, aided by a local mercenary group with an excellent reputation and good relations with the council. These are the Black Swords, run by an old half-orc named Riggen. The Black Swords work as guards for hire throughout the Dockside neighborhoods, and Martyn's Nest thieves and ne'er-do-wells know better than to bother anyone with Black Swords in their party. Even if you can beat them now, the rest of the Black Swords will track you down later to protect and avenge their own. Some have called the Black Swords just another gang and accused Riggen of running a protection racket (and Augusthir Megson of being in Riggen's pocket), but no evidence of wrongdoing on Riggen's part has ever come to light, and Black Swords caught committing crimes are run out of the organization and Martyn's Nest for good.

Temple of the Sea God

Quell is usually referred to as "the Sea God" along the Westmarch coast, with worshippers speaking his name only in reverent whispers out of respect and superstition. Said Sea God is by far the most popular deity in the entire Martyn's Nest region. No matter what other gods one might worship, or other religious practices one might espouse, everyone pays homage to the Sea God. It may seem strange then that the single most popular, best-funded temple in Martyn's Nest (and all the Westmarches) looks a bit like a pile of flotsam crossed with a sinking ship.

This forbidding and even shabby-looking structure, however, is designed as a deliberate acknowledgement of the Sea God's power, a humble fatalism in the face of the capricious sea. Inside, the temple is more obviously stable and well-built. Its materials remain simple and modest, but all is well-crafted and comfortable. Shrines all around the walls display relics from famous sailors, the saints of the local version of Quell's worship. These relics are also humble in materials and appearance, displayed for their legendary significance rather than their beauty or ostentation.

Obslyn, the elderly gnomish head priest, is much like his temple. Dour, grouchy, and forbidding on the surface, he is known to work night and day healing the sick and injured, blessing ships for travel, and otherwise ministering to the beleaguered Dockside community. Beyond the basic needs of the priests and of temple upkeep, all funds donated to Obslyn's temple are wisely invested in philanthropic efforts, providing for retired or disabled sailors and dockworkers, keeping the local waters clean and healthy for fishing, and anything else that might aid the poor of the Dockside District.

Eastlake

Across Martyn's Lake from smelly Dockside lies the pristine upper-class district known as Eastlake. The wind patterns across this saltwater lake are such that the aroma of the docks never reaches the wealthy merchants, nobles, and artists that make their homes in Eastlake. Pleasure craft and lake sports of every kind fill Martyn's Lake throughout the good-weather months, and inexpensive ferries serve as a quick and pleasant form of transport between Eastlake neighborhoods — and back to the Dockside, of course, but who wants to go there?

Beyond the lake itself, Eastlake is something of a fictional small town for rich city people to feel as if they're getting in touch with the sea. Oh, many commoners also live in Eastlake, if they can at all manage to afford to do so. The wealthy of Eastlake welcome these poorer neighbors, as the "small town feel" requires quaint small-town folk to run the small town shops and say folksy small town things at the taverns or when one hires them to clean one's house.

Eastlake residents are only willing to take their "small town experience" so far, however, and all the amenities of the big city are expected by the wealthier inhabitants. Given that this is a port city, and given the sprawling proximity of a number of other nearby towns, the folk of Eastlake have found that, for the right price, they can conjure whatever mixture of small town and big city best suits their individual tastes, ranging from the wildly decadent all the way to the almost plausibly rustic. Such comforts and extravagances, however, take a toll on the rest of Martyn's Nest and are often blamed for the squalor and peril of the neglected Dockside across the lake.

All three council ministers work constantly to balance and ameliorate the various troubles caused by the rather literal gentrification of the Eastlake district, but the poor of Martyn's Nest suspect that said ministers are also wooed by the grand events, expensive gifts, and fine dining offered them by the Martyn's Nest elite. They would try harder to fix things, the poor believe, if they were not so fond of remaining in the gentry's good graces. Others suspect that old former-Baron Lerwen Gummel is still a major power in the region behind the scenes. Though stripped of his title and holdings, Gummel remains a wealthy man and grows more bitter with age about his loss of status. Through years of strategic moneylending in the region, he is believed to hold most of the Martyn's Nest landowners deep in his debt, perhaps intending to reinstall himself as the de facto baron before he dies.

The Gemcutters Guild

The Martyn's Nest Gemcutters Guild grows more famous every year — around the Crescent Sea and beyond — as it is a unique structure in all the world. The specific geography of the Baronswood Peninsula, combined with the coastal current flowing ever northeastward from the Strait of Gehenna with its constant volcanic activity, has led to a prevalence of sheltered grottoes, caves, and tunnels all over the peninsula itself, which some scholars believe was formed by a buildup of volcanic detritus not long after whatever earthshaking, ancient event first created the Hellsgate Peaks.

These sheltered, rocky areas grow a type of crystal found in many parts of Akados — so common as to be nearly worthless — but here they are likelier than usual to grow to vast sizes, larger than the oldest trees in the region. These giant crystal formations are a wonder all their own, and local guides are happy to take visitors on short "crystal excursions" to the nearby, tamer wilderness areas. The largest and most beautiful giant crystals are harder to get to, and are found near the southern edge of the Baronswood itself, north and east of Martyn's Nest.

One of the most impressive giant crystal formations, however, is located in the Eastlake market district of Martyn's Nest and has been expertly carved to house a small gemcutters guild. Normally, these crystals crack or shatter easily when cut, and they have certainly never been considered a viable building material, but the expert gemcutters that founded the Martyn's Nest guild were so skilled that with a combination of patience, complex geological knowledge, and secret alchemical agents they were able to carve out this particular crystal formation to create a remarkably sturdy and beautiful structure that glows like flame during sunrise and sunset, especially in the winter, when the angle of the light comes more from the south.

In addition to the Green Mountain emeralds, local pearls, and other fine gems sold in the guild, visitors can purchase little chips "of the guild" as mementos. These are hand-cultivated crystal shards from the sheltered rear of the shop, which still boasts some living crystal. Guild mementos are ridiculously expensive for this type of crystal (up to 2 gp in peak trade months), and bear the guild's insignia in silver settings. Guild-members also advertise that they could quarry tiles from other large Baronswood Peninsula crystals to make for sturdy and decorative building materials, but the prices they charge, ostensibly for labor and secret alchemical ingredients, are so high that it is believed that no one has ever yet purchased such a service.

The guild itself is emptied of all gems at night, and their nighttime lockbox's location is a closely guarded secret. Few even know how or when the transport takes place — only that thieves targeting the guild have repeatedly been shocked to find it empty at night. Despite this, however, the Gemcutters Guild is heavily guarded at all times, because even at night the structure itself must be defended from vandals who have been known to chip pieces off the walls for bragging rights. The living crystal garden at the rear of the shop is especially well-defended, as portions of it have been lost to inexpert handling in the past and no longer grow new crystals.

Outside the guild, especially in some of the kitschier Dockside District shops, bits of cheap, ordinary crystals are sold to the ignorant as "guild chips," usually with brass settings and all manner of different (often inexpert) insignia, though the Gemcutters Guild doggedly pursues legal recompense from any and all who use the guild insignia outside the guild. These unofficial "guild chips" are usually about one-quarter the price of those sold in the guild, but still absurdly expensive for the materials and labor involved in their crafting.

Glondarr and Sirin

Down the coast from Martyn's Nest, a mere few hours walk in either direction (and closer still by sailing skiff), lie the villages of Glondarr to the northwest and Sirin to the southeast. Though officially separate towns in their own right, many from outside Martyn's Nest see both places more as Martyn's Nest neighborhoods, and even locals know that the Glondarr thieves' guild operates throughout the Martyn's Nest region, very much like a larger city's thieves' guild.

To most visitors, Glondarr feels like a continuation of the Dockside District (if a bit less smelly due to luckier weather patterns), while Sirin is where many of the servants and workers for Eastlake live if they can't afford the high prices around the neighborhoods where they work. Sirin is also home to a large and successful winery and a hilltop inn known for an excellent view of the sea from almost every room.

Appleton and Beyond

Out past Glondarr, to the north and west of Martyn's Nest, the entire coast of Martyn's Bay is settled, ostensibly by a series of separate fishing villages, though the larger Martyn's Nest grows, the more these villages bleed together at the edges. Appleton is the closest of these to Glondarr and Martyn's Nest. Appleton apples, apple butter, and cider are sold throughout the Martyn's Nest region, and each of the little towns farther down the coast tend to have their own little signature goods that are popular in the Martyn's Nest markets. When Appleton and the other Martyn's Bay towns are included as part of the same larger settlement, Martyn's Nest is arguably the largest city in the Westmarches.

Reference Sources

A Family Affair, Razor Coast

Fenria

Alignment: Neutral
Ruler: Countess Sevlania Fenrith-Dragul
Government: Feudalism
Population: 7,232 (mixed ethnicity human 3,428, Foerdewaith 1,536, hill dwarf 1,422, gnome 304, 239 elf, halfling 196, half-orc 102, other 5)
Languages: Common, Dwarven
Religion: Freya, Mithras, Solanus, some animism
Resources: Alchemists guild, college of wizardry, bard college
Technology Level: Medieval to Renaissance

The county of Fenrith (or earldom, as male Fenrith-Dragul lords style themselves earls instead of counts) is a long slender march in the eastern Westmarches that stretches from just north of Caer Dire in the north all the way to the coast in the south, and bordering on grand ducal lands the whole way. The seat of the Fenrith Earldom is Fenria, for which the original Fenrith family was named many centuries ago.

Fenria is located about halfway between Eckland and Gilboath, and about halfway between the Western Reme Road and the southeasternmost tip of the Green Mountains. It borders a small lake and a pretty little wetlands between itself and Eckland that are known as Brightfish Lake and Birdsong Marsh respectively. Since the end of the Westmarch civil war, a road-building project has begun from the Western Reme Road out to Fenria, though there has, of course, long been a hard-packed dirt road for trade and transport.

Fenria is a strange city and highly reflective of the strange and often secretive Fenrith-Dragul clan. It is the oldest city in the Westmarches, having been continuously settled since even before the Hyperborean expansion through the region. The oldest foundations in the center of the city are of elven origin, and the oldest surviving temple in the city is an ancient elven-style animistic earth temple. Some of the later temple additions indicate to scholars that Loreclannic humans and elves lived together peacefully here for perhaps a century or more before the warfare between humans and elves reached Fenria.

Scars in the ancient stonework and destruction of other elven temples indicate that the conflict eventually reached Fenria as well, and that the elven inhabitants were either driven away or massacred by hostile human invaders, but the city as a whole was not destroyed and was never abandoned through all the long centuries since its founding.

Some say the Fenrith family is just as old as the city and has always been there since its founding. Scholars find this highly improbable, but no solid proof can be found in either direction. What is known is that the Fenrith family were once very small-time landowners, baronets at most, but that through thick and thin, throughout recorded history, their power and wealth slowly and steadily grew until just the last few centuries.

The Dragul family, by contrast, enjoyed a meteoric rise from near anonymity, until they claimed the status of duke and took authority over their former rivals, the Dunavens. At that time, the Fenrith family were indirect vassals of the Draguls, beholden, in fact, to the Dunavens. The Draguls' fortunes changed, however, after the tragic events that led to the downfall of the Dunaven house, and some say that the murderous Lord Dunaven laid a powerful curse on the Draguls before drinking himself to death in his rapidly deteriorating castle.

It is true that Dragul fortunes plummeted after Dunaven's death, though whether these two facts are in any way related is unknown. The Lord Dragul of that time was a known gambler, so it is not surprising that he found himself deeply in debt and ultimately falling from the king's and the grand duke's good graces. By the time Reme declared its independence from Foere, the Dragul family holdings were reduced to little more than the Dunavens had held as their former vassals, and their lands were impoverished and sickly, with one exception: Fenria.

However bad things got, Fenria continued to prosper, and the Fenriths, having founded a small bard college and a college of wizardry in their city, grew significantly wealthier than their lieges, and were promoted to the lesser peerage as barons. During that era, which also corresponded with a spate of petty (and bloody) intrigue-feuding between the Draguls and Harrings (relatives by marriage to the fallen Dunavens), a lesser Dragul daughter and Fenrith son fell in love and secretly married, much to all four parents' fury. This young couple moved to Eckland, where they and their descendants (the first Fenrith-Draguls) gained a reputation as canny diplomats and wily economists. They made many connections with other nobles of many houses and were well-liked in all the most powerful circles (other than among the Harrings, of course). Meanwhile, the main Dragul family continued to decline.

Eventually, only one Dragul countess remained, childless and twice widowed, while the Fenrith-Draguls (and the Fenriths) still prospered. The last Countess Dragul was said to hate the Fenrith-Draguls passionately, and she wrote in her will that no scion of the Fenrith-Draguls should inherit her title and holdings under any circumstances. Unfortunately, the same pox that killed her also killed her adopted heir, leaving her march without a head. The grand duke and the duke of the Westmarches weighed the deceased countess's will against the Fenrith-Dragul's claim, and ultimately decided, in the name of expediency, that the will should be disregarded and the well-respected Fenrith-Draguls granted the march seat. The first Fenrith-Dragul count of Dragul March styled himself an earl, as a playful dig at the Harrings who'd been making fun of the Brodcheks for calling themselves earls instead of counts.

Within a single year of the Fenrith-Draguls accepting the Dragul county seat (at that time nearer to the coast, in Sheffen), their fortunes plummeted as the other Draguls' had. Their ventures lost money, their allies deserted them, and their reputations fell. In each individual case, the causes seemed normal and coincidental, but taken in total, it was, indeed, an eerie pattern. It is said that the earl's personality changed dramatically as well. Before his title as a peer, he was cheerful, witty, charming, and known for his lilting and insightful poetry. After becoming an earl, he grew withdrawn, unreadable, his wit sarcastic and biting, and his poetry lost all popularity.

The Fenrith-Draguls mended fences with their Fenrith relatives generations previously, but now Earl Dragul became strangely obsessed with his distant cousins, visiting their home in Fenria for months at a time and prowling their baronial mansion at all hours of the night. He took a younger Fenrith cousin (a very distant cousin) to be his wife, and their marriage seemed happy enough, but after a few years and a few children with her, he became obsessed once more with the Fenrith family home. Eventually, he frightened the Fenrith baron, and they quarreled. Earl Dragul went home, apologized to his in-laws and distant relatives by letter and gifts, and his apology was accepted.

Then a plague hit Fenria. As the disease spread with unnatural swiftness, Fenria's healers soon discovered that their magics did them no good. The greatest healers in Reme were called to intervene, but to no avail. It seemed this plague could not be cured by magic, and several who came to aid the sick fell ill themselves and died. It was the worst and deadliest disaster to touch this otherwise ever-fortunate city in all of its recorded history, and the nobility were for some reason the worst affected. The grand duke quarantined the city, and the plague took three years to finish running its full course. By the time it was done, two-thirds of the population of Fenria had died, including every single member of the Fenrith family other than the earl's wife.

Earl Dragul and his family went into public mourning for their cousins and vassals for three years, and the rest of the Fenrith-Dragul clan followed his lead. To honor his fallen family members, he said, the earl requested and received permission from the duke and grand duke to change the earldom's name to Fenrith and his own title to Earl Fenrith. After this mourning period, he held a great ritual of "life and peace" in Fenria, to which he invited priests of every religion in the region, dignitaries from all over the Crescent Sea, and even the Harrings, who did deign to send a lesser daughter to the event. The ritual is recorded to have been beautiful, and all who wrote about it claimed to feel the blessing of the gods upon them that day, though three also recorded disliking Earl Fenrith and shivering as he passed them.

Earl Fenrith then moved his earldom's seat to Fenria and invited many of the other Fenrith-Draguls to join him there. Many accepted his offer. He also expanded the bardic and wizardry schools and founded an alchemy school in the same part of town, then sent messages far and wide to draw students from all over the world. Though the Fenrith-Dragul coffers were somewhat diminished since his ascension to the nobility, they were still at that time quite wealthy. They offered monetary incentives to artisans and teachers, craftsfolk and even serving staff from many lands and cultures to help repopulate poor Fenria.

And Fenria, once again, prospered. More interestingly, the strange descent of the Fenrith-Dragul fortunes seemed to cease. The family, when asked, laughed it all off as an unlikely series of coincidences, and resumed their former dealings, seeming to prosper once more. Less than two years later, a terrible earthquake struck the former Dragul seat in Sheffen. The old palace crumbled to the ground, killing three of the newly-appointed baron's family. Hundreds of others in the town lost their lives as well. Sheffen was rebuilt but has remained underpopulated and rarely visited by outsiders in the following years.

Since that day, Fenria itself has continued to prosper, and its people are known to be happy and well-off, nearly untouched by the war. It is currently at the highest population it has ever known, and its bards, wizards, and alchemists are employed far and wide when they leave their respective schools.

The Fenrith-Draguls, on the other hand, largely keep to themselves. They are known now for intrigues and mystery instead of diplomacy and finance, and no one really knows for sure how wealthy they are, as they seem to have mastered the art, as a family, of always appearing wealthy regardless of the reality. The rest of the Fenrith Earldom is doing better under the Fenrith-Draguls than it did under the Draguls after the fall of the Dunavens, but outside Fenria, it can't truly be said that Fenrith lands are prosperous. The people mostly get by, sometimes better than others, and they are glad the war is over. No more, no less.

Many in the Westmarches and beyond suspect some eldritch mystery to the bizarre fortunes of the Dragul and Fenrith families, but if such a thing exists, the Fenrith-Draguls guard the secret jealously. Nothing of import has ever been found in the ruins of the old Dragul palace outside Sheffen, and no one has ever been permitted to search the Fenrith mansion as the first Earl Fenrith did before it became his own home. If someone were to investigate the place, perhaps the secret history would finally be unlocked, or perhaps it really all has just been coincidence.

FERDOZAN

Alignment: Chaotic Evil
Ruler: Queen-Matron Helsass
Government: Absolute monarchy
Population: 4,943 (drow 1,124, driders 1,358, slaves, many species 2,461)
Languages: Drow, Undercommon
Religion: Queen of Spiders
Resources: Weapons, magic, slaves, assassins
Technology Level: Medieval

Ferdozan is one of the best known drow cities in the northern Akadonian Under Realms. Situated deep beneath the Green Mountains and accessible by tunnels opening into the Quail Valley, word of the might of Ferdozan has reached far and wide, and some believe that this has been its undoing.

Ferdozan has access to a *gateway* to the remains of faraway Barakus, and in recent generations has been exploring the possibility of founding a new city there. Many Ferdozan troops have been committed to this project, and perhaps that is part of the explanation for Ferdozan's currently diminished state, but some suspect, rather, that the whole purpose of this attempt to start anew in Barakus is that something has gone terribly wrong in Ferdozan.

Queen Matron Helsass and her consort and vizier, Tiernant, as well as her various commanders, all take great pains to hide Ferdozan's weakness from outsiders, but anyone gaining entrance to this vast and sprawling underground city can see that most of its homes and streets are empty and abandoned. The city is designed to be easily defended by very few troops and a scattering of mages, such that every entrance tunnel remains secure from all incursion, even with such diminished forces, but the population of Ferdozan is declining rapidly. If this trend continues, it may not be long before the city falls.

Threatened from all sides by every manner of other Under Realms' denizen, it is difficult to discern clearly what has led Ferdozan to this pass. Certainly most of the once-mighty city's inhabitants have been kept in the dark, as it were, and those few who might know more are not sharing their knowledge. Rumor speaks of incurable disease, curses, the withdrawal of the Spider Queen's blessing, derro plots and poisons, unimaginable horrors from the depths beneath the city, and even the work of unknown adventurers. Whatever the case, it is not impossible that Ferdozan's fall would mean something much worse for Quail Valley and the rest of Reme.

There are entities dwelling in the darkness, deep beneath the bright, upper world, that are far more terrible than mere drow, after all.

REFERENCE SOURCES

The Vault of Larin Karr, The Lost City of Barakus

FORSWEN

Alignment: Neutral
Ruler: Count Geossep Harring
Government: Feudalism
Population: 6,213 (Foerdewaith 4,226, Loreclans 1,987)
Languages: Common
Religion: Freya, Mithras, Solanus
Resources: Grain, berries and preserves, other foodstuffs, river pearls
Technology Level: Medieval

Harring County is somewhat like a half moon in shape nestled between the eastern Green Mountains and the Quail River in the north and stretching down to include a short stretch of the Westmarch coast in the south, encompassing on the way the majority of the land between the Quail and the county's shared border with the Fenrith Earldom to the east, with the exception of the duke's lands, which hug the river between Eckland and the sea.

Forswen, the Harring County seat, sits on the Quail River some ways north of its confluence with the Aciier, and just south of the Western Akadian Forest. It is known as the best place in the Westmarches to buy raspberries, raspberry jam, raspberry wine, and really any food involving raspberries. Unfortunately, it is also known for some terrible recent injustices.

The Harring family has always had a strange set of values as the Westmarches go. They did not support Reman secession from Foere, and though they have always sworn fealty to the grand duke of Reme and have never shown any lack of Rhemish patriotism, they have, as a family, historically retained a sort of kneejerk Foerdewaith purism, affecting a lifestyle they believe (some scholars have said wrongly so) to be traditional Foerdewaith culture (foods, fashion flourishes, holidays, etc.). With staggering inattention to history, they claim they do this to honor Reme's glorious origins.

For the most part, this attitude has been little more than a pretentious family quirk over the generations, but in the recent Westmarch civil war, this "quirk" took a truly unfortunate turn, with damaging consequences for Forswen, Eckland, and many thousands of Westmarch citizens. Indeed, Geossep Harring has only been count for five years, and his youth and inexperience are really the only thing that has protected the Harring family from major censure by not just Duke Wylan but the grand duke himself.

The previous count was Geossep's grandfather, Theswick. Theswick Harring was always an arrogant man with little compassion for the common folk of his county, and though he never said so publicly, some close to him, including his son, Gavrus, have admitted since the war that he hated non-humans of all kinds. Though many believed he treated non-humans unfairly as count, his early injustices were never so egregious that one could say for certain he wasn't simply unkind to all commoners equally.

Late in the civil war, however, during a period in which the Harrings had taken over occupation of Eckland, the count's family say he came home from one river battle just outside Forswen forever changed in some way that he never articulated to anyone else. All those around him could see was that he suddenly refused to tolerate non-humans anywhere near him. First, he fired all of his non-human servants, and when others protested, he doubled down, ordering that all non-humans of all species be driven from Forswen and Eckland.

Only those who protested the deportation were harmed in any way, and very few lives were lost to violence in this mass-exile, especially in comparison with the rest of the bloodshed going on elsewhere in the Westmarches at that time. Nevertheless, some 6,000 or more people were driven from their homes, out into the countryside, and told simply to "find another liege." This forced a tide of what were effectively refugees out of Harring County and into surrounding regions during an extremely unstable time, which in turn weighed upon the already war-strained resources of other communities. It also, of course, grossly disrupted the lives of the victims. Many have argued that although the death toll from the original exile was very low, perhaps as low as four, the deaths ultimately resulting from the count's actions — due to exposure, starvation, or lack of safe shelter in a wildly unsafe-at-the-time world — were eventually much higher, in the hundreds at the very least.

As the exiles continued, a brave coalition of humans stepped forward. These were mostly humans of non-Foerdewaith or mixed heritage — though many were entirely Rhemish of culture, some for generations. These courageous Rhemishfolk signed a collective letter to the count that stated that non-human Rhemish were exactly the same as they were: peoples who had joined Reme from other cultures and become part of Reme and made Reme richer and better for their contribution. In a fit of rage entirely uncharacteristic for the normally stuffy and formal count, he publicly tore up the letter in question and followed this shocking tantrum with a proclamation that all non-Foerdewaith humans were also to be exiled as the non-humans had been.

This second proclamation affected a larger number of higher-ranking aristocrats than the first had, and was therefore the final straw for the rest of the Harring family. With the first exile, they'd trusted that the count had some purpose or plan in his terrible treatment of his non-human subjects, but with him extending the behavior to include fellow humans, they decided he must have gone mad. They requested he change his mind, and he refused. They pleaded and attempted to bargain with him, and he refused. All this while, the victims were already being driven from their homes and out into the countryside with only what they could carry, just as the non-humans had been.

Harring family internal loyalty and fixation with tradition and propriety were such that it took more than two years of back-and-forth wheedling as well as failed attempts at diplomacy and manipulation before the rest of the Harrings finally gave in and openly argued with their count. In response, he flew into a monstrous, destructive rage, screaming, cursing, and destroying things — all behaviors far above and beyond anything anyone who knew him would ever have thought him capable. At the height of his tantrum, he suddenly collapsed in a seizure and died before a healer could even reach his side.

In examining the count's corpse, the healer informed the family that a swelling in his brain had been driving him mad for years and had finally grown large enough to kill him. A simple spell to remove diseases could have saved him at any time, but no one had realized he needed a healer.

Shamed by their public support of a madman — especially when standing up to him sooner could not only have saved thousands of people from losing their homes but also have led to the curing of the old count's madness — the Harring family, under the direction of Gavrus, the new count now known as "the three-day's count," immediately rescinded the banishment of all citizens of Eckland and Forswen. Count Gavrus then abdicated to his 19-year-old son in atonement for having himself obeyed Count Theswick's cruel orders.

Young Count Geossep has governed Harring County and the city of Forswen since then with what some call remarkable humility and maturity for his age, and the current residents of Forswen are thus far pleased with his largely circumspect governing style, but his path is unlikely to be an easy one. He is now by far the youngest of the duchy's march heads, widely believed to be outmatched in authority, experience, and sheer wiliness by his various peers, and his situation grows more complex from there.

Barely a year after Geossep's assumption of the title of count, the old duke of the Westmarches was murdered, and Duke Wylan was appointed by the grand duke. Geossep Harring immediately swore fealty to the new duke and is said to have been very helpful in negotiating the end of the long civil war.

Nevertheless, in the five years since the revocation of Count Theswick's disastrous exile decrees, very few of those banished have returned to Forswen. In many cases, they simply settled elsewhere and do not wish to be uprooted again, but most of the surviving victims remain angry with the Harring family and feel that not nearly enough punishment took place for their complicity in Count Theswick's crimes. Sentiment against the Harrings in surrounding marches is very high among dwarves especially, who were among the most grievously impacted communities. Relations between Forswen and the city of Gemtown in the Green Mountains are more strained than they have ever been, which is bad news for Forswen's jewelers, glassmakers, and many other artisans who rely on materials from the dwarven mines.

Forswen's streets are all but empty of traffic, and many homes and shops stand vacant. Even if Geossep Harring were to initiate a sponsorship program to entice former residents back "home," many feel that a simple apology of that nature would not be enough to balance the scales of the harm done. In any case, the question is moot, as the Harring family are currently struggling for funds for their investments and county upkeep, and may never again have the kind of power and wealth they once did.

Those in Forswen whose beloved friends and neighbors were driven away — and in some cases died before they could find new homes — would like Duke Wylan to find some solution, some way to heal their city's still-open wounds, but in 20 years of war, many atrocities were committed on all sides, and the new duke has his hands full solving all of them. There is also fear that should Wylan Rogers appear to show any favoritism at all among the four primary contributors to the duchy's internal strife, resentment and wounded pride would ultimately lead to a resumption of the violence. Whatever Duke Wylan decides, the people of Forswen only hope to see their home thrive once more. They just don't know where to begin.

THE GALLOWS

The Gallows is a teardrop-shaped island some 450 miles to the southwest of Martyn's Nest in the Crescent Sea, with an extension on the northern end that gives it the vague resemblance of a hangman's noose. The island runs 20 miles north to south and eight miles east to west. A light pine forest dots the entire island except for the center, where a craggy hill known as Dead Man's Head resides. The eastern beach holds the remnants of a village and cemetery of unknown origin.

Previously known as God's Tear Island, for many years it was an important trading port and safe haven for merchants in the midst of the Crescent Sea. Though surrounding reefs make the waters around the island perilous to navigate, the islanders learned the passages and would row out to ships arriving at the island and lead them safely to the docks.

About 100 years ago, however, the baron at Martyn's Nest learned that the island was the haven of a group of fierce pirates that had been terrorizing the sea lanes out of Reme. The baron mobilized a large fleet and seized the island. The islanders mysteriously vanished before he arrived, but four months later, the baron's fleet sank or captured each and every one of the pirates' ships in a battle. It is said that, as they looted the vacant island, the baron's soldiers reportedly saw strange shapes lurking in the shadows and heard disturbing noises. At first, these reports were dismissed, but then soldiers began to disappear in the night. Their bodies would eventually be found with fearful expressions on their faces, but no marks on them to indicate how they had died. By the time the baron's soldiers left the island, rumors spread that it was haunted by the ghosts of the dead pirates. The baron's soldiers returned to tell the tales to their families, and the name of the island became known as the Gallows. To this day, the island remains uninhabited, and sailors refuse to go there, as they believe the island is cursed.

GREEN MOUNTAINS

The Green Mountains are named for the Green Mountain Clan of hill dwarves, who in turn named themselves for the emeralds they mine in their Green Mountain towns. A now-extinct volcanic range, the Green Mountains are known primarily for these emeralds, which are said to be of particularly desirable brightness and clarity. Relations between humans and the Green Mountain dwarves have always been reasonably good, perhaps because the dwarves' stone cities — carved directly into the mountains as they are — are so well defended that the humans could never have profitably threatened them. Instead, human settlers brought only trade and increased prosperity for the Green Mountains, and as such, the Green Mountain Clan has long sworn fealty to the grand duke of Reme and to the duke of the Westmarches in which the Green Mountains are located.

Due to this relationship, much intermingling of dwarf and human cultures has taken place in the Westmarches and, aside from war-ravaged Eckland and Forswen, most central Westmarch cities and towns have a sizable population of dwarves living among the humans. The reverse is also true in the Green Mountains, as the Green Mountain Clan has welcomed humans and other Reman citizens to live in the dwarven cities. Humans are less suited, however, to spending weeks at a time underground in tunnels, no matter how palatial they might in some cases be. Without regular sunlight, most humans (and elves) grow dissatisfied and unhappy, something most dwarves find unfathomable. Nevertheless, the dwarves in and around the Green Mountains are more integrated into Reman culture than any other dwarves in the region.

Aboveground, the mountains are not particularly habitable, with the sole exception of the fertile Quail Valley just east of the range's heart. Nevertheless, certain sections of the mountains, particularly the southeastern spur, seem to be crawling with orcs and hobgoblins, and some suspect that the Green Mountains may be full of tunnels and caverns even outside the dwarf cities, built by creatures on much-less-friendly terms with Reme than are the Green Mountain dwarf clan.

Rocs also nest in the Green Mountains, preying primarily on the bighorn sheep that thrive there. The rocs have an important ecological niche, as this particular species of sheep has a tendency to overbreed and starve without natural predation. That being said, the rocs are extremely troublesome to the residents of the Quail Valley, and in the spring and summer are sometimes known to harass mountain travelers as well.

A local legend surrounding the Green Mountains sprang up not long after they were first accurately mapped and has clung to them ever since, though no evidence for such a tale exists. The claim is that the mountain range is in the shape of a truly massive dragon. The northwest spur is its head, the southeast spur its tail, and the north and southwest tips of the range are the wings. This, says the legend, is evidence that the largest green dragon that ever lived was slain here, and that the entire mountain range is, in effect, its burial mound.

Since the dwarven stone experts that live in the mountains say that the range was formed by volcanic activity — as were many of the smaller mountain ranges in western Akados — this tale seems highly unlikely, little more than wild imagination. That doesn't stop the commonfolk from frightening one another with tales of evil wizards come to raise the undead dragon from its grave, or other such horrors. Earl Brodchek is known to have a peculiar phobia of the mountain dragon, however, to the point that at least one of the battles between himself and Count Mercier is said to have begun because the count was teasing the earl about the dragon's imminent return.

Use the **Mountains Encounter Table** for random encounters in the Green Mountains and within any half-hex around them.

REFERENCE SOURCES

The Book of Taverns, *A Family Affair*, *Town of Glory*, *The Vault of Larin Karr*

KEMRESEN

Alignment: Neutral
Ruler: Count Regdel Mercier IV
Government: Feudalism
Population: 9,839 (Foerdewaith 5,956, Loreclans 2,315, hill dwarf 1,537, elf 26, other 5)
Languages: Common
Religion: Freya, Mithras, Solanus
Resources: Arms and armaments, cattle
Technology Level: Medieval

Kemresen is the county seat of Mercier County, located on the south bank of the southeastern Aciier River, about halfway between Silverlight and Eckland. A previous count installed a movable bascule bridge over the Aciier at this point, some say primarily to irritate the earl of Brodchek whose march also borders the southeastern Aciier to the north. The Kamresen bridge floods out at least twice a year and until recently has rarely been safe to use even when dry because of the sporadic warfare across it between Mercier and Brodchek forces. For some years near the end of the war, it simply stood open and useless.

Aside from its bridge, Kemresen is a heavily fortified town known for constructing cheap and relatively high quality arms and armaments, as well as for passable beef cattle. Decades of civil war have left the city struggling, impoverished, and rife with intrigue, but since Duke Wylan's new peace and the grand wedding between Lusea Mercier and Relm Brodchek, local morale is improving. For reasons few understand, the current Count Mercier is very popular with his people, who mostly supported the civil war despite the way they suffered for it, and who now support the end of it as a rousing victory for Mercier, despite all evidence to the contrary. Some say that Regdel IV is simply that good at oratory and propaganda.

The Kemresen bridge, however, has been wildly unpopular with the common folk since its first construction, generations ago. Considered an annoyance to river traffic and not particularly useful for foot traffic, it has long been colloquially known as the "Fool's Dam." Sometimes an "n" is affectionately added at the end when the nickname is written down. Since the new peace, however, and the marriage alliance between Mercier and Brodchek, trade traffic has been crossing the bridge for the first time in many decades, and some talk is circulating of replacing the Fool's Dam with a larger and better-conceived Kemresen bridge in the near future.

KHAZFRECHT

Alignment: Lawful Good
Ruler: Baroness Mesha Greenmountain (hill dwarf)
Government: Feudalism
Population: 6,879 (hill dwarf 5,756, Foerdewaith 736, Loreclans 315, half-orc 63, other 9)
Languages: Common, Dwarven
Religion: Freya, Mithras, Solanus, Dargath
Resources: Emeralds, jewelry, feldspar, simple glass, other gems and metals as available
Technology Level: Medieval

Khazfrecht, or "Gemtown" in Common, is the largest of the surviving ancient dwarven settlements and mines in the Green Mountains. It is carved directly into the mountains themselves and situated near the top of Emerald Falls, a long and lovely waterfall along the northern Quail River. Famous primarily for their emeralds, Gemtown residents collect and experiment with uses for many minerals they find in their mines and have been making some interesting innovations in the field of glassblowing.

Though the city itself is very old, having existed for centuries or perhaps millennia longer than the nation of Reme, the culture is unusually cosmopolitan for a mountain fastness of its kind, and offers music, cuisine, and other amenities from all over Reme, especially in the summers when trade up and down the Quail River is at its height.

Like most of the Westmarches, Khazfrecht has suffered economically over the last few decades in the civil war, but — having remained both neutral and unassailable throughout the conflict — this ancient city suffered fewer losses than much of the rest of the duchy. Many dwarven refugees from the purge years in Eckland and Forswen have relocated here, however, so the city is more crowded than it has ever been, and as belts and purse strings have tightened, both crime and civil unrest have grown. Nothing has ever quite tipped over the edge into riot or worse, but Gemtown citizens tend to have very mixed feelings about Baroness Mesha, who is said to have been too harsh with the poor, especially near the end of the duchy's long crisis.

Since Duke Wylan managed to bring about the end of the civil war, however, Gemtown has been in a prime position to take advantage of the newly resurging Westmarch economy, and the baroness is doing her best to use this opportunity to move public opinion back in her favor. She is not hated, but she has not yet succeeded in making herself loved, and much intrigue and rebellion is whispered in Gemtown's shadows, even now that prosperity is once more beginning to reign.

Another crisis may yet loom on the horizon for Khazfrecht, as more than a dozen miners in the deepest mines on the city's east side report hearing sounds in the tunnels that, in these miners' expert opinions, are not normal. To her credit, Baroness Mesha is handling this situation with appropriate care and caution. Work in those mines ceased and a team of specialized stone scholars was called in to investigate. However, no one yet knows what they will find regarding these strange sounds, and some residents fear that whatever built the tunnels the orcs and hobgoblins are using in other parts of the Green Mountain range may now be trying to tunnel its way into Gemtown as well.

KNIFE'S EDGE RIDGE

Out in the middle of Mercier County, smack in the center of one simple farmer's plot of fields, stands a rock formation that locals have known for time out of mind as Knife's Edge Ridge. The ridge does indeed look very much like a knife blade in shape, thin and long and somewhat triangular, as if someone had buried a dagger on its side and left a third or so of the blade sticking up from the earth. The ridge is as tall as an ogre at its tallest point, where it drops off in a sheer and improbably flat line on the southern edge. It is as long from there as four horses standing end to end, tapering slowly until it vanishes into the earth in the north.

Several farmers have tried to dig the ridge up over the years, both out of curiosity to see how deep it went and also simply to get it out of the way of their ploughs, but none has ever succeeded at unearthing the thing. Several generations back, the countess of Mercier declared it a county treasure and made tampering with it or harming it in any way a fineable offense. A small wooden sign posted next to it explains as much.

What is far stranger, however, is what the current tenant of the property discovered about the ridge just last year. She decided to build a nice fence around the ridge to discourage potential vandals and to stop her dogs from digging next to it. As she sank in her post hole digger in preparation for raising the fence, however, she very shockingly heard the clang of metal on metal. Digging further, she found what seemed to be a large bronze sheet buried at the back of the ridge behind the sheer drop at its tallest point.

Growing ever more curious, she called over a few of her friends, and they all began digging furiously, revealing a longer bronze slat, several inches wide, buried in the earth. Suddenly, one of her friends stopped digging and stared up at the Knife's Edge Ridge, suggesting that everyone take a few steps back. The diggers all did so, and soon all were staring in amazement.

If one imagined the stone of the ridge to be an earthen crust hardened around a metal core …

… then the bronze slat in the earth was of the perfect size and placement to be the tang of a truly titanic bronze dagger.

Knife's Edge Ridge, indeed.

The farmer and her friends informed Count Mercier immediately, who gave permission to investigate further, and even sent a wizard to examine the ridge. Further digging northward toward the ridge revealed that the buried slat was, in fact, connected to the ridge, and that the ridge itself contained a core of ancient bronze beneath its stony crust. The count's wizard consultant did not believe the gigantic dagger to be magical, but digging farther south, away from the "ridge" and toward the end of the tang, revealed something more bizarre still: enormous bones, shaped exactly, the wizard claimed, as if they were the bones of a hand large enough to grip such a dagger.

Further excavation is ongoing. The count's wizard would like to find the giant's skull in the hope of learning more about what sort of being lies buried here, but the count's pockets are not especially deep so few years after the end of the long war, and he worries that Duke Wylan would prefer for his vassals to concentrate on restoring the Westmarches, not digging them up. Only time will tell what the people at Knife's Edge Ridge may discover about the ancient dagger and its fallen owner, or how long the count will permit them to remain at their task.

MUSEIDS

A single ancient monolith stands in the center of the southwestern Aciier floodplain in the middle of nowhere and covered in water for at least a month out of every year. Carved into the monolith are ancient symbols from an unknown language, as well as old Hyperborean letters reading a nonsense word that might be "musedzeko," and in Common, the word Museids. No one knows who placed the monolith there or what the words chiseled into it might mean, but many in the local region, even as far off as West Fortress, believe the monolith to be cursed and advise travelers to give it a wide berth should they happen upon it.

Several nearby villages have a tale, usually about someone's great-grandparent or great-great aunt or uncle, but the tale is always the same: Almost 100 years ago now, someone from the village became suddenly obsessed with "going to Museids." Those affected claimed they could feel it in their bones and in their blood; they could hear it singing inside their heads. They had to go to Museids. This persisted for three days and three nights, with the affected villagers growing increasingly unresponsive to any topics other than their ever more desperate need to go to Museids. Then, sometime on the third night, most of them slipped away from their homes and loved ones and were gone by morning, never to be heard from again.

Several were last seen wandering in the general direction of the Museids standing stone. Three were followed for miles before giving friends or family members the slip without apparently trying to. One, a young boy, was locked up by his parents and denied the ability to leave the house. He was found dead in his bonds at dawn the next day. Finally, one single affected villager, so the tale goes, was followed all the way to the standing stone, or at least to where the standing stone should have been. Instead, the Museids-obsessed villager's daughter described seeing a large and half-ruined city full of happily talking and laughing ghosts, and also with terrible, prowling shadows like those of hunting beasts.

This witness said that in a single glance she knew she should not set foot within the city. She chased her father to the edge, clinging to him in an attempt to stop him, but she wasn't strong enough. He stepped onto the half-ruined cobbles, and some power she couldn't explain threw her back away from him, into the mud of the surrounding, ordinary countryside where she lost consciousness. Other family members who'd been out searching with her found her half frozen the next morning. At 13 years old, every hair on her formerly red head had turned pure white overnight. The strange city was gone without a trace, and neither she nor anyone else in the village ever again saw any sign of it. All that remained was the lone monolith in its field of mud.

The woman lived to a ripe old age and passed the tale on to her grandchildren, but when she grew very old indeed, she began to wander in her mind, as some old folk are known to do. She frightened her family, however, when in the last month before her death, she woke weeping and shaking from terrible nightmares and spoke of Museids as if it were her home, as if she needed to get back there. A priest was called without delay to remove any curse placed on her mind, but the family were informed, upon examination, that the only magic clinging to her was that of divination. She might be confused, but she suffered from visions, not a curse.

For the last three days of her life, she said only these words, over and over: "Museids. One hundred years. Museids. One hundred years."

Next year will be the 100th since the incident, if these tales are to be believed. Many in the region are concerned that the phenomenon will repeat itself, but no one has any idea what they might do to stop it. Some suggest destroying the monolith, but others fear that the monolith might be a ward of some kind, and that the problem would only grow worse if it were gone. Four village elders petitioned Countess Aciier to hire a band of heroes to wait for the city of Museids to appear once more and to enter it of their own free will to discover its mysteries and learn how to stop it from ever returning again. It is unknown as yet whether the countess will grant such a strange request.

QUAIL RIVER

The Quail River has its source in the Quail Valley, high in the Green Mountains. Fed by several mountain tributaries, the Quail goes on to pass the dwarven fortress of Khazfrecht (also called Gemtown) and from there plunges down a cliff face to the fields and forest below in the beautiful Emerald Falls. A large and sturdy platform attached to massive ropes and pulleys allows for ease of transport and trade up the cliff near the falls, or a stone-paved path, full of switchbacks and steep stairs cut into the rock, serves as a longer path around the falls and lacks the toll fee of the elevator platform.

Passed the Emerald Falls, the Quail River becomes a major trade route, often busy with barges, fishing craft, and all manner of other river commerce, as the people of the central Westmarches move their goods southward to the markets in Eckland and Martyn's Nest. About halfway between the Emerald Falls and the sea, the Quail meets up with the temperamental Aciier, flows passed (or rather, through) the Westmarches' capital of Eckland, and thence down passed the Baronswood to Martyn's Nest and the Crescent Sea. From the Emerald Falls to the sea, the Quail River is prone to flooding, like most other major rivers in the region, though in the Quail's case this usually takes place in predictable and manageable amounts, without interfering too terribly in the central Westmarches' farming, trade, or transport.

The Quail is also a well-managed river in a populated area, for most of its length, meaning that it is relatively free of monsters and other major dangers (with the possible exception of roc attacks during their autumn migration). It is, however, well-stocked with fish of several varieties, including a delicious species of bluegill, as well as a freshwater mussel known for fine river pearls.

The most dangerous area on the Quail (with the possible exception of its source in the Quail Valley) is in the south as it flows passed the Baronswood. Whatever mysterious horror lurks in that wood has yet to make a documented attack on a craft in the Quail River, but bandits are sometimes known to lay ambushes among the trees at the forest's edge along the river's east bank in the hope of stealing cargo and coin from wealthy travelers. It is wise, therefore, to be wary of narrow bends in the river as it passes the Baronswood, and to look out especially for signs of the large nets some bandits are known to stretch across the river from bank to bank in order to trap a vessel for boarding.

Use the **River (General) Encounter Table** for generating random encounters on and near the Quail River.

REFERENCE SOURCES

The Vault of Larin Karr, A Family Affair

QUAIL VALLEY
N
W
E
S
1 Hex - 5 Miles
River Wren
Bostwick
B
K
H
G
I
J
F
Forest of Nin
C
D
E
A
Pembrose
Quail River
Twain
M
L
O
N
Gaskar Hills

Quail Valley

Quail Valley divides the eastern and western ranges of the Green Mountains. An exceptionally fertile, sheltered valley near the center of the Green Mountains, Quail Valley was formed by a massive volcanic explosion not long before the Green Mountains ceased all volcanic activity. The nutrient-rich ash left behind in the resulting crater turned over time into exceedingly productive soil, and eventually this apparently idyllic little valley was discovered and settled by humans and others.

Quail Valley is quite difficult to access, even from the dwarven settlements within the Green Mountains, and the monster population of the valley is also unusually high. In addition to its three, small, mostly-human villages, Quail Valley is also the site of a hobgoblin keep, an orc village, a young adult green dragon's lair, and a great many other monstrous inhabitants, including ogres, trolls, ettins, ettercaps, wyverns, and more. Thus, despite the valley's richness, the humanoid population has never risen high, and trade with the rest of the Westmarches is sparse, though with its excellent source of iron ore in the northeastern Gaskar Hills, a few courageous merchants do risk the trek every year.

Geographical features within the valley include the source of the Quail River, as well as the confluence between the Quail and the River Wren, its first tributary. Most of the valley's monstrous inhabitants dwell in either the Gaskar Hills south of the valley or the Forest of Nin to the northeast. The Quail's source is in the Gaskars, and its early course runs primarily westward between the hills and the forest, while the Wren's source lies north of the valley. It runs primarily southwestward, bordering both the Forest of Nin and the Gaskar Hills on the west side. The village of Bostwick lies on the upper Wren, Twain on the eastern Quail, and Pembrose near the confluence of the two, dangerously close to the hobgoblin keep.

In addition to all these, the Quail Valley is, unbeknownst to most, the site of not one but several entrances to Akados' extensive Under Realms. These entrances are all hidden and generally guarded by denizens of the lands below. They are, in all probability, one of the major factors in the Quail Valley's monster population being so high.

All told, the Quail Valley's pleasant climate, rich soil, and generous beauty are all to some extent belied by the region's many perils. Valley residents are tough, stubborn people, territorial and determined. Anyone would have to be to live in so perilous a place.

Judging by the patterns of monster attacks in the region, it is likely that at least two — if not as many as five — more Under Realms' entrances exist, even aside from the two or three in the wilderness areas described above. As many are beginning to realize, the eastern Green Mountains seem to be riddled with ancient tunnels into the depths, and the Quail Valley is no exception to this trend. Should all the competing monstrous factions of the region ever be united under a single leader, Quail Valley could make an excellent staging ground for a full-scale invasion of Reme. It is very likely that the situation in Quail Valley should be more closely monitored than it is, and that even the valley's stalwart residents are not prepared to stem whatever tide may be bubbling up from below the Green Mountains.

Reference Sources
The Vault of Larin Karr

Locations in Quail Valley

Gaskar Hills

Though arguably less inherently perilous than the Nin Forest to their north, the Quail Valley's Gaskar Hills are where its orc village can be found, as well as a nest of wyverns and most probably one of the Under Realms' entrances, though its exact location is not known by the locals. The Gaskar Hills are also home to innumerable other monsters, including something of an undead problem during the nighttime hours.

Nin Forest

In addition to its other monstrous inhabitants, the Nin Forest is the territory of the green dragon Lerentis. Lerentis is neither the largest nor the most dangerous green dragon to have ever lived, but he is nevertheless a dragon and not to be trifled with. The hobgoblin keep stands at the opposite end of the forest, not far from Pembrose, and at least one, if not two, additional entrances to the Under Realms can be found elsewhere in the Nin Forest, most likely in the lower eastern section.

Seaside

Alignment: Neutral
Ruler: Mayor Sharsai Kaveen
Government: Feudalism
Population: 1,416 (1,320 half-elf (?), 58 Foerdewaith, 38 Loreclans)
Languages: Common
Religion: Quell (see below)
Resources: Fishing
Technology Level: Dark Ages

The westernmost coastal town belonging to the nation of Reme is an eerie little place called, simply, Seaside that lies directly in the path of the heated and magical currents flowing northeastward from the Strait of Gehenna. Many believe that Seaside's strangeness can be explained by its exposure to these waters and their occasionally impenetrable, sauna-like fogs, and perhaps by the fishing and consumption of unnaturally magical species washed northward as well. Others whisper that Seaside was always strange, and that the villagers of this settlement are not at all what they seem. The town is in a state of poor repair, its temple to Quell largely fallen down and tenanted by a single priest whose sanity is questionable.

Passage to Seaside from other parts of the Reman coast is not difficult, especially by sea, and yet, most visitors find the place to be surprisingly insular, almost foreign of culture compared to even its nearest neighbors. Most Seasiders appear to be half-elves, implying a surprisingly long history of intermarriage with the normally standoffish elves of the nearby Green Warden Forest. But if this is the case, the residents of Seaside are uglier-than-average half-elves, possibly inbred or in some way deformed, with too-large eyes and strangely jagged teeth. No clear records exist of the town's founding or history, yet regional bookkeeping lists the town as loyal to the Westmarch duke for as long as any Westmarch duke has kept such records. The town pays its taxes every year and asks little of Reme in return.

Visitors to Seaside often report a sense of being watched the entire time they were there, and of strange-tasting food and water. Others report nightmares all night while sleeping at the inn, while others still speak of a strong sense of unwelcome, as if they should leave before dark at all costs. Disappearances in the area are no more common than in any other part of this dangerous world, but when they do occur, many people in a 50-or-so-mile radius around Seaside tend to blame the strange denizens of that town.

One particularly bizarre account that came out of Seaside was from a man claiming to be the sole survivor of an adventuring party that went to the town pursuing rumors of a cursed treasure hoard hidden in the waters nearby. The survivor was clearly out of his mind by the time he told his tale, often hallucinating people and creatures who were not there, or breaking into uncontrolled fits of weeping, screaming, laughter, or frenzied cursing. As such, none knows for certain how much of his account even really happened.

According to the madman, he and his companions annoyed the Seaside villagers by asking too many questions about ancient treasures and underwater tunnels. The party could tell their hosts wanted them to leave, but they stubbornly stayed and persisted in their inquiries, poking around the town and the waters beside it. As relations with the townsfolk grew ever more hostile and two of the adventurers fell ill from an unknown disease that their cleric couldn't cure, they finally discovered, at a particularly low tide, a series of caverns set into a low outcropping of rock on the beach.

Armed with water-breathing magics in case the tide should turn while they explored, the adventuring party chose to make one last attempt to uncover the town's secrets before retreating to regroup and allow their companions time to heal from their mysterious illness. Before that day was out, before the tide even turned, they found themselves wandering into what the survivor believed to have been another world.

Here, he claimed, time and distance did not function as they should, and traversing an eight-foot stretch of tunnel could take what seemed to be hours or days. High ledges could be stepped upon like shallow stairs, and shadows did not fall in the proper directions. At one point, a large and broad-shouldered member of the party fell into a crack in the tunnel no wider than a finger's width and was swallowed up as if he had never been. While the others scrambled to understand this puzzle and if it was possible to save their friend, they were set upon by creatures the survivor did not recognize but that bore some resemblance to sahuagin.

The tale grew increasingly incoherent and hallucinatory from there, but the survivor plainly believed that his companions died suffering horribly and that only his own skills at stealth and at slipping through bonds allowed him to flee from their captors, back the way they had come. The route out was, he claimed, shaped entirely differently than the route in, despite the fact that he had seen no side passages or forks of any kind. He remembers making his way, eventually, to a cave full of water and swimming as hard as he could until he passed out some time after reaching the sea. Miraculously, a fishing boat from another village rescued him before he drowned, and thus was he able to tell his tale. The night after he told it, he contracted a terrible fever that no priest in the village could cure, and he died screaming.

Duke Wylan recently hired another adventuring party to investigate the madman's claims. They returned unscathed and said only that Seaside was a weird but harmless little village, and that some curse must have befallen the poor "survivor" to make him hallucinate such a terrible tale. They had, in addition, found no evidence of tidal caves anywhere along the Seaside coast.

Ruins of Sheffen Palace

The town of Sheffen is small and unassuming, like any normal, slightly impoverished Westmarch town. It doesn't look like a baron's estate, though it is, and Baroness Lemren is folksy and humble as are most of her vassals. Sheffen definitely doesn't look like a county seat, but if asked, the locals gladly share that it was once the home of the counts of Dragul. During daylight hours, they even guide visitors to the centuries-old ruins of "the old city" that was destroyed in an earthquake.

The former city of Sheffen was much larger than the current town, and most of it is crumbling away and covered in vines and foliage. During daylight hours only, townsfolk happily (for a modest fee) offer tours of the ruins, and guide visitors to the old Dragul palace, which is remarkably grand in scale, even for a count's home. Little is left of the place, as it has been well picked-over for hundreds of years, but some of the remaining structure is of interest to historians and students of architecture, and the vine-covered ambiance is pleasant enough. As many have said over and over since the palace first fell, there is nothing mysterious here to find.

No native resident of Sheffen, however, goes within a hundred yards of the ruined city after dark for any amount of money, and many weep and beg or scream shamelessly if forced there at night against their wills. They don't want to talk about why, but if pressed or impressively bribed, they admit that a powerful undead being has taken up residence somewhere under the palace, but that it seems to be allergic to even the thinnest of rainy-day sunlight. It has also shown no interest in leaving the ruins, which is the only reason anyone has ever survived its attacks to tell the tale.

The villagers don't know what the undead creature is doing there or where it goes during the day, but no one in the village believes it has been there longer than a few generations, and certainly not as far back as when the palace fell. Having grown up with it next door, the people of Sheffen seem remarkably accustomed to its presence near their homes. After all, it only hurts people who are stupid enough to go into the ruins at night.

Shining Temple

A legendary temple — or perhaps a very impressive permanent illusion of a temple — stands atop a wide ledge cut into the tallest peak in the southwestern Green Mountains. This is, according to local guides or maps, the Shining Temple, the Temple of the Spark, or sometimes the Blinding Temple. No one knows where the names come from.

The temple itself is simple, with clean, elegant lines reminiscent of — but not wholly identical to — the architecture of many nations in the world. A statue of a howling wolf stands in front of it. The wolf appears to be made of a reddish metal, like copper, but it remains as polished and shining as if brand new, no matter how many centuries it spends exposed to the elements on top of a mountain.

Climbing to the temple is very difficult and requires specialized climbing equipment, though, of course, flying up the mountain is quite possible with magic or a winged mount. Most who approach the temple, however, notice as they draw nearer that the temple grows transparent the closer they come. By the time they might be able to see inside the open front doors or make out details of the size, layout, or architectural flourishes, and certainly by the time one might be able to read any signs or symbols marking the place, the temple has grown so indistinct as to make such observations impossible. Those who approach closer still find that by the time they arrive on the temple steps, there is no longer any temple upon that ledge. It is simply an empty ledge on the mountain, apparently a natural formation.

According to some versions of the legend surrounding the Shining Temple, it is dedicated to the refinement of the soul through perfection of the body. Others say it belongs to a fierce wolf-warrior who teaches those who enter the temple many secret warrior arts from a far-off plane (or sometimes a mighty wolf-sorcerer who commands fire and lightning at whim). Others still claim it to be a kind of ship in disguise that travels at will through time and space.

The legends all agree on one detail, however. For those worthy to enter, the temple remains solid, and all who are able to train there return home one day as mighty warriors (or sorcerers or priests), both wise and bold, heroes among heroes.

Silverlight

Alignment: Chaotic Neutral
Ruler: Headwoman Febba (half-orc, female)
Government: Protection racket
Population: 2,800 (human [mostly Foerdewaith 1,875], dwarf 580, half-orc 328, orc 8, other 9)
Languages: Common, Dwarven, Orcish
Religion: Mithras, Solanus, Dargath
Resources: General trade hub
Technology Level: Medieval

Silverlight sits in the foothills of the southwestern Green Mountains above a large bend in the eastern Aciier river. The town began as a small trading post for travelers coming eastward through the Windreft or explorers and trappers returning from expeditions in the mountains. Its location also sheltered it neatly, allowing it to benefit from the Aciier flow without too much risk of the unpredictable flooding so common along the Aciier's banks. During the flooding season, too, Silverlight retains a reasonably secure overland path eastward to more populated areas and, eventually, to the tamer Quail River with its constant river traffic down to Eckland and beyond.

Over time, this strategic location expanded to become quite a large trade town, though its development has regressed significantly since the start of the Westmarches' long civil war. It lies in disputed territory between Brodchek and Mercier lands and became an open battleground for much of the first five years of the region's sporadic warfare. Once this bloodshed left the town broken and defenseless, a mountain bandit horde came raiding and decided to move in and take over. Headwoman Febba (formerly the bandit chief) ran the Brodcheks, Merciers, and any stray allies of theirs out of town, then put the townsfolk to work building a better palisade while her bandits guarded the place.

The noble families had their hands too full with fighting each other to take back Silverlight, so while they moved their warfare farther west into the edge of the Windreft, Febba and her bandits dug in and made themselves at home. Febba is technically, therefore, the tyrannical usurper of Silverlight, but her taxes are not higher than the old lords' taxes, her justice is not much more arbitrary, and her bandits not particularly worse-behaved than common soldiers. The only major difference the people of Silverlight saw during the war was that the fighting in the streets finally stopped, and they could go back to their lives.

Of course, since the civil war continued all around them, the Silverlight economy was still negatively impacted by the violence, but Febba's contacts in the Green Mountains allowed the town to expand its commerce to a dwarf village and even a pair of orc tribes living up in the peaks, and in this way Silverlight survived the civil war. It has become a more exciting place since being taken over by a gang of bandits, a bit rougher around the edges, perhaps a bit less friendly. Now that the war has ended, business is booming once more, and Febba is no more hated than any other authority figure in living memory.

Febba has petitioned the Westmarch duke to grant her official legal status as the town's liege, perhaps as a baroness, in light of her excellent stewardship in protecting Silverlight. Naturally, Earl Brodchek and Count Mercier also petitioned Duke Wylan to lend forces to "return" Silverlight to the Brodcheks or Merciers. Duke Wylan has put them all off time and again, saying that he must visit Silverlight in person before making a final decision, and that he still has too much to do, post-war, to make such a trip to a town that seems to be running just fine in the meantime.

It is unknown as yet what his final decision will be, but it seems clear that he is aware of several things: Febba's 15-year occupation of Silverlight does not appear to have negatively impacted trade or security in the Westmarches, and worse things could have happened to the people of Silverlight during the civil war. Whatever Duke Wylan decides, he is likely to weigh the situation most carefully.

REFERENCE SOURCES
Town of Glory

TANNER'S GREEN

Alignment: Neutral Good
Ruler: Mayor Rutiger
Government: Elected Mayor
Population: 309 (Foerdewaith 198, Loreclans 101, halfling 10)
Languages: Common
Religion: Freya
Resources: Farming, ranching, some trade
Technology Level: Medieval

Tanner's Green seems to be a quiet, peaceful little town in the middle of nowhere right outside the eastern edge of the Westwood. It is technically the northernmost settlement in the vast and sparsely-populated Aciier County, though the Aciier countess's patrols rarely reach so far into the wilderness. Thus, the little town fends for itself,

making decisions by consensus or by casting lots, including the election of a mayor every three years.

The region around Tanner's Green is so sparsely populated that the villagers rarely encounter outsiders, either travelers or raiders. The former tend to be welcomed and pressed for news or tales, and then politely encouraged to move on as soon as the reason for their visit is complete. The latter have little to gain from humble farmers and ranchers like the folk of Tanner's Green, and generally find the inhabitants to be of sufficient courage and stubbornness to make raiding them more effort than it would be worth. All in all, Tanner's Green is primarily remarkable to travelers in the region simply because it is the only village at all for several dozen miles in all directions.

That said, however, terrible rumors are emerging from the Westwood of late, rumors of ghastly cults and of ancient evil returning to life. The folk of Tanner's Green, according to these rumors, seem to be somehow caught up in whatever is happening in the woods near their home.

REFERENCE SOURCES
Demonheart

TOWER OF JHEDOPHAR

More than a thousand years ago, a school of magic was built at the westernmost edge of the Green Mountains by a great mage named Jhedophar. Some centuries later, he closed the school, drove his students away, and sealed himself within his tower, never to emerge. Though the tower has largely passed from history and memory, it does yet stand, only recently rediscovered by intrepid adventurers.

Inside, over the centuries, the tower has become a veritable labyrinth of terror packed with undead monstrosities, perilous eldritch mysteries, and a dragon who claims a portion of the tower for himself. Little else is known, as no one has yet penetrated to the tower's ancient heart — none, anyway, who have escaped to tell the tale.

REFERENCE SOURCES
The Tower of Jhedophar

WESSEM

Alignment: Neutral
Ruler: Earl Evrus Brodchek (mixed Foerdewaith/Loreclans ethnicity)
Government: Feudalism
Population: 9,334 (Foerdewaith 3,723, Loreclans 3,231, hill dwarf 1,940, elf 426, other 14)
Languages: Common, Dwarven
Religion: Freya, Mithras, Solanus
Resources: Grain, cattle, cloth
Technology Level: Medieval

Situated on a lone hilltop near the center of the Brodchek Earldom stands the fortress city of Wessem, where Earl Brodchek and his close family make their home. Its walls are thick and strong, its architecture dull and practical. In all but the wettest and coldest months, the cheerful tents and stands of farmers and craftspeople, merchants and entertainers cluster near the city — scattered around the walls, especially near the lone front gate — all offering their goods and services to any who pass though their throng. The area is well-peopled by the Brodchek-allied Loreclans who sell cattle, horses, and leather goods.

These brightly-colored tents and often-aromatic stands are still a very welcome sight to the citizens of Wessem and surrounding settlements. It is only in the last two years, since young Relm Brodchek's wedding with Lusea Mercier, that Earl Evrus has once more allowed his people to hold their outdoor markets beside the city walls. During the long civil war, the dour fortress walls stood bare and forbidding year round, and the majority of the region's commerce ground to a halt.

The Brodchek lands extend from the southernmost edge of the Green Mountains in the north down to the Aciier River in the south. West to east, they stretch again from the Green Mountain foothills eastward to the Quail River. Nearly all of this land is among the most prized farmland in the entire Westmarches, with excellent soil, largely predictable and beneficial flooding, and only the gentlest of rolling hills. For this reason, it is something of a relief and a boon to all of the Westmarches that the Wessem markets are once again running at peak capacity. It is through Wessem that much of the duchy trades for the food its people need to survive.

Inside the Wessem walls, however, only the locals can even tell that the war has ended. They know that far fewer soldiers are now seen parading in the streets, and that far fewer young warriors are being brought home dead or dying. They know also that they are once again able to purchase fine goods and even luxuries from neighboring counties. Things have improved. However, the earl has been in a foul mood for some months and makes no attempt to hide this from his people.

Thus, to an outsider, the city streets of Wessem seem tense and hushed, lacking in all cheer or even artistry. Loud performances, bright colors, or even excessive laughter might provoke the lord of the land, and he is not particularly known for his mercy or restraint. Oh, he isn't truly evil, and his fits of temper rarely lead to bloodshed (at least, not the blood of his own citizens), but many a family income has been destroyed, many a reputation shattered, and many a property confiscated in the name of the earl's foul moods.

Few speak aloud of what they fear the earl to be angry about, but everyone knows that his new Mercier daughter-in-law gave birth just a bit early after her marriage to his young heir. Relm Brodchek is known to have an entirely different temperament than his father and is keeping his feelings on the matter to himself, appearing publicly, at least, to still be committed to his new wife and their baby son. Servants, however, have heard raised voices on the subject between Relm and Earl Evrus, and report also that relations between Relm and Lusea have grown awkward and tentative.

Everyone fears what will happen if Evrus Brodchek discovers (or invents) some sort of proof that Lusea's child is not Relm's son. Despite the pretty tents and cheerful market outside the city, inside the city, Wessem's populace is walking on eggshells everywhere they go, taut with the fear that they may soon be going back to war. Unpopular as the Merciers (and Harrings, and Fenrith-Draguls) have always been with the common people of Brodchek lands, these same common people have found over the last decades that they loathe war even more.

It is true that only Duke Wylan may keep a large standing army in the Westmarches at the moment, and that Earl Brodchek therefore cannot simply sally forth to begin a new conflict, but many suspect that their earl yet harbors armed forces in secret or that he might even hire mercenaries to attack the Merciers from the sea. If such a thing were to take place, no one in Wessem knows how Duke Wylan would respond or how it might ultimately impact the lives of Wessem's people.

This growing fear among the populace — of any sort of return to violence — has led to an aura of intrigue and counter-intrigue among the city's wealthy and powerful, and rumors whispered in the shadows speak of possibilities as dire as even assassination. After all, everyone knows that Relm Brodchek has a cooler head and a kinder heart than his father. Surely he would sue for peace regardless of what his new wife may or may not have done before their marriage. Would it not be better to trade the life of one earl for the lives of however many people might be killed in his inability to let the past be past?

The earl is not widely hated, however, despite his mercurial temperament. His father was worse, so the old folks say, and his grandmother as well. Besides, centuries of loyal tradition stand between the people of the Brodchek lands and any kind of treachery against their lord. If cooler heads prevail, it is likely that all these murmurings will die away and be forgotten, and in the end, that's what everyone would prefer.

And so the people of Wessem go anxiously about their business and wait to see what the future will bring.

WEST FORTRESS

Alignment: Neutral Good
Ruler: Countess Gemra Aciier
Government: Feudalism
Population: 4,378 (human [mixed ethnicity] 2,105, halfling 1,465, elf 455, gnome 232, dwarf 96, other 25)
Languages: Common, Elven
Religion: Freya, Mithras, Solanus, many others
Resources: Horses, donkeys, mules, sheep, cattle, wool, granite, river transport
Technology Level: Medieval

The West Fortress was once the westernmost settlement in all of Reme. While many settlements exist farther west now, West Fortress remains the county seat for the Aciier family, one of the few noble houses in the Westmarches to avoid becoming embroiled in the recent and lengthy Westmarch civil war. West Fortress also remains the westernmost major trade hub in Reme, as well as the best place in the Westmarches to buy tough work-ponies, donkeys, Loreclan-bred horses, and mules. Finally, West Fortress is known for fine sheep, wool, and excellent cheeses.

Located on the west bank of the Aciier river, about halfway between the Windreft and the northern edge of the Westwood, the West Fortress riverboat pilots are some of the most skilled in the world, with intimate knowledge of the mercurial Aciier's many moods. The Aciier is prone to unpredictable flooding, especially during winter and spring, and also varies in depth and speed (and even course from year to year due to its flooding habits) while maintaining a deceptively placid surface. Many a supposedly experienced river pilot from other parts of the world has lost cargo or even lives trying to navigate the Aciier, but the West Fortress pilots teach their apprentices to notice every last detail of weather and water flow, taking clues from the surrounding wilderness and more in predicting when transport is advisable and where to play it safe and portage one's craft for a day or so. West Fortress rivercraft are designed with shallow, flat bottoms and built light with attachable cart wheels for easier portage where necessary.

For similar reasons, West Fortress itself boasts an impressively high wall built of granite and sealed watertight all the way around the city. When the Aciier's floodwaters reach all the way to the city, various extendable or floating ramps are deployed to allow any necessary traffic to and from the fortress, while the majority of citizens remain snug and dry in the elevated and granite-paved streets inside. The city was built atop a low but wide granite tor near the river, one of three such tors in the general West Fortress region. Between the flooding and a minimum of good farming soil nearby (everything being too rocky), the city is already at its maximum population capacity, and Aciier's countess funds settling expeditions to the less-populated regions of her nominal territory whenever she can afford to do so.

Fortunately for West Fortress, the Aciiers are currently in high favor with the grand duke and the duke of the Westmarches due to their neutrality in the long war. Thus, ducal funds have been allocated for improving crowding issues within the fortress itself, as well as several new sponsored settling expeditions to wild areas, taking the pressure off the residents somewhat. Also, with the war finally abated, and pitched battles between the Brodcheks and Merciers no longer a common occurrence in the eastern Windreft, West Fortress is now once again more easily able to send large granite-barges down to Eckland in the late summer when the Aciier is tamer. The granite from quarries south of West Fortress has long been one of the region's best exports, but between the Aciier's unpredictability and the violence in the Windreft, transporting the stone to market has been hazardous. Now that profits are up again, the countess is said to be in a generous and optimistic mood, more beloved by her people than ever.

Of course, another reason the countess might be happier than before is her growing friendship with Hana, a young ward of hers. No one knows why the countess took in this apparently clanless orphan, but the two are as close, it is said, as mother and daughter. Countess Gemra Aciier has never birthed children of her own, though she was married for many years, and she has never stated publicly why this is. Her title and lands will pass to her niece, Kemmin Aciier, with whom both the countess and West Fortress have a basically pleasant relationship. Everyone adores young Hana, however, who is cheerful, intelligent, hardworking, and always helpful to those around her without the slightest regard for class. Some fear that Hana's popularity is causing a jealous rift between the countess and her heir, but others believe that Hana is so likable that even Lady Kemmin can't help but dote on her as a young cousin. Thus far, Countess Aciier has made no move to officially adopt her ward.

Many are curious about Hana's origins, however, and some say she bears a startling resemblance to the old Decian duke and his wife. If Hana is somehow the child or grandchild of the last duke, some believe that would make her, by rights, the true grand duchess of Reme. Countess Aciier gives every sign of being loyal to Grand Duke Iltobarus, but some say that the old duke's Northmarch Decian cousins, though not themselves eligible for the grand ducal throne, have sent agents to sniff around West Fortress in case Hana might be their ticket back into power. According to Countess Aciier, Hana is the orphan of someone to whom Gemra Aciier owed a boon, and she is raising the deceased woman's child in order to pay her debt. Hana is now 14 years old, pale, small and slim, the perfect opposite in appearance of coppery Gemra Aciier who stands taller than most men, with broad shoulders and a surprisingly heavy sword arm.

Western Akadian Forest

This forest lies north of Eckland, east of the Quail River, and south and west of the Green Mountains. Its eastern edge is plagued by hunting rocs in autumn during their migration, but by very few orc raids from the mountains, unlike the Dunavenwood to the east. The Green Mountains end in sheer cliffs where they border with the Akadian, making climbing down there nearly impossible. Other sorts of monsters do sometimes nest in cracks in the cliff faces, but the duke's armies do their best to keep the forest safe for travelers, and, indeed, it is one of the safer forests in the Westmarches. The forest provides the more populated central Westmarch areas with meat from wild boar and forest buffalo hunted there, as well as truffles and mushrooms. Some lumber is cut, though since the forest is primarily hemlock and the trees are full of knots, it is not as sought after as timber from some other woods.

Perhaps for this reason, some of the northeasternmost reaches of the Akadian are old growth, with massive ancient trees and cathedral-like branches high overhead. In this region, a small but beautiful stone shrine has stood for untold generations. No one knows who built it or to what religion it was dedicated. Its style is different from any other extant shrines in the region. The locals believe that it is appropriate to worship any god there so long as that god is good to trees, and the humble offerings one can find on and around the little shrine reflect this interdenominational approach.

Local legend says that anyone who leaves a genuine and heartfelt offering at the shrine will be blessed with long life and great wisdom. If such a thing is indeed true, those who benefit from said blessing are wise enough not to say anything, as the shrine is not well known outside the forest. Some years ago, the wizard Rithirioth did visit it from Eckland and asserted firmly that the shrine had no magical aura of any kind. The locals don't believe a word of it, and they still leave their offerings whenever they journey far enough into the wood to pass nearby.

Use the **Forest Encounter Table** for generating random encounters in the Western Akadian Forest.

Westwood

Bordering on the Endless Hills, the Westwood is a tangled forest in the far western portion of the Westmarches. It was once part of the Great Akadonian Forest, but was separated from the rest during a devastating magical battle between elves and humans. Though the few miles of open meadowland that today stand between the Westwood and the remains of the Great Forest have long since healed from the scars of battle, for some centuries after the erecting of the powerful ward-stones known as the Green Warders, this stretch of blood-soaked and magic-ravaged land would grow nothing at all. As grasses and wildflowers slowly returned, now a few trees, too, dot the land between the Westwood and what has come to be known as the Green Warden Forest, but it will be many generations yet before the two forests grow back together as one, assuming they ever can.

The Westwood is populated primarily by elves of the Forest Wolf wood-elf clan. Millennia ago, this clan was an offshoot branch of the same family who later founded the Kingdom of Wolves in the Green Warden Nations, but there has been little contact between the two peoples for well over a dozen centuries, and their cultures and appearances have diverged widely since, though both retained their symbolic and spiritual connection to wolves.

Gnolls dwell in small bands in the Westwood as well. They are a recent arrival to the wood from their ancestral homeland in the Endless Hills to the west. These are a gnoll subspecies known as western hill gnolls who are a little bit taller and stockier than average, and who grow long, shaggy coats in the winter. Their faces are a bit more canine than the average gnoll's as well, and their coloration is black and tan like some dogs. Like most gnolls, these western hill gnolls are territorial and violent, and their elven neighbors consider their presence in the Westwood quite troublesome.

In the Westwood's distant past, elven chroniclers say it was once inhabited by an ancient elven race known as the Trae'este (Shadows of the Forest). The Trae'este, they say, faced a terrible gnoll invasion from the Endless Hills, back when the gnolls were far more numerous than they are today. The Trae'este held back the invasion, but only by calling up forces they found themselves unable to control. In order to save the forest from their own mistake, they sacrificed themselves and merged their souls with the Westwood forever. Some of the Forest Wolf elves believe that the souls of the Trae'este still guard the wood around them to this day. Of these, some even believe that if the souls of the Trae'este were to leave the Westwood, the evil they put down would reawaken, even now.

Finally, in the southern corner of the Westwood, an unusually high feral cat population has been observed, for reasons unknown.

Use the **Forest Encounter Table** for generating random encounters in the Westwood.

Tree of the True Heart

Deep in the center of the Westwood stands an ancient camphor tree, one of the few of its species in the entire wood. This particular specimen is unusually large and is said to take seven elves with their arms stretched wide to reach all the way around the trunk. Near the base on the east side of this tree is a massive and strangely-shaped concave knot that on moonless nights appears as an open gateway into the inside of the tree.

Peering through the opening, one sees a simple, irregularly roundish, wooden room with a dirt floor, exactly as if the tree were genuinely hollow inside. Indeed, if one were to happen upon the ancient specimen for the first time on a moonless night, having never seen its normally solid state, one would have no reason to suspect that it was not an ordinary hollow tree.

Stepping inside the hollow, however, is an entirely different experience. To outside observers, anyone entering the tree's open "mouth" simply disappears without a trace, instantly. Some who enter never again emerge. Others emerge months or years later, and a rare few after mere hours. All who emerge say that within the tree they found a labyrinth of wonders, beautiful and terrible, but most will offer few, if any details of their wanderings beyond that, and those who do all contradict one another, telling entirely unrelated tales.

What those who emerge from the tree have in common, however, is that they are all profoundly changed by the experience, and usually those around them agree that the change is for the better: unhappy people emerge happier; violent people emerge gentler; foolish people emerge wiser; and so on. No one understands how or why this occurs, or where the tree came from. The elves of the forest say it has always been there, immortal.

Westwood residents guard the tree with their lives, for it is dearer to them than their families, but they never attempt to stop anyone from entering its inner chamber. Indeed, marauding gnolls who attack on moonless nights might be deliberately led to the tree and tricked into entering. The elves know that even gnolls — assuming they ever emerge at all — will be better, more agreeable beings after their adventures inside the Tree of the True Heart.

Some local elf tribes use the tree as a punishment for crimes, forcing criminals inside against their wills. More commonly, elves struggling with despair or crushing grief enter the tree as an alternative to suicide. Some holy people or seekers of knowledge in pursuit of wisdom enter the tree as a kind of pilgrimage.

If two to seven people enter hand-in-hand or lashed together, those who emerge (at all) emerge together and usually forge an unshakable bond of friendship in the course of shared adventures in the labyrinth. With more than seven people at a time, any bindings that hold them together break, and all of those who enter experience their journeys separately. There is no known limit to how many people can journey inside the tree at one time, but only two elf-sized people can fit through the door at once.

REFERENCE SOURCES

Demonheart

THE WINDREFT

Though not the farthest place from civilization in western Reme, the Windreft is among the wildest and least settled. Orc tribes control much of the nearby Green Mountain foothills, while hobgoblins camp in the north. Boggards infest the Windreft wetlands areas known as the waterwoods, and a tribe of gnolls has recently moved into the region, though no one knows for certain whence they came. Trolls sometimes wander down from the Green Mountains, as do migrating rocs in the autumn, and various types of fey and undead sometimes emerge from the Green Warden Forest to the south.

As if all these monstrous inhabitants weren't enough, both human and elven groups of roving bandits sometimes attack travelers or shipping in the region, and the Aciier river that runs through the heart of it all is dangerously swift here and prone to flooding.

Nevertheless, since the end of the Westmarch civil war, the Windreft is at least no longer the site of regular pitched battles between factions. For some reason, Grand Duke Iltobarus has taken this as a sign that it is time for Reme to settle the Windreft. To this end, he sponsored the establishment of a tiny new town there called Glory, certainly in the hope of decreasing the risk of transporting goods to market through the Windreft, but perhaps also simply to keep a few of the Westmarches' young hotheads busy with a new project in the interest of maintaining Duke Wylan's hard-won new Westmarch peace.

Then again, it may also be possible that the clever grand duke has sponsored this project because he acquired evidence to support an old rumor in the region: that a glorious realm known as the Kingdom Beneath somehow lies hidden under the Windreft itself. A new rumor has sprouted up since the founding of Glory as well: that Grand Duke Iltobarus chose Glory's location because it sits directly atop this same mythical Kingdom Beneath. Perhaps the grand duke has plans to unlock the secrets of the fantastical kingdom before any other powers in the region can seize them.

Although much of the Windreft is the plains, use the **Hills (General) Encounter Table** to generate random encounters here.

REFERENCE SOURCES

Town of Glory

ASHEN HILLS

Alignment: Lawful Evil
Ruler: None
Government: Tribal warlords
Population: 35,550 (orcs 33,200, gnomes 2,350)
Monstrous: Orcs, wolves, worgs, bulette, griffons, hobgoblins, chimera, ogres, hill giants, wyverns
Languages: Orcish, Common
Religion: Orcus
Resources: Chalk, copper, quarry stone, tin
Currency: Various coinage, barter, gems
Technology Level: Medieval

   This area of rocky, largely barren hills contains no known veins of precious ores, though some of the gray stone here can be quarried for use in building. Tribes of orcs roam these hills, and some have grown quite powerful and strange. In addition, it is said that ancient tunnels, possibly dug by a prehuman race, can be found beneath these hills. Several of these tunnel complexes have been found and occupied by the Ashen Hills orcs, but rumors persist of other lost networks and of magnificent temples or other wonders still hidden from view.

History and People

The Ashen Hills were once heavily forested and part of the Namjan Woods that adjoined the divine elven realm of Alathanar. The various conflicts that tore at Alathanar also affected this region, and much of the forest was destroyed in the war with the usurper Taloran. The influx of humanoids from the Deepfells and south out of the Great Steppes in the late 600s I.R. drove the last elven settlers from the hills and finally finished the destruction of the old forest and cut the Haunted Wood off from the Namjan Forest for good. A few minor copses remain, but the ancient and mystical woods that once filled the area are now gone.

In their place are arid, rugged hills covered in hardy grasses and scoured by the winds. Only the strong survive in this environment, and with the retreat of the other humanoid tribes and the rise of the Hyperborean Empire, several especially tough and resourceful orc bands remained behind, making the Ashen Hills their permanent home.

Initially there were five major tribes: the Zighoom (Night Bulls), the Pargh'kandul (Bloodstained Sun), the Ashk'mak (Bonebreakers), the Agdha'sakk (Mountain Axes), and the Gnaukkaz (Gnashing Fangs). These groups were of roughly equal size and capability and divided the Ashen Hills among them. It was the Zighoom who first discovered the subterranean passages and began to explore, setting them up as living quarters and citadels. Ancient treasure and magic were also found in the labyrinth, and the strange sorceries associated with their finds began to steadily affect the Zighoom orcs' minds and bodies. Elsewhere, other tribes made their own discoveries, gaining powers and abilities as a result.

These various finds and the modifications meant that no tribe could overwhelm the others, and a continuous stalemate began, not dissimilar to what happened to the Deepfells hobgoblins after the fall of their demonic leader Kakobovia. The Ashen Hills' orcs continued to hone their fighting skills over the centuries, and whenever they grew bored fighting each other, they raided into the Frontier and the Northmarches beyond, sometimes allied with each other, sometimes individually.

The five tribes remain equally influential, each with its own unique abilities. Despite these oddities, they remain orcish to the core, devoted to war, violence, and the accumulation of power and martial glory. The tribes and their unique qualities are described below:

Zighoom (Night Bulls): No one is certain who built the network of tunnels and chambers that honeycomb sections of the Ashen Hills. The Zighoom were the first to explore them and found odd paintings of minotaurs and human or elven figures dancing with gigantic bulls. The Night Bulls took this as a sign of the gods' favor and occupied the tunnels, finding many old weapons and strange ritual objects. In time they grew taller, stronger, and more ferocious. Some began to grow horns and oversized fangs. Soon they began to resemble the beasts for which they were named.

Pargh'kandul (Bloodstained Sun): The Bloodstained Sun orcs happened upon a cache of elven weapons and armor and adapted them to their own purposes, going into battle armed with the elegant gear of their ancient enemies. Like the Night Bulls, the Pargh'kandul have also begun to change, growing taller and slenderer, but also faster, nimbler, and with more acute senses. Rival tribes claim that the Bloodstained Sun orcs are slowly transforming into elves, but such assertions drive the Pargh'kandul to frenzy as they strive to prove that they are every bit as bloodthirsty as other orcs, if not more so.

Ashk'mak (Bonebreakers): Like the Night Bulls, the Ashk'mak discovered ancient ruins and tunnels and also found inscriptions and monuments that seemed to grant them arcane powers. Those Ashk'mak priests who studied the inscriptions found themselves gaining potent necromantic powers, with the ability to commune with spirits, raise the dead, and inflict the curse of undeath on others. Many of these priests live on as liches and act as the spiritual leaders of the Bonebreakers, who now believe that death holds no power over them. A Bonebreaker warrior's fondest desire is to die in battle and be raised in undeath to continue to fight for the tribe.

Agdha'sakk (Mountain Axes): The Agdha'sakk hunted then domesticated the giant elk that migrated into the hills from the forests and foothills of the Deepfells, eventually creating a new breed of powerful war beasts that they continue to ride into battle to this day. These creatures, known to the outside world as orcish war-elk, are the object of considerable scholarly and scientific scrutiny, and the Reman government has expressed an interest in obtaining breeding pairs for study and possible use in human armies, especially those subject to ice, cold, and other harsh weather conditions.

Gnaukkaz (Gnashing Fangs): The Gnaukkaz found the remains of old gnomish mines and mining equipment, which they transformed into powerful armored vehicles and weapons of war. Most of these vehicles are muscle-driven, often by goblin slaves, and are equipped with various ranged weapons such as ballistae or flamethrowers. They are slow and ponderous but well-defended, though getting them out of the hills and into the realms targeted for raiding can be challenging. Once in battle, however, the Gnashing Fangs' war engines are greatly feared.

Religion

If the orcs are united on one thing, it is their faith. Loyal followers of Orcus, the Ashen Hills orcs praise the Lord of Undeath and dedicate every death (including their own, if necessary) to him. Orcish priests strive to reflect their tribes' character — Agdha'sakk war-clerics ride the largest and fiercest war-elks, Gnashing Fangs' priests have personal war-machines crewed by fanatical Orcus worshippers, Bonebreaker priests are masters of necromancy and the dark arts, and so on. Shrines to Orcus can be found throughout the Ashen Hills, where on dark nights rites of bloody sacrifice and torture are performed.

Loyalties and Diplomacy

The Ashen Hills' orcs have about as much interest in loyalties and diplomacy as most other orcs, which is to say not very much. Their ultimate loyalty is to their tribes and to Orcus, but even their common religion does not keep them from each other's throats, as the Lord of Death prefers to see his followers fight it out to prove who is strongest and most capable of delivering fresh blood and souls. The orcs' interactions with other kingdoms such as the Alathi elves and the humans of the Northmarches always involves warfare and bloodshed, and the outside world's only interest in the orcs is the hope that one day the world will be rid of them.

The orcs are only marginally more diplomatic with each other, to the extent that tribes may declare common cause when raiding outside of the Ashen Hills. Though the prospect of allied orc tribes plundering other lands is indeed frightening, such alliances are usually doomed, for the participating triumphs invariably fall to bickering with each other over the division of the spoils, which often leads to more and bloodier battles before they even return to their home territories.

Government

Orcish rule is by the strongest. Chiefs rise purely through violence, and subordinates serve their rulers only so long as they are powerful and able to fend off pretenders. Orcish society is also quite egalitarian, as any orc, regardless of sex, age, or social standing, has the right to challenge a chieftain for dominance. Once elevated to the position of chief, orcish rulers must constantly fight to remain in power, for peaceful transfers of rulership are unheard of and, in fact, considered to be a sign of weakness.

While in power, a chief's word is absolute law and is carried out by his or her (temporarily) loyal minions. Opposition is ruthlessly stamped out, hesitation or outright refusal to obey commands is punishable by immediate (or sometimes prolonged) death. Rebels, enemies, troublemakers, and those who do not fully support a chieftain may indeed find themselves bound for ovens or cooking pots, for the orcs have no qualms about eating whatever meat is available.

MILITARY

The Ashen Hills' orcs are organized into ruthless hordes of warriors, each commanded by its most powerful and ruthless officer. These officers are constantly on guard against their subordinates in much the same way as tribal chieftains. This is good practice, for successful war leaders may have the opportunity to overthrow and replace a less-capable or aged chieftain.

Battle tactics and troop types vary from tribe to tribe. The Night Bulls are primarily powerful armored infantry with little in the way of missile or mounted troops. The Bloodstained Suns use ancient elven armor and weapons and have learned many of the techniques of creating elven-style magical items. Their lightly-armored but mobile infantry fights with bows, and riders mounted on worgs attempt to duplicate elven envelopment and mounted archery tactics. The Bonebreakers' necromancers summon regiments of walking dead, and even raise the slain of both sides mid-battle to bolster their own forces. The Mountain Axes maintain large numbers of fearless and deadly war-elk cavalry supported by heavy crossbow and spear. The Gnashing Fangs' war engines and vehicles form the core of their battle lines, reinforced by heavy infantry with jagged falchions and sturdy polearms.

MAJOR THREATS

Few outside forces threaten the Ashen Hills, safe as they are behind walls of thick forest and high mountain ramparts. The orcs are not without their enemies, however, and the shadow creatures of the Haunted Wood and the Namjan Forest have been known to make incursions into the hills to seek out the living and to destroy orcish settlements. The Alathi elves are weak and their numbers are few, but they also sometimes venture into the hills on punitive expeditions, especially if the orcs have taken prisoners or plundered important treasures.

The duchy of the Northmarches is well aware of the threat that the Ashen Hills' orcs represent, but has so far been unable to dislodge them. Several plans are on the drawing board for military expeditions into the hills, but so far these have not been put into action due to lack of resources and the inability to fully persuade officials of the Grand Duchy of Reme about the magnitude of the danger that the orcs represent.

WILDERNESS AND ADVENTURES

The northern region of the duchy is an especially dangerous place, and the Ashen Hills are more dangerous still. Orcish bands roam the region freely, fighting each other and seeking out opportunities for bloodshed. Adventurers and other travelers who are unfortunate or foolish enough to venture into the hills are ideal victims, and without proper precautions find themselves captured, facing death by torture for the amusement of the tribe, or being used for fodder by hungry and indiscriminate orcs.

Few adventurers visit the hills for this reason, but a handful are drawn there, risking death or worse at the hands of the orcs. Some come to seek out riches, hoping to plunder the orcs' treasure vaults or to explore the ancient and largely unplumbed tunnels that wind beneath the weathered hills. Others may be recruited by the gnomes of the Namjan, the Northmarchers, or even (rarely) the Alathi elves to reconnoiter and learn about the orcs' activities, to rescue prisoners, or to retrieve stolen wealth.

The orcs are not the only danger to visitors, for the hills also swarm with a number of other hostile creatures, including such beasts as minotaurs, manticores, owlbears, peryton, leucrotta, and packs of wild dogs. These and other creatures are usually quite hungry and willing to attack even well-equipped enemies.

Use the specific **Ashen Hills Encounter Table** to generate random encounters in this area.

REFERENCE SOURCES
The Six Spheres of Zaihhess

KINGDOMS OF THE DEEPFELLS

Alignment: Lawful Evil
Ruler: None
Government: Monarchy
Population: 122,430 (hobgoblins)
Monstrous: Kobold, centipede swarm, derro, giant centipede, giant slug, black pudding, cave fisher, centipede swarm, cloaker, roper, otyugh, duergar, rust monster, gelatinous cube, violet fungus
Languages: Goblin
Religion: Kakobovia
Resources: Gems, gold, iron, lead, silver
Currency: Each kingdom has its own currency
Technology Level: Dark Ages

HISTORY AND PEOPLE

This mountain range, despite its isolation, has played host to a number of momentous events in the history of Akados. In −6484 I.R., the Obsidian Vault plunged into the range, creating the strange structure known as Devil's Finger. In those days, dwarves inhabited portions of the Deepfells, and the arrival of the vault prompted some of them to begin worshipping the demon known as the Faceless Lord. The dwarves were largely displaced by hobgoblin clans who began to move into the region, and by 1548 I.R., under the leadership of the demigod Kakobovia, the Hobgoblin Kingdom of the Deepfells had grown powerful enough to threaten the Northmarches of Reme, eventually reaching its tendrils as far east as the Starcrag fortresses. Kakobovia was eventually defeated and banished at the Battle of Ironhill in 1573 I.R., and the hobgoblins were pushed back into the mountains over subsequent decades.

Today, the hobgoblins are splintered into several smaller kingdoms, each competing with the others for dominance. Nevertheless, the hobgoblins still dominate the Deepfells. Smaller powers such as the Stoneaxe dwarves, the Dragonrock kobolds, and the derro of the deep caverns also exist, but the hobgoblins are the clear masters of the Deepfells.

Organized into various kingdoms, each with its own warlord-ruler, the hobgoblins inhabit the various caverns and subterranean fortresses of the old united Deepfells kingdom. They have no relations with the outside world save for when they emerge to raid and plunder the Northmarches, taking whatever they need in the form of supplies, food, and slaves.

Within their own kingdoms, the hobgoblins raise their own food in the form of subterranean cattle bred over generations to be blind and docile. Underground fungi as well as edible slimes and oozes form the remainder of the hobgoblins' diet. They are a versatile species, however, and also subsist on foodstuffs plundered from the Northmarches and the Frontier.

While concepts of romantic love and marriage are foreign to the militaristic hobgoblins, they do live in family groups consisting of mated pairs and their offspring. These families are considered almost like small military cadres, raising youngsters until they are old enough to join their kingdom's legions.

Religion

Though they are bitterly divided, the hobgoblins continue to be united by their devotion to their old demon-god ruler, Kakobovia. Though he was defeated and banished back to his home plane, the hobgoblins fervently believe, and with good reason, that Kakobovia lives on, and will one day return to unite his shattered people and lead them once more on the path of conquest. This time, the hobgoblin priests declare, he will not be defeated. This time, Kakobovia's path to true godhood is clear, and his people will be invincible.

Of course, each hobgoblin kingdom is convinced that it is the one true kingdom, to which Kakobovia will return and whose banner he will carry into battle. When that great day comes, they say, all of the other hobgoblin monarchs will see the truth and join together in a new union. Then, the priests proclaim, the world will tremble before Kakobovia's might and fall one by one to the swords of his armored legions.

While the glorification of Kakobovia and their chosen kingdoms certainly are part of the hobgoblins' priestly class's major duties, they provide numerous other resources for their nations as well. Priests are all expected to be highly skilled in combat, and most serve as officers or even generals, leading their warriors into battle while shouting the praises of Kakobovia. When not in combat, Kakobovian priests oversee the interment of the dead, the blessing of weapons, performing marriages, selecting names for newborn children, and issuing titles to adult warriors based upon their accomplishments.

Ordinary hobgoblins believe that they serve Kakobovia by fighting fearlessly and accepting death as warriors. Those who perish in battle are believed to travel immediately to Kakobovia's home plane where they serve as his personal guard, and will return with him when he finally comes back to lead his people. Those who die in less violent or militaristic fashion are thought to be reincarnated so that they may have another chance to glorify Kakobovia in battle. Cowardice, excessive greed, treachery, and disloyalty are all hateful qualities to the hobgoblins, and those who committed such sins in life are cast into the abyss and left to the demons of evil and chaos, for their souls are not wanted by Kakobovia or his people.

Loyalties and Diplomacy

The hobgoblins are loyal to no one outside their own kingdoms, though the return of Kakobovia and his consequent reunification of the Deepfells kingdoms would eliminate any existing divisions. Until that time, however, the various kingdoms remain in a constant state of warfare, both cold and hot, each seeking to overcome the others and claim supremacy. Outside of the Deepfells, the hobgoblins are seen only as raiders and a constant threat to life and peace. The ferocity of the old invasion is still heralded in story and song, and the hobgoblins emerge to raid and destroy with sufficient frequency that they cannot be forgotten or ignored.

While they remain in a constant state of warfare with each other, the Deepfells hobgoblins are also at war with their neighbors, contending with the kobolds and dwarves in the upper regions of the mountains and with the derro and other, stranger creatures in the pitch-black depths below. For their part, the dwarves survive in their fastness, and conflict with the hobgoblins has become a fact of their existence, while the kobolds move constantly, relocating as the hobgoblins advance then surging back when they withdraw. To the hobgoblins' intense annoyance, they have so far proved unable to rid themselves of either of these foes, though the struggle continues and has grown into a generational and all-but-endless conflict.

Government

The hobgoblin kingdoms conduct themselves in accordance with their old ways, when their demigod was an absolute ruler. Today, the hobgoblin monarchs (both kings and queens, for there is little difference between males and females, and both fight with equal skill and ferocity) operate in a similar manner, exercising all but complete authority and demanding unquestioning obedience. Rulers are supported by a largely loyal corps of generals, marshals, and officers who have been raised to obey superiors without hesitation. While this makes hobgoblin rulers both ruthless and efficient, they can sometimes go too far — incompetent or especially greedy warlords may find themselves the target of coups and be quickly and decisively overthrown and replaced by more competent and respected leaders. This is in fact the most common way short of death in battle or from natural causes that hobgoblin rulers are replaced.

Those more successful rulers who die on the throne are replaced by a general or senior officer who is chosen by the monarch's inner circle of advisors. While the hobgoblins are indeed violent, bloodthirsty, and utterly without mercy, they are at least an honest and straightforward people who select their leaders with complete confidence. Petty politics, manipulation, and the intrigues of the surface world have no place in hobgoblin society, where ruthless honesty is respected and strength is rewarded. A hobgoblin monarch is guaranteed the loyalty and obedience of his or her subjects and advisors, unless of course he or she stumbles or grows too drunk with power, in which case violent overthrow is always an option.

Military

Hobgoblins do not simply *have* a military — they *are* their military. Trained almost from birth in myriad forms of slaughter and destruction, hobgoblins live in a society geared toward war and conquest. Their very martial excellence keeps them from uniting, as each kingdom believes itself to be superior to all the others. Only a powerful and charismatic ruler of the status of a Kakobovia or an especially legendary warlord can unite all hobgoblin nations into a single unit. And when this happens, the results are nothing short of terrifying.

Hobgoblin legions number 1,000–2,000 individuals that are organized into regiments of 100–600. Most hobgoblin legions are infantry, but many kingdoms maintain regiments of cavalry — albino worgs raised in the underworld and trained to be carnivorous and utterly vicious. Kingdoms also employ other creatures such as giants, ogres, trolls, and slave soldiers of various races.

Major Threats

The hobgoblins' greatest threat is their disunity, for without a single leader they are doomed to fight each other in an endless series of wars with no clear winner. Though they emerge from time to time to raid the outside, and sometimes form temporary alliances, the hobgoblins are actually caught in an eternal cycle of violence that will eventually end in either destruction or their reduction to utter and final barbarism.

The Deepfells still swarm with traditional foes, however, though none has the ability to truly threaten the hobgoblins on their own. Highly mobile kobold clans move quickly from place to place, raiding and annoying the hobgoblins, often entirely out of spite. Unable to fully exterminate these pests, the hobgoblins often overreact to their provocations and send massive punitive expeditions against the kobolds that more often than not encounter empty caverns and vanished foes.

The dwarves of Stoneaxe Caverns are of course the hobgoblins' most hated enemies, for they have fought with each other for millennia. Triumphant, the hobgoblins fought the dwarves to the very threshold of the caverns, pushing them out of their traditional homelands. At Stoneaxe, however, the hobgoblins have been stopped cold, and the continuing irritation of an independent dwarvish kingdom infuriates them. So far, however, dwarven steel and resolve have kept Stoneaxe free.

There are numerous other tribes, clans, bands, and even petty kingdoms throughout the Deepfells, including the derro of the deep caverns, orcish tribes, goblins, trolls, ogres, and other subterranean creatures. Battles with these foes keep the hobgoblins in shape and help them win the martial glory that they so crave. All the same, for all their prowess, the hobgoblins can never truly rid themselves of their various petty foes, and their frustration with these enemies, and with each other, continues to grow and fester, leading to even greater rivalry and distrust between the hobgoblin kingdoms.

Though the outside world, especially the folk of the Grand Duchy of Reme, sees the Deepfells' kingdoms as a threat and knows that war and destruction will follow if they ever reunite, the hobgoblins are dug in too far and the Deepfells are too extensive to ever dig them out. The Northmarchers' best hope for avoiding the nightmares of the past is for the hobgoblins to continue fighting among themselves, and see to it that Kakobovia never returns and that a single warlord never gains absolute power.

Through their contacts with the dwarves of the Stoneaxe Caverns, the Duchy of Northmarch is aware of at least some of the divisions among the hobgoblins, and Duchess Candrella Iskadar is taking steps to help keep them at each other's throats. Her schemes, so far unsuspected by the hobgoblins, are subtle and of increasing levels of sophistication. Initially, adventurers and other skilled scouts were sent into the Deepfells caverns simply to observe and gather information on the hobgoblin kingdoms. Then, as the Remans gained more knowledge, these scouts became provocateurs, committing acts of mayhem, vandalism, and destruction on various hobgoblin kingdoms, then leaving behind evidence that the perpetrators were rival states. These acts of provocation have grown in size and complexity, including several raids by Reman agents disguised or magically altered to resemble hobgoblins that target especially sensitive areas or influential kingdoms. Several hobgoblin alliances have been shattered by these acts, and so far the hobgoblins haven't suspected that they're being had by the wily surface dwellers.

WILDERNESS AND ADVENTURES

The Deepfells are honeycombed with tunnels, chambers, galleries, and various structures that date back to the old kingdom. With the fall of the great Deepfells Kingdom, many of these areas were abandoned by the hobgoblins and fell into ruin, overrun by subterranean vermin — insects, slimes, oozes, and other creatures of the dark underworld. Other areas were occupied by goblins and kobolds, whom the hobgoblins themselves regularly attempt to root out with military expeditions.

Those caverns not patrolled by the hobgoblins are truly dangerous places, with dangers both natural and unnatural. Darkness, deprivation, lack of food and water, predatory creatures of the depths, unexpected encounters with goblins, hobgoblins, kobolds, derro, and other denizens and the constant threat of falls, cave-ins, or becoming hopelessly lost all combine to make the Deepfells one of the most challenging and intimidating places in the entirety of the Northmarches.

Why then do adventurers seem drawn to the place? As always, it is the challenge of the unknown and the gaining of bragging rights, but the Deepfells have legitimate attractions as well. It is known that the old hobgoblin kingdom plundered much of modern-day Reme and even made contact with the hobgoblins of the distant Starfell Mountains, and brought back almost unbelievable amounts of treasure and plunder. The fragmented hobgoblin kingdoms of today retain some of that wealth, but some of it remains hidden, locked away in lost chambers or buildings, awaiting discovery. Gold, magic, weapons, the art, and treasure of a dozen kingdoms may still lie here for the taking, so long as those who seek it are bold and resilient, capable of withstanding the dangers of the underworld.

Kingdom of the Chosen: The largest and most influential of the hobgoblin kingdoms, the Chosen occupy a central portion of the Deepfells, close by the ancient and sacred caverns of Dragonbone Citadel. Despite their proximity and their absolute confidence that someday they will regain control, the Chosen have for centuries proved unable to take Dragonbone and are content to simply keep its rulers in check.

The Chosen are led by Queen Avordandra, a powerful warrior who claims to be more than 300 years old, sustained by the magic of her two most important advisors, the priest Odolos and the priestess Khezavaza the Repentant. Both are fanatical Kakobovia-worshippers who specialize in battle magic and creating potions that enhance health and lengthen lifespans. These potions, using as they do rare and exotic ingredients from all across the world and beyond, are reserved for them and their monarch, and are forbidden to ordinary hobgoblins.

Crimson Caverns: In the south of the Deepfells, near the border with the Frontier, the Crimson Caverns are home to this powerful hobgoblin kingdom ruled by the ferocious King Mandar and his countless sons and daughters. Though smaller than many other kingdoms, the Crimson Caverns are located in an old string of military strongpoints built by the Deepfells Kingdom and so are highly secure and all but immune from direct assault. The hobgoblins of this kingdom are among the finest warriors in the Deepfells, and their corps of albino worg-riders is the largest and best-trained.

Steelblade Depths: As its name implies, the Steelblade Kingdom is centered on the deeper caverns under the Deepfells, even to the point that it extends beneath the regions of the Chosen and the Dragonbone hobgoblins. Steelblades are a grim group within a larger grim species, and are known to fight ferociously even after taking mortal wounds or while dying. Their worship of Kakobovia shocks even the fanatics of the Chosen, and in some cases takes the form of extreme body modification, with limbs replaced by weapons, armor physically bolted to flesh, sharp jagged shards of metal grafted into hands, shoulders, or even faces. The Steelblade priests — who are known to be the most heavily mutilated and modified — claim that this reflects the suffering of the god Kakobovia, and that pain and wounds are sure ways to find favor with him, especially when they are self-inflicted. The Steelblades are nightmarish dwellers in deep darkness, but they sometimes form temporary alliances with other kingdoms and go on to raid the surface, riding white worgs that have also been extensively modified. Even other hobgoblins consider the Steelblades hopelessly mad, but are willing to fight alongside them nevertheless, at least for a time.

The Depths are ruled by priests, and led by the Priest-King Navokut, a towering and terrifying creature given to fits of rage in which he kills and, it is said, devours underlings who fail him.

Use the **Mountains Encounter Table** for generating random encounters anywhere in the Deepfells.

DEVIL'S FINGER

This bizarre tower resembles a great bony finger rising 750 feet above an isolated valley in the Deepfells. It was formed 10,000 years ago when the demon lord Jubilex's Obsidian Vault crashed into the mountains. Within the tower, a clan of dwarves built the citadel of Dwurschmiede. The dwarven god Dwerfater ultimately trapped Jubilex in the vault some 9,000 years ago. Three thousand years ago, Orcus, rising in power in the Abyss after his humiliation by the Three Gods, sent forth an army of demons in an unsuccessful attempt to invade Dwurschmiede. Finally, some 1,300 years ago the citadel fell to undead legions of the necromancer Giltz after being betrayed from within by a dwarf priest follower of Orcus.

Dragonbone Citadel

The central core of hobgoblin power in the Deepfells was also once home to mighty Kakobovia himself, and the Dragonbone Citadel today represents the true capital of the hobgoblin state. The great mountain is riddled with tunnels and chambers, and under control of a very old kingdom that represents the remnants of the old dynasty, still bound to the mountain where their god once dwelled.

While they are just as violent and militaristic as their fellows, the hobgoblins of Dragonbone Citadel are a cut above the others in terms of sophistication and "civilized" behavior. Though warfare is still their major motivation, Dragonbone hobgoblins continue to use their ancient written language to produce treatises on history and military tactics or to contemplate the lessons of Kakobovia and the ways that he may one day return. The Dragonbone hobgoblins also are the only ones of their kind in the Deepfells to compose and perform music, though unsurprisingly it is considered another way to motivate and excite their warriors in battle. Weapons and armor are of functional design, but are also works of art that rival even the craftsmen of Xha'en, and are highly prized outside the Deepfells. Some well-known adventurers, rulers, and generals possess arms or armor created by hobgoblin craftsmen from Dragonbone Citadel.

Queen Nashrahlu and her husband Crown Prince Chaixhul rule with more wisdom and less brutality than some other hobgoblin monarchs, but they are a thoroughly evil pair nonetheless, always seeking ways of overcoming their rivals and also wrecking damage on the outside world. They and their priests, who unsurprisingly take a far more philosophical and thoughtful approach to the memory of Kakobovia, are serenely confident that when their demon god does finally return, he will come to Dragonbone and elevate the descendants of his old rulers to their former glory. Mind you, this is no different than the beliefs of all the other hobgoblins, but the folk of Dragonbone have never once entertained a doubt of their destiny.

Dragonbone Peak

This high peak lies at the eastern edge of the Deepfells mountain range. Although it is still a citadel of the Deepfells hobgoblins, Dragonbone today is a mere shadow of its former greatness when it served as home to the demigod Kakobovia and his powerful hobgoblin empire. Kakobovia's power reached its zenith in the late 1500s I.R., but the demigod was finally defeated by Grand Duke Borell II of Reme at the Battle of Ironhill. Without a leader, the Deepfells hobgoblins splintered into competing factions and scattered throughout the mountains, though the Dragonbone hobgoblins remain influential due to their control of the citadel.

Eamonvale

Alignment: Lawful Good
Ruler: Lord Arb Angus
Government: Feudal
Population: 46,505 (Uplander 29,606, Foerdewaith 4,979, mountain dwarf 4,226, half-elf 2,921, human mixed ethnicity 1,818, gnome 912, hill dwarf 716, halfling 676, high elf 401, other humanoid 250)
Monstrous: Wolves, great cats (including jaguars), bears, serpents, girallons, dire animals, smilodons, kamadans, dryads, sprites, oakmen, brownies, and buckawns
Languages: Common
Religion: Thyr, Sefagreth, Belon the Wise, Stryme, Kamien, Dre'uain, Pekko, Solanus, the Green Father
Resources: Trade, Lumber, Agriculture
Currency: Eamonvale (though Rhemish currency is widely accepted)
Technology Level: Medieval
Demonym/Adjectival Demonym: Eamonvaler

Eamonvale is a long fertile valley through which runs one of the few trade roads across the Stoneheart Mountains. The valley, the forested mountain slopes that flank it, and its deep swamps and boggy moors are governed from the Grey Citadel of Dun Eamon. The authority of the lord of Eamonvale extends from the mountain passes near the river's headwaters to the trading center of Broadwater at the edge of the foothills of the Stonehearts.

For reasons that remain unclear, the Grand Duchy of Reme has never laid claim to the lands of Eamonvale, even though it is the source of a major tributary of the river that at its mouth empties into the Crescent Sea at the city of Reme itself. Rumors suggest that Eamon Angus, the original lord of Eamonvale, performed some critical service to the grand duke centuries ago and was rewarded with a permanent writ to hold Eamonvale free of the authority of Reme. Whether or not that is the case, neither the grand dukes nor the dukes of the Northmarches have ever attempted to annex the valley, though that has not stopped Rhemish merchant houses from seeking influence over this key trading route.

History and People

In 3238 I.R., Eamon Angus founded a small trading post at a ford near the end of a valley in the western eaves of the Stoneheart Mountains, south of the High Downs. As it became apparent that the trading post and the growing community on the ford were in a position to influence trade across the mountains, the community attracted the attention of several merchant families from the heartland of Reme. As the number of caravans moving across the ford and stopping to trade within the walls of the city steadily grew, the merchants sought a toehold in the thriving economy. Angus and his descendants forbade their emporiums in the city that would become Dun Eamon, so the merchants were forced to barter their goods and collect their tariffs before the caravans entered the valley.

At the mouth of the valley where the River Eamon calmed and widened into a navigable waterway, the tent cities and caravan camps of the traders grew into the town of Broadwater. It was here that the powerful Reman merchant house of Drenwall established an emporium and dominated the smaller independent traders. With total control of the movement of goods up the valley, House Drenwall taxed goods so heavily that they became unmarketable in the frontier communities. The merchant dynasty bought out caravans of certain critical supplies to deny the settlers the tools for their survival. When Eamonvale had been weakened by their actions, a scion of the Drenwall empire led an army of mercenaries upriver to sack the Angus trading center at the ford and seize the lucrative position on the trade road for themselves.

Angus and his supporters raised an army of woodsmen and settlers and engaged the merchant prince with a ferocity and tenacity that surprised even the seasoned mercenary generals. The battles of the Frontier War were hard-fought and costly, but the people of Eamonvale drove the army of House Drenwall from the valley to secure their economic freedom and gain effective control over the trading center of Broadwater. House Drenwall withdrew from the economics of the region but never forgot the chagrin of their defeat in the campaign and still covets the valley's flourishing economy.

The frontiersmen of Eamonvale have fought for generations to preserve their rights in the valley, first wresting their sustenance from the untamed wilds, then defending their homes against humanoid onslaughts and, most recently, dealing with the political machinations of greedy merchant empires. The people of Eamonvale are hardy and self-sufficient, hardships are taken in stride, and respect is reserved for those who earn it. Two dominant social groups exist in the valley, and are usually at odds with each other. The woodsmen who people the fertile slopes and forested glens of the valley regard the merchant class as arrogant foreigners from pampered lowland cities; the merchants regard the woodsmen as savages whose uncouth lifestyle they tolerate only in the interests of profit.

Religion

Among the merchants, Sefagreth is worshipped, and a temple to this god can be found in Broadwater. The locals generally prefer Dre'uain (particularly among the craftsman), Kamien, Pekko, and Thyr. Many travelers also sacrifice to Belon the Wise, seeking protection as they travel into the wilds beyond the valley. The Angus family, rulers of Eamonvale, have typically honored Stryme, and Lord Arb Angus' brother, Cael Angus, currently serves as the master of the Temple of Fortitude and high priest of Stryme in Dun Eamon. Rumor has it that the Angus family adopted Stryme as their patron after a long-ago battle where they fought alongside dwarves who honored that god.

Trade and Commerce

Eamonvale is a key location on one of the few commercial trading routes over the Stoneheart Mountains. Caravans, traders, explorers, and more take the Eamonvale Trade Road, and Dun Eamon and Broadwater are the last safe havens before entering the deep mountains. This has made the valley a target of many merchant houses over the centuries, though the Angus family has fended off all threats to the independence of their domain. Other than trade, the valley also produces fur and timber that is sent downriver to Yalendir and beyond into the heartland of Reme.

Loyalties and Diplomacy

Eamonvale is isolated, on the very limits of civilization, several hundred miles from Quintas, the nearest Rhemian city. It remains on friendly terms with the grand duchy, having apparently been guaranteed its independence around the time it was founded. On rare occasions, ducal patrols visit Broadwater or Dun Eamon on their way to assignments along the Stoneheart foothills, and they treat the locals with care and respect (with the Eamonvalers responding in kind). The only real diplomatic challenge to the Angus family comes from Reman merchant houses — particularly House Drenwall — that continually seek to influence or control the trade routes through the Stonehearts.

Government

For almost three centuries, rule of Eamonvale has passed by hereditary descent through the Angus family, beginning with Eamon Angus, the founder of Dun Eamon. The current ruler is Lord Arb Angus, a tall, robust man with thick brown hair and a well-trimmed beard. The region has developed well under his reign. He is young, having just entered his 30th year, and he rules with the confidence and vigor of youth tempered by the strict discipline and wisdom of his father. His policies on trade and tax ensure a place for the local farmers and craftsmen in the economy, and his strict prohibition on foreign guild influence has drawn much controversy. While many abroad would see him overthrown, he is well loved by his citizens.

Arb Angus remains unmarried, and it is well known in the valley that he intends to wait until later in life to take a wife. He has two younger brothers, Bron Angus, who serves as captain of the Mist Watch in Dun Eamon, and Cael Angus, master of the Temple of Fortitude and high priest of Stryme in Dun Eamon.

Military

The maintenance of law and order in and around the Grey Citadel is the responsibility of the Mist Watch, which is over 200 strong. The force is made up of career soldiers, citizen militia, and wilderness outriders. There is no law of mandatory service for the citizens, but any man living within the city walls is subject to conscription in times of war.

Bron Angus, Arb Angus' younger brother, is the captain of the watch and has been highly successful despite his young age. His experiences as a young man in a mercenary company taught him to be intolerant of sloth, insolence, and drunkenness, and his strict orders have resulted in an elite fighting force. The members of the Mist Watch are trained to a basic level with all weapons and tactics, but many of them have additional areas of expertise. All the Watchmen are rotated through various duty stations to avoid boredom and complacency.

Another 200 soldiers serve in the Broadwater Guard, a standing military force garrisoned at the Old Keep in Broadwater. These guardsmen, under command of sergeants and captains, are charged with safeguarding the town from external threats, a duty that includes manning the walls and gates, patrolling the immediate vicinity and responding to any apparent threat in the small communities immediately outside the gates. As the largest armed body of troops in the city, they may also be called upon to respond to any large disturbance within the walls, but they do not operate regular patrols in the town (which is the province of the Broadwater Constabulary).

Major Threats

There are many threats to Eamonvale that require the continual vigilance of the Angus family. The mountains contain many perils, including the orcs of Og-Brethos to the north and the other monsters that call the Stonehearts home. But historically, the greatest threat to Eamonvale has come from the merchant families of Reme, who continually seek to take control of this critical juncture on the trade road across the mountains. It is said that House Drenwall, in particular, holds a deep grudge against the Angus family for evicting them from Broadwater in the Frontier Wars several centuries ago.

Broadwater

Alignment: Lawful Neutral
Government: Council manipulated by merchant dynasty
Population: 2,268 (1,898 human, 100 dwarf, 60 gnome, 70 half-elf, 70 half orc, 70 high elf)
Languages: Common
Ruler: Councilman Alfgar, Councilman Drust, Councilman Herward, Master of House Gastone-Sheshek, Councilman Thorald, Councilman Galfridous.
Notable NPCs: Constable Maehil, Manwead, Uthno Abecar, others.
Resources: Ore, stone, weapons
Technology Level: Medieval

Overview

Like Dun Eamon, Broadwater sits at a key position on the trade corridor of the foothills of the Stoneheart Mountains. From its walls, four gates open to the world. One gate leads up to Eamonvale along the Trade Road to the Grey Citadel and the mining operations beyond. Another opens to the vast grasslands of the Marches of Reme. A third gate opens to the pontoon bridge that crosses the River Eamon and provides access to the road that winds its way along the back hills of the Stonehearts. The fourth gate opens to the Docks of Broadwater where waterborne trade crosses from Eamonvale to the capital in Reme.

Broadwater is built partially on top of a high sandstone bluff and partially below it on the banks of the River Eamon. The upper portion of the city is referred to as High Town. It is the location of the Mercantile quarter where representatives of the numerous trade emporiums maintain a presence throughout the year.

It is here that agents of Lord Angus operate a customs warehouse for oversight and taxation of trade in the region, a part of which is tithed to the overlord in Reme. High Town also holds a fort known as the Militant Quarter that holds a garrison of Lord Angus' troops who are there to safeguard the mouth of the valley.

A variety of mercenaries and roustabouts occupy the city's Adventurers' District and offer their services as sell-swords working river and caravan traffic. Bandits and river pirates are a common occurrence in the region.

Low Town is found closest to the River Eamon and is the location of the Artisans' District, which produces various items for trade. The district's wares typically include goods and services that apply to the shipping industry and include everything from wagon wheels to saddles, bridles, bits, and horseshoes. For shipping, yards manufacture and repair keelboats and barges, and a plant manufactures pitch and tar for chinking boats that navigate the waterways.

The Paupers' Quarter in Low Town is home to a variety of beggars, thieves, and scoundrels. Rundown pleasure houses and gaming halls are found here in abundance, servicing the needs of the rough-and-tumble drovers and barge-folk.

Here too are the docks known as the Flotilla and the notorious Broadwater Corral that is maintained throughout the year by various of the plains' Loreclans under a treaty devised to keep the peace.

People

The folk of the region are predominantly human of Foerdewaith descent, though the lunar cycle brings members of the plains' Loreclans who manage and maintain the corral. Ethnically, the folk of Broadwater have a distinct cast to their features that is common among the folk of Eamonvale and differs slightly from the broader population of Waymarch and the Grand Duchy of Reme in general. The folk of Broadwater are, in general, hard workers, though they have a strong element of corruption and a thriving criminal undercurrent that feasts upon the trade from Eamonvale to Reme.

Trade

Trade in the city is closely monitored on several levels. Overseers at each gate inspect every wagon, cart, and handbarrow that enters the city. The only streets wide enough for dray traffic lead to the trade grounds where additional agents review and tax the cargoes passing into the market. All other streets are intentionally narrow to prevent merchants from sneaking goods around the local tax collectors to avoid paying the tariff. For this reason, the criminal activity in black market and smuggled goods is higher than the average town of its size as the grift on trade is much smaller when dealing with the thieves' guilds than it is in dealing with the government. Unfortunately for the folk of Broadwater, it is the merchant league that is taking the lion's share of profit from the city. The denizens of Broadwater are beginning to bare their teeth against the yoke of the council. Many hope that Earl Angus comes to Broadwater for an audit of profits and exchanges and throws the whole lot of the council in stocks until their behavior improves.

Government

The government of Broadwater is ostensibly administrated via a charter between the earl of Eamonvale and his extended allegiance to both the duke of Waymarch and the grand duke of Reme. In truth, the city is run by a series of corrupt officials of the various trade houses who manipulate one another as an oligarchy of distrust and avarice. None of the noble powers that be seems to take much notice or pay much attention to the situation in Broadwater as long as their own tithes are always paid on time and in full.

Threats

Threats to Broadwater come in the form of bandits, politicians, and river pirates who brazenly raid merchants almost as soon as they leave the city, returning to the very city of Broadwater itself to resell the goods that had only recently passed through customs.

The various council members are constantly attempting to sabotage one another, which destabilizes the local economy and threatens the general peace as they hire rogues and mercenaries to attack one another's caravans.

Furthermore, an active slave trade within the city is unknown to all but a very few. Newcomers and travelers who go missing often end up in the slave pits of the Underbluff.

Dun Eamon

Alignment: Lawful Good
Ruler: Lord Angus of Dun Eamon
Government: Feudal
Population: 5,722 (Uplander 4,323, mountain dwarf 312, gnome 229, half-elf 209, human [mixed ethnicity] 183, halfling 171, high elf 115, hill dwarf 87, half-orc 51, Foerdewaith 42)
Languages: Common
Religion: Stryme, Dre'uain, Belon the Wise, Kamien
Resources: Trade, furs, and pelts
Technology Level: Medieval

The city of Dun Eamon is the center of government for Eamonvale. Located high in the mist-shrouded mountain crags of the Stoneheart Mountains, it is a city like no other. Locally known as the Grey Citadel, it is an important trading city that sits on a broad ford at the base of one plunging waterfall and at the head of another. Midway across the ford, a huge slab of bedrock divides the river into two channels. On the island between, many generations ago, Eamon Angus staked a claim and founded a tiny trading post. Now, centuries later, expansion of the duchies and kingdoms on either side of the Stoneheart Mountains and development of trade between them have caused the tiny trading center and waystation to grow into a heavily fortified citadel, with the lordship still in the hands of the Angus family. Three brothers of the Angus clan currently rule over the city and valley with strictness and compassion, and have seen it flourish under their authority.

The Grey Citadel is renowned as the location of some of the finest forges in the land. Nearly any tool, weapon, or other metal item can be crafted there, and the quality of their alloys and strength of their castings are unsurpassed. Due to its critical location at the ford and its safety relative to the perils of the frontier, the Grey Citadel is a popular stop on the route to the passes of the Stonehearts. It is a hiring point for caravan laborers and guards for the dangerous journey over the mountains to the distant kingdoms beyond. Many hunters and trappers pass through the gates every season to sell their pelts and to resupply for another trip into the wild mountains beyond. Traveling minstrels, adventurers, and highwaymen all call the city home from time to time.

A rampart wall surrounds the entire island, with watchtowers evenly distributed along it, and a massive gatehouse guards each entrance where the road rises up from the ford. Where the divided channels of the river spill over the lower falls, the island rises steeply to a flat-topped promontory. On this slab of rock sits the upper city, which consists of the craftsman's district, the vast market, and the largest taverns. The stone buildings are quarried from the same gray basalt as the bedrock they sit on, as are the city walls and keep. The rest of the buildings are half-timbered two- and three-story structures, with roofs of thatch or shingle. The cobblestone streets and alleys are always shiny and damp, and everything in the city hosts at least a thin sheen of green moss; many buildings have thick clumps of ferns growing on the roof. Amid the green-forested slopes and drifting gray rainclouds, the gray-green edifices of the citadel blend right in.

According to rumor, a network of caves and caverns and even an underground river lie beneath Dun Eamon.

EAMONVALE TRADE ROAD

Winding a course through Eamonvale's mountainous wilderness, this road is the chief artery of transit for the valley. It runs from the town of Broadwater, passed several villages, through the gates of the Grey Citadel of Dun Eamon and beyond, until it slips into the snow-clad passes of the Stoneheart Mountains. At the Feirgotha Plateau, it connects to the Southern Pass that leads to the eastern eaves of the Stonehearts. Traffic on the road includes mercantile enterprises ranging from large caravans to tiny farm carts, as well as travelers, military forces, homesteaders, pilgrims, and indigenous creatures.

Use the **Roads Encounter Table** to generate random encounters on the Eamonvale Road.

RIVER EAMON

The River Eamon flows down out of the Stoneheart Mountains, first through snow-fed mountain streams, then crashing down through rocky gorges and finally calming and widening at the town of Broadwater where it enters the plains of the Northmarches of Reme on its eventual way to join the Remenos River to the Crescent Sea.

Use the **River (General) Encounter Table** to generate random encounters on the River Eamon.

THE HAUNTED WOOD

Alignment: Chaotic Neutral
Ruler: None
Government: Elder and council (Golden Oak)
Population: 5,430 (wood elf 3,610, shadow elf 1,820)
Monstrous: Wolves, giant rats, giant weasels, giant spiders, dire wolves, giant owls, ogres, trolls, green hags, wereboars, werewolves, shambling mounds, treants, will-o'-wisps
Languages: Elvish, sylvan
Religion: Shalraei (Golden Oak elves), Sha-yen-maar (shadow elves)
Resources: Furs, timber
Currency: Barter, ancient elvish coinage
Technology Level: Dark Ages

The Haunted Wood is a last remnant of the old wood elf kingdom of Alathanar that was felled centuries ago by the Hyperboreans. Today it is a dense, forbidding old growth forest crossing northern stretches of the Duchy of the Northmarches between the Deepfells and the Stoneheart Mountains. This woodland has always been considered fey and strange, and it is believed that large portions of it currently lie under a shadowy curse. It was never actually a part of the Great Akadonian Forest that once swathed much of the continent, always having been separated by the Ashen Hills to the west and the Green Mountains and chalky High Downs to the south. Tribes of reclusive dark elves still live in this forest but are largely confined to the settlement of Golden Oak as a consequence of the shadowy curse that besets the woodland.

HISTORY AND PEOPLE

Five thousand years ago, the region that came to be known as the Haunted Wood extended all the way to the Namjan Forest on the border of the Ashen Hills. It was then part of the elven kingdom of Alathanar, home of the Alathi tribe of wood elves. These elves, who worshipped the goddess Shalraei, were advanced in arcane knowledge and lived in homes melded from the living trees and rocks of the forest.

Almost nothing is known today of what transpired during that time, for the land-hungry Hyperboreans had little concern for the traditions and stories of the people whom they replaced, or for the true significance of the ancient forest that fell beneath their axes. Most of the elves of the region departed during the Third Exodus and, though they didn't know it, the advancing humans founded the Duchy of the Northmarches on the corpse of an ancient and sacred land.

For many generations, the Alathi dwelled in peace alongside their goddess. Even after her departure during the Age of the Gods, Shalraei's divine presence continued to be felt, and she is worshipped to this day by the remaining Alathi, as well as many other fey creatures, including the Vaeltaia centaurs of the Frontier.

It was long before the Hyperboreans' arrival and the final decline of the kingdom that a stranger arrived in the lands of the Alathi. Those few who are even aware of the story from fragments of epic elven verse or overgrown monuments and tablets glimpsed deep within the Haunted Wood estimate that it was around –5,000 I.R. when an individual calling himself Dyraxl Uhl-Kal-Totten established a stronghold deep in the Namjan Forest, defying the protective magics that had long guarded the realm. This sorcerer-warlord may have hailed from the far south, or possibly even far Libynos, and was probably a member of the old human race known only as the Ancient Ones. He revered an especially foul deity, Sha-Yen-Maar, The Masked Mistress, She of the Nine Eyes, whose worship he had imported from his homeland.

In those days, the Namjan Forest was inhabited by the Thistlehill gnomes, but soon their mines, farms, and villages fell to the warlord. Dyraxl began to delve into secret, forbidden rites of magic, summoning creatures of shadow, demons, and worse from distant planes of existence and worshipping gods that were utterly alien and inimical to the elves of

Alathanar. His magic proved stronger even than that of the Alathi druids, who had little familiarity with many of his arcane powers. Alarmingly, Dyraxl's realm began to spread into Alathanar, and he attracted all manner of foul creatures, not the least of which were orcs, goblins of the hills, and summoned horrors from beyond normal time and space. When some of their own people began to fall under the sorcerer's domination, the chieftains of the Alathi knew that something had to be done. The call to battle went out, and soon the entire nation of Alathanar rose against the Ancient One and his nightmare army.

Battle raged in the peaceful forests, and in some cases, elf fought elf as Dyraxl's corrupt minions stood against their own kin. The Ancient One was powerful, but his magic was still limited, and the Alathi still wielded much of their old goddess's power. The conflict lasted years, but in the end the Alathi advanced to the gates of Dyraxl's fortress. Completely surrounded by enemies, the warlord prepared to cast one great ritual that would blast the elven armies even as they besieged him. With the enemy's armies destroyed, Dyraxl could return to his schemes unmolested and spread his dominion over all Alathanar.

Fate, luck, or possibly a final blessing from their lost goddess intervened in the Alathi's favor, as the normally-infallible Dyraxl made a single tiny error. His ritual backfired, and the sorcerer was consumed by his own fell magic. Many of his summoned creatures vanished, their ties to their master broken, while others lost heart and fled into the woods. The elves stormed the battered Shadowhold and swept through it, scattering the last of Dyraxl's minions before returning in triumph, bearing loads of stolen riches and powerful magical artifacts back to their capital at Golden Oaks. Shadowhold was still a threat, however, and the region remained subject to incursions from the Shadow Plane. The wild elves avoided the place and surrounded it with wards and magical protection.

For a time, the kingdom prospered under the rulership of Queen Phaerela, a devout and faithful priestess of Shalraei. As her long life ended, she passed the throne to her young son Marolan, who was a studious and thoughtful elf with a great interest in magic and the arcane. All was well for the first few decades of his rule. He married the druidess Sylaea, who gave birth to their daughter Aurea, a widely beloved princess.

Alas, though the evil was bottled up and contained in the Shadowhold, Dyraxl's evil survived him as the magical tomes and items looted from his stronghold made their way into the realm of Alathanar, eventually falling into the hands of the greedy and weak-willed. Soon, a dozen or more secretive groups were exploring the forbidden secrets of Dyraxl's lore. Arcane magic — long shunned by the Alathi druids — grew more powerful and prominent, encouraged by the king. It was centuries after the Ancient One's fall that a tall, elegantly-clad sorcerer named Taloran arrived at the king's forest palace and offered his services as a court magician. It was this moment, unheeded by most, when the downfall of the realm began.

Taloran didn't wait long to reveal his true colors. He was, it seemed, not even an Alathi, but had traveled to the region from a distant Green Realm kingdom seeking to learn more of the rumored powerful spells and rituals now being developed. With the resources of King Marolan and Queen Sylaea at his disposal, Taloran dispatched bands of handpicked warriors to seek out the various spellcasters and circles that possessed Dyraxl's old artifacts and books, ruthlessly seizing them and killing anyone who stood in their way. In time, Taloran accumulated a sizable collection of the old warlord's objects of power and began to delve into controlling them.

Taloran's merciless amorality quickly transformed into untrammeled cruelty and sadism as his increasingly savage warriors roamed the land, bringing him young elves for sacrifice and experimentation. Despite his bloody excesses, Taloran was careful to maintain the good will of the royal couple, passing on treasures, magical blessings, and wealth along with sycophantic fawning and declarations of eternal loyalty. King Marolan's fascination with arcane magic grew to an obsession, and his psyche, always somewhat fragile, finally began to give way.

Soon he was the de facto ruler, having bent both king and queen to his will. The sacrifices grew in size and brutality as creatures of shadow were once more drawn to the region, along with summoned fiends and gateways to realms of unimaginable horror. Taloran began to regularly venture into the Namjan Forest, defying the old wards and defenses, returning with still more objects of power and dark knowledge. It was said that Taloran has actually spoken with the shade of the Ancient One Dyraxl Uhl-Kal-Totten and plotted to return him to some semblance of life.

Ensnared and utterly under Taloran's influence, King Marolan announced that the realm would now worship Sha-Yen-Maar, shunning the gentle faith of Shalraei. Pushed beyond their limits, the common people finally rose up in rebellion under the banner of Princess Aurea, Marolan's own daughter who finally rejected her parents' wickedness.

Soon, terrible civil war wracked the land. Towns and citadels were sacked, vast stretches of forest were ruined, and thousands perished. Now that the monarchs' usefulness was at an end, Taloran finally ended the charade, killing the royal couple and declaring himself monarch. His followers were scarcely elven anymore, for many had fused their essence with the creatures of shadow or taken on the aspects of demons. These shadow-elves were a new elven people, different from the dark elves of the deep reaches and possessed by the essence of distant, alien planes of existence.

The fight went on for years as countless Alathi and their shadow-elf foes perished in desperate battle. In the end, the shadow-elves' power was broken, but Taloran's body was never found, nor were those of many of his followers. The realm was devastated and most of its inhabitants slain, leaving the survivors to rebuild. At this time, the settlement of Golden Oak was founded as a new central town in the depopulated kingdom. A sad, dispirited Queen Aurea returned to her palace with a heavy heart, knowing in her soul that the last days of the realm were upon them.

Her premonition proved true in the following years as the humanoids of the mountains and forests descended on the depopulated realm. Many brave battles were fought in those days, and the Alathi experienced some epic triumphs. In some ways, it was their finest hour, but in the end it was for naught, for Queen Aurea finally decided in the late 600s I.R. to withdraw to the Crynnomar Gap along with the other elven refugees. A handful of her subjects remained behind in Golden Oak to continue guarding the old ruins and to try to maintain at least a semblance of the old ways. They remain there today, the last survivors of Alathanar, in the place called the Haunted Wood by outsiders.

The wood is generally left alone by the modern Reman Northmarchers, save for the town of Nerimar located a half day's march from the forest's edge. Those with the courage to venture deep into the woods speak of hostile wood elves, shadow creatures, and tribes of hostile goblins. It is known that the settlement of Golden Oak still exists, but few know its location, and some even claim that the ruins of the ancient elven kings who delved into evil magics and triggered their land's civil war also lie hidden in the depths of the Haunted Wood.

The surviving members of the old Alathi tribe are an insular lot who meet intruders with open hostility, usually giving them a chance to leave before they attack. However, some more fanatical Alathi shoot first and ask questions later, making the woods an even more dangerous place for outsiders. What most outsiders don't know is that the old conflict still lingers in some places, and the seemingly hostile wood elves are actually holding back a fearsome and dangerous enemy. The old ruins do exist and are still occupied, and their inhabitants are not friendly.

The shadow elves persist in the deep woods. Some are the descendants of the old enemy, while others are quite old and fought alongside Taloran the usurper and his horrors. Some few of his old shadow-demon-elf hybrids persist as well, still preying on the Alathi elves and the occasional unfortunate adventurer. The shadows' presence in the forest and in the nearby Namjan Forest is part of the ancient curse that plagues the region, haunts the dreams of its inhabitants, and sometimes even drives ordinary souls to madness and murder.

Religion

The Alathi wild elves are all that remains of the great tribe that once controlled nearly all of the modern Northmarches nearly three millennia ago. Today only a handful remain, but they continue to follow the old ways and worship the goddess Shalraei who once dwelled in the forests alongside her people. Rites are performed by druidic priests and priestesses who still utter prayers in ancient tongues and preside over animal sacrifice on both equinox and solstice nights. The corrupt nobles who spread the rites and teachings of the Ancient One Dyraxl Uhl-Kal-Totten perverted the old rituals and began to sacrifice their fellow elves to the horror of the uncorrupted Alathi who, despite their often violent natures, would not even consider such terrible acts.

Isolated as they are in their cursed settlements and ruins, the shadow elves of the deep forest still persist, following their own old ways as well and revering Sha-Yen-Maar, The Masked Mistress. One of the infamous Unholy Three whose worship was outlawed in Foere, her worship seems to have originated in distant Libynos and was brought here by the Ancient One sorcerer-warlord Dyraxl Uhl-Kal-Totten. Also known as the goddess of vice and pain, Sha-Yen-Maar is portrayed as a comely female with either a masked face with nine eyes or a nightmarish demonic visage. She is also worshipped by shadow creatures and evil beings of all sorts, and her rites invariably involve blood sacrifice and excesses of all kinds.

Trade and Commerce

The remaining elves of Golden Oak and the other small settlements throughout the Haunted Wood do not trade with the outside world. A small amount of trade occurs between communities, but for the most part they remain self-sufficient, as travel through the woods, especially at night, is hazardous even for the elves who have lived in the forest for millennia. What trade exists is in food, clothing, weapons, and handcrafted goods.

Loyalties and Diplomacy

Having experienced the horrors of Dyraxl Uhl-Kal-Totten's evil magic, then seen their forest felled by the axes of the Hyperboreans, the Alathi have little interest in diplomacy or even contact. A few hardy Northmarchers or adventurers have made their way into the forest, but with rare exceptions, these individuals are not welcome. The Alathi's struggle against the shadow has continued for countless generations without assistance from the outside world, and today they are loath to even consider asking for it. Humans, dwarves, halflings, and other outside peoples rarely venture into the woods, and when they do, they are usually asked to leave, often urged along by flights of elven arrows.

Government

The glorious days of the ancient kings and queens are long past. With the passing of Aurea, the last queen, governance of the Alathi elves passed to tribal and village leaders. The highest-ranking elf in the Haunted Wood is probably Elder Sarim Oakleaf, who ascended to leadership after he and a band of adventurers unmasked the elves of House Shadowleaf — the former elders of Golden Oak — as corrupt servants of the shadow demons. Relatively young, he is more open to outsiders than his fellow elves and has proven himself a capable leader. Others in the region look to him for leadership, but the various small villages and bands of the woods usually see to their own affairs. Invasions, disasters, or other significant threats to the forest and the Alathi can stir the various communities to come together, however; in times of crisis, villages and bands send representatives to meet in Golden Oak to discuss common action and defenses.

Military

Any Alathi capable of holding a weapon or casting a spell fights, and their old traditions of wilderness scouting, hunting, and irregular combat all serve them well. Villages and tribal groups are skilled in camouflage, archery, sneak attacks, and misdirection, and are commanded by war leaders drawn from the best hunters, rangers, or fighters. The Alathi elves' main weakness is their numbers — despite their determination, the Alathi cannot hope to stand against a determined foe such as the Remans or the Deepfells hobgoblins, though they will inflict casualties far beyond their population. These days, they must rely on the dangers of the woods, the threat of the shadow, and outsiders' fear of the very real curse that affects the land. So far, this has kept them relatively secure in their wilderness fastness.

Major Threats

The handful of wild elves who persist in the Haunted Wood are the last of their kind. When they are gone, the ancient Alathi will truly be extinct. Most modern Alathi acknowledge this and know that soon their time will end, but they continue to fight on against the shadow nonetheless.

Their evil counterparts also dwell deep in the forest, clinging to the ruins and remains of Taloran's old kingdom. These creatures — whom the Alathi do not even consider to be elves anymore — are the greatest threat to the realm. Some are simply elves who bear the essence of the shadow in their souls, which grants them unusual powers such as innate shadow magic, the ability to conceal themselves or vanish altogether, or alter their enemies' memories and mislead them with false thoughts. Others are the very shadow sorcerers and priests who fought alongside Taloran, while still others are more demon than elf — dark beasts who exist to kill the living and extinguish the hated scourge of light and life. All still live in rough bands and small communities, worshipping the wicked Sha-Yen-Maar and striking at the Alathi any chance they get. Attacks on isolated villages have been growing recently, along with elves who cannot dream or recuperate from injury or trauma. Some of these have been known to go mad and kill their families or fellow villagers, and these incidents too have been spreading. The Alathi periodically venture into the shadow ruins to push back their enemies, but centuries of battle have not eliminated the threat.

While the shadow is indeed the worst threat that the Alathi face, it is not the only one. The woods also contain tribes of murderous goblins and wicked shadow fey. Orcs and hobgoblins from the Gryphon and Ashen hills or even from the distant Deepfells sometimes venture into the woods as well, heedless of the dangers. In such cases, these invaders face the wrath of the Alathi and the shadow elves, who both hate the humanoids intensely.

Wilderness and Adventures

The Haunted Wood is well named, for with the exception of the islands of relative safety represented by the Alathi elven settlements (where outsiders are usually only grudgingly tolerated at best, or outright attacked at worst), the realm is truly a place of shadows, monstrous predators, hostile humanoids, and ancient curses. The ancient and twisted shadow elves are probably the most overt threat, as their hatred of the Alathi is equaled only by their hatred of outsiders. Infused with shadow and reinforced by powerful ancient magic, creatures of the shadow planes and their own demon-possessed warriors, the shadow elves are eager for blood and sacrificial victims. Woe unto the traveler or Alathi hunter who blunders into their ruins or encounters one of their raiding parties, for their end is certain to be bloody and painful.

There is reason to seek out shadow elven ruins however, for many old and powerful magical items can be found there, along with various items of treasure such as artwork, weapons, and everyday objects crafted of gold, silver, electrum, and fine hardwoods. Even mundane items gleaned from shadow ruins can fetch a high price in the Northmarches, but magical objects are sometimes infused with dark and cursed sorcery, leaving looters vulnerable to demonic possession, disease, madness, hauntings, and other misfortune.

The tangled forests between elven settlements are wild and evil indeed, with murderous goblins, giant spiders, and wandering shadow creatures being the least of a traveler's worries. The spirits of ancient warriors, spellcasters, and druids also wander the forest, lost and unable to find peace, their immortal minds driven to madness by the influx of evil magic that wracked the land. Gates to the planes of shadows or chaos open randomly, allowing access to hostile and alien creatures whose very presence heralds madness and fear. Alathi wards and magic provide some protection from these incursions, but the spells of today are increasingly feeble, especially in comparison to the mighty enchantments once woven by the wild elves' ancestors.

Old ruins dot the landscape, which is mostly overgrown and lost. These ruins may contain wealth and magic, but as previously noted, these prizes often come with a steep price and may also be guarded by shades, shadow beings, demons, or incomprehensible horrors from alien realities. The evil of these ruins can ensnare even the most faithful and benevolent of victims, as they did the ruling Shadowleaf clan of Golden Oak.

Lycanthropes of all sorts lurk in the depths of the Haunted Wood, for the dark energies that suffuse the place seem to suit evil shapechangers particularly well. The Golden Oak elves and others who venture into the woods are strongly advised to carry silver weapons and exercise caution around nights of the full moon. There are tantalizing rumors, however, that not all of the shapechangers in the forest are entirely evil. Surprisingly, a band of benevolent wereboars is said to sometimes be encountered in the woods, aiding travelers and even driving off evil lycanthropes. No one is entirely sure exactly who or what these strange creatures — whom the stories call "Bristlebacks" or "Brightboars" — are, especially since wereboars are traditionally an especially wicked lot, and many think that their existence is a wild travelers' myth.

The old royal palace of Alathanar, once a giant and glorious tree equipped with vast chambers, temples, and living quarters, lies somewhere in the depths of the forest. Where, the Alathi are unable (or unwilling) to say, and it forms the center of shadow elf power in the region. The Alathi themselves speak of the cursed place only in hushed whispers, but some claim that the minions of shadow, and possibly even their high priest and leader, the evil usurper Taloran, live on as ghosts, undead horrors, or demon-possessed hulks. The Shadow Palace, as the Alathi call it, is also said to be full of potent spells and magic, though as is typical with such things in the forest, much of the wealth and arcane treasures of the place bears terrible curses.

Use the **Forest Encounter Table** for generating random encounters in the Haunted Wood.

REFERENCE SOURCES

Curse of Shadowhold

THE HIGH DOWNS

Alignment: Neutral Good
Capital: Royal Bluff (rock gnome 3,221)
Notable Settlements: Chalktown (rock gnome 1,150)
Ruler: King Oron Granith
Government: Monarchy
Population: 9,265 (rock gnome 8,100, humans of mixed ethnicity 655, half elf 510)
Monstrous: Kobolds, goblins, ankheg, cockatrice, hill giants, zombies, ogres, peryton, trolls
Languages: Common, gnomish
Religion: Michol Stoneshaper (gnomes), Solanus (humans)
Resources: Chalk, gems, livestock, furs
Currency: Reme, ancient gnomish currency
Technology Level: Dark ages

The High Downs are a natural chalky highland area of central Reme between the Green Mountains and the Stoneheart Mountains. While the downs are considered to be the southern boundary of the Duchy of the Northmarches, they are nevertheless technically an independent kingdom and the historic site of ancestral rock gnome homeland, specifically the royal gnomes of Clan Granith. Though Reman domination essentially reduced the High Downs and its gnomes to the status of ducal subjects, the gnomes themselves continue to practice their old ways. For the most part, the Northmarchers maintain the pretense of their independence.

HISTORY AND PEOPLE

The High Downs have been inhabited for millennia. The Phoromyceaen founders of the ancient city of Barakus wrote of a "distant kingdom of the rock gnomes" that had built cities and mines in and around a hilly region far to the west. It is almost certain that these ancient gnomes were the ancestors of today's inhabitants.

The gnomes themselves tell their own history through the story of Clan Granith, who have ruled the kingdom literally since its founding. Clan Granith may in fact be the longest uninterrupted dynasty in all Akados, if not the world, a fact of which the gnomes are exceedingly proud, and which contributes to their unwillingness to simply acknowledge Reme's rulership. For their part, the Remans have little desire to conquer or otherwise disturb the gnomes and let the dynasty continue.

For many generations, the rock gnomes lived in close proximity to the wild elf kingdom of Alathanar. Forbidden from entering the sacred forest, the gnomes contented themselves with developing their homeland and occasionally trading with wild elves who sometimes deigned to journey into the downs (apparently the forbiddance on travel was one-way only). When the wild elves were beset by civil war, the gnomes struggled to stay out of the conflict, but as it grew worse and the Alathanar region fell into chaos, horrors and strange beasts began to appear in the forest and grew emboldened, sometimes marauding into the High Downs.

In response, the rock gnomes — normally peaceful and provincial — were forced to form defensive militias equipped with locally-produced weapons and armor. Initially, these militias met with little success due to their lack of training and experience, but slowly they began to grow more effective, finally helping to keep the rock gnomes' homeland safe as Alathanar descended further into disorder.

This training served the gnomes well, for the humanoids of the north followed, ravaging elven lands and forcing the final evacuation of the sacred Alathanar realm. Several gnomish songs and stories tell of battles between the gnomes of the High Downs and the hordes of goblins that tried to plunder their realm, with most ending (at least as the gnomes tell it) in gnomish victory.

During this time, the advance of the human-ruled Hyperborean Empire reached the High Downs and the forests of Alathanar beyond.

Even after their successes against the humanoids, the rock gnomes found themselves unable to face the humans and though alarmed, did nothing to interrupt the founding of the Hyperborean settlement of Ironhill. After negotiation, the gnomes were granted autonomy and generally left in peace by the humans, but by this time the writing was on the wall, and the decline of the gnomes' kingdom had begun.

Years passed and the gnomes traded with the humans, providing chalk, minerals, and metals while Ironhill grew in size and influence. Beyond the Downs, the humans settled the Northmarches and grew prosperous, only to be interrupted by a massive invasion of hobgoblins from the Deepfells. Humans were driven from their lands, and the invaders even swept into the High Downs, killing and enslaving gnomes, burning their settlements, and plundering the entire land. The gnomes fought back as best they could, sometimes fighting shoulder-to-shoulder with the humans, and several gnomish companies were there on the day that Duke Borrell finally broke the power of the hobgoblins at the Battle of Ironhill.

Bruised and battered, the gnomes were reduced to a shadow of their former glories, but returned to their burned towns and once more took up their old trades. Humans returned under the rulership of Foere, but few wished to settle the Downs, preferring instead to seek their fortunes to the north in the Great Steppes. The invasion by the Shadow Horde in the 2940s I.R. was a distant tragedy, and the gnomes of the Downs were affected only by the arrival of countless refugees. An inherently kind and peaceful people, the gnomes tended to the human refugees and did their best to provide. With the raising of the Wizard's Wall and the defeat of the horde, life slowly returned to something resembling normalcy, but it was clear that the old kingdom was gone in all but name.

Most gnomes today acknowledge that their kingdom is only a pale shadow, and that true authority lies with the humans of Reme. A handful, including a group of expatriates in the city of Castorhage, are calling for a return to the old ways and an aggressive reclamation of their homelands, but so far these calls have come to nothing. It remains to be seen what exactly the future holds, but some of the dissidents have even called for an end to the ancient Granith dynasty and its replacement with a more vital and modern ruler.

For all the violence of the past, the gnomes remain a friendly and peaceful people, though centuries of conflict have taught them how to defend themselves, and hostile raiders or invaders of the Downs can expect a warm welcome. When not fighting for their survival, the gnomes are pleasant and have little problem with their human neighbors, so long as they are left in peace and their largely illusory independence is maintained. They live in villages of 20–200 individuals, with most citizens engaging in chalk mining, farming, or herding goats. Transportation is on foot or by goat cart. Most structures are built in the old style, resembling stone beehives or longhouses, though a few human-style houses and manors do exist, scaled down to smaller gnomish size.

RELIGION

The gnomes of the Downs still follow their old faith, worshipping the deity Michol Stoneshaper, who is said to have crafted the rock gnomes out of the native bedrock of the primal world. Like their rulership and government, the gnomes have remained consistent since the earliest days of their kingdom. They maintain small roadside and household shrines at which they sometimes leave small carved stones and statues as offerings to their deity in recognition of the divine craft that he used to create his favored people. Not all priests of Michol are true clerics or cast divine magic; some are simply devout individuals who tend to the spiritual needs of their families or communities. A few are gifted with divine magic, and these tend to be community leaders and particularly influential members of the kingdom.

TRADE AND COMMERCE

In their earliest days, the gnomes were largely self-supporting. They lived in stone huts, raised their own food, and saw to their own needs in a surprisingly peaceful corner of a violent continent. When approached by wild elf traders from the realm of Alathanar, the gnomes traded their food and chalk for wood, metal tools, ceramics, and other useful items. Today, they continue to raise their own food and livestock, but they trade mostly with humans in exchange for the chalk that they mine from the hills. Their trade relationships are of course primarily with the Northmarchers of Reme, but a few hardy Foerdewaith merchants make the long trip to the High Downs for chalk, providing the gnomes with much-needed gold and various staples.

The gnomes trade a few exotic items as well, including gemstones that are occasionally found in the chalk mines. A few ranches in the downs also specialize in raising animals for fur, specifically ermine and mink, providing a small but significant flow of income to wealthy clients in Reme and Foere. The successful breeding of such mustelid creatures also led to the gnomes most impressive military force, the giant weasel riders of Chalktown (see below).

LOYALTIES AND DIPLOMACY

The gnomes of the High Downs are fairly isolated, and those who are even aware of their existence think of them as subjects of the grand duchy. While this is in essence true, the gnomish kingdom officially retains its independence and maintains an official embassy in Ironhill. Beyond the Northmarches, the gnomes have very little influence, though the city of Castorhage harbors a significant number of gnomes, some of whom have started a movement to return to the High Downs and restore the old glories of the gnomish homeland.

GOVERNMENT

For all intents and purposes, the rock gnomes have always lived in the High Downs. It is indeed their ancestral homeland and for the most part has always been ruled by royal gnomes of Clan Granith. In the past, the kings and queens of the High Downs had considerable power, but today only a few of the old monarchs' traditional powers have been retained by King Oron.

Oron is nearly 200 years old and has seen many changes in his lifetime. He himself is little more than a successful farmer and owner of a number of prominent chalk mines, and his status as king seems less significant with each passing year. Oron is a friendly and imminently approachable monarch, with little power beyond the authority to settle disputes between subjects and perform marriages.

MILITARY

Though peaceful, the gnomes learned to fight and have defended their land against a number of powerful enemies over the years. While they have no standing military, the gnomes have adopted the humans' militia system, with able-bodied adults expected to drill with weapons and basic tactics at least once per year. In battle, the gnomes deploy crossbows, spears, and slings. They try to avoid direct combat with larger, better-equipped troops.

The gnomes also have a few surprises up their sleeves in the form of various traps, pitfalls, and other defenses around their larger settlements. However, their most impressive — and in many ways, most terrifying — defensive measure is their giant weasel cavalry, an elite band of riders based in Chalktown. Over the centuries, the gnomes bred stoats and weasels for size and ferocity, eventually creating an especially large species of weasel that they train for battle. Extensive training also allows certain brave or possibly foolhardy gnomes to actually ride these undulant, ferocious beasts and guide them in combat. These weasel riders are considered especially wild and dangerous individuals, for most gnomes are quite staid and peaceable. The weasel riders occasionally get to ride into battle, for the Downs are sometimes subject to humanoid raids.

Major Threats

Standing at a crossroads between the old wild elf kingdoms and various humanoid raiders meant that the ancient gnomes sometimes had to defend themselves. Initially, the peace-loving gnomes fared poorly, but as time passed they grew more capable of self-defense while retaining a surprising amount of their welcoming nature. Today, what remains of the old kingdom is under the protection of the Grand Duchy of Reme — a relatively generous and benevolent state in an increasingly chaotic world. All the same, the gnomes do face challenges, including raids by the orcs, goblins, hobgoblins, and other humanoids who periodically ravage the region. There is considerable antipathy toward the Deepfells hobgoblins due to the great violence and destruction that their predecessors inflicted on the Downs and on the surrounding human regions, and the rock gnomes fight them with unparalleled ferocity. Against other foes such as goblins or human bandits, the gnomes favor hit-and-run tactics, giving up territory in exchange for time and letting their enemies overextend themselves. If necessary, the gnomes make a stand at larger communities but rarely engage in pursuit or punitive attacks, preferring that their foes simply leave as soon as possible.

Wilderness and Adventures

Though long-settled, the High Downs have grown wilder in recent centuries as gnomish authority declines and the gnomes stay closer to home. A network of roads connects the small gnomish towns and hamlets, and are traveled by small groups of gnomes on foot or on goat-drawn carts. The gnomish militia patrols some of the most widely-traveled roads, occasionally aided by human legionnaires from Ironhill. Gnomes prefer to travel by day and try to make it to shelter in towns or the occasional roadside inn by nightfall. While this is mostly out of basic common sense, the dangers of being abroad at night can be considerable in some places, particularly on the edges of the Downs, farther from the central towns and patrolled regions.

As an especially ancient and storied part of the continent, the High Downs has its share of secrets, including abandoned gnomish towns, temples, and palaces, many of which have been buried beneath the rolling hills and can still be excavated and explored. Despite their consistent good alignment and demeanor, the gnomes were not without wicked individuals. Some of their cautionary tales speak of gnomes who dabbled in necromancy, demonology, and other forbidden lore, unleashing disaster on themselves and their communities. From time to time, outsiders have brought chaos and destruction to the Downs as well.

Though millennia have passed, the remnants of some of this evil may still be found in obscure and forgotten corners of the High Downs. One such place is called the Six Stones, where it is said that the wicked half-elven sorcerer Neávar once settled, far from civilization and the threat of exposure, to perform experiments on the living in an effort to live forever by transferring his life essence to other bodies. In this fashion, he hoped to avoid the curse of undeath and an eternity as a lich, and in doing so caused vast suffering and loss to the surrounding gnomish communities. Though the gnomes eventually took matters into their own hands and destroyed the sorcerer, they continue to avoid this place centuries later, fearful of Neávar's curse. Some claim to have ventured here and report that the place still contains extensive underground tunnels where some of Neávar's creations, twisted and deathless, still lurk, along with various riches left behind by the superstitious gnomes.

Various creatures wander the downs and can pose a threat to travelers as well as the gnomes who live there. This includes packs of worgs and wilderness-dwelling predators such as perytons and leucrottas. As noted, hobgoblins and orcs sometimes raid into the Downs, but the most persistent humanoid threat comes from the bands of kobolds that live in lairs and tunnel networks beneath the hills. These kobolds tend to avoid combat with capable foes, but they will creep into gnome settlements to steal and despoil. Gnomes, often aided by Northmarch troops, sometimes venture into wilder areas to root out especially troublesome kobolds. They also hire outside contractors to take care of the dirty work for them.

Use the specific **High Downs Encounter Table** for generating random encounters in this area.

Chalktown

The settlement of Chalktown is in some ways as mundane and dull as its name suggests, but while the town continues to mine for the chalk that gave it its name, it is also at the heart of gnomish mink and ermine breeding. Relatively prosperous, Chalktown has a population of more than 200 and is also well-known as the home of the High Downs' fearsome weasel cavalry. An elite group of 20 riders and their gigantic mustelid mounts, the weasel riders spring into action if summoned to battle. They have played an important role in driving off goblins, human raiders, and even orcish mercenaries.

Royal Bluff

Long the capital of the High Downs, Royal Bluff is a picturesque cluster of stone huts that surround a single hill topped by the royal palace, the traditional home of Clan Granith. The palace is a wonder, extending above and below the hill, and displays many antique and largely-forgotten architectural features. Today, King Oron spends only part of his time here, preferring instead to remain on one of his various goat ranches or overseeing operations at one of his family chalk mines. In his absence, a devoted staff keeps the palace clean and in good repair, though like the king himself, it remains little more than a symbolic reminder of the gnomes' ancient glory and prosperity.

Royal Bluff is also the only major settlement in the Downs equipped to accommodate humans and other larger peoples, with several larger inns and taverns managed by humans with gnomish staff. With a population of more than 300, Royal Bluff also hosts several marketplaces. Gnomes from the Downs and outsiders come here to trade for chalk, exotic furs, and goats.

Reference Sources
The Blight

KYTHERAX'S KINGDOM

Alignment: Lawful Evil
Capital: Flamespire (2,000)
Notable Settlements: Ruby (500), Rockpile (300), Stoneskull (300)
Ruler: Kytherax the Dragon Goddess
Government: Tyranny
Population: 7,374 (ancient red dragon 1, kobolds 6,160, dragonborn 1,213)
Monstrous: Kobolds, dragons, salamanders, earth elementals
Languages: Draconic
Religion: Kytherax
Resources: Gems, gold, iron, silver
Currency: None
Technology Level: Dark ages

The ancient red dragon Kytherax abides in the heart of the Deepfells, well away from the bickering hobgoblin kingdoms, besieged dwarves, and monstrous humanoids. With the dragon are the kobold minions who worship her like a goddess and her corps of loyal, deadly dragonborn warriors. Kytherax has lived in these mountains for time immemorial, predating even the ancient Phoromyceaen civilization. Few suspect how ancient she truly is, or know the secrets of her true nature.

HISTORY AND PEOPLE

Before the modern kingdoms of Akados, before Foere, before Hyperborea, before the vanished splendors of Phoromycea, even before Riann cast down Pazuzu, the primal dragons came to the world from the inner planes, displacing and defeating the inhuman civilizations that came before to establish the Age of Dragons. It was then, in a vanished time far beyond memory or even myth that the being named Kytherax first walked the world. In those days, like the other primal dragons, she wielded powers that rivaled the gods themselves.

The Age of Dragons is so impossibly ancient that few if any reliable histories exist. If anyone were so fortunate as to actually talk to the Dragon Goddess, Kytherax herself would profess little memory of the time, for though the primals were all but immortal, their minds are not infinite, and are ultimately vulnerable to the same ravages of age as other material creatures. That Kytherax even exists after such an impossible stretch of time is miraculous; that she can remember only scattered fragments of her early days is not surprising.

There were conflicts in those days, to be sure. The primal dragons were proud creatures, each with its own unique character and powers, and they quarreled at times. For such powerful creatures, however, simple disagreement could result in world-shaking consequences, and the few elven myths that deal with the Age of Dragons suggest that they remade the world several times — sometimes out of spite, sometimes from curiosity, and sometimes simply out of boredom. Kytherax also remembers struggles against other entities, possibly the mad gods of primitive chaos that still persisted in dark corners of the world, possibly against such known beings as Pazuzu, Tsathogga, or other even stranger alien deities.

In time, the dragons settled into their world, each claiming its own corner, watching intently as civilizations grew and new beings evolved. The kobolds who today worship her claim that Kytherax created their race from fire, rock, and her own blood as her personal servitors. It is known that even the priest-kings of ancient Xantollan inscribed stone tablets that spoke of powerful dragons and their diminutive servitors, which can only be kobolds, suggesting that their kind has existed for a very long time. Other inscriptions from the time of Xantollan tell of a great fire goddess, "the winged fire serpent that the small crimson ones worship, and call Mother Dragon, bringer of fire, builder of mountains, shatterer of gods."

Despite Kytherax's vast powers and vast antiquity, she finally saw her power wane with the end of the Age of Dragons and the beginning of the Age of Kings. Most of her kin had departed the world, and some few had died in their internecine conflicts or in battle against the Old Ones and their allies. Their descendants still soared in the skies as the dragons that are still known today — powerful beings of awesome strength, violence, and wisdom, but even they were only shadows of their ancestors. It soon became apparent that Kytherax was alone in the world; other primals certainly existed among the inner planes and some slumbered in secret places throughout the world, but for all intents and purposes she was the last of her kind.

She was not idle in those days, and with the rise of the Phoromyceaens, reliable descriptions of her and her powers began to appear. Most of these exist in fragments, but some indicators of Kytherax's role in the old world can be gleaned from them.

The Dragon Goddess ruled openly in regions of modern Akados. Her kobolds kept to themselves, though from time to time she bestirred herself to participate in conflicts, allying herself with various factions as it suited her mood and her needs. In those days, she also commanded many of the world's dragons, particularly those of lawful or evil inclination. Good and evil were of course foreign concepts to such an ancient and alien being, but as time passed and she grew more self-centered, focusing her efforts on survival and preservation, she came to behave in a way that was inimical to most other peoples. Evil may have been a mere word and a concept developed by weak, short-lived mortals, but after a few millennia it became clear that Kytherax was no benevolent goddess, and her people, though orderly and lawful, were enemies to the world.

This did not stop some Phoromyceaen rulers — wicked creatures themselves — from seeking her out and asking her for aid, which she provided in exchange for gold, slaves, and magic. During his reign around −6,000 I.R., the Phoromyceaen god-king Xarideos sent a delegation bearing 1,000 human slaves and 1,000 chests of gold westward for the Dragon Goddess in exchange for her assistance in his war against the stubborn city-states of Eileinethys. If Kytherax helped Xarideos triumph, he promised another 10,000 slaves and 5,000 more chests of gold.

Intrigued and somewhat amused at the offer, Kytherax considered it for a year before agreeing. A hundred red dragons flew to Xarideos' aid and utterly demolished the Eileinethys cities, burning them to the ground and slaying virtually every inhabitant. Kytherax followed the atrocity by having her kobold priests summon storms and great waves to drown the ruins, sinking them forever beneath the Sea of Baal.

Xarideos was furious, for he had wanted the cities as prizes, their people as slaves, and their gold for his own. Kytherax's kobold emissaries replied that he should have been more specific in his requests, then noted that the agreed-upon payment was still due. Xarideos understandably, though somewhat foolishly, angrily refused. Within a few months, Xarideos perished in the ruins of his palace as Kytherax's dragons treated him to the same fate as his Eileinethyan enemies. Some believe that this disaster, which resulted in a prolonged civil war as Xarideos' successors fought for control of the empire, probably hastened the fall of the Phoromyceaen civilization and brought about the subsequent rise of the Hyperboreans.

Human civilization took the event as a warning and never treated with the Dragon Goddess again, which somewhat disappointed Kytherax, who had thoroughly enjoyed the experience with the same cruel joy as a sadistic child stepping on an anthill. She turned her attention inward, focusing on her own kingdom and amusing herself with the 1,000 human slaves she had obtained. Impressed by their hardiness and adaptability, she used them as the basis for a new race of servitors, the creatures now known as dragonborn, who were to become her personal servitors and favorites, replacing her beloved kobolds in importance.

To Kytherax's chagrin, some of the ants that she had found so entertaining resisted her power, and in numbers they proved able to defeat even a goddess of her age and power. The elves of Akados, weary of the kobolds' constant provocations and determined to stamp out the evil dwelling so nearby, marched to war against the Dragon Goddess in the mid −4,000s I.R. Today, this great war is scarcely known save to some of the more ancient elf priests and storytellers, but in sheer violence and intensity it rivaled any conflict up to that time. The Dragon War (actually a series of wars that took place over nearly eight centuries) was costly, but the elves were aided by the divine power of their gods and eventually pushed Kytherax's forces back into the mountain range now known as the Deepfells.

The war was long and bloody, with both atrocities and acts of noble sacrifice on both sides. Kytherax's newly-created dragonborn fought with skill, intelligence, and savage intensity, bred as they were for war and the defense of their Great Mother. Countless kobolds swarmed across battlefields, sacrificing themselves in the tens of thousands, for though they had been supplanted in the Dragon Goddess' eyes by her newest children, the kobolds remained loyal and ferocious in their defense of their realm. Elven magic was truly powerful in those days, and massive spells shook the very land itself while elegant armored elven warriors fought across the disputed lands.

Kytherax's dominion over the other dragons had been shattered for centuries by this time, and now the elves had their own dragons. Noble elven princes and warlords rode the winds, unleashing endless destruction upon the kobolds and dragonborn below, and engaged in ferocious aerial battle against those dragons who remained loyal to Kytherax. At sea, elven warships, armored marines, and sea-mages delivered destruction to coastal citadels, pushing the enemy inland.

The Dragon Goddess did not give up, but in her ancient soul she knew she was defeated. In the end, she surrendered the lands to the elves and pulled back to the heart of her realm, where she remains today, still surrounded by her favored children, though in greatly reduced numbers.

Many in the outside world are unaware of her kingdom's existence, for at her incredible age even a goddess has begun to feel the ravages of time. Kytherax dwells in her central citadel, a deep cavern heated by magma, attended by hordes of kobold and dragonborn servants. The hobgoblins of the Deepfells are aware of her existence and extend her significant respect, for though they are proud and self-centered, the hobgoblins recognize the Great Mother's vast power and the significance of her long existence.

The Dwarves of Stoneaxe Caverns also know of the Dragon Goddess and her continued existence, for their ancestors fought alongside the elves in the Dragon War, engaging in brutal tunnel fighting against persistent and numberless kobold antagonists. They do not openly speak of Kytherax, however, for they do not think that the outside world should know of her existence lest foolish humans seek her out to obtain her aid or to plunder her riches. Such an event might well reawaken the sluggish goddess's resolve and result in a terrible disaster for both the dwarves and the world at large.

Religion

As they dwell in the presence of what they consider to be a literal goddess, the kobolds' reverence for Kytherax is understandable. While kobolds elsewhere may dispute it, the Deepfells kobolds fervently believe that Kytherax literally made their species from rocks, fire, and her own blood, binding them to her forever. Kobold priests call upon her for aid and thank her for their own divine magical abilities. Warriors praise her in battle, and her image or sigil is inscribed on every kobold weapon made. Worship consists of solemn prayers and stories of personal struggle and triumph, as well as the recounting of ancient tales of Kytherax and her people's successes and failures. A lawful folk, the kobolds do not engage in sacrifice, but see bravery in battle and loyalty to the goddess as the greatest virtues.

The dragonborn, the results of Kytherax's experimentation on human slaves thousands of years ago, are surprisingly less fanatical in their devotion to the goddess than their kobold brethren. Bred for war, the dragonborn acknowledge the Dragon Goddess' supremacy, but they are a singularly unemotional and passionless race, seeing it as their duty to simply serve and be silent. This suits Kytherax just fine, as in recent centuries she has begun to find the kobolds' mindless devotion and fanaticism a bit tiresome.

The dragons who remain with Kytherax are not at all inclined toward religious faith and see her as another dragon, albeit a big, dangerous, and powerful one whom they owe their loyalty and support. Many of these dragons are old enough to remember the old days when Kytherax was more powerful — these choose to remain by her side and slumber along with their mistress. Younger dragons sometimes grow dissatisfied with this arrangement and depart, striking out on their own and leaving Kytherax and her ancient kingdom behind.

Loyalties and Diplomacy

As noted, few outside kingdoms even know that Kytherax exists, let alone that she still commands thousands of minions in her hidden fastness. The Deepfells hobgoblins are the only major entity that has attempted contact with the goddess, as several kingdoms have sent emissaries to treat with her and ask if she and her minions are interested in mutually-beneficial cooperation. So far they have not met with success, though they have developed a working relationship with some of the kobolds and have brought a few dragonborn back to observe the inner workings of the Deepfells kingdoms. These visiting dragonborn sometimes even participate in combat, more out of their own interests than out of any desire to ally with the hobgoblins.

Government

A government headed by a being who may be a literal goddess can be considered the ultimate theocracy. While Kytherax spends most of her time in slumber or alone in her chambers, her word is still absolute law, obeyed by all. In most cases, however, governance is left to her priests and priestesses, all kobolds of considerable divine skill and knowledge. The dragonborn have little interest in government and rarely participate, though they are quick to obey the decrees and judgments of Kytherax and her kobold priests.

Lawful and fair, the priests oversee a strongly loyal populace. Kobolds are a cunning and obedient people with a millennia-long history of faithful service to their goddess. Few if any choose to disobey or rebel, and those accused of misdeeds nearly always accept their punishments without complaint. Crimes such as robbery, murder, and assault are all but absent from kobold society, where the ultimate crimes are cowardice and disloyalty. Accordingly, the death penalty is almost unknown in kobold society, and most crimes are punished by imprisonment or deprivation.

Kobold society is also largely self-governing, with the priests generally making decisions only over internal matters such as where to dig new burrows, when military cadres are ready for service, how to divide supplies, schedule watches and foraging parties, command in battle against goblins or other foes, etc.

Military

Kobolds are known for their cunning tactics, and in the past few thousand years have adapted to their underground environment by becoming skilled guerilla fighters, trapsmiths, and subterranean tacticians. In the old days before the Dragon War, kobolds also dwelled aboveground and fought with more conventional tactics, but those days are long gone.

A typical kobold warrior is lightly armed and unarmored save for occasional leather harnesses or small shields. Favored weapons include slings, shortbows, short swords, and spears, but most kobold formations try to spend little time in direct combat, preferring battles of maneuver intended to draw enemies into ambushes or traps.

The dragonborn form the hard-edged, armored professional core of Kytherax's army. They are powerful, well-protected, and highly disciplined. They are usually deployed against especially stubborn or powerful foes, or sent to pursue and destroy retreating enemies. Fighting both armored and unarmored, dragonborn prefer to fight with polearms, heavy cutting weapons such as falchions, and crossbows.

The most powerful of Kytherax's forces are her dragons. Perhaps a score of various ages remain, with the oldest able to remember the great battles of the past and the glories of their mistress's old empire. These dragons tend toward lawful and evil alignment, but a few neutral or good individuals may remain, still holding to ancient oaths and willing to fight for Kytherax despite their misgivings about her as an individual.

The Dragon Goddess herself is naturally the most powerful and terrifying creature that intruders will encounter. Though she is weary and rarely stirs from her central caldera-citadel, she retains all of her ancient powers, far beyond that of even the most ancient of worldly dragons. She is also a potent spellcaster — possibly the most knowledgeable and deadly in the world — with access to spells and rituals that predate even the Phoromyceaens and date back to the Age of Dragons when magic was truly epic and capable of reshaping an entire world. How well these spells work today is uncertain, but if provoked, the Dragon Goddess may well call upon strange powers from the dawn of time, an act that could have world-spanning consequences.

Major Threats

Safe in their fastness at the heart of the Deepfells, Kytherax's followers have little to fear from the outside world. Only the most determined and costly of military campaigns could possibly dislodge them, and even that is likely to fail in the deep, well-defended tunnels of the Dragon Goddess' kingdom.

The kingdom still faces challenges, for the Deepfells are full of hostile creatures, including subterranean horrors and aberrations such as ropers, aboleths, mushroom folk, ratfolk, and derro. Kobolds regularly patrol tunnels to keep these intruders out, and pitched battles between Kytherax's forces and raiding parties of rival humanoids are not uncommon.

The only true threat to Kytherax may come from the drow realm of Nyctosea located some distance north in and around the hidden Ebonmark Vale. Scouts from both realms have encountered each other, and occasional skirmishes have arisen, but so far neither group seems interested in open conflict. Kytherax's dragonborn advisors are alarmed by the drow plan to ring their valley with Blackflame temples linked to their goddess and their distant homeland, as it may draw unwanted attention to the region and possibly threaten her kingdom's security. Kytherax herself is less aggressive than she used to be, and she wishes to avoid conflict if at all possible. The threat of a rising drow kingdom nearby might be enough to stir her from her slumber, however, and war between the two realms may prove unavoidable.

Wilderness and Adventures

The depths of Kytherax's kingdom are well-patrolled and secure, and as noted above, constant patrols keep them relatively free of dangerous creatures or invaders. Only the hobgoblins and the Stoneaxe dwarves are fully aware of the kingdom's existence, and neither of these groups is likely to freely share their knowledge about the Dragon Goddess.

The existence of the kingdom certainly would present a significant temptation to adventurers, for Kytherax is one of the oldest living creatures on the planet and has spent literal millennia accumulating a vast and almost endless horde of treasure, magic, and secret knowledge. She herself is a powerful spellcaster with access to magic lost since the Phoromyceaen Age.

Her kobolds are a cut above the ordinary. They are smart, tough, and motivated, having honed their skills at repelling enemies over thousands of years. The tunnels of their goddess's realm are crammed with traps, dead-ends, and ambush points, all intended to defeat enemies without direct face-to-face combat. The kobolds themselves are skilled at surreptitious, highly-mobile combat, hitting enemies hard then falling back into labyrinths of tunnels that they know intimately.

Intruders who challenge the kobolds find themselves facing even greater challenges in the form of dragonborn warriors who cannot even conceive of the concept of retreat, and Kytherax's own dragon allies — fewer in number than in the glorious past, but equally determined to fight any intruder in the name of their mistress. These dragons also have their own hordes of treasure. Some of the younger dragons may be persuaded to give up the fight and strike out on their own, but the oldest and most powerful remain unshakably loyal and willing to fight to the very end.

Caldera Citadel

In the far distant past, Kytherax herself constructed a perfectly cylindrical cavern in the center of her realm. It is ringed with secondary chambers, each large enough to accommodate the Dragon Goddess as well as several other huge dragons. The shaft extends nearly a mile beneath Mount Dracoris, the highest peak in the Deepfells, until it meets with a subterranean magma flow that keeps the entire citadel hot enough to suit Kytherax and the legion of kobolds and dragonborn who serve her and live in barracks attached to the central shaft.

The heat here is enough on its own to kill any unprotected outsider, save for fire-dwelling creatures such as salamanders. It also contains vast libraries of wisdom scribed on metallic sheets and stored on great scrolls gleaned from a score of ancient civilizations and from the old primal dragons of the inner planes, proportional to the Dragon Goddess' own vast size. Here also is her horde, and it is a vast and almost infinite mass of gold, silver, gems, weapons, armor, jewelry, clothing, crowns, staves, scepters, and almost anything else imaginable, accumulated over the entire history of the world. Robbing such a horde is an all-but-impossible task, and Kytherax's powerful senses inform her if even the smallest gem or single coin is stolen from all of her possessions.

The Dragon Goddess dwells here, sleeping in various chambers, or perched upon a vast metal platform magically suspended in the middle of the shaft. The platform is able to move up and down at her whim. Though she spends most of her time alone or sleeping, Kytherax has been known to directly meet with visitors — be they spirits, gods, or emissaries from the hobgoblin kingdoms — on the platform, where her magic can be used to protect them from the terrible heat. These days, she rarely actually talks to anyone, and when she does, it is with an impossibly ancient sense of weariness, cynicism, and bitter humor. Kytherax is a very, very old being to whom the world and existence itself has become a bitter joke that grows less funny with each passing era.

Nyctosea

Alignment: Chaotic Evil
Capital: Blackflame
Notable Settlements: Ebonmark Vale (3,500)
Ruler: Princess Nyossa Dargoth
Government: Monarchy
Population: 25,451 (dark elf 20,400, fey 5,051)
Monstrous: Fey creatures (all sorts, evil alignment), giant boar, giant owls, cockatrice, giant wolf spiders, peryton, ettercaps, owlbears, giant weasels, wraiths
Languages: Aklo, Elvish, Sylvan
Religion: Tar'liante (the Spider Queen, drow), the Lady of Shadow (fey)
Resources: Alchemy, electrum, magic items, mithral, platinum, silver, timber
Currency: Silver, electrum and platinum drow coins and gems
Technology Level: Dark ages (fey), Renaissance (dark elves)
Demonym/Adjectival Demonym: Nyctoseans

Ebonmark Vale, a valley concealed by magic and thick with dark conifers interrupted occasionally by lush meadows, is in the north of the Deepfells. A cold river runs through the vale and mountain crags rise on all sides, cutting the vale off from the outside world. It is always cold in the vale, even in the bright sunshine of summer. In winter, the vale is thick with snow and the river is frozen. The place is utterly inaccessible from the outside, save by magic or flight. Here dwell the dark fey, and in the tunnels and chambers beneath the mountains live their masters, the drow of Nyctosea.

History and People

Ebonmark Vale lies at a thin place — a crossroads between the realms of fey and the material world. It has always been a place of dark magic and evil such that it draws to it wicked fey and monstrous sylvan creatures. The good fey shun the place, leaving it to its cruel inhabitants. Portals to the dark fey places are scattered throughout the vale, appearing and disappearing at random, or on certain nights sacred to the evil sylvan folk. Its connections to other realms make time pass strangely — sometimes slowly and sometimes quickly. Those mortals who come here by magic sometimes discover that years pass in a matter of moments or that they can spend a lifetime there and have only a few minutes pass back in the ordinary world.

The drow have likewise dwelled in the Deepfells and their environs for many centuries. The mountains surrounding Ebonmark Vale are riddled with their tunnels and chambers, and the vale is collectively under the governance of the drow realm of Nyctosea.

The realm had its beginnings in the elven First Exodus and the catastrophic impact of the Obsidian Vault in the southern Deepfells. These twin events disrupted the drow's existing settlements and forced many to relocate, fleeing farther into the Deepfells. The mountains were especially cruel that year, and the subterranean realms were still controlled by the kobolds who served the Dragon Goddess Kytherax.

The drow suffered during those days, and a battered group of refugees stumbled upon Ebonmark Vale and its evil fey inhabitants. After some initial struggles, the drow worked together to pacify the fey and soon controlled several strongpoints throughout the valley. Angry and frustrated, the fey were forced to accept drow authority, and within a year the drow began to excavate in the surrounding mountains, drawing supplies from the valley.

The new kingdom grew, new traditions formed, and new dark elven houses formed in the millennia that followed. Wards and concealment spells protected the vale and, after initial conflict and suspicion, the realm became a place where drow and dark fey could live safely. The fey began to serve in the citadels and underground settlements of the dark elves, while the drow established towns and palaces in the vale itself, eventually connecting the place with the main drow regions via new underground passages.

Today, Nyctosea is a safe haven for the drow, allowing them to control their own base of operations while venturing beyond the Deepfells to seek out magic, wealth, and knowledge, to make contact with other drow groups and potential allies, and to raise havoc among the humans, dwarves, and their hated elvish cousins.

Numerous dark fey creatures dwell in the valley and consider themselves to be full partners in the state that the dark elves founded. Wicked sprites and pixies, boggards, redcaps, gremlins, spriggans, phooka, and others can be found here, often moving between the fey planar realms and the valley through the various planar gates found in the area. They are a chaotic, capricious, mischievous, and often cruel lot who derive great amusement from the discomfort, injury, and sometimes even the death of outsiders. They have over the centuries developed a protective fondness for dark elves but are especially savage in their attacks upon high and wood elves and against good-aligned fey.

Religion

Nyctosean drow are quite faithful despite their intensely chaotic nature. Since their people's arrival in this world countless centuries ago, they have remained steadfast in their worship of the Spider Queen, whom they consider to be their race's creator and prime patron. Isolated from the rest of drow culture, the Nyctoseans drifted somewhat in their devotions, and today the Spider Queen (known locally as Tar'liante) is served by male and female priests and is worshipped in several forms, including that of a giant spider, a cruelly-beautiful drow woman in diaphanous silken garments, or a simple sphere that appears to radiate a cold and strangely dark light. Her shrines and temples are located throughout Nyctosea, lit by glowing blue or purple crystal, and decorated with terrifying sculptures of the goddess and her servants. Larger temples also feature sacrificial altars that are used on holy days or for important occasions.

The fey are too chaotic to practice any real religion, but most speak reverently of what they call their "Lady of Shadow" who may be an amalgam of Tar'liante and a powerful ruler on the fey planes. As a rule, the dark fey don't talk about religion (or much of anything else) with outsiders.

Trade and Commerce

The fey of the vale don't usually trade with mortals, but they have been known to strike deals with those who stumble into their realm. As might be expected, these deals don't usually end well for the outsiders, but these don't enter into the actual realm of trade and commerce. The fey usually leave contacts with the world outside the Deepfells to their drow allies.

The drow do leave their kingdom from time to time to seek out various exotic and needed items that the Deepfells can't provide such as rare herbs, spell components, magic, exotic creatures, and body parts from various creatures that are useful in alchemy and arcane research. To this end, they may contact humans, dwarves, or their fellow drow who live in other enclaves throughout Akados. Nyctosean drow may also make themselves available as mercenaries or adventurers to clients seeking employees for illegal, illicit, or morally questionable acts. They do such things discreetly and in exchange for the exotic materials that they need. They swear clients to secrecy, for it is in their interest that no one ever learn about Nyctosea's existence, lest the realm be threatened by outside forces.

Loyalties and Diplomacy

Nyctosea is in an interesting position, essentially a point where several planes of existence overlap. The kingdom maintains far more contacts in the dark fey planes than on Akados, and dark elven or fey ambassadors frequently make the trip to treat with these planes and their inhabitants, including the wicked unseelie court, the powerful and capricious kings and queens of the dark fey realms, and even demons and devils if they are able to contact their realms. These contacts can result in even stranger and more powerful fey visiting the vale, or with the exchange of goods, services, and knowledge, bringing weird chaos magic and otherwise unknown spells to the material world. Some of the magic that the drow obtain from the fey realms is questionable and highly volatile, often having unexpected effects on Akados that it does not have in the dark fey's planes. This can be either good or bad, for a malfunctioning fey spell can be quite dangerous and lead to dire consequences if not properly controlled.

Government

The Nyctosean state is officially a principality, with its ruler crowned as prince or princess. This is something of an affectation on the part of the drow, for they don't feel that the region is either large or influential enough to officially be declared a kingdom, keeping their ruler's title relatively modest.

The drow monarch is not as powerful as some rulers on Akados, for his or her decisions must always be approved by a grand council consisting of the realm's grand sorcerer, army commander, high priest, senior elder, and a vizier appointed by the king or queen. In practice, the monarch's decisions are almost always approved unanimously, and a number of mundane decisions are exempt from consideration by the council unless at least one council member demands it.

Nyctosea's current ruler is the charismatic and outwardly charming Princess Nyossa Dargoth, a relatively young drow (only 99 years old) who took the throne when her great-grandmother passed away of (supposedly) natural causes. While she is clearly as twisted and evil as other drow (she enjoys watching her torturers work and occasionally arrests a random individual to give her an excuse), Nyossa is also a highly intelligent and capable woman who knows when to put her foot down and when to let the realm manage itself.

Military

The realm's army is relatively small and serves primarily to keep the various unorganized subterranean races at bay. Though the fey assist if asked, the kingdom's military is almost entirely made up of drow, most of whom are equipped as light or medium infantry. Light infantry wear silken tunics and fight with bows or crossbows and swords, providing a fast and professional strike force that can quickly move to places of crisis. A few nobles and wealthy drow ride trained cave lizards into battle, and the drow magical corps is often critical in turning the tide of battle.

The drow have also come to rely on the natural creatures of the caverns such as ropers, piercers, cave fishers, and the like, treating them with enchantments that prevent them from attacking drow. These creatures guard important passages and chambers, making attacks from outside far more complicated for invading forces.

Nyctosea is an egalitarian state, which means that anyone can succeed especially if they murder someone and take their place. The army and the government are near-evenly divided between males and females, and either sex can be found in command of the drow's army and regiments.

Major Threats

The nagging raids of derro, goblins, and other subterranean races cause the Nyctoseans little distress, but the presence of an entire kingdom of kobolds led by an incredibly ancient dragon whom many consider to be a goddess is a vexing threat that the drow would be fools not to be aware of.

The kingdom of Kytherax predates every other nation on Akados, and though it is smaller and weaker than in the past, it still represents a very real threat in the minds of the princess and her advisors. Armed patrols are especially vigilant in the vicinity of the Dragon Goddess' tunnels, and though open warfare has never flared between the two states, the drow have good reason to distrust the kobolds and their near-immortal deity.

Like Kytherax, the drow benefit from the fact that few people are even aware that the kingdom exists. While drow have been found in the region — lurking in the Ashen Hills and the Sternwood — there is still no general knowledge about where they come from. Even the name Nyctosea isn't widely known.

Even if Nyctosea is ever revealed to the human kingdom, it's unlikely that a distant realm such as Reme or Foere could do much about a drow kingdom that is based at the heart of a forbidding mountain range with legions of evil fey at its command. If Nyctosea is ever found out, the greatest danger is not invasion and siege, but isolation and being cut off completely from the rest of the world. Even then the realm would survive, but drow ambitions and desires from the lands beyond Deepfells would be frustrated.

Wilderness and Adventures

The aboveground portion of Nyctosea is the region known as Ebonmark Vale. It's a forbidding place even from a distance — thick with shaggy green-black conifers, with a small cold river running along its length. Simply getting far enough to glimpse the vale is almost impossible without flight or magical assistance, and descending the sheer slopes of the mountains that surround it is perilous in the extreme.

Narrow trails created by the fey crisscross the vale, and cold meadows offer some respite from the crowded masses of ancient, black-barked firs and pines. Trees are often home to various fey creatures that usually simply lurk and observe outsiders during the day, whispering among themselves and planning mischief. They creep out at night, and their visitations are usually confusing or annoying at first — spoiled, damaged goods, cut straps, frightened pack animals, etc. As each night progresses, the fey grow bolder, eventually attacking outright, intent on murder or capture. Captives are kept for the fey's amusement or taken to the dark elves for further "investigation." Such unfortunates are rarely seen again.

The wildlife of the vale presents further challenge, as they are often influenced or outright controlled by the fey and engage in behavior that is at first strange, then disturbing, and finally violent. Birds sing strange songs that may be familiar to visitors and fly in complex patterns above the trees. Deer and bears may engage in elaborately choreographed dances, mice may march through camps on their hind legs, wolves may utter poetry, etc. Eventually, the wildlife act as the fey's allies, sometimes attacking alongside them.

While the vale is definitely a dangerous place, it's not without its rewards, for the fey have been known to carelessly pile treasure in clearings, stash magical items in caves and crevices, or hide riches in their various dwellings. This wealth is gleaned from the drow, from the occasional unfortunate visitor, or brought directly from the planes of the dark fey. These last items are of special interest, for they often harbor wild magic, unknown powers, or secret curses. Those who plunder fey hoards are advised to use caution, for the wealth gained there often comes at a steep price.

The drow carved out a subterranean realm beneath the mountains, a place isolated from the rest of the world and safe from incursion by most surface powers. The passages are well patrolled, and the drow settlements are often located in vast cave complexes with wondrous formations, luminescent rocks and fungi, and exotic cave-dwelling creatures. The drow have made some of these creatures into guardians, with such creatures as ropers, gelatinous cubes, piercers, and mimics located in various places throughout the complex, each one under magical compulsion not to attack drow but to deal violently with outsiders.

As with the vale, the caves of Nyctosea are a potent lure to adventurers. The drow prefer to hoard wealth in the form of gems, silver, electrum, and platinum — gold is considered somewhat gauche and gaudy. Drow magic artifacts, weapons, armor, and clothing can be found here as well and bring high prices in the markets of Foere, Xha'en, Reme, and elsewhere.

BLACKFLAME

Alignment: Chaotic Evil
Ruler: Princess Nyossa Dargoth
Government: Monarchy
Population: 3,743 (dark elf 3,132, fey 611)
Languages: Aklo, Sylvan
Religion: Spider Queen
Technology Level: Renaissance

When the drow first arrived in Ebonmark Vale, they began construction on a new network of tunnels and settlements in the mountains that surrounded the valley. They dubbed the peak of the mountain Runya'mor, or Blackflame Peak. The mountain was named for the eternal dark flame that burned at the center of the drow's old homeland that they occupied before their arrival, and within the peak itself the drow constructed a great conical chamber. There they brought precious blackflame crystals and other exotic, arcane objects to kindle their own smaller version of the sacred dark fire. This flame has burned there ever since, radiating a cold radiance from which the drow draw much of their arcane power. The flame remains a tenuous but very real connection to both their old homeland and their strange spider goddess, Tar'liante. On particularly sacred occasions, drow priests gather in this chamber to commune with Tar'liante, and with proper sacrifice, propitiation, and ritual, her visage appears in the flames to talk directly to her people.

The realm of Nyctosea spread out from this sacred space, first filling Runya'mor then expanding into the adjoining mountains. The drow built hidden entrances throughout the range, including many connecting to Ebonmark Vale below, to allow the fey access to their dark kingdom. Today, the settlement of Blackflame extends beneath the peak, with level upon level of vast, cunningly-built chambers and winding passages. Viewed from above, each of the numerous levels resembles a labyrinth intended to confuse outsiders. But to the drow, it is home, and the city's inhabitants know its many twists and turns intimately.

A single long central shaft extends from the upper temple chamber down to the last level below. Staircases wind around its inner surface and, along with various mechanical and magical elevators, these provide access to all levels. The drow have also harnessed a subterranean species of floating scyphozoa (jellyfish) that can be compelled to rise and fall through the central shaft as living elevators that also provide dim bioluminescence. More accomplished arcanists dispatch with artificial transport altogether and simply levitate from floor to floor.

More than 3,000 drow live in Blackflame, dwelling in chambers hollowed out from each level. They are limited in overall area by the mountain's circumference, so when one level is excavated to its limits, new chambers are dug farther down. Drow engineers have painstakingly crafted the city, being careful not to overly weaken the mountain's structure, which is one reason for the labyrinthine layout of streets and buildings. Levels vary in their function, contents, and level

of security. The chaotic drow do not spend too much time enforcing order on these many levels, leaving it to the inhabitants to police their own neighborhoods. Many levels are wild places full of crime and corruption, while others are more serene and beautiful depending upon the attitude of their inhabitants.

Despite its successes, several engineers have determined that Blackflame may be at its limit, and that even deep excavation may weaken the structure so that it might actually collapse in an earthquake or other disturbance. Accordingly, new cities are now planned, either based upon existing settlements or freshly dug in the heart of other mountains. The drow envision a network of Blackflame chambers, each the peak of its own mountain and ringing the entire vale, providing an unprecedented amount of arcane energy and also a significant increase in protection for the drow and their fey allies.

STONEAXE CAVERNS

Alignment: Lawful Good
Ruler: King Theonos Steelbrow
Government: Monarchy
Population: 10,125 (mountain dwarf)
Monstrous: None (occasional incursions by subterranean creatures)
Languages: Dwarvish
Religion: Dwerfater
Resources: Copper, gems, gold, iron, silver, tin
Currency: Gold bar (5 gp), gold circle (1 gp), silver square (5 sp), silver orb (1 sp), copper cylinder (1 cp)
Technology Level: High middle ages

The Deepfells is a subterranean wilderness rife with danger and treacherous unexplored regions. For the surface folk it's a place of nightmares, but for the dwarves who have lived here for countless generations, it is a home, and it is under siege.

HISTORY AND PEOPLE

The struggle for control of the Deepfells goes back to before even dwarven memory. The mountains, called Kheláduban (Mirror Mountains) by the dwarves, are believed to be a gift from the Dwerfater himself, granted to his people for all eternity. Much to the dwarves' displeasure, the hobgoblins took issue with Dwerfater's decree and began to raid into the mountains a number of centuries later (most historians date the earliest hobgoblin incursions at around the time of the Hyperboreans' arrival in Akados, around −100 I.R.). By the time the Hyperboreans reached the Northmarches in the late 600s I.R., the conflict had entirely moved underground, with the fecund and aggressive hobgoblins pushing the stern and sturdy but outnumbered dwarves back into their core kingdoms.

The struggle continued unseen by the outside world, though at one time the dwarves mounted a diplomatic mission to Curgantium to ask for imperial aid in fighting their foes. The mission met with frustrating delays and bureaucratic complications and finally returned emptyhanded, an event that convinced the remaining dwarves that they would never receive aid from the humans or any other outside force. They settled in for a long conflict in the unspoken knowledge that they were doomed and that the only question was how long their final extermination would take.

Interestingly enough, this attitude seemed to almost hearten the dwarves, and their fatalistic conclusion that no one would ever help them hardened the resolve of individual warriors. Finally, after several more centuries of near-constant conflict, the hobgoblin advance was finally checked.

At this point, however, only a single center of dwarven resistance remained — the well-defended reaches of Stoneaxe Caverns. The dwarves made their last stand there, and the struggle has continued for more than 300 years, with the dwarves holding their precious caves, corridors, chambers, and strongholds against inexorable pressure from the hobgoblins.

Though they remain as cynical and grim as ever, there are reasons for the dwarves to see some hope after all these centuries. The Duchy of the Northmarches, long indifferent to the dwarves' plight, now sees the hobgoblins as a real threat, and even the most disinterested scholar admits that unification of the hobgoblin kingdoms would be a bad thing. At last, Reman agents have made contact with the Stoneaxe dwarves, offering aid and assistance in the struggle. For their part, the dwarves remain gruffly suspicious of the humans, but view their efforts to turn the hobgoblins against each other with amusement and even grudging approval. A small group of Stoneaxe dwarves has even begun to wonder whether maybe, just maybe, some surface-dwellers can be trusted after all.

Like others of their kind, the Stoneaxe dwarves are tough, hardy, and warlike. They have been engaged in a centuries-long fighting retreat against the inexorable pressure of the Deepfells hobgoblins, and this has cultivated a wide sense of fatalism and a grim determination to go down fighting, taking as many of their foes with them as possible. Their stubborn resistance has kept them free of hobgoblin domination, and try as they might, the enemy has been unable to decisively defeat or uproot them.

The dwarves have developed a highly efficient culture based upon their own siege mentality. The Stoneaxe Caverns contain everything they need for survival, including veins of iron, copper, silver, and gold, great caverns where edible fungi are grown, and other areas where the dwarves raise the same blind cattle as their hobgoblin rivals. Elsewhere, mighty forges help craft arms and armor, barracks house companies of skilled dwarven warriors, schools teach youngsters the basics and tell them of the dwarves' long history, temples are filled for worship services dedicated to the Dwerfater, and surprisingly-comfortable living quarters are home to hundreds of dwarven families.

Access to and from the caverns is strictly controlled at massive iron portals — round, riveted gates of iron and bronze that defy even the mightiest of war machines. A few smaller passages allow access to other regions, but these are heavily patrolled and set with demolition charges every few hundred yards so that they can be completely sealed in the face of attack. So far the hobgoblins have been unable to force entry through any of these access points, and none has had to be collapsed.

RELIGION

Deeply faithful, the dwarves of Stoneaxe Caverns pray to Dwerfater thrice daily and typically carry numerous holy symbols, tokens, and runic charms in his honor. Statues and shrines to Dwerfater can be found throughout the Stoneaxe caves. Dwarf priests are also stern warriors, leading Stoneaxe warriors into battle armed with great two-handed warhammers or mauls. The battlecry "For the Dwerfater!" echoes throughout the Deepfells when the Stoneaxe dwarves go to war.

For all this, however, the dwarves have as little confidence in their maker-god as they do in the rest of the world. While Dwerfater created his people and granted them the Deepfells (or Kheláduban) as their eternal homeland, the Stoneaxe dwarves know that he will not aid them in their struggle, and that their best hope is to perish bravely in battle then be admitted to the afterlife to stand beside him during the final battle with the lords of evil and chaos.

Dwerfater is a distant god to the Stoneaxe dwarves. He loves his children, it's true, but he also demands that they stand on their own without help from him, or from anything beyond their own courage. The dwarves' isolation has gone on for so long that many believe acceptance of outside help to be sacrilege. Fortunately for the dwarves, enough are willing to treat with the Northmarch humans that their isolationist attitudes may finally be ending.

TRADE AND COMMERCE

The Stoneaxe dwarves trade with no one. They are an island of dwarven society surrounded and besieged by thousands of hereditary foes in a fight that can end only with the dwarves' extinction. Food, clothing, weapons, and armor are all crafted and created locally within the Stoneaxe Caverns exclusively for use by the dwarves themselves. Tentative contact with the Northmarch humans has opened the door to limited trade, and some dwarves have considered asking for material aid, though such requests are anathema to the independent dwarven spirit.

LOYALTIES AND DIPLOMACY

In diplomatic relations as in trade, the Stoneaxe dwarves consider themselves alone in the world. The most fanatical followers of Dwerfater go so far as to believe that seeking out allies or even making contact with the outside world is a grave offense that suggests the dwarves cannot take care of themselves. For literal centuries the dwarves have fought beneath the mountains, stung by their early dismissal by the Hyperboreans, convinced that no one (even their beloved god) will help them, and that it would be better to die fighting nobly than to demean themselves by begging for aid.

This attitude may be changing, for a few dwarves have declared it is time to end their isolation and seek allies, for the final end of their dynasty may be in sight as the hobgoblins gather and attack in ever-increasing numbers. Emissaries of the human duchy have made tentative contact with the Stoneaxe folk, gaining valuable intelligence about the Deepfells hobgoblins, and allowing them to use cunning provocations to keep the enemy fighting with each other. Seeing the Northmarchers' success, some Stoneaxers have begun to wonder whether their traditional isolation may finally be ending, but the harder and more traditional dwarves reject this as utter folly and a heretical denial of Dwerfater's authority.

GOVERNMENT

The king of Kheláduban sits upon a throne carved from living rock in the center of the Stoneaxe Caverns. A hereditary monarch whose line has continued for the past 1,000 years, King Theonos Steelbrow is a grizzled, cantankerous, stubborn, and impossibly brave dwarf who lost an eye to a hobgoblin spear and his left hand to a white worg. Refusing magical healing, he sports an elaborately etched eyepatch and a cunningly-designed mechanical hand that functions with absolute natural precision. He has two sons and two daughters, and by dwarven tradition must choose one of them as his successor; seniority is of little significance in the Stoneaxe Caverns, taking a distant backseat to competence, wisdom, and skill in battle.

The king has no official advisors — every Stoneaxe dwarf has the right to approach him and speak freely, so long as he or she does so with honesty and forthrightness. Theonos often seeks out his people to ask those with expertise in important matters their advice and guidance. While he has a company of dedicated and near-legendary bodyguards, Theonos knows that he has nothing to fear from his own people. His guard serves only to defend him in battle, but is usually left behind by their monarch who frequently leads the attack against the enemy, armed with his battleaxe *Tharuk'nahd* (the Black Axe) and clad in the shining mail of King Azaband, which was forged in the ancient time before the coming of the hobgoblins. Though many feel it inevitable that the king will one day fall heroically in battle, so far he has survived and continues to rule.

Military

Every dwarf able to hold a weapon is considered part of the caverns' military, but the core of regular warriors is actually relatively small — no more than 2,000 out of a population of 10,000. Yet the very size of their regular army makes Stoneaxe dwarves some of the finest fighters in Akados, each highly skilled in tactics, close combat, missile combat, siege and countersiege, scouting and stealth, demolitions, and guerilla warfare. The Steelaxers claim that a single dwarven warrior is worth a thousand hobgoblins, though there is probably a fair amount of dwarf pride and hyperbole in that statement.

A typical Stoneaxe warrior is clad in knee-length mail crafted of the finest dwarven steel, and equipped with a sturdy helmet, gauntlets, greaves, and heavy leather or iron-shod boots. Each warrior is expected to excel in all forms of weapons, and generally carries one or two handaxes, a large round steel shield, and a sling or crossbow along with sufficient ammunition for a full battle. Those without shields are armed with two-handed battleaxes, warhammers or mauls.

The dwarves' specialty is tunnel-fighting, and their tactics usually involve unbreakable shieldwalls backed up by heavy missile fire and magic. Narrow, easily defended passages allow the dwarves to absorb attack after attack from the enemy, then follow up with a ferocious charge to shatter the bruised and hopefully demoralized enemy.

As direct assault has proven ineffective, the hobgoblins have increasingly turned to small unit actions, with elite groups of scouts or assassins sneaking into the caverns to commit acts of sabotage or open the main gates to allow a full-scale invasion to take place. This has in turn led to the Stoneaxe dwarves training and deploying their own specially-trained scouts to counteract the new threat, and battles between small highly-trained squads of dwarf and hobgoblin elites have become far more common in recent years.

Major Threats

The greatest threat to the Stoneaxe dwarves may be the hobgoblins, but other foes exist in the twisting corridors of the Deepfells as well. The wily kobolds raid the dwarves as frequently as they do the hobgoblins and treat the dwarves with equal hatred. Elsewhere are ogre clans, orc tribes, and the mad derro of the deeper caverns. While the hobgoblins represent an inexorable and daily danger, these other groups combine their forces to sap dwarvish resolve and resources, making the Stoneaxers' situation even more perilous.

Wilderness and Adventures

The caverns of the Stoneaxe dwarves are well patrolled and settled. While hobgoblins, kobolds, and orcs sometimes are able to gain entrance in small numbers, the corridors and chambers of the area are kept scrupulously free of dangers by squads of tireless guards constantly on patrol.

That is not to say, of course, that there is any lack of potential for enterprising adventurers. The Stoneaxe dwarves have of course developed a long and abiding distrust for the outside world, though they sometimes accept aid from adventurers in the defense of their realm (a few hidebound priests and fanatics disdain even that much assistance, however). A slow thaw in relations between the dwarves and the Northmarches has begun as well, but non-dwarves are still treated coldly and with at best grudging cooperation. The dwarves are good, however, and if outsiders were to prove their mettle, they may be treated better and actually given some measure of trust. Dwarves from other realms receive warmer welcomes as well, though the Stoneaxers are clannish and tend not to confide even in others of their own kind.

Adventures include defense against incursions, exploration of surrounding caves, and performing scouting missions on behalf of the Northlands duchy. This last is especially challenging and dangerous, for the hobgoblins are wary and alert to any attempts at spying. Should adventurers gain important intelligence regarding hobgoblin intentions, they may be given even more dangerous (but rewarding) missions in the form of provocation and planting of false evidence to convince the hobgoblins that their own rival kingdoms are behind acts of sabotage and destruction. Those who assist in such intricate plots will win the gratitude of the Northmarchers and the reluctant respect of the Stoneaxers, who may warm enough to start sending adventurers of missions of their own.

Tulidor Vale
(Too-LE-door)

Alignment: Neutral Good
Capital: Maldran (1,350)
Notable Settlements: Council Grove
Ruler: High Lord Athe Sutherle
Government: Monarchy
Population: 3,595 (high elves 2,750, aarakocra 625, centaur 220)
Monstrous: Sprites, pixies, aarakocra, centaurs, blink dogs, dryads, nereid, satyrs, treants, pegasi, unicorns, faerie dragons
Languages: Sylvan
Religion: Wayland the Smith
Resources: Fruits, grains, cloth, mithral, weapons, armor
Currency: Ancient elvish coins
Technology Level: Renaissance

The hidden land of Tulidor Vale is a last remaining fragment of a grand and ancient elvish culture, left behind after the elves departed in their three great exoduses. Guardians of the last fane of Wayland the Smith, the elves of Tulidor have protected their enclave with powerful magic and live in a manner that preserves many of their old traditions, including potent rituals, ancient sorceries, and elven artifacts of significant power. Needless to say, the folk of the vale guard their realm jealously and, despite their good alignment, they are reluctant to let any unauthorized visitors leave.

History and People

The vale was originally home to a great temple dedicated to the elves' most powerful and respected god, Wayland the Smith. The sacred crystal anvil of Wayland was a huge carved shrine located in the center of the fane where elven priests and priestesses could commune directly with Wayland and actually view his sacred planar realm. The anvil was immovable, hewn from the very living bones of the land, and could not be moved, even in the face of the elves' tragic exoduses. Rather than abandon their holy temple, the elves of Tulidor chose to remain here, directing the anvil's potent magics in a series of elaborate and perilous rituals, linking the vale to Wayland's realm while also shielding it from the view of outsiders. Since the completion of these rituals nearly 5,000 years ago, the vale has remained isolated and essentially frozen in time, with the sacred energies of Wayland's plane suffusing the place and transforming it into a realm of beauty and magic, with a population of serene high elves, wild but good-hearted centaurs, and winged aarakocra who live in the surrounding highlands and occasionally scout the Deepfells to make certain no enemies are coming near.

High Lord Athe Sutherle has ruled the vale for over two millennia, having taken the high seat in the White Palace of Council Grove from his mother High Lady Genela after she entered her final slumber and faded into Wayland's eternal realm. He is aided by a council of almost mythically-powerful sorcerers and priests who still command significant divine and arcane magic due to their connection to their god.

Religion

No living elf remembers the oldest days of the vale when priests could communicate directly with Wayland and his holy servants through the crystal anvil at the center of the great fane. All the same, their devotion to Wayland remains unbreakable, and the folk of the Vale are an especially devout people. Worship for all who live in the vale, including centaurs, fey, and aarakocra are held once per week, while the fane is available to all who wish to go there to pray, study, consult with priests, or simply to contemplate Wayland's holy words.

Government

The vale operates as a monarchy, with a single ruler who consults with and is advised by a council of powerful spellcasters and clerics. As the high lord or lady rules for the duration of their lifetime, this can extend for millennia, and indeed it has, for the vale has had only two rulers since its magical isolation from the rest of the world. High Lady Genela Sutherle ruled for more than 3,000 years before finally passing into the holy realms. She was succeeded by her son Lord Athe.

All citizens of the vale have the right to address the high lord or lady and present petitions or requests to the high council. The very nature of the vale's elven culture makes such events relatively rare, as nearly all those who dwell here respect the authority of the high ruler and the council. In the past few centuries, however, a few individuals have begun to question the vale's isolation and have requested that the council begin to study the possibility of emerging from isolation. So far they have not been rejected outright, but as with everything else in the vale, the council's decisions are slow and deliberate, as might be expected from beings whose lives are measured in epochs rather than simply years.

Military

While the vale remains safe from discovery, the tradition of elven military excellence has not declined, and every citizen of the vale is skilled in arms and combat, and many are accomplished spellcasters powered by the divine and arcane energies that flow through the crystal anvil in the fane of Wayland.

The vale's regular army consists of 300 stern, armored warriors equipped with bow, spear, and sword, each of whom is easily worth a hundred times his or her number in lesser human, orcish, or other warriors. A potent regiment of 100 armored riders mounted on ancient elvish steeds forms the elite core of the army. They too are skilled with bow and sword, and their lances are magical artifacts of the highest order.

The vale's greatest asset slumbers beneath the palace in Council Grove. Three ancient dragons — Alechar the Golden, Melichan the Silver, and Galdrax the Bronze — were chosen by Wayland himself to guard the vale. They entered into a magical slumber from which they will awaken should Wayland's fane ever be threatened.

Major Threats

Tulidor Vale is technically surrounded by threats, for any outsider would desire the riches and secrets that the vale hides. Fortunately for the elves, few if any have ever suspected the vale's existence, and to this day the vale's wards and concealments remain strong.

That said, some ancient elvish documents or artifacts may provide clues to the vale's existence should an especially enterprising scholar ever investigate thoroughly enough. Even if the vale is found to be real, it would take a very powerful spellcaster (or group of spellcasters) to breach the realm's protections. Should that happen, the elves would respond severely, and any hostile intruders would face a strong response indeed

Wilderness and Adventures

The vale is a place of extraordinary beauty and serenity, with few if any real dangers to travelers or to the elves and others who live there. While visitors to the vale are extremely rare, there are tales of outsiders who have found the place and discovered various secret means of entry, some of which may be found in ancient tomes or carved into extremely old elvish monuments. Despite their relative benevolence, the elves are not likely to allow visitors to enter freely, and those who do manage to access the vale will never be allowed to leave.

A few stories exist of adventurers, wanderers, or others who stumbled upon a hidden elven kingdom and were allowed to stay, even to the point of being rewarded with extreme longevity and a life of beauty and enlightenment to prevent them from ever leaving. Most of these stories end sadly, with the visitors growing homesick and making their way, with great difficulty, out of the vale, only to find that the outside world has changed beyond recognition, with their homes long gone and their loved ones old or dead.

Needless to say, the treasure, magic, wisdom, and artifacts that the elves have at their disposal would lead even the most cautious of adventurers to at least consider risking the potential consequences of finding the vale. Such an adventure would require individuals of the highest levels of skill and daring, as well as certain ethical flaws that would allow for theft from an ancient and benevolent group. Those who attempt to steal from the elves may face harsh punishment, regardless of the vale folk's relative peacefulness and serenity.

Council Grove

Alignment: Neutral Good
Ruler: High Lord Athe Sutherle
Population: 1,350 (high elves)
Languages: Sylvan
Religion: Wayland the Smith

Council Grove is a serene and ancient settlement located at the southern end of Tulidor Vale, where it serves as the seat of government for the valley's ancient elvish civilization. A vast palace here houses the realm's high lord. A city full of gleaming structures of gray and white marble surrounds the palace and houses the high council and hundreds of other high elves.

The grove houses barracks for the vale's regular army. Beneath the palace are vast tunnels where the three ancient dragons charged with defending the vale slumber.

Appendix A: Primary Gods of Reme

Dame Torren
Goddess of the Four Winds
Lesser Goddess

Alignment: Neutral
Domains: Air, Animals, Tempests, Travel
Symbol: Four wavy lines, one over the other
Garb: Flowing robes
Favored Weapons: Scimitar, lance, pulled bows (long or short)
Form of Worship and Holidays: Small but regular private sacrifices, with four holy days in the year, linked to the seasons
Typical Worshippers: Barbarians, sailors

Dame Torren is the Goddess of the Four Winds, and is generally perceived as a goddess of freedom as well. She is worshipped by barbarians (especially the Loreclans of Reme) and by sailors. Her temples are usually simple circles of standing stones or columns that are open to the air. In the case of large temples, the stones might circle an entire temple complex or might be placed atop a large temple building. There are traditionally four "gates" to these temples, and it is said that to pass through any stones other than the gate is to incite the wrath of the goddess. The gates are demarcated by symbols: a horse to the west, a hawk to the east, a gaunt woman's screaming face with flowing hair to the north, and a beautiful woman with flowing hair to the south. One of the mantras of the clerics of Dame Torren is "Horse from the west, hawk from the east, mouth from the north, beauty from the south."

While Dame Torren is neutral in alignment, she is an unforgiving deity and one of changeable temperament. Another saying that is important to her clerics in this regard is that "the goddess has a short memory for favor, and a long memory for scorn." It is acceptable to offer her small sacrifices, but important never to stop honoring her once one starts. Asking the favor of the goddess is a permanent and irreversible decision; once one has asked her favor, one can never stop sacrificing to her for the rest of one's life, or retribution is quite likely.

As the goddess is worshipped in Reme and in many other cities, designated priestesses ride in a column through the settlement during extremely high winds. A high priestess mounted on a sacred horse leads the column, with a second sacred horse beside her, saddled but without a rider. This second horse is reserved for the goddess herself, should she deign to join the procession. The column of priestesses carries banners and long poles mounted with ratcheted wheels that are designed to produce a loud, clicking whir. The eerie noise carries far into the wind, informing all that the priesthood of the goddess is abroad upon the wind. This is for the most part an urban tradition; it is not widely practiced as a religious ritual by the Rhemish Loreclans, although some Loreclans practice a much less dramatic version of it.

Halatra
The Horse, Lord of the Sea of Grass
Lesser God

Alignment: Neutral
Domains: Animal, Community, Earth, Travel
Symbol: Horse
Garb: Sacred garb is usually a bead-embroidered yoke with curling patterns on the back (symbolizing a mane) and the image of a horse on the front. Other than sacred garb, there is no traditional clothing associated with the god.
Favored Weapons: Lance
Form of Worship and Holidays: Halatra's worship has no holy days associated with it; the god is usually honored with small sacrifices when worshippers entreat his aid or enjoy a victory of some kind.
Typical Worshippers: Barbarians, plains-dwellers, riders

Halatra is a major deity of the Loreclans of the Rhemish plain. Halatra has very few clerics, for the deity seems to be more shamanic and even druidic in nature. He is even known to make pacts with benevolent witches and warlocks. This is a deity of the open air who has no true temples. A number of places on the Rhemish plains and in other open regions are sacred to Halatra, and are traditionally maintained by druids.

Halatra and Dame Torren share some association. In a very few stories, the Goddess of the Four Winds rides Halatra into battle. However, the connection is more visible in the sense that clerics of Dame Torren and the various holy people serving Halatra tend to have similar visions and oracles at the same time, and are often directed to work together when there is direct communication from the gods themselves.

Mithras
The Bull, God of War
Greater God

Alignment: Lawful Neutral
Domains: Law, War
Symbol: Bull's Head
Garb: Armor
Favored Weapons: Not applicable; Mithras favors all weapons
Form of Worship and Holidays: Various holy days are observed in underground spaces, with practice varying by the level of initiation of those present
Typical Worshippers: Soldiers

Mithras (not to be confused with Mitra) was the primary war god of the Hyperboreans and is worshipped to greater or lesser extent almost everywhere conquered by the Hyperborean Empire. Mithras is a bitter enemy of Demogorgon, and priests of the god drop almost anything to hunt down Demogorgon cultists if a nest of them is suspected in the vicinity.

Mithras is a god of attack more than a god of defense, which distinguishes him from Vanitthu and Vanitthu's followers.

SOLANUS

Goddess of the Sun and Healing
Greater God

Alignment: Neutral Good
Domains: Life, Light
Symbol: A blazing sun inscribed with an open palm
Garb: Pale robes bearing the symbol of Solanus. The color of
robes changes as adherents progress through the hierarchy of
the church. Initiates wear robes of red that are then changed
to those of orange, then yellow, and then white for the high
priest. There are even multiple subtle shades between these
main colors to denote gradations within their ranks.
Favored Weapons: Mace, quarterstaff
Form of Worship and Holidays: Regular worship on the first
day of the week (Solsdag), special observances for the clergy at
each dawn, major holidays on the summer and winter solstices
(High Sol and Low Sol, respectively), and the Ides of the eighth
month is devoted to Solanus as well.
Typical Worshipers: Rangers, bards, healers, soldiers, undead
slayers

Solanus is the benevolent goddess of the sun, Sol as it has traditionally
been named in Akados. She is a goddess of ancient Hyperborea who, as
a founding deity of that culture, has known great popularity in Akados
across the breadth of the empire. Her priests have often served as
field medics in armies and once made up an entire legion of ancient
Hyperborea. They have also commonly been the local healers in
villages and small towns. Some hospitals were established in Solanus'
name in certain imperial centers (namely Remenos and Curgantium),
but the practice never caught on in more remote settings where
sufficient funds from the imperial coffers were frequently unavailable.
As a result, her rural clergy remained principally scattered as individual
practitioners while her central high church maintained a rigid hierarchy
that often looked with disdain upon the rural church as disorganized
or even bumpkins. Perhaps the church's greatest claim to notoriety
over the centuries, however, has been the propensity for members of
her rural clergy to join adventuring bands. At one time in the empire's
history, it is likely that as many as eight out of 10 adventuring parties,
mercenary companies, or freelance knights was accompanied by a cleric
of Solanus, bringing great acceptance and goodwill among the common
folk far beyond what could have been managed by the central offices of
the church tucked away in the great cities of the empire. Many of the
older bardic hero tales composed in the classical style of those times
include a warrior of Thyr, a wizard of Jamboor, a paladin of Muir, and
a cleric of Solanus as heroic archetypes. (They also typically include a
scoundrel character devoted to Moccavallo, though this is less likely to
be acknowledged in polite company.)

In recent centuries, the church of Solanus has seen a steady, and in
some cases precipitous, decline. This can be directly attributed to the
equally steady rise in the encroaching faith of Mitra from the far reaches
of the east after being embraced by the Foerdewaith overkings several
centuries ago. In general, her worship becomes more common the
farther west one travels across Akados, as the faith of Mitra has not yet
spread that far. Solanus is one of the three matron/patron deities of the
great city of Reme (alongside Dame Torren and Mithras) and still enjoys
a great degree of popularity and worship there. Her high altar remains
in that city at the venerable Hospital of St. Jethra the Martyred, which
still maintains 1,220 beds and accepts the sick and infirm from all over
Akados who make their way to its doors.

REFERENCE SOURCES

Solanus first appeared in *The Lost City of Barakus* by **Necromancer
Games**.

Appendix B: Encounter Tables

Ashen Hills Encounters

Check three times per day of travel or rest, using percentile dice, with a result of 01–25 indicating an encounter. If an encounter occurs, roll on the following table to determine its nature (if the encounter takes place during a time when the characters are simply resting, ignore results of settlements).

1d100	Encounter
01–15	Bears
16–20	Bulette
21–25	Chimera
26–45	Flying Monster (General) Encounter Table
46–50	Griffon
51–55	Hill Giant
56–65	Hobgoblins
66–70	Ogres
71–75	Orcs
76–77	Small settlement (Gnomes)
78–80	Troll
81–90	Wolves
91–95	Worgs
96–00	Wyverns

Endless Hills Encounters

Check three times per day of travel or rest, using percentile dice, with a result of 01–25 indicating an encounter. If an encounter occurs, roll on the following table to determine its nature (if the encounter takes place during a time when the characters are simply resting, ignore results of settlements).

1d100	Encounter
01–10	Bears
11–15	Ettin
16–30	Flying Monster (General) Encounter Table
31–35	Giant Boar
36–40	Giant Hyaena
41–42	Gnoll Tribe
43–60	Gnoll Warband
61–65	Hill Giant
66–70	Hyaenas
71–80	Lycanthrope
81–85	Snake
86–90	Wild Cattle
91–95	Wild Horses
96–00	Wolves

Flying Creatures (General)

1d100	Encounter
01–10	Blood Hawk
11–12	Dragon
13–30	Eagle or Hawks
31–40	Giant Eagle
41–45	Giant Owl
46–50	Harpy
51–55	Hippogriff
56–60	Manticore
61–75	Pteranodon
76–86	Ravens
87–90	Roc
91–00	Wyvern

Forest Encounters

Check three times per day of travel or rest, using percentile dice, with a result of 01–25 indicating an encounter. If an encounter occurs, roll on the following table to determine its nature (if the encounter takes place during a time when the characters are simply resting, ignore results of settlements).

1d100	Encounter
01–20	Special by forest (Baronswood: Ancient Green Dragon Aureensaador; Westwood: Wood Elves [Forest Wolf Clan]; Eisenwood: Cute squirrels; Sternwood: Zombies; Haunted Wood: Creatures of Shadow; Namjan Forest: Creatures of Shadow; Western Akadian Forest: Roc; Dunavenwood: Humanoid Warband)
21–25	Bandits
26–35	Bears
36–40	Bugbears
41–42	Dragon, Green
43–47	Elves
48–52	Giant Badger
53–57	Giant Spiders
58–60	Giant Wasps
61–62	Lycanthrope
63–70	Owlbear
71	Satyr
72–80	Snake
81–85	Stirges
86–90	Treant
91–95	Wolves
96–00	Worgs

High Downs Encounters

Check three times per day of travel or rest, using percentile dice, with a result of 01–25 indicating an encounter. If an encounter occurs, roll on the following table to determine its nature (if the encounter takes place during a time when the characters are simply resting, ignore results of settlements).

1d100	Encounter
01–05	Ankheg
06–10	Bears
11–15	Bulette
16–20	Cockatrice
21–35	Flying Monster (General) Encounter Table
36–45	Giant Mountain Goat
46–55	Gnomes
56–60	Hill Giant
61–65	Kobolds
66–70	Ogres
71–75	Peryton
76–80	Small settlement (Gnomes)
81–82	Small Settlement (Human)
83–93	Traders
94–97	Troll
98–00	Zombies

High Plains Encounters

Check three times per day of travel or rest, using percentile dice, with a result of 01–25 indicating an encounter. If an encounter occurs, roll on the following table to determine its nature (if the encounter takes place during a time when the characters are simply resting, ignore results of settlements).

1d100	Encounter
01–03	Ankheg
04–07	Bulette
08–28	Caribou
29–34	Centaurs
35	Chimera
36–50	Flying Monster (General) Encounter Table
51–55	Giant Boar
56–60	Hobgoblins
61–65	Humanoid Warband
66–70	Loreclan Riders
71	Pegasus
72–80	Small settlement (Centaur)
81–90	Wild Horses
91–00	Wolves

Hills (General) Encounters

Check three times per day of travel or rest, using percentile dice, with a result of 01–25 indicating an encounter. If an encounter occurs, roll on the following table to determine its nature (if the encounter takes place during a time when the characters are simply resting, ignore results of settlements).

1d100	Encounter
01–08	Bears
09–10	Druid
11–20	Elk
21–22	Ettin
23–40	Chimera
41–45	Fur Trappers
46–50	Giant Boar
51–55	Giant Elk
56–59	Hill Giant
60–70	Hobgoblins
71–73	Lion
74–78	Ogres
79–85	Small settlement (Foerdewaith)
86–90	Werebear
91–00	Wolves

Mountains

Check three times per day of travel or rest, using percentile dice, with a result of 01–25 indicating an encounter. If an encounter occurs, roll on the following table to determine its nature (if the encounter takes place during a time when the characters are simply resting, ignore results of settlements).

1d100	Encounter
01–20	Special by region (Green Mountains: Dwarves [Encounter 41]; Deepfells: Humanoid Warband [Encounter 72]; Stonehearts: Humanoid Warband [Encounter 72])
21–25	Bears
26–30	Dwarves
31–33	Ettin
34–35	Fire Giants
36–50	Flying Monster (General) Encounter Table
51–53	Frost Giants
54–65	Giant Mountain Goat
66–75	Hobgoblins
76–77	Kobolds
78–82	Ogres
83–86	Orcs
87–88	Roc
89–98	Saber-toothed tiger
99–00	Stone Giants

Plains (General) Encounters

Check three times per day of travel or rest, using percentile dice, with a result of 01–25 indicating an encounter. If an encounter occurs, roll on the following table to determine its nature (if the encounter takes place during a time when the characters are simply resting, ignore results of settlements).

1d100	Encounter
01–04	Ankheg
05–06	Bulette
07–27	Flying Monster (General) Encounter Table
28–32	Giant Hyaena
33–35	Humanoid Warband
36–37	Lion
38–55	Loreclan Riders
56–57	Lycanthrope
58–64	Pashtar Druid
65–70	Pashtar Ranger
71–75	Small settlement (Loreclan)
76–85	Wild Cattle
86–95	Wild Horses
96–00	Wolves

River (General) Encounters

Check three times per day of travel or rest, using percentile dice, with a result of 01–25 indicating an encounter. If an encounter occurs, roll on the following table to determine its nature (if the encounter takes place during a time when the characters are simply resting, ignore results of settlements).

1d100	Encounter
01–05	Barge
06–10	Bears
11–20	Crocodile
21–25	Deer
26–28	Fishing Boats (Foerdewaith)
29–30	Fishing Boats (Loreclan)
31–40	Flying Monster (General) Encounter Table
41–45	Giant Crocodile
46–50	Giant Snake
51–55	Giant Toad
56–58	Loreclan Riders
59–63	Small Settlement (Foerdewaith)
64–68	Small settlement (Loreclan)
69–75	Traders
76–80	Troll
81–94	Wild Cattle
95–00	Wolves

Road Encounters

Check three times per day of travel or rest, using percentile dice, with a result of 01–25 indicating an encounter. If an encounter occurs, roll on the following table to determine its nature (if the encounter takes place during a time when the characters are simply resting, ignore results of settlements).

1d100	Encounter
01–05	Ankheg
06–15	Bandits
16–20	Caravan
21–30	Cattle Drive
31–35	Cavalry Troop
36–45	Flying Monster (General) Encounter Table
46–50	Foot Patrol
51–55	Giant Hyaena
56–60	Loreclan Riders
61–65	Pashtar Druid
66–70	Pashtar Ranger
71–75	Small settlement (Foerdewaith)
76–80	Small settlement (Loreclan)
81–90	Traders
91–95	Wolves
96–00	Wyvern

INDEX

A

Aciier River, 63, 89
Acropolis of the Four Winds, 35
Albion, 51
Alliances, 73
Angry Gull, 39
Appearance, 72
Appleton and Beyond, 106
Arcanum Collegium, 31
Armory of the Militia, 57
Ashen Hills, 51, 119
Ashen Hills Encounters, 144
Avenue of Eternal Warning, 29

B

Baronswood, 90
Beast Takers, 84
Beast Takers' Camp, 73
Blackflame, 138
Breastplates by Beatrix, 80
Broadwater, 126
Brokerage League, 75

C

Caer Dire, 90
Caldera Citadel, 135
Carnival's End, 96
Castle District and Yalendir Gate, 78
Castle Qellinroque, 78
Cattle Bridge, 29
Central Market, 78
Chalktown, 132
Chapterhouse of the Solari Templars, 33
City of Cats, 96
City of the Lost, 96
City Palisade, 56
Civil Unrest in the Westmarches, 16
Council Grove, 141
Crossroads Center, 72
Crynnomar Gap, 53
Culture of the Loreclans, 10

D

Dame's Gowns, 81
Dame Torren, 142
Devil's Finger, 123
Dockside District, 105
Docks of Yalendir, 24
Downriver in the Westmarch Region, 89
Dragonbone Citadel, 124
Dragonbone Peak, 124
Dreikeng, 63
Ducal Palace, 54, 78, 100
Ducal Theater of Panetoth, 82
Duke Borrell's Victory, 55
Dunavenwood, 98
Dun Eamon, 126
Durgam's Folly, 52

E

Eamonvale, 124
Eamonvale Trade Road, 127
Eastlake, 105
Eckland, 99

Eisenwood Forest, 65
Endless Hills, 64, 102
Endless Hills Encounters, 144

F

Fallenhouse, 42
Fareme, 73
Fehlween River, 66
Fenria, 106
Ferdozan, 107
Field of the Sirkan Pashtars, 43
Fivestone Distillery and Brewery, 76
Fivestones, 75
Flint Faces, 83
Flying Creatures (General), 145
Foerdewaith Era, 15
Forest Encounters, 145
Forswen, 108
Fort Sod, 72
Fortress of the Bandi, 38
Four Winds Bridge, 29

G

Gardens, 56
Gaskar Hills, 113
Gauldark, 65
Gilboath, 19
Glondarr and Sirin, 106
Gnomish Quarter, 55
Golden Oak, 52
Grand Duchy of Reme, 1, 7
Grandmaster of Smiths Silanus Otiak, 32
Grass Sailors, 83
Green Mountains, 109
Gryphon Hills, 53
Guild House, 32

H

Halatra, 142
Hall of the Red Thumb, 44
Hall of the Terriers, 43
Harrowfar, 66
Hauk Skarpson's Feast Hall, 40
Hauk Skarpson's Feast Hall Menu, 41
Haunted Wood, 53
High Altar of Solanus, 32
High Downs, 53
High Downs Encounters, 145
High Plains Encounters, 145
Highwaymen, 73
Hills (General) Encounters, 146
Hol-Hebar, 39
Hospital of St. Jethra the Martyred, 32
House Drenwall, 37
House Gastone-Sheshek, 37
Hyperborean Era, 15

I

Ice Palace of Perfidium, 77
Independent World Power, 16
Inn-at-the-End-of-the-Road, 79
Ionkri Hall, 53
Ironhill, 53

J

Jousting Lists of Panetoth, 83
Judiciary Complex, 30

K

Kemresen, 110
Khazfrecht, 110
Kheled'khaduin, 55
Kingdoms of the Deepfells, 121
Knife's Edge Ridge, 110
Kytherax's Kingdom, 133

L

Lancers' Hall, 41
Lantern Bridge, 29
LeCroiy Linens, 24
Lich's Rest, 35
Livonia's Park, 35
Locations in Eckland, 100
Locations in Martyn's Nest, 105
Locations in Quail Valley, 113
Locations in the City of Reme, 54
Locations in the Frontier, 63
Locations in the Grand Ducal Territory, 19
Locations in the Kingdom Beneath, 103
Locations in the Westmarches, 89
Locations in Waymarch, 72
Locations within the Namjan Forest, 66
Lord Mayor's Manor, 33
Loreclannic Knights, 13
Loreclan of the Quick Knives, 11
Loreclans of the Waymarch Grasslands, 83
Lost and Found, 94

M

Martyn's Nest, 104
Mayor's Manor, 79
Merchant Hall, 56
Military Barracks, 78
Mithras, 142
Mountains, 146
Museids, 111

N

Namjan Forest, 66
Naso Drenwall, 37
Nerimar, 56
Nin Forest, 113
North Gate, 36
Notable Inns and Taverns, 79
Notable Locations, 24
Notable Locations, 75
Nyctosea, 136

O

Order of the Bull's Hooves, 34
Order of the Orphans of Mithras, 34
Organized Crime, 24
Origin in the Frontier, 89
Outer Lawns, 78
Overview of the City of Reme, 27

P

Panetoth, 77
Panetoth Road Agency, 81
Plains (General) Encounters, 146
Prairie Fire Theater, 74
Prairie Gate, 78
Pre-Hyperborean Period, 15

Q

Quail River, 111
Quail Valley, 113
Quick Knives, 83
Quill House, 41
Quintas, 19

R

Red Thumb Adventure Hooks, 44
Reme, Ducal Lands, 18
Reme Gate and Gatehouse, 78
Remenos River, 20
Rhemish Barons, 13
Rhemish Dukes, 13
River Eamon, 127
River (General) Encounters, 146
Riverside, 67
Road Encounters, 147
Roost of the Owls, 41
Royal Bluff, 132
Ruins of Sheffen Palace, 114
Runya'mor, 57

S

Sand and Flame, 24
Sea Power, 13
Seaside, 113
Shadowhold, 57
Shining Temple, 114
Shops and Amenities, 80
Shrine of the Earth Spirit, 75
Silverlight, 114
Sir Beefheart's Chevalier Tavern, 79
Slavery in the Sujabi Quarter, 40
Smoke and Urine Street, 29
Solanus, 143
South City, 78
South Gate, 36
Sternwood, 57
Stillwater, 66
Stoneaxe Caverns, 138
Stoneheart Glacier and Shengotha Plateau, 77
Stone Tap Tavern, 75
Street of Decadent Stenches, 29
Street of Stampedes, 29
Street of the Martyr Lanterns, 29
Street of the Sun, 29
Streets and Bridges, 29
Stronghold of the Sea Tigress, 30
Student Orders, 31
Sunbreath Quartz, 67
Switchgrass Forge, 73
Sword of Borell, 80

T

Tanith, 58
Tanner's Green, 115
Temple of Dame Torren, 54
Temple of Mithras, 33, 54, 74, 82
Temple of Sefagreth, 82
Temple of Solanus, 54
Temple of the Sea God, 105
Temple of Vanitthu, 55
Temple of Vanitthu, 82
Temple Street, 29
Terrier Adventure Hooks, 43
Theater, 56
The Bawdy Centaur, 80

The Blue Man, 95
The Blue Rooster, 39
The Brims, 81
The Brokerage House, 81
The Brokerage League, 81
The Carnival, 92
The Carnival at the End of the World, 91
The Castle of Reme, 30
The Citadel, 55
The Cliff, 92
The Compass Tower, 82
The Dagger & Rose, 73
The Deeper Carnival, 95
The Deepfells, 63
The Duke's Market, 101
The East Bank, 100
The East Docks, 100
The End of the World, 94
The Forbidden City, 103
The Gallows, 109
The Gemcutters Guild, 105
The Gilded Chicken, 55
The Gladiatorial Ring, 95
The Great Jousting Pitch, 74
The Grimburg, 76
The Grounds, 31
The Haunted Wood, 127
The Hedge Apple's Bite, 81
The High Downs, 19, 130
The House of Horrors, 95
The House of Oron, 36
The Ice Cult, 42
The Ice Floe and Deceiver's Pass, 77
The Ice Tower of Kal-Tior, 77
The Island of Heroes, 29
The Kingdom Beneath, 102
The Kirimaji Loreclan, 11
The Knights of St. Longus, 34
The Kujuk (Gate), 42
The Lore, 11
The Loreclan of Tabaj, 10
The Loreclans and the Shattered Folk, 16
The Mask Booth, 94
The Old Oak, 57
The Order of St. Jethra, 32
The Path of Blood, 65
The Path of Shadow, 65
The Pit of Yar-Mith, 20
The Pit of the Lizards, 42
The Plains, 83
The Quojo, 43
The Rathole, 24
The Red Elk Inn, 72
The Red Plumb, 24
The Rise of Reme, 11
The Road Agency, 75
The Road Gate, 101
The Shining Altar, 103
The Singing River, 103
The Standing Stones, 75
The Star Walkers, 83
The Strangeness, 64
The Sujabi, 40
The Temple of the Retinue of Ice and Snow, 43
The Token Booth, 93
The Village, 91
The West Bank, 101

The Western Winds Tavern, 80
The Windreft, 118
The Wizard's Wall Inn, 56
Thistlehill, 66
Thunder Head Bar, 74
Thunder Riders, 83
Tower of Jhedophar, 115
Tower of Law and Order, 79
Town and Gown, 32
Tradeway Ale, 80
Tradeway Brewers, 80
Trailblazer's Inn, 74
Tree of the True Heart, 117
Tulidor Vale, 140

U

Underwall, 36
Uphill, 36

V

Varazath, 20

W

Wayland's Fane, 58
Wessem, 115
Western Akadian Forest, 117
Western Reme Road, 29
West Fortress, 116
Westwood, 117
Wheelwrights, 75
Wheelwrights Guild Hall, 25
Wheelwrights Outpost, 81
Whiterush, 23
Whiterush River, 23
White Squirrel Inn, 22
Wild Rye Estate, 80
Wind Keep, 74
Wizard's Wall, 58

XYZ

Yalendir, 23
Yalendir Keep, 25
Yalendir Pitch, 25
Yorwich Imports, 81

Legend

- **●** Town or Village
- **◉** City
- **✪** Capital or Free City
- **⊛** Imperial Capital
- **■** Fortress or Citadel
- **⁂** Ruins
- **▲** Place of Interest
- **~** Road
- **⌇** Trail or Unused Road
- **⋯** Mountain Pass

Albion
Tanith
Northmarch
High Downs
Ironhill
North Trade Road
Dun Eamon
Broadwater
Eamonvale
Quintas
River Eamon
Northway Road
Trade Road
Yalendir
Remens River
Duchy of Waymarch
Dagger & Rose
Panetoth
The Tradeway
The Tradeway
Duchy of Ysser
Pirwatch Keep
Old Tors
Elderwood
Whiterush River
Whiterush
Kingdom of Foere
Nains
Farall Hold
Pentals
Châlaix
County of Coutaine
Tourse
Hogshead Bend
Curgant
Cantelburgh
Great Amrn River
Aixe
Vermis
Aachen Provi
The Wa
The C
Cretian Mountains
Volk
Mons Terminus
Lost Boy Byrn Mountain
Stoneheart Forest
Fairhill
Stoneheart Valley
Fareme
Ruined Keep
Gr
Ur Quash
Citadel of the Griffon
Stoneheart Mountain
Dungeon
Citadel
Bard's Gate
Plai
Stoneheart River
Glendovel Close
The Grimburg
Fivestones
Ice Tower
Thane's Road
Abad Durdhai
The Ice Palace
Alesardin
Azure Mountains
Old North Road
Arano
T A
Hazed Canyon
Elise
Glaiv
Eng Wood
The Desolation
Carter's
Oxibuul
Black Forest
The North Cut
The Fingers
Thumb
Index
Middle
Ring
Little
Southern River
Frenzied Crossing
The Camp
Tsar
Stoneheart Escarpment
Cold Iron Pass
Stoneheart Grade
Southern Pass
Stoneheart
Ice Plateau
Shengotha Plateau
Eamonvale Road
Og Brethos
Miners' Refuge
Mithral Mtn.
Erod Flan
Baen's Pass
Tyr Whin
Ohl Rennal
Stoneheart Mountains
Feingotha Plateau
Koristaell the Silent Lake
Toh
Pelthean Pass
agotha Plateau
Exon
Dea
Starc
Baen's Keep